Pride Publishing books by KD Ellis

Out in Austin
Teddy's Truth

Out in Austin

TEDDY'S TRUTH

KD ELLIS

Teddy's Truth
ISBN # 978-1-83943-941-4
©Copyright KD Ellis 2021
Cover Art by Erin Dameron-Hill ©Copyright January 2021
Interior text design by Claire Siemaszkiewicz
Pride Publishing

TEDDY'S TRUTH

Dedication

To Susan and Courtney, my beta readers who stuck with me through every misplaced word and sentence fragment, and whose suggestions made this book one thousand times better, and to Jamie, who caught the ten million errors we all missed.

To Anna, who told me in the first place that Teddy needed a book.

And to the Flint Area Writers who stuck with me through the painstaking process of editing and re-editing.

You're the best!

Chapter One

Teddy tugged at the hem of his overlarge sweatshirt then discreetly scratched beneath the band of his sticky sports bra. As far as he was concerned, breasts were disgusting lumps of fat that hoarded sweat, bounced like painful beanbags on his chest when he was busy catching a football and strained the front of any button-down he tried to wear. He couldn't understand why boys were so obsessed with them. He personally couldn't wait to get the damn things cut off.

Hormone therapy had deepened his voice and given him a shadow of patchy fuzz on his jaw. Clippers had sheared him of his blond hair and his mother's Italian heritage had blessed him with broad shoulders and narrow hips.

It was unfortunate that it had also cursed him with breasts that not even puberty blockers had been able to thwart.

He wished he could blame her awful time-management skills on their heritage as well, but he knew better. The fault lay with either Jack or John—the bottle or the boyfriend, whichever she was currently in bed with.

He'd been sitting on the hard, concrete steps of the high school for almost an hour. It wasn't like he could call her. His cell was out of minutes, and hers was probably dead on the nightstand.

Just as the final school bus trundled back onto the parking lot and Teddy was about to give up on waiting, someone stepped up beside him, casting him in shadow.

"Stay there," Teddy ordered, craning his head back until he could grin at his best friend. "Perfect. Be my sun block."

Shiloh, still in his leotard, laughed and nudged Teddy's hip with his shoe. "If you don't think I shine brighter than the sun, then clearly I'm not wearing enough glitter."

"Shine as bright as you want, but just keep standing there. Fuck, it's hot!" Teddy gripped his collar and tugged at it repeatedly, trying to stir a breeze. All it ended up doing was wafting the stench of boob sweat up into his face.

"Well, duh, it's ninety degrees—and you're in a sweater." Shiloh rolled his eyes and dropped onto the curb beside him. "And it's not even pink."

Teddy opened his mouth, his usual response dancing on his tongue—that boys don't wear pink—but he swallowed it. Shiloh was currently in a hot pink leotard and pink Chucks.

Instead, Teddy shrugged and glared down at his baggy jeans and boring blue sweater. "You know why." It was hard enough getting people to call him Teddy instead of Thea. Or, worse, Theodora.

"I'm going to make you a shirt. It's going to be pink and fabulous. It's going to say, 'Call Me Teddy'. *And* it's going to be in glitter." Shiloh threw an imaginary handful into the air, then fell back to lie on the sidewalk, his arms flung out.

"With your handwriting, they'd probably think you wrote 'Daddy'." Teddy dropped back to use Shiloh's arm as a pillow.

Shiloh shifted but didn't pull away. He just rolled onto his side, his blond hair flopping into his eyes. He left his arm beneath Teddy's head, bringing their faces close enough that their noses nearly touched. "It's not *that* bad. Besides, you're clearly not a *Daddy*."

Teddy rolled his eyes. Ever since he'd borrowed Shiloh's laptop to finish up his college application essays — and forgotten to clear his search history after falling down the rabbit hole of kinky porn — Shiloh's teasing had been less than subtle. Teddy refused to be embarrassed, though, especially since the only reason he'd stumbled onto that website in the first place was because Shiloh had left three separate bookmarks for it.

It reinforced everything Teddy knew about their relationship. They were destined to be the bestest of friends — but nothing more. They were both too attracted to the same type of man — tall, dark and dangerous.

Still, knowing his friend was into the same kinks that he was didn't mean they needed to talk about it. He ignored the leading comment and switched back to the far safer topic of handwriting. "Remember when Mr. Carmine thought you wrote an essay on *Storage Wars*?"

"Hey, Mr. Carmine also thought you wrote an essay about Quasimodo."

"I did write him an essay about Quasimodo. Well, really about how the novel by Victor Hugo helped raise the money needed to restore the cathedral, and—" Teddy felt the beginnings of a spiel on gothic architecture creeping up.

Shiloh interrupted, "Yeah, buttresses...a rose window. I remember. I still think the gargoyles are creepy."

"You said buttresses," Teddy snickered, shoving Shiloh's shoulder.

"Teddy, can I touch your *buttress*?"

"Your hand can stay far away from my *buttress*, fuck you very much."

"It's like a butt fortress. I just want to invade your buttress! Why are you so mean to me?" Shiloh rolled onto his back and kicked his feet against the sidewalk like an angry toddler, except for the smile on his face.

"No, it's impregnable!" Teddy stuck out his tongue.

"Well, duh, you're a boy. Of course you're impregnable."

"Something tells me you don't know what that word means."

Immediately, Shiloh rattled off the definition. "Impregnable. Unable to be captured or broken into. Also, unable to be defeated or destroyed. But you have to admit that it sounds an awful lot like it means you can't make babies."

"And thank God for that," Teddy shivered at the thought of being responsible for a little, squalling, helpless baby. "I might miss wearing pink, but I won't miss *that*."

Teddy froze at the accidental admission. His therapist had told him that it was normal, that gender was a spectrum and that just because he still liked feminine things didn't make his desire to transition less valid. Still, it was the first time he'd admitted it to anyone except his therapist.

Shiloh sat up slightly to face him better. "You can still wear pink. You can wear whatever the fuck you want." Shiloh's voice hardened. "And if anyone bothers you about it, I'll cover their lockers in gay porn. Just say the word."

"The poor football players won't know what to do with themselves. Think of all the spontaneous erections." The few he'd dated had been far more interested in his ass than a straight guy probably should be — not that he'd obliged, since he refused to be anyone's dirty little secret.

Shiloh sighed. "It would be a beautiful gift to all of us."

A black Mercedes pulled up to the curb, barely parking before the driver was leaning on the horn.

"Impatient bastard," Shiloh grumbled. "I don't know why he's in a hurry. He gets paid by the hour."

"Well, that stick is so far up his ass it has to be uncomfortable sitting down." Teddy sat up and straightened his sweatshirt. The Becketts' driver was a homophobic dick. He didn't understand how the man hadn't been fired yet.

Shiloh pushed himself to his feet. "I bet he has hemorrhoids. That's probably where he rushes off to every night."

"Ew. You picture him rubbing cream on his ass?" Teddy teased.

Shiloh gagged, shoving Teddy to the side. "Gross. You're such a dick. I don't know why I hang out with you."

"Because you love me."

The Mercedes blared its horn again, a demanding series of honks that only ended when Shiloh threw a hand up in acknowledgment. "I gotta go. Do you have a ride?"

Teddy shrugged. "Yeah. She must just be running late or something. I'm sure she'll be here soon." He knew she wouldn't be, but he'd rather walk than listen to the driver sling slurs. He didn't understand how Shiloh dealt with it.

Shiloh hesitated on the bottom step, looking like he wanted to say something, but all he did was give a small nod and say, "Okay. See you Monday?"

"Yeah, see you."

* * * *

Teddy dropped his backpack beside his front door and toed off his trainers. He was halfway up the stairs when he heard his mother calling from the living room.

"Boo Bear, is that you?"

Teddy rolled his eyes to the ceiling, debating ignoring her, but she'd only keep yelling until he answered. Instead, he turned back and dragged his feet into the living room. "Stop calling me that."

His mother was draped over the loveseat. She was still in the same faded red pajamas he'd left her in that morning, her hair the same twisted mess of blonde knots. She rolled her head back over the armrest and gave him a lazy smile. "You'll always be my Boo Bear, Boo Bear." She giggled. It dwindled after a second and her forehead wrinkled with thought. "You're home early." The wrinkles faded quickly, though, leaving her glassy-eyed.

Teddy moved toward the couch, cringing at the stench of stale urine. "You were supposed to pick me up from school. It's past dinner time. Have you eaten?"

"It's Saturday, Boo." She reached out like she was trying to pat his shoulder, but wobbled precariously close to the edge of the couch.

"Friday, Mom." He untangled the blanket from around her feet. "You've pissed yourself again."

His mom blinked owlishly. "No, Boo, I'm sure it's Saturday. I had a lovely talk with Mr. Thompson across the street. Did you know his daughter is coming in next week? Lovely girl. She's about your age."

Teddy sighed. Mr. Thompson was a crotchety old man whose daughter was easily a decade older than him, and even if Teddy decided to give girls a try—which he wouldn't—Heather was a bitch. He couldn't count on one hand the number of times she'd called him 'dyke'. The last time, he'd told her that if she were going to insult him, she could at least do her research.

"Come on. Let's get you to the shower." Teddy levered her off the couch.

"Don't want to." His mom pouted but leaned against him, allowing him to guide her into her bedroom and through to the bathroom. He propped her against the counter. Her mouth formed a moue as she rubbed her palm over the prickly stubble on his scalp. "You're getting shaggy, Boo. I can clean this up with the clippers." She turned too quickly, catching her elbow on the toothbrush holder and sending it scattering into the sink.

"I'll take care of it later…after your shower. Come on, Mom." Teddy urged her away from the cabinets she was rooting around in. She hadn't helped him shave his head since he had been twelve—the last time he remembered her having a steady enough hand.

"I don't want to shower." She resisted his attempts to help her out of her piss-soaked pajamas, swatting at his hands.

"Let me take them off or you're wearing them in the shower," Teddy finally snapped, losing his patience with the fight. If he searched the living room, he'd find Johnnie Red somewhere—likely nearly empty and shoved beneath a cushion.

She quieted down long enough for him to unstick her clothes and drop them in the sink. He helped her into the shower, closing the curtain partway for privacy. She pouted quietly beneath the water for the first few minutes then started belting the lyrics to *Singing in the Rain*.

"Come on, Teddy," Mom broke off the tuneless belting for a second, "Sing with me."

"Did you wash your hair?" he asked instead, tracing a small crack in the countertop.

"I can't. I'll get soap in my eyes."

"So close them."

A few seconds later, "It's too dark."

Teddy closed his eyes and rubbed them. "Fine." He tugged open the shower curtain and was immediately pelted by stray drops of water. "Turn around."

She turned away from the spray and started humming again. He poured a dollop of soap into his palm and carefully worked it through her hair, trying to untangle as many knots as possible. "Maybe we should take a clipper to *your* hair, instead," he muttered.

"We could be twins." She smiled and started swaying to inaudible music as he worked the lather around. He grimaced. She wasn't even joking. His mother had only been sixteen when she'd had him, a whole year younger than he was now. At thirty-three, she looked too young to have a kid his age. The alcohol had added wrinkles, but not enough to stop people from calling her his sister — or enough to stop the dicks at school from making crass jokes.

She reached out to touch his hair again. He cringed away from the wet fingers. "Mom, stop."

She pouted but refrained from wetting his scalp further. He helped her rinse the soap clean then grabbed a towel. She stumbled slightly climbing over the side of the tub but managed to steady herself before falling.

He got her into a pair of clean pajamas and tucked her into bed. "I'll make you something to eat."

"It's too early to eat. I'm not hungry." Mom tugged the blanket up to her chin. Her eyes slid from his, darting surreptitiously to the nightstand and away. Habit made Teddy want to snag the hidden bottle and take it to the sink to empty. He ignored the urge. He was tired of making the effort when she wouldn't, and besides, she'd just use money that should be spent on groceries to replace it.

Instead, he set her alarm and headed to the kitchen, making her a sandwich and bringing it back to her room. Maybe the bread would sponge up the liquor.

She shoved a bottle under the covers like she thought he wouldn't see it — or smell it, since she'd sloshed a good few swallows on the pillow.

"Here." He passed her the sandwich.

She took a bite then crinkled her nose and threw the sandwich, plate and all, on the floor. "Not hungry."

Teddy clenched his fists, not bothering to clean the scattered bread. "Fine."

So much for sobering her up.

Chapter Two

The next morning, Teddy banged on his mother's bedroom door. "You're going to be late." He grabbed the knob and twisted, not honestly expecting it to turn this time when it hadn't the last three, and he was, sadly, correct. "Mom!"

He had to leave to get to his janitorial job at the local community college in twenty minutes. If she wasn't up and dressed by then, she wouldn't make it to her shift at the hospital, and she was already on thin ice with her boss.

The door flung open just as Teddy was about to start banging on it again, but it wasn't his mom on the other side. Instead, Teddy was face-to-face with a rotund, red-faced man in a stained white tank top and sweats. His bare feet ended in thick, yellowing toenails. Teddy was going to have to steam clean the carpets. Twice.

"Who the fuck are you?" The stranger grunted, scratching the patch of hairy skin peeking out the bottom of his shirt.

"When the fuck did *you* get here?" Teddy asked instead of answering. When he'd crashed last night after finishing his English essay, his mother had been dead to the world in her bed...alone.

The fat man frowned and looked back into the darkened bedroom, where Teddy could just barely see the sprawled form of his slumbering mother. "Libby—"

"It's *Livy*, dumbass. Short for Olivia," Teddy corrected. He leaned around, crouching to see beneath the man's wobbly, out-flung arm, which was currently propping up the doorframe. "Mom, you gotta get up or you'll be late."

She just groaned and tugged her pillow over her head.

"Damn. You've got a kid?" The man turned to eye the mound of covers, then scanned Teddy. "Thought she was younger."

"Pervert." Teddy scowled and gave his mother a final look, hoping to see her stirring. He didn't, so he crossed his arms and straightened to his full, barely over five-foot height. "Time to go, John."

The man started to say, "It's Jack—"

Teddy swallowed a laugh, and muttered, "Ironic." Louder, he added, "Whatever, *Jack*. You gotta go. I have to get to work."

"I wanted to make her breakfast..."

Teddy didn't know why. It wasn't like he was ever going to see Mom again. She had more men in her bed than a Motel 6.

"Yeah, yeah, you're a real gentleman. Leave your number on the fridge with the others. I'm sure you'll be the one she calls back." Teddy ushered the man out of the house and shut the door in his face. He opened it a second later to toss a pair of cowboy boots he didn't recognize onto the porch. He slammed it shut again and pulled the deadbolt.

When he got back to his mother's room, the door was locked again. Teddy kicked it. "Fuck!" He cursed, rubbing his bruised toe.

He'd have to deal with the fallout later. He grabbed his sneakers and tugged on his sweater. He left the house, grateful that John, or Jack, or whatever his name was, had finally left. Shoving his useless phone in his pocket, just in case he had to call the police—the only number it would let him dial out—he started down the sidewalk for the college.

He couldn't help glancing up to stare at the house next door. Twenty years before, it had probably been identical to his. They were both two-story Craftmans, both with the same off-gray siding and covered porch. But the Romeros had added a white picket fence that separated their yard from Teddy's, with a neat row of well-kept hedges alongside it. It was clear from the sparkling windows and stone garden by the steps that the Romeros lovingly cared for their home. Teddy glanced back at his own house.

The porch sloped slightly to the right and the small front lawn was overgrown. Spring had come, but there were no flowers to show it, just patchy dirt and a single, overgrown shrub. Their recycle bin overflowed with glass bottles. Teddy's lips tightened and he turned back to the Romeros.

Mama R was probably cleaning up from breakfast, and he heard the sound of a saw from the workshop out back. Despite telling himself not to, despite knowing he shouldn't, Teddy's gaze darted over to the open garage, where a beat-up red Chevy truck sat, its hood open. A pair of legs, jeans stretched over firm thighs, was the only thing he could see of the man lying underneath the truck. Faintly, he heard the *tinging* of a wrench on metal.

Teddy's heart thumped faster in his chest. He should walk away before he got caught staring — he knew it — but his feet were glued to the sidewalk.

Ian Romero was four years older than he was. At twenty-two, his body had filled out in all the right places, but when he smiled, his eyes still held the laughter of youth.

Teddy had been coming to the Romeros' house since they had moved in when Teddy had been five — first for play dates with Lucas, the Romeros' middle child, back when Teddy's asshole of a dad was still alive and his mother wanted him out of the house, away from the screaming and swinging fists. Later, after his father had died, he'd come over nightly after Mama R heard he was home alone while his mother went to work.

He remembered the first time he'd seen Ian as more than just his friend's annoying older brother. He and Lucas had been twelve, Ian sixteen, and they'd been playing tag in the back yard. He remembered Ian had been chasing them and laughing so hard that Teddy had tripped over a clump of loose dirt, crashing to the ground with Ian in a tangle of limbs and laughter. Then, he'd felt *it* — the way his heart *thud-thudded* harder at the feel of Ian's hands pinning him down, the heat in his groin as he'd straddled him.

Not that Ian had noticed. Ian had just laughed, apologizing as he stood and helped Teddy up, looking him over to make sure he wasn't hurt. Teddy had felt both childish and cared for as he let Ian smooth a Band-Aid over his knee. He'd been in love — with a capital

L—with Ian ever since. It was a pity Ian would never see him as anything but his younger brother's friend.

One of Ian's cowboy boots shifted against the pavement, digging his heel in to drag himself out from under the car, and Teddy yelped, scrambling down the sidewalk before he could get caught staring.

* * * *

Later that night, sore from hours of mopping and sweeping and cleaning whiteboards, faintly nauseous from the strong odor of bleach and antiseptic, Teddy closed the door to his room behind him and gathered his kit from the dresser. He cleared off the small desk in the corner of his room and flipped on the desk lamp.

He went through the routine of setting up with the ease of practice. He'd been doing it on his own for nearly two years—ever since he'd turned sixteen and gotten off puberty blockers and onto Delatestryl. His mother had sobered up enough to help for the first month, but, like all the other times, the sobriety hadn't lasted.

Washing his hands, checking the date on the vial, examining the contents for discoloration... The rubber stopper on the vial had to be cleaned with an alcohol swab, the packaging on the needle checked for tampering. He did it daily, though he'd never found a problem, because his hormones were too important to risk screwing up over something stupid. Satisfied that everything was clean and prepped, he plunged the 18-gauge needle into the rubber stopper and cleared the syringe of air.

Holding the vial tightly, he turned it upside down and positioned the needle, slowly depressing the plunger until he'd pulled the correct dose. With the needle still safely in the vial, he tapped the side of the syringe and removed the last few air bubbles. It used to make him cringe, watching the bubbles float to the top so he could push them back into the vial. He'd been afraid he'd miss one and end up hemorrhaging on the floor, like in those detective shows on TV. It had never happened, and now the step was simple.

He pulled the needle out of the vial, setting the little bottle back on the desk far enough from the edge that he wouldn't knock it off by accident, then disassembled the needle, dropping it into the little red home sharps kit on the floor beside his desk. He attached the injection needle in its place.

It was easy now to find the injection spot. At first, he'd had to mentally plot a grid on his thigh, three squares by three, to find the outer middle that marked the best spot. A new alcohol swab sanitized the skin, then he took a deep breath before pinching the muscle. Careful to keep the syringe at the right angle, he quickly injected it into his thigh before he could tense too much. He hated needles with a fiery passion — just not nearly as much as he hated who he'd be without the testosterone.

After checking the syringe for blood — there wasn't any — he finished the injection and removed the needle. He cleaned up the injection site, the alcohol stinging his skin, all while trying to avoid looking. After he disposed of the needle in the sharps container, he breathed a sigh of relief. He was done with the chore for the next two weeks.

He was even more glad that he turned eighteen in a few days. He'd already talked to his gender therapist and had received her letter of recommendation for medical transition.

The house phone started ringing in the living room. Teddy ignored it. Nobody but Shiloh called him anyway, and Shiloh only called him on his cell. When the phone stopped then started again then stopped and rang a third time, Teddy sighed and headed downstairs to snatch it up, his thigh burning.

"De Luca residence."

A familiar voice spoke through the phone, "Teddy? It's Maria. Olivia didn't show up for her shift today."

Teddy's shoulders tensed immediately. "Oh, I meant to call. She's…sick. She's got the flu, hasn't been able to get out of bed." He crossed his fingers at his side.

Maria was silent on the other end of the line. Maria was his mother's supervisor at the hospital and the closest thing she had to a friend. If Maria didn't know or at least strongly suspect that he was lying, he'd be shocked. Already this month, he'd fielded her call three times.

"Teddy, dear, have you seen my red dress?"

Teddy closed his eyes as his mother yelled from upstairs, doubting it was quiet enough not to be heard through the phone. He covered the base to avoid screaming in Maria's ear. "You threw up on it this morning. Remember? It's in the wash."

"Oh. Are you sure? I don't remember…"

"Teddy. Tell your mother to see me in my office tomorrow morning," Maria sighed. "I can't keep covering for her."

"I'll let her know. I gotta go." Teddy hung up and slammed the receiver down. He glared at the ceiling and counted.

He waited until he was calmed down a bit, then headed back upstairs to his mom's room. She was standing in her underwear in front of the floor-length mirror, a towel swaddled around her hair, still damp from a shower.

"Why do you need your red dress?" Teddy asked from the doorway. "You're not leaving, are you?"

"I have a date. A nice man from the coffee shop." Mom lifted a blue dress and held it against her body, then a pink one. "What do you think?"

"I think you have to work at eight tomorrow and should stay home," Teddy answered, rather than pick a dress.

"Oh, Teddy, it'll be fine. Stop worrying."

"Maria called." Teddy crossed his arms over his chest. "She wants to see you first thing."

It was almost enough to get through. He could see her waver, the hesitation that flickered over her face before she buried it with a smile. "I'm sure it's nothing important."

"It will be if you're late. Please stay home." They couldn't afford for her to lose her job again. She'd only been working there for a year, after teetering between unemployment and part-time work and back again. He'd seen the stack of bills growing steadily on the counter, the red stamps on the envelopes. It was only recently that they'd stopped coming—and only because Teddy had picked up a job.

His mom reached out and patted his cheek. "Boo Bear, you worry too much. Come out with me. I'm sure you'd like Mike." She winked. "I'll slip you a beer."

Teddy gave up. "I've got homework." He turned to head back to his room.

"Teddy," his mom called after him. He paused, shifting his eyes to the ceiling for a moment before he turned around. She lifted the two dresses. "Which one?"

"Blue," Teddy conceded, then headed to his room.

Chapter Three

Ian considered himself an equal opportunity lover. Pansexual and proud, he didn't give a fuck what was between someone's legs as long as they had a good personality and a dirty mouth. The man sitting across the bar from him had too much of one and an unfortunate lack of the other. Ian had, of course, noticed the man when he'd entered. Seeing his lithe body and sculpted cheekbones, Ian would have had to have been blind not to. It also meant, unfortunately, that he'd seen the man who'd entered on his arm, his hand possessively planted on the smaller man's ass — the one who was temporarily ensconced in the bathroom.

Which apparently meant to the pretty boy who had introduced himself as Sam that he had free rein to flirt with the bartender. Ian didn't know if Sam was angling for a hookup or just discounted drinks, and he didn't really care. He didn't dip his dick in taken holes. It was his rule *numero uno*.

Silently, he slid a cosmo across the bar to the man, then resolutely ignored any further attempts at conversation, pointedly turning his back to start wiping down the many glass bottles stretched along the bar-back.

"Have you worked here long?" Sam said, not taking the hint, his voice loud and whiny to be heard over the pounding bass line. Ian glanced at the mirror, watching the man's lips thin when he realized Ian was ignoring him. "Fine. Fuck this, I got better things to do. Don't expect a tip next time."

Ian just tugged the single dollar bill the man had tossed on the bar out of his pocket and dropped it in front of him. "No problem."

Sam slid off the stool with a dramatic huff that was ruined when he had to tug his glittery silver Spanx out of his ass crack. Ian's lips quirked up in a smile that made the man glare before storming back to his date.

"And good riddance," Ian muttered to the man's back.

His buddy Zak, the other bartender, laughed as he stepped up beside him. "Letting the boys down hard again?" Zak was even taller than Ian, his shoulders small mountains over a well-built chest. Ian preferred his men smaller than himself, but even he couldn't help but take a second look the first time he'd seen Beast, as the patrons called him, behind the bar.

"You know me. I don't do anything the easy way," Ian took the good-natured ribbing for what it was and grinned. He tucked the towel back into his apron strings, letting it dangle over his hip, and stepped aside to let Zak take his place.

Prism was busy, even for a Friday night, and Ian felt guilty for leaving the other two bartenders on their own. "Want me to wait a bit?"

"Nah, man, go take your break. If you could hold the place down, so can I. We all know I sling better drinks," Zak teased, already working on pouring a round.

"Better slinger my ass." Ian pulled the key to the back room out of his pocket and passed it over.

"Finger your ass? In public? Damn, who knew you were kinky." Zak winked, then shooed him around the bar. "Go take your break before I change my mind."

Ian gave a half-assed salute. "Sir, yes, sir."

Zak's eyes darkened slightly. "Careful, boy, or I'll be tempted to show you how good it feels on your knees."

Ian just laughed, not at all scared by the threat. "I can Dom from my knees. Come out back and I'll prove it." He waggled his eyebrows salaciously.

It was Zak's turn to laugh.

Ian slipped into the stockroom, navigating the tightly packed shelves to reach the back door. He left it propped open by a box of olives and stepped into the Austin air. Even at night, it was hot, but at least it was a crisp heat, no humidity to weigh him down. He pulled out his phone and spent a few minutes absently scrolling through Facebook, reading other people's posts and stories.

He had one more semester left to finish his degree. He felt like he was the only one of his high school buddies still stuck. He was still working the same job he'd worked since he'd turned eighteen and could legally serve alcohol, still drove the same beat-up Chevy—though he wouldn't trade Sally in for the devil's own ride—and still lived in the same room he'd grown up in. He could move out if he had to, but the cost of living in Austin was only one reason he stayed at home. Lucas, his younger brother, was quickly becoming a handful.

Ever since his papa's heart attack had forced him to retire, Lucas hadn't been the same. Ian suspected much of Lucas' acting out was a response to his papa's growing distance. His dad spent more and more time out back in his workshop or planted in front of the television. It was like living with a ghost.

The only one who seemed unaffected was Noa. His younger sister — not quite a child, not fully a teenager — was the same brightly smiling girl as ever. He was afraid that if he left, that would change. Sometimes he felt like he was the only thing holding their family together. He didn't mind the weight on his shoulders, but he hated the uncertainty. They couldn't stay like this forever. Eventually, he would finish his business degree and open his own bar, like he'd always dreamed of, and move into his own house, with a husband or wife of his own. He felt the change coming the way he sensed a tornado. The air held the same stillness, the same undercurrent of static raising the hair on his arms.

He closed Facebook and shoved his phone back into his pocket, crossing his arms instead to stare at the dark sky. The only stars he saw were the constellation of fears hiding behind his eyes.

* * * *

It was late when Ian quietly shut the front door behind him. He was halfway upstairs when he heard a loud *thunk* from the kitchen. He sighed, already knowing what he'd find. He turned around and followed the noise. In the shadows of the kitchen archway, he leaned against the doorframe, his arms crossed.

His brother Lucas was sprawled across the kitchen tile, the window over the sink open, the screen out. Ian could smell the alcohol from where he was.

"The door's unlocked, you know," Ian said, his voice dry. This wasn't the first time he'd found his brother like this. He wasn't old enough to drink, but that didn't seem to stop him.

Lucas jerked at the sound of Ian's voice, rolling to his feet before swaying. He squinted and lifted a hand to shadow his eyes, as if the little bit of light from the stove clock was too bright. Ian leaned in, his frown deepening when he noticed his brother's blown pupils. *Great. Drunk* and *high.*

Sighing, he uncrossed his arms and stepped forward, taking his brother by the elbow. "Come on. Let's get you cleaned up."

"I'm thirsty." Lucas tried to pull his arm away, but Ian didn't let him.

"I'll get you some water after you take a shower." Ian steered him up the stairs, catching him when he tripped partway, then ushered him into the bathroom. It was a struggle getting his younger brother undressed, since Lucas kept stopping to try and pull the clothes back on. Finally, though, he was able to shove the kid under the lukewarm water.

"Shit, it's hot! Why are you burning me? Am I a lobster? Fuck, are you going to eat me?" Lucas flinched back from the water, arms flailing like he could divert the spray. Whatever his brother was on, it had fucked him up good this time.

"Hold still," Ian grumbled, not bothering to do more than give his brother a cursory wipe down and a quick lather of shampoo. He knew, unfortunately from experience, that Lucas would soon be racked with sweats and shivers that would render the shower pointless anyway.

After turning off the water, he helped Lucas climb out of the tub. Lucas' eyes were drooping now. The water had succeeded in sobering him up at least slightly. Ian wiped him down with a towel and escorted him back to his bedroom, helping him into a pair of gym shorts and a nightshirt.

"Get in bed and I'll get you some water."

For once, Lucas obeyed without argument, sliding beneath the sheets, his jaw gaping in a yawn. He was asleep by the time Ian brought him up a glass, so he left it on the nightstand. In the morning, he'd talk to Mama again at breakfast about a rehab facility — or at least trying to get the young man into a support group — not that it would help.

Lucas didn't want to change, and nobody could force him to. Ian felt guilty about it, but sometimes, he thought that it would be best for everyone, his brother especially, if the next time the police found him, they just locked him up. At least he'd get clean in jail.

Chapter Four

"She lost her fucking job." Teddy kicked his heels against the dark shingles. It was Sunday morning, and he was on the roof of the pool house at the back of the Beckett estate. His head was nestled in the hollow of Shiloh's hip. A pilfered cigarette dangled between Teddy's fingers. He dragged in a small puff of smoke, holding it in his chest. The burn centered him. "It took her fourteen months to get this one and she goes and throws it away."

Shiloh ran his fingers through Teddy's hair. "That's what alcoholics do."

"She's not an alcoholic," Teddy snapped instinctively.

Shiloh's hands stilled against his scalp. "Oh, sorry. Are we still lying about it?"

"She's not a bad mom," Teddy shifted against Shiloh until he could look up at him.

The look Shiloh gave him was more tender than pitying, and it was the only thing that kept Teddy from pulling away. "I didn't say she's a bad mom. I said she's an alcoholic."

Teddy was quiet until the silence grew too heavy. "Yeah."

"Is she coming to graduation?" Shiloh asked.

Teddy had worked his ass off to get a scholarship to Griffin. They couldn't have afforded the tuition otherwise. While Teddy had a tidy trust fund left over from his father's life insurance policy, he couldn't access it until he was eighteen without his mother's authorization. Besides, it was already earmarked to pay for his surgery. Without the scholarships, he'd have ended up in public school. He liked to think his mother would be proud enough of his accomplishment to show up, but he honestly doubted she'd remember.

Teddy shrugged, then asked, "What about your dad? Is he coming?"

"Nah. He's got a conference in New York this weekend." Shiloh's thigh shifted beneath Teddy's head. "Which means I'll have the house to myself. You're going to come to my party, yeah?"

"That depends. Are you going to try blowing Matt in the dining room again?" Teddy asked.

"Why? You wanna watch?" Shiloh teased, "Dirty little voyeur…"

Teddy scrunched his nose. "Hmm-m. Do I want to watch my best friend try and swallow a dick, or would I rather shove a curling iron up my ass? I think I'll take the curling iron for five hundred, Alex."

"Try? He's not that big, darling." Shiloh crooked his pinky for emphasis.

"You say tomato, I say 'still feels like incest'." Teddy waggled his brows.

"Will you come if I promise to keep my shenanigans behind closed doors?"

"Only if you promise to never say 'shenanigans' again."

"Deal." Shiloh tangled his pinky around Teddy's and shook. "I'll scratch voyeur off the list." Shiloh shot him a considering look, "How about exhibitionism? *You* could blow Matt while *I* watch…"

Shiloh screeched, ducking Teddy's attempt to swat him.

* * * *

Teddy craned his neck to see around the curtain into the audience. He was next up to accept his diploma but he hadn't spotted his mother anywhere. The school had set up the ceremony in the auditorium, and it was already packed with parents.

"Teddy De Luca," Principal Harris read.

Teddy climbed the stage. The principal shook his hand and handed over the diploma, then Teddy walked off the other side. It was a rather anticlimactic end to four years of hard work.

A crowd of students who'd already crossed the stage lingered in the back. Most had stripped clear of the robes and were chattering excitedly in small groups. Teddy picked his way over to Shiloh. Like the others, Shiloh had removed his robes. Unlike the rest, though, Shiloh had not worn dress attire beneath it. Instead, he wore skin-tight pink leggings and an off-the-shoulder blouse, complete with heels.

Shiloh glanced up from his phone and grinned. "Ready to go?"

"You're not staying for the brunch?" Teddy asked before pulling off his robe and shoving it into the backpack he'd left by the lighting booth.

"Why would I want to do that?" Shiloh visibly shuddered, like the thought of eating would kill him.

Teddy rolled his eyes. He'd seen Shiloh eat almost a whole pizza by himself, but heaven forbid he try a buffet. "Did you see my mom out there?"

Shiloh's smile slid off his face. "No. But maybe I just missed her."

"Yeah. Maybe." Teddy plastered on a grin. "I'm ready."

Teddy followed Shiloh into the hallway. He paused partway down to peer through one of the side entrances to the auditorium, scanning the chairs again.

"Coming?" Shiloh called from the exit.

"Yeah." Teddy stepped away, knowing his mother wasn't out there, and followed Shiloh into the student parking lot. It wasn't hard to find Shiloh's car. The yellow Cobra stood out among the black sedans predominantly filling the lot.

Shiloh spun the radio dial up then checked the lot behind them before pulling out and onto the street. Teddy hummed along to the music. Shiloh bleated the lyrics off-key at the top of his lungs while his blond hair whipped around his face.

Shiloh passed the entrance to his subdivision and Teddy frowned. "I thought we were going to your house?"

"Gotta get the liquor first," Shiloh answered, angling the car into a lot behind a small liquor store.

Teddy's frown deepened. "You have a fake ID?"

"Nope. The cashier and I have an arrangement."

Nerves coiled in Teddy's stomach. "What kind of an arrangement?"

"I give him a blow job and he ignores the date of birth on my license." Shiloh slid out of the car and went inside before Teddy could do more than grimace.

Teddy ran a nervous hand over the bristles on his scalp, debating on whether or not he should go in and stop Shiloh. It wasn't like he didn't know Shiloh was sexually active, but exchanging blow jobs for beer was not the same thing as a fumbling hand-job underneath the bleachers. Before he'd made up his mind, Shiloh exited the liquor store with a smirk and a cart loaded with liquor and beer. Teddy helped Shiloh transfer everything to the back.

"You think you got enough?" Teddy asked sarcastically.

"Probably not, but I told everyone it was a BYOB party, so whatever." Shiloh shrugged and started the car.

Teddy was quieter than usual on the ride back to Shiloh's house, still running circles around the ethics of Shiloh's deal with the cashier.

Shiloh misread his silence and said, "Don't worry. I got you Coke back at the house. And I think there's some Dr. Pepper too."

"Thanks," Teddy sighed and made an attempt to stop thinking. There wasn't anything he could do about it, and if Shiloh wasn't concerned, maybe he shouldn't be either.

* * * *

Teddy curled up in the armchair next to the cold fireplace. It was stacked high with abandoned paper plates and red Solo cups. Teddy and Shiloh would have to burn them tomorrow. With this many drunk people on the estate, starting a fire now would only lead to a call to the fire department. Teddy was certain he was the only sober one left at the party. He'd already witnessed two girls throwing up in planters and at least one fumbling hand job in the shadows by the stairs.

His eyelids were heavy. Heels on the edge of the seat, he tucked his knees beneath the hem of his sweater, resting his chin atop them. He smothered a yawn. The liquor had emptied over an hour ago, and only a handful of beers still floated around, so surely the party would start to die soon.

A girl in a too-short skirt laughingly swayed her way through the game room. The heel of her shoe caught in the carpeting and she stumbled, landing painfully on top of Teddy. He grimaced as her pointy elbow jabbed into his thigh, but she just giggled, her eyes glazed as they skimmed him up and down.

"Oops! Sorry." She contorted herself around as she struggled to stand.

He half-helped, half-shoved her off his lap then stood up himself. He left the room and headed upstairs. He followed the hall for several feet until he found Shiloh's room. The door was open and the light off, so Shiloh must still be downstairs somewhere.

Teddy went inside and closed the door. He dug around the bottom drawer of the dresser, the one that was unofficially his, and pulled out his most comfortable pair of basketball shorts and a baggy shirt. He left his party clothes in a neat stack on the floor.

After flipping off the light, he slid beneath the coverlet. Strands of music drifted up from downstairs, along with intermittent laughter. Teddy pulled the blanket over his head in hopes of filtering out the noise and tried to sleep.

He must have succeeded, because the next thing he knew, he was awakened by the mattress dipping as someone climbed in beside him. Teddy blinked open his eyes and rolled onto his side, coming face-to-face with Shiloh.

The blond boy was smiling sleepily, cinnamon whiskey on his breath as he asked quietly, "Did I wake you?"

"It's okay. Wasn't really sleeping," Teddy murmured back.

It was a sign of how much alcohol remained in Shiloh's system that he slid closer and asked, voice pleading, "Can we cuddle?" Shiloh always played the tough guy sober, the one who didn't need anything or anyone—the strong shoulder to cry on, because he *never* cried.

Teddy nodded and allowed Shiloh to tangle himself around him. There were a messy few moments of drunk and half-sleepy rearrangements before they ended up with Shiloh's knee tucked between Teddy's, with Teddy's head on Shiloh's arm. Shiloh's other arm tightened around Teddy's waist.

"Do you think everyone had fun?" Shiloh asked after several minutes, just as Teddy was nearly drifting off. His voice was quiet, but not soft—brittle, like old glass, like a misstep could shatter it.

"Yeah. I think people had fun." Teddy smoothed away a strand of Shiloh's hair in reassurance.

Shiloh shifted closer, pressing his face into Teddy's neck. His breath was warm against Shiloh's skin. "Love you," Shiloh muttered.

"You, too."

* * * *

"Goddamn it, Shiloh," a voice bellowed from the doorway, "what did I say before I left?"

Teddy rocketed up, his heart thudding in his throat. Shiloh jerked up as well, knee digging into Teddy's thigh hard enough to for it to immediately blossom into a bruise. Shiloh's hair was a halo around his startled face.

"Dad, don't you know how to knock?" Shiloh asked, clutching his chest.

"Why should I care about your privacy? I walked into my bedroom to find a bevy of drunk teenagers passed out in my bed!" Mr. Beckett bellowed.

"You weren't supposed to be home until tomorrow. I was going to change the sheets." Shiloh slid off the mattress, and after grabbing his discarded jeans from the floor, tugged them on. Teddy stayed where he was, hoping that lack of movement would mean lack of notice, as well.

It did, in part. Mr. Beckett didn't comment on his presence in Shiloh's bed, but that meant Teddy had to sit through several long minutes of yelling back and forth, until finally, Mr. Beckett slammed his fist down on the nightstand. The alarm clock rattled. "I am done arguing with you. You will clean up the mess your so-called friends left behind when they scattered this morning."

"Whatever. I was going to do that anyway." Shiloh crossed his arms mulishly.

"And you're grounded."

"Fine!"

"I have another conference tomorrow in Amsterdam. You'll stay here with Sam. Maybe he can keep you in line." Mr. Beckett didn't wait for a response before he stormed out.

Shiloh grew pale. He stared silently at the bedroom door for several seconds before he set his jaw and spun. "Can I stay at your house?"

Teddy shrugged. "I mean, of course you can, but you know it's not all that...nice."

"Better than staying here with *Sam*." Shiloh's mouth twisted as he said the lawyer's name. Teddy didn't know the story between them, except that whenever Shiloh talked about him, he got a look on his face. Teddy had only met the older man once. He'd seemed pleasant enough.

Teddy helped Shiloh throw clothes into a duffel bag. It seemed like more than he would need for a week, but then, Shiloh liked to change his clothes often. Teddy was worried that they would get caught sneaking out, but nobody was paying attention to them.

They drove several neighborhoods over to Teddy's house. Here, the average family income was at least two zeroes smaller than the one they'd just left. Despite that, Teddy knew he was lucky. If his mother hadn't gotten an inheritance after her parents had passed, they'd have been on the streets by now. Thankfully, she had bought the house outright when Teddy had been hardly more than a toddler, nearly a decade before his father passed and she started drowning her sorrows in a bottle.

Shiloh parked his car behind the rusty 1998 Plymouth Chrysler Teddy's mother had bought the previous year, after she'd crashed their far-more-reliable Corolla. The Rustbucket, as Teddy called it, was missing the passenger side rearview mirror and a third of its fender. The vents insisted on only blowing out hot air, and two of the four windows didn't roll down. Teddy was waiting for the day that the spring-laden seats succeeded in fully deflowering him. He didn't count a few fumbled blow jobs and some half-assed fingering.

Shiloh, at least, was polite enough not to comment. He just grabbed his bag and followed Teddy up the porch steps. Teddy shoved his hands into his pockets and struggled not to defend the sorry state of his house. Shiloh had never come to visit before.

The house itself was a small but solid two-bedroom. The paint was faded but not peeling, the house number hanging by a single screw — but hanging on — and the yard was green, if overgrown. It could be worse. They could live near Rosewood, or over by Twelfth and Chicon, like they would if they were relying on their current income to pay for housing, instead of resting on the laurels of his grandparents' generosity. Although both neighborhoods had been slowly getting better, he still wouldn't want to walk home there at night.

Compared to the Beckett mansion, his house was a dump. Teddy's cheeks burned as he twisted the knob on the front door and found it already unlocked. He held it open and gestured for Shiloh to go in first.

"Come on. You can throw your stuff in my room," Teddy said, moving past Shiloh to lead him farther in. The entryway was barren except for the shoe rack against the wall. It opened into a short, narrow hallway. The kitchen was on the right, as was the dining room, though it was currently being used as a junk room. His mother's old treadmill had been converted to a clothing rack — shirts that no longer fit, pants that needed hemming and mismatched socks dangling from the armrests. A few boxes of old magazines lined the wall with records stacked on top. They didn't have a record player. He didn't know what else was in there, since he pretended the room didn't exist.

To the left was the living room. Teddy couldn't help glancing in as he walked by. His mother was asleep on the couch again, surrounded by half-drank bottles and empty glasses. A mostly full pack of cigarettes sat near the edge of the table. Teddy wondered if she'd notice if he took them.

Instead, Teddy hurried past, taking the stairs at the end of the hall to the second story. "This is mine," he said as he pushed his door open. At least he'd straightened up a few days before. It was messier than he'd have liked if he'd realized he was going to have company over, but his underwear had found its way to the hamper and his dirty magazines had been placed back beneath the mattress.

Shiloh dropped his bag on the floor by the closet and collapsed onto his back on the unmade bed. "I like your house," Shiloh said, his arms flung out.

"It's shitty," Teddy corrected, going over to pull the blinds on the window, unleashing a bright stream of sunlight into the small room. "The only good part is the view."

Shiloh rolled onto his stomach and craned his neck to see around Teddy out of the window. There was a three-foot gap between Teddy's house and the one next door. His window looked right into the neighbor's bedroom.

"He doesn't close his blinds," Teddy sighed dreamily, staring into his favorite place in the whole world...Ian's bedroom. Not that he'd ever been in it, except in his dreams. Ian always kept it locked. Teddy used to think he had a superhero lair hiding behind the door. As he got older, he realized it was locked just because Lucas liked to steal his older brother's shit.

"Creeper." Shiloh grabbed Teddy's pillow and chucked it at him.

Teddy ducked, laughing as the pillow hit the window and slid to the ground. "Have you *seen* him?"

Teddy's excuses to visit had dwindled since Lucas had dropped out of school and started hanging with some sketchy kids, and he'd been left getting his Ian fix through the window. His neighbor worked as a bartender and, the last Teddy knew, he was taking online management classes, which was why he still lived at home. Teddy hoped he never moved out.

"You could leave him notes on the window if you want to go full stalker," Shiloh mused, folding his arms like a pillow beneath his chin.

Teddy's cheeks flamed. He had a stack of sticky notes on his desk, and he couldn't honestly say that they'd never made their way onto the glass.

"Oh, you *already* leave him notes, don't you?" Shiloh chuckled. "Oh, *Ian*, I wanna suck your —"

"I do *not* say that!" Teddy burst out, embarrassed. He'd certainly thought about it often enough.

"Oh, *Ian*, I left my back door unlocked for you. Come pound me into the mattress," Shiloh rolled onto his back, fisting the sheets as he grinned like a maniac.

"I don't sound like that!" Teddy grabbed the pillow and chucked it at his friend.

"Oh, *Ian*!" Shiloh continued moaning, but Teddy stopped listening as he caught movement through the window out of the corner of his eye. He turned to find Ian staring at him, a smirk on his perfectly formed lips. He was shirtless, every ridge of his muscles on perfect display, his jeans riding low on his sharp hips. The button was undone, leaving a V of tan skin that drew Teddy's eye before he could help it.

He couldn't tear his gaze away until Ian moved, stepping closer to the window and wrenching it up. He leaned on the frame with a smirk. Teddy's skin heated further when Ian pointed at Teddy's window, clearly laughing, and waved his hands like he was gesturing for Teddy to follow.

"Be quiet," Teddy said to Shiloh before struggling to push up on the glass. It hadn't been opened in forever. Not since he'd repainted his room, at least, and apparently he'd managed to paint the window shut. It cracked as the window snapped up.

Shiloh smothered his laughs in the pillow. He was thankfully out of sight.

Ian smirked. "Get your phone out."

Teddy's heart thumped in his chest. Why did Ian want his phone? Was he finally going to give him his number? Teddy had tried to be subtle in his crushing, but maybe Ian had noticed anyway. Ian was observant. He grabbed his phone and waved it as proof.

"Does it have a camera?" Ian asked.

"Um…yeah." Teddy fiddled with the app, brow lowering as he wondered why he needed it.

"Good. Why don't you take a picture?"

"Of…of you?" Teddy stuttered, face flushing.

Ian just smirked. "Well, unless you'd rather take one of my bedroom. I can just step out of frame…"

Ian went to step back but Teddy, half shouted, "Wait!" He snapped a photograph of the drop-dead gorgeous man before he could move too far.

"Got it?" Ian asked, brow lifting.

Teddy nodded, his phone clasped in his hand.

"There. You can stare at that next time you get the...*urge* to peek." Ian winked then retreated into his own room, laughing as he closed the window.

Teddy... Well, now Teddy had to go shove his head in the oven and just *die*. He slammed his window closed and, for good measure, tugged down the drapes.

"You are so *busted*," Shiloh teased.

Chapter Five

Ian laughed at the expression on Teddy's face as he slammed the window shut. The shocked embarrassment was nearly as amusing as the lust that had preceded it.

Ian finished getting dressed and left his room — and his not-so-secret admirer — behind. Following the sound of laughter, he made his way to the kitchen. The back door was open to the small patio that comprised much of the back yard. Mama leaned against the doorframe, a cup of black tea in her hand. She was smiling fondly.

She turned to look at him as he entered, her smile brightening.

"Mama." He leaned down to kiss her right cheek in greeting.

"*Mijo*. I made tea." She gestured to the kettle on the stove.

Ian made himself a cup and carried it over to stand beside her, following her gaze into the back yard. It wasn't large, and the patio swallowed most of it, but the little bit of property they called their own was enclosed in a white picket fence. His mother had insisted on it when she and his father had first immigrated from Bolivia, several years before Ian had been born.

"She's growing like a weed," Ian said, watching his sister dance. Noa was thirteen, though in his mind she was still barely knee-high. He still expected to see her gap-toothed smile when she looked at him. Instead, she looked far too old in her pink-striped leggings and racer-back tank top, her MP3 player tucked into the pockets. White earbuds traced their way up to her ears. Her face was fixed in concentration. Her heels sank into the dirt with each step.

"She wants to dance for the talent show," Mama murmured, voice proud. "And she chose the *Caporales*."

Ian remembered learning it at her age and wondered if he could still do it. He knew he couldn't fit in the shoes, for sure. The low-heeled boots had bells on the ankles. He'd worn them everywhere for a month.

Noa ended with a flourish and Ian and his mother both clapped loudly. Noa grinned, bounded up the stairs and threw her arms around Ian's waist. "Did you like my dance?"

"Of course, *hermanita*." Ian ruffled her dark hair, careful not to disturb the handful of colored ribbons she had strung through the braid.

She beamed up at him. "You'll come to the show, right?"

"Of course. I wouldn't miss it for the world," Ian promised. He was about to ask when it was when he heard the thundering of footsteps down the stairs, followed by the front door slamming.

Mama sighed and muttered a prayer below her breath. "That boy, I swear."

"I'll go talk to him," Ian replied. Mama had flatly refused to even consider hearing him out about Lucas going to rehab. *'Not my baby,'* she'd said. Ian supposed he'd just have to do his best to bring his brother around on his own.

"Tell him I'm making *saltenas*," Mama said as Ian placed his cup in the sink and headed for the front door.

His younger brother was several feet down the sidewalk. Ian shook his head as he hurried to catch up. It had been bad enough when Lucas had dropped out of school the past year, only a handful of months from graduating. Ian blamed it on the hooligans his brother called friends. Most of them came from broken families, so it was hard to blame them for taking to the streets, but Lucas didn't have that excuse.

"Lucas!" Ian jogged up beside him, grabbing his brother's arm to get his attention. "You didn't say goodbye to Mama."

Lucas rolled his eyes. "It's not like I'm moving or nothing."

"Where are you going? I know you don't have a job."

Lucas glowered, crossing his arms. It made him look like a child preparing to throw a tantrum. In his defense, however, he was. "I could have a job...if I wanted one."

"But you don't. You spend all day roaming town with your merry gang of assholes while Papa pays your rent and you don't even have the decency to kiss Mama goodbye."

Ian was tired of his younger brother's tantrums and childish rebellions. He'd skipped from throwing fits to petty theft and vandalism. Just last week, the police had picked him up at a convenience store. Even if it wasn't for the fact that it gave all of them a bad name, it pissed Ian off personally because it was so stupid. Their parents made good money. Lucas still got an allowance, though he did no chores and didn't look for work. He could have paid for the stupid DVD if he'd wanted it so bad, but he'd stolen it just for street cred.

"You're not Papa, so fuck off, yeah?" Lucas turned his back on Ian and started down the sidewalk, his shoulders set.

Ian grabbed his brother's arm and spun him around, anger flaring. "No, I'm not Papa. I can still put you on your ass, though." Ian wasn't prepared for his brother to cock back his fist and let it fly toward his face. It struck him hard on the chin. Ian's head snapped back and he winced, rubbing the already-swelling skin.

"Thought you said you could put me on my ass," Lucas egged him on, his feet planted. He shoved Ian backward, but Ian refused to budge. "Well, come on then. Prove it, *pendejo*."

"I don't have to prove it to make it true. Come home. Have breakfast. Mama's making *saltenas*." Ian reached for his brother, who cringed away.

"Whatever. I gotta go." The look Lucas gave him practically dared him to stop him again. Ian gave up. If his brother wanted to screw up his life, then so be it. He wasn't going to waste his breath.

* * * *

Maybe Ian was biased, but Mama made the best *saltenas* he'd ever tasted. She'd learned the recipe from her mother, who'd learned it from hers and so on. She didn't make them often anymore, since they were pretty much a whole weekend project, so when she did, he made sure to be home.

He helped Mama clear the plates after breakfast. His sister kissed him goodbye then headed out of the house to meet her friends at the museum. She said she was studying for a project. With only a week left before school was out, he suspected there was less studying going on then she pretended.

He knew Mama suspected it as well, but when he'd brought it up, she'd just smiled and shrugged. "She's growing up. It's good for her to get out of the house. I'll be at my book club anyway."

After his mother left, Ian grabbed his laptop and carried it out onto the front porch. Sitting on the steps, he leaned against the siding, his computer open in his lap. The sunlight made seeing the screen more difficult, but he learned better in the fresh air.

He was in the middle of a boring lecture on *Creating a Culture of Health in Your Business* when two boys spilled out of the house next door. They were both laughing. He recognized Teddy, of course, in his signature oversized sweater and jeans, but the second one was a mystery.

He wondered if Teddy had a boyfriend and immediately glowered at the thought — then had to kick himself for feeling something far too close to jealousy. Teddy was his brother's friend. Even if he wasn't, he was too young, only barely graduated. Maybe the four-year age difference wouldn't seem so bad later. At the moment, staring after Teddy and his friend made him feel like a pervert.

He forced his attention back to the lecture as the pair climbed into the fancy car outside Teddy's house and drove away.

Eventually, he gave up on the lecture and closed his laptop, resolving to watch it later when he was less distracted. Maybe his preoccupation with the boy next door was a sign. It might be his night off, but *Prism* was as good a place as any to spend it. At least he knew he wouldn't go home alone.

* * * *

The nightclub wasn't strictly queer, but over the years, it had acquired a reputation. Gays and their allies had commandeered it, drawn by the glitter and the rainbows and the relatively tolerant owner — an aging man who spent more time in his office than on the floor, but whose managers and staff waved more flags than just Old Glory.

One of the perks of tending bar there four nights a week was bypassing the line that weaved along the sidewalk. Some nights, like tonight, were busier than others. The bouncer, Zadrien, pounded Ian's fist before unclipping the frayed rope and letting him through.

The club was dark. He'd seen it with the lights on and no amount of money could make him eat the food served, but he hadn't come here for that purpose anyway. He flagged down Zak at the bar and ordered a drink. Glass in hand, he turned to scan the dance floor. It was crowded with college students on break and businessmen off for the weekend. There were more men than women.

One in particular caught his eye. From the back, he saw only a lithe neck thrown back and a pair of slender legs in jeans that cupped an ass so perfect that Ian knew it would fit his palms like they were made for it. An overly large glitter top hid what Ian suspected was a lissome torso. The man's arms were cast above his head. Ian pictured gripping the narrow wrists in his larger hands to pin the man under him, the willowy frame swallowed beneath him. Imagined the taste of sweat dripping down into the hollow of the man's throat, and how his moans would taste on Ian's mouth.

But then a blond boy separated from the crowd and draped an arm over the other man's shoulders, and Ian flinched as he recognized him.

He'd seen the blond earlier that morning, leaving his neighbor's house. And when the man Ian had been fantasizing about turned, his face brilliant beneath the strobe lights, Ian was shocked to recognize him as well.

The man of his fantasies wasn't a stranger Ian could take home and fuck into the mattress. It was a bright-eyed, scantily clad Teddy.

Chapter Six

Ian stood stunned, a statue in a sea of gyrating bodies, until Teddy threw his head back and laughed. Ian could almost hear the bell-like sound being carried over the throbbing bass. It stirred him from his stupor and he frowned, pushing his way through the crowd to get closer.

He told himself it was because Teddy was too young to be there and that if he saw his brother here, he would do the same thing. But he knew that if he saw his brother here, he would be worried about what trouble the kid was trying to get into. When he saw Teddy, he had an entirely different worry—because Ian wasn't the only one watching him.

Ian came up behind him and gripped his arm, spinning him around. Teddy looked startled as they came face-to-face. Face-to-chest, rather, as the younger man was quite a bit shorter.

Teddy's throat bobbed as he swallowed, his chin lifting as he looked up, then up some more. "Ian?"

"What are you doing here?" Ian growled, keeping his grip on the boy, who looked ready to run.

Teddy's friend stepped forward, puffing out his chest. "What do you care? It's a free country."

Ian gave Teddy's friend a once-over before dismissing him, turning his attention back to Teddy. "You're too young. How'd you even get in? Zade cards at the door."

"I'm eighteen," Teddy grumbled. "As long as I'm not drinking, I'm allowed."

Ian hesitated but finally released the younger man's arm. "Huh. Eighteen? Really? When did that happen?"

"It's his birthday, asshat." Teddy's friend rolled his eyes. "And you're ruining it, so…fuck off."

"Shiloh!" Teddy's face heated.

"Teddy!" His friend rolled his eyes. "Just because he's hot doesn't mean you have to let him manhandle you."

Teddy's blush deepened to full crimson. Shiloh eyed Teddy as well then laughed. "Or maybe you do." Shiloh shoved Teddy forward until he bumped into Ian's chest.

Ian instinctively gripped Teddy's arm, keeping him from tumbling over.

"Have fun. Be safe." Shiloh waved and disappeared into the crowd, leaving Teddy and Ian staring at each other. Ian wasn't sure which of them seemed more startled.

"I can—" Ian started, just as Teddy said, "Do you want—?"

"Oh, I *want*," Ian muttered, unable to resist. He drew Teddy closer, out of the path of a drunk man pushing his way through the tightly packed bodies behind him.

A grin spread across Teddy's face. It was hypnotic. Ian couldn't look away. "The picture was blurry, you know," Teddy finally said, his voice breathy.

"Should've been faster," Ian replied. He lifted his hands from Teddy's arms. He didn't think he imagined the disappointment that colored the young man's face. It faded when Ian curled his hands around Teddy's hips, tugging them closer to his own.

Teddy's breath escaped in a moan. Ian knew the young man could probably feel the effect it had on him where they were pressed together. "Say the word," Ian said, his face tilting down. "Tell me to give you back to your friend. Tell me to leave you alone."

"No," Teddy said on a sigh, tipping backward and parting his lips.

Ian longed to capture them, to steal his breath into his mouth, to explore the taste of his skin. Then he realized there was nothing stopping him. Teddy was a consenting adult—a consenting adult who was currently leaning into his embrace, all but begging for him to close the scant few inches that separated them.

So Ian did. He took what Teddy was offering so sweetly. He caressed the seam of Teddy's lips with his tongue until they parted, granting him entry. He tightened one hand on the boy's slender hips like he was afraid of letting go and lifted the other to gently clasp the back of Teddy's head. Ian used it to angle him back, opening his mouth farther. He tasted of mint, but when Teddy moaned, it became fire.

Until Teddy's mouth broke from his and he was tugged out of Ian's grasp by his friend.

"TMZ is here," Shiloh said, tugging on Teddy's arm. Teddy blinked, looking for all the world like Ian was the sun and he'd been caught staring at him too long, until his gaze sharpened and he blinked.

"Shit," Teddy breathed, breaking the intense stare he and Ian had been tangled in to turn to his friend. "Did they spot you?"

"I don't know, maybe. We gotta go." Shiloh tugged on Teddy's arm, glancing nervously over his shoulder.

Teddy turned back to Ian, an apology in his eyes.

"Don't worry," Ian said, lips curving up. "I know where to find you."

Teddy flushed at the reminder but allowed his friend to grab his hand and lead him off the dance floor. Ian watched until he was out of sight, regret burgeoning in his chest. He didn't mind going home alone, but going home alone and knowing that Teddy was right next door might kill him.

* * * *

Ian spilled his release into the shower drain, telling himself it was the last time he was going to use thoughts of his sexy neighbor to get off. At least, it was the last time he was going to use thoughts of his sexy neighbor to get off *alone*. The next time, he fully intended the young man to be there with him—preferably naked.

He spun off the shower and wrapped a towel around his hips, heading back into his bedroom. He paused in the doorway, a smirk crossing his mouth. He hadn't drawn his curtains yet, and while the darkened room would keep him in shadow, if he turned on the light…

He crossed to his window, the one that faced his not-so-secret admirer. He leaned his forehead against the cool glass.

He'd never really paid attention to the room across from his, except to notice that he could see into it, and occasionally to read a note or two Teddy had left — usually, some message he wanted Ian to pass on to his brother. He'd never dared stare longer.

He remembered when he'd first noticed that the walls were pink and the curtains were lacy, and that far too often, the girl on the other side had looked sad.

But he couldn't pinpoint when that had changed. At some point over the years, the window on the other side of his had become just a window. Looking now, he noticed the changes. The walls were a not-quite-blue, not-quite-gray shade that looked perfectly bland, and posters he couldn't quite make out were scattered across them. He couldn't see the bed, but he saw that the vanity had become a dark oak dresser.

While he didn't know when the room had changed, he remembered the exact moment when the girl had.

Ian had been fourteen and finding himself more interested in boys as well as girls. He'd never paid his younger brother Lucas' friend Thea much attention. She had been a kid, too young to be much fun, even if she did follow him around a lot while Mama was babysitting her. And she was always pouting — not whining, not really bothersome, just generally unhappy. Ian hadn't known much about girls, except that normally, they got a pinched sort of look on their face when they were talking to him and he wasn't really listening, so maybe *unhappy* was the default setting for girls.

But then one day, he'd come home from football practice and stood, confused, in the doorway to the living room. His younger brother hadn't had a lot of friends. He'd been overweight and acne-spotted. Neither were what had kept him from making friends, though. It was the fact that his brother was so concerned about both of those things that he lashed out at classmates before they could lash out at him for either.

So, he had been surprised to see a beaming boy lying on his stomach on the carpet, cheerfully inspecting a collection of Pokémon cards spread across the floor. It took him an uncomfortably long time to realize that his brother's friend Teddy, the happy boy with the shaved head and the obsession with 3D puzzles, was the same friend who used to be called Thea.

He'd long ago stopped thinking of the sad shadow of a girl who had followed him around like a puppy.

He didn't miss her.

Through the other window, Ian saw the door crack open and the bedroom light flick on. Teddy and his friend were both frowning as they entered Teddy's bedroom. Ian found himself frowning as well. He didn't like the jealousy that reared his head at the thought of Teddy being with someone else, though he knew they owed each other nothing. A single kiss did not a relationship make.

The frown vanished, though, when Teddy's eyes lifted immediately to the window in a way that spoke of routine, as if his first thought upon entering was to seek Ian out for comfort—though Teddy's eyes widened, like he hadn't actually expected to see Ian peering at him through the glass.

Ian knew that the towel wrapped around his hips provided enough privacy that he didn't need to be concerned about showing too much. Even without it, he doubted his room was light enough to reveal more than a suggestion anyway. It didn't stop the red tint from filling Teddy's cheeks, nor did it stop Ian from wanting to see it closer. He wanted to trace the blush with his fingers, follow its path along Teddy's skin and see just how low it went.

Instead, he lifted his fingers to his lips and blew the young man a kiss, then winked.

That night, he left the blinds open.

Chapter Seven

"Your neighbor is *hot*...with a capital H-O-T," Shiloh said, the morning after Teddy's semi-disastrous eighteenth birthday. Only semi, because kissing Ian might have been the highlight of his decade. It more than made up for the drunken fit his mother had thrown the morning before, and the high-speed chase that had ended in a high-priced ticket for Shiloh afterward. Today, they were in a little boutique in the Second Street District, one Teddy wouldn't have stepped foot into without Shiloh's urging. He preferred the vintage shops on South Congress or other, less expensive stores.

"I know," Teddy sighed, his mind already pulling up a dreamy image of Ian, as if he could have possibly forgotten what he looked like already.

"I am sorry I interrupted your big moment, though," Shiloh added, twisting his face slightly. "I probably could have waited a few more minutes... Let you at least get his pants off."

Teddy chucked the blue button-down he'd been holding up, still on the hanger, at his friend with a huff. "If I'd already had his pants off, you'd have been shit out of luck."

"But you wouldn't have been." Shiloh grimaced at the shirt Teddy had been considering buying, the one that Teddy had used as a projectile, and hung it back on the rack. "I am not letting you wear that. Try this one." He held out a fuchsia pullover instead.

Teddy fingered the soft material regretfully. "It's pretty," he admitted.

"So buy it." Shiloh held it out.

"It's too thin," Teddy said, dropping his fingers.

"Wear your binder. No one will notice." Shiloh shrugged and waved it at him again.

"It's too bulky." Teddy turned away from the offering and pulled out a different shirt. It was not quite so vivid and the material wasn't as soft, but it had more drape and less cling. "How about this one?"

"I guess it's not horrible. Did you schedule your surgery yet?" Shiloh eyed the fuchsia shirt, then shrugged and draped it over his arm instead.

"It was technically already scheduled. I just had to call and confirm that I hadn't suddenly changed my mind because my age changed." Teddy rolled his eyes and grabbed a pair of black basketball shorts to go with the shirt. "I'll be going under next month."

Shiloh beamed. "Then you can totally buy this shirt. It's not like it'll be languishing in your closet for the next ten years." He held it out again then pouted when Teddy refused. He knew without even looking that the price tag was way over his budget. He was already pushing it with what he had.

"I'm going to go check out. Meet you by the entrance?" Teddy asked.

"Sure. I just have to grab one last thing." Shiloh headed toward the lingerie.

Teddy got in line. He set his purchases on the counter and waited while the cashier removed the anti-theft devices and scanned the tags.

"That'll be seventy-two dollars and ninety-eight cents," The woman said, her voice bored.

Teddy pulled out his debit card and swiped it. The machine issued a loud siren of beeps, the screen flashing red, and he frowned. "Um, can I try it again?"

The cashier sighed. "Of course."

He waited then swiped his card again when prompted. It was declined, again. He frowned, flipping the card over to examine the shiny magnetic strip on the back. It looked fine. It was brand new. He'd only just gotten it the day before. It must not have been activated correctly. That was the only thing he could think of. It wasn't like he'd spent almost a hundred thousand dollars in two days. This was the first time he'd touched the account with his trust money in it.

"Sir, if you can't pay, I'm going to have to ask that you step out of line. There are people waiting."

Normally, the cashier's automatic use of 'sir' would have been the highlight of his day, but he hardly noticed. He was certain he'd called to activate it. They'd given him a pin number and everything. Frowning, he headed to the front door empty-handed.

Shiloh met him a few minutes later. His friend frowned, "What happened? Change your mind?"

"I gotta run to the bank real quick. Something's up with my card," Teddy answered.

Immediately, Shiloh's face grew wary. "Oh. Um, did you want me to go with you?"

"No, that's okay. I'll meet you back at the house, okay?" Teddy knew Shiloh had hang-ups when it came to money. They were the opposite ones that Teddy had, but that didn't mean he didn't understand. He'd been friends with Shiloh long enough to see people come and go from his life, nearly all of them users, looking for handouts. Shiloh, after all, was the only son of the CEO of BeckTech, a giant in the technology industry. A lot of kids seemed to think that meant Shiloh owed them somehow.

"Okay." Shiloh, voice muted, agreed.

But everything wasn't okay, because fifteen minutes later, Teddy was staring stupidly at a man in a sweaty polo shirt who was holding a receipt that couldn't be right.

"What do you mean, there's no money?" Teddy asked, not quite able to comprehend the teller's words.

"I can go get my manager, if you'd like. She can explain it to you," the man said, clearly exasperated.

Teddy nodded. "That would be great."

The teller had to be wrong, because a hundred thousand dollars didn't just vanish overnight. The manager emerged from a door behind the desk a few minutes later. She was tall and lanky, her blonde hair limp around her face, but she had a kind smile. "Ms. De Luca?"

"Mr.," Teddy corrected.

The woman glanced down at the paper with a frown that cleared a moment later. "Oh, I'm so sorry, I didn't notice the name change form. It's right here. Well, *Mr.* De Luca"—she shot him a bright smile—"I see you have some questions about your account. Let's see what I can figure out for you, hmm-m?"

She tapped the keys on the computer. "So, your ending balance for May, it looks like, was…seventeen dollars and forty-two cents. There have been two withdrawals this year, one for May and one for April, each totaling twelve hundred ninety-two dollars and forty-seven cents to PennyMac Loan Services. It looks like there were…three payments last year to the same firm, and… Well, actually, there have been a total of…twenty-three payments over the past six years. There appear to be payments out to the City of Austin, as well as several dozen payments to Austin Energy." She clicked a few more times on the computer. "The payments were authorized by Olivia De Luca."

Teddy clenched his hands tightly into fists and sucked in a breath. He closed his eyes to try to steady himself. "Okay, thank you. I didn't realize."

Teddy left the bank in a daze. He'd planned on calling an Uber, but with the only money he had the little bit he'd saved from his after-school job, he no longer felt comfortable spending it. Instead, he spent the walk home running his mother's betrayal over in his mind.

She knew what he wanted that money for. He didn't understand why she'd paid almost thirty thousand dollars to a loan service. The house was supposed to be paid off. If she'd taken out a mortgage, she would have told him, right? And the rest, the payments to the energy company and the city of Austin? Well, it sounded like she'd used his trust on bills. He wondered if that was the reason all the red-stamped envelopes had stopped coming.

Had she been funding her employment gaps with his inheritance? Each time she'd fallen back into the bottle hard enough to lose her job, had she done so because she knew his money was just there, conveniently waiting to bail her out?

The more he considered the possibility, the angrier he grew. It was like molten lava swirling in his chest, so hot that he knew his bones couldn't contain it. His hands shook at his sides, even when he shoved them into his pockets, and his jaw clenched together so tightly that he thought for a moment he could feel his teeth cracking.

He was angry, but beneath the fury he felt a riptide of guilt, preparing to take his feet from under him. A small voice whispered in his mind that he couldn't be angry. What right did he have to be pissed that she'd taken the money, since she'd spent it on bills? But he would have given it to her, freely if not happily, if she'd asked.

If she'd just sat him down like the adult she pretended he was and explained.

"Fuck," he cursed, then bent, hands on his knees, at the sharp pain that swarmed his stomach. He had no idea how he would pay for his surgery now. It was only a month away and, even with a payment plan, they needed half up front.

He hadn't come up with any solutions by the time he reached his house.

"Boo Bear," his mother called from the living room. He ignored her, taking the stairs two at a time. He slammed his bedroom door behind him.

Shiloh looked up from where he was reading on Teddy's bed. "You look like someone stole your lunch money."

Teddy tugged off his sweater and threw it as hard as he could at his hamper, then stared at it. He kicked the damn thing over. He grabbed his shirt and pulled it tight across his chest. "Might as well get used to these…these…*things*, since they're never going away." He slammed his head angrily back into the door, ignoring the tears it brought to his eyes, then slid down it to the ground. "Fuck!"

The mattress groaned as Shiloh shifted, moving to a seated position perched at the edge. "What happened? Did your doctor call?"

"No. Fuck, I almost wished it was something like that, then I could just find another doctor or something. No, my fucking drunk of a mother emptied my trust." Teddy shoved off his shoes, chucking them at his closet door, finding a dark enjoyment in the satisfying *thud* as they struck.

"She can't do that," Shiloh said immediately, before hesitating. "Well, I mean…not unless she was the executor, but…"

Teddy laughed coldly. "Yeah. Fuck my life. All this time I thought we owned the house free and clear and she took out a goddamn *mortgage*."

Shiloh sat in uncomfortable silence for a long moment. "That sucks."

"Yeah. Tell me about it. She could have at least fucking told me. All this time, letting me talk and talk about my surgery, letting me think that there was actually a chance of me getting to be *me*." Teddy jerked to his feet and crossed to his closet, tugging it open. "Might as well get rid of all of this shit. No point in being a boy with boobs." He grabbed a handful of his clothes and started angrily stripping them off hangers, letting them fall haphazardly to the floor. He knew he was being over-dramatic and that he should stop and find a solution that didn't involve him devolving into a dysphoric mess on his bedroom floor, but if he stopped, he was going to start thinking, and if he started thinking, he'd start feeling — and that would hurt.

It wasn't even that he would have to postpone his surgery that hurt, though he had to admit it was frustrating, but he'd been living like this for six years. Another few wouldn't kill him. He was stronger than that. What hurt was that his mother, who had promised and promised to support him, who had told him over and over that she loved him and that she wanted what was best for him, had betrayed him, had stolen from him not once, or twice, but dozens of times over the past half-dozen years.

"Teddy, stop." Shiloh tugged him back from the closet. He couldn't see the clothing anymore, not through the haze of tears blurring his eyes. "Teddy, it'll be fine. You're just working yourself up now. Come on. Breathe with me."

"I don't want to breathe!" Teddy couldn't stop his outburst. "You can't say it's going to be fine. I don't have seventy thousand dollars just…just sitting around, and I can't go to my daddy and ask for more. That money was all I had. You don't understand."

He registered the frozen, pained look on Shiloh's face immediately and horror bloomed in his chest. "I'm sorry. I didn't mean… I shouldn't have said that."

Shiloh shrugged, the motion stiff. Teddy, more than anyone, knew that Shiloh didn't have an easy life, even if his problems were rarely about money.

"Whatever." Shiloh pressed his lips together so tightly they turned white at the edges before the expression softened, hidden beneath a mask Teddy thought would *never* be used on him. "Do you want money, then? I can talk to my dad. It's not like I don't have it. He likes you. I'm sure he'd help."

"No, Shiloh, *no*." Teddy stepped forward, wanting to soothe the wound his words had caused, but Shiloh jerked back, out of reach. "I'm sorry. I didn't mean it. I was just angry and I shouldn't have taken it out on you."

"It's fine. I gotta go, though. Thanks for letting me stay, but my dad is probably worried." Shiloh gave a stiff smile and started packing his duffel, shoving his clothing inside with little care. "Let me know if you change your mind. I really can help."

"I don't want your money," Teddy said, shame burning him. Shiloh didn't answer. He just carried his duffel bag downstairs and gave a halfhearted wave before heading to his car.

Teddy followed him out onto the porch, wanting to say something...anything. Wanting to take his words back, but he couldn't. Instead, he watched Shiloh leave.

He sank down onto the porch steps and buried his face in his hands. He'd really fucked up everything.

Chapter Eight

"Hey, Teddy? Everything okay, man?"

Teddy looked up, blinking his eyes clear and shrugged. He didn't have the energy to fake a smile, especially not for his old friend, Lucas. Lucas had seen him cry before.

"Nah, man. Not really," Teddy admitted.

Lucas hesitated then sank onto the step beside him. "I know I haven't been around much, but I'm still a good listener if you want to talk."

"Not much to say. I'm an asshole." Teddy swiped at the dampness on his cheeks, embarrassed.

"Yeah right." Lucas bumped shoulders. "You *like* assholes. That doesn't make you one. What happened?"

"I fucked up. My mom spent the money I had planned to use on my surgery and I took it out on one of my friends." Saying it out loud didn't help. It just reemphasized the epic mistake he'd just made.

"If he's really your friend, he'll understand." Lucas shoved his hands in the pocket of his baggy pants. "Did you talk to her about it? See if she had a good reason?"

"No. I went to the bank. I feel… God, I'm so pissed, but I feel like I don't have the right to be, you know? She used it on bills. How can I be pissed for that? But…" Teddy hunched inward. "But then I keep thinking that, you know, she used the money on bills because she kept getting fired, and that was because she couldn't keep her hands off the bottle. And that pisses me off because I shouldn't have to support her addiction. It's not fair. But I *know* it's a sickness. She can't help it, you know?"

"God, man, that's rough. I'd be fucking pissed if someone did that to me." Lucas frowned. "What about a loan? Can you get one of those?"

"With what credit? I don't have collateral or a credit history. They'd laugh me out of the bank. And it's not like my mom could co-sign."

"What about your friend? The one with the fancy car?" Lucas suggested, his face creased in thought.

"He's the one I just stepped all over, and even if I hadn't, I can't ask him. He already thinks everyone is using him for money." Teddy certainly hadn't helped with that, either.

They sat in silence for a while, both just staring at the cracked sidewalk in front of him until Lucas jerked then nudged him excitedly in the side. "Come with me. I know someone who can help."

Teddy stared blankly at his old friend. "You know someone…who would just lend a complete stranger thousands of dollars."

"Yeah, my *cabeza*, Julian. He's always talking about wanting to make the city a better place, and he gives out loans to people all the time. I bet he'd give you one."

"Not exactly legal, is it?" Teddy asked. It sounded sketchy.

"Why not? It's not like it's hurting nobody. Just a bit of borrowing between friends." Lucas' smile dimmed slightly and he nudged Teddy's shoulder again. "We've been friends for years, right? I know I haven't exactly acted like one lately, but I want to help. Let me help."

"It's just a loan, right?" Teddy hedged after a stretch of awkward silence.

"Yeah, just a loan."

* * * *

Teddy wasn't happy about it, but in the end, after a couple days of arguing with himself, he agreed to go meet Lucas' so-called-friend, Julian. The man wasn't as old as Teddy expected, only in his late twenties, and Teddy couldn't help but wonder how a man that young had enough money floating around to hand out loans left and right.

Fortunately, Julian seemed nice enough. He laughed easily and shook Teddy's hand readily enough, after having him sign a rather straightforward contract. "Don't worry, *compañero*. Get your surgery, rest, recover. Six months, no payment, yeah? Sounds good, right?"

Teddy had to admit it sounded good. He wouldn't be able to work for at least six weeks after his surgery. Not having to worry about making payments would be a godsend. He left the warehouse they'd met in — an odd meeting choice, but who was he to judge? — and headed home, in a better mood than he'd been all week. He didn't even care that it was pouring rain, plastering his sweater to his sticky skin.

He was surprised to see a small figure huddled on his porch, a hood pulled up over his head to keep him dry, though he doubted it helped much. Teddy stopped at the foot of his stairs. He and Shiloh stared at each other for a few moments, neither willing to break the silence.

"Do you want to come inside?" Teddy finally offered, climbing the steps. He unlocked the door and held it open.

Shiloh was shivering as he followed. It wasn't that cold, at least not in Teddy's mind, but he didn't really know how long Shiloh had been waiting, so he supposed, if he had been out there a while, that he was chilled from the rain.

"I'll get you a towel," Teddy offered, leaving Shiloh in the entryway to grab one from the downstairs bathroom. He brought it out and passed it over.

"Where were you?" Shiloh asked, tugging his hood down to run the towel vigorously over his hair.

"I got a loan for my surgery," Teddy said. "I was just signing the papers."

Shiloh's hands slowed in his hair for a moment. Teddy wished he could see his face to read his expression but the towel blocked it. "That's...that's good, I guess? Did you get good interest rates?"

Teddy shrugged. "I think so." He wasn't actually sure. Financial things weren't his strong suit, but a six percent interest rate seemed low. The banks he'd looked at all spoke of interest rates upwards of ten, so it had to be good.

Shiloh lowered the towel and shook the last few drops of water from his hair. Teddy got his first glimpse of Shiloh's face and cringed.

A dark, black bruise darkened Shiloh's left eye, turning purple over his cheekbone, and his lower lip was split—like someone had bit it, hard.

"What the hell happened?" He reached out to grab Shiloh's arm, keeping him still for him to look him over, but Shiloh jerked back.

"Nothing. Had a bit of an accident, no big deal. That's not why I came here, anyway. I just…I wanted to make sure you were okay…after everything. I left a bit abruptly last time and…I wanted to make sure you knew I wasn't mad at you."

"It was my fault." Teddy shrugged the apology away, more worried about the bruises than their stupid fight anyway. "This doesn't look like an accident. What did you do, fall face-first into a fist?"

Shiloh's face darkened, the tendon in his jaw clenching. "I don't want to talk about it. Leave it alone."

"Shiloh—"

"I said *no*, Teddy." Shiloh's words were sharp, forcing Teddy to let the subject drop whether he liked it or not.

Teddy bit his lip, turning his words over in his mouth. "I'm sorry about what I said. You have every right to be mad at me. I shouldn't have taken my anger out on you." Teddy looked down. "I'd take it back if I could."

"Can we just…agree to let it go?" Shiloh asked, his voice hopeful.

"Yeah, yeah. That would be great." Teddy felt the last remaining tension in his shoulders uncoil. His strained relationship with Shiloh had been the only thing marring an otherwise-bright week. Or it had been, until Teddy had seen the bruises.

"Have you talked to your mother yet?" Shiloh asked.

Teddy shook his head. "She's been so drunk that I wouldn't get anything rational out of her anyway. Wanna come upstairs? I can kick your ass at Mario Kart."

"I was gonna go to Vibe. You can come with if you want." Shiloh twisted the hem of his sweater in his hands.

A night of dancing seemed like the perfect way to reconnect. Teddy grinned. "I have the perfect outfit."

"Do my makeup?" Shiloh asked.

Teddy's eyes drifted to the bruising. He nodded slowly. He wondered if he could get a picture of it before it was hidden under foundation. This wasn't the first time Shiloh had shown up with suspicious injuries. It had happened more times than Teddy could count. He'd been trying to document them, storing the photographs in a file he'd hidden in his bottom dresser drawer. Shiloh refused to explain. He always brushed away Teddy's concerns like they were nothing, but Teddy wasn't stupid. He doubted they were caused by Shiloh's dad. Mr. Beckett was controlling, but Teddy'd never seen him lift a hand in anger.

But someone was hurting Shiloh, and the injuries always coincided with Mr. Beckett's trips out of town. Shiloh could claim they were accidents all he wanted—that he'd tripped down the stairs or walked into a door...or stemmed from a hookup gone bad—but Teddy wasn't stupid. He was no stranger to using those same excuses, back when his father had still been alive.

The only good thing the bastard had ever done for him and his mother was die.

"Come on. My mom won't care if we borrow her makeup."

* * * *

Later that night, Teddy closed the front door quietly and twisted the lock. Shiloh, more than a little buzzed from the shots he'd conned out of the bartender, had shoved a small wad of bills into Teddy's hand and told him to call a taxi. His friend, despite Teddy's protests, had gone home with a stranger.

"Boo Bear?"

Teddy froze at the sleep-mumbled words. He turned to find his mother blinking blearily at the bottom of the stairs. She was in a silk sleep set, and for once, it didn't look rumpled or piss-stained. "Boo Bear, it's late. Don't you have school in the morning?" She asked, then frowned. "No, that's not right…"

"I graduated. Remember? Oh, wait. You missed it." Teddy clenched his fists for a second then let them uncurl. He repeated the gesture again once he found it soothing. He almost wished the smell of alcohol didn't make him nauseated. Maybe he could make it through this conversation if he were drunk.

She frowned, frowning in confusion. "Did I? Oh, Boo, I'm sorry… I'll make it up to you. We'll go out for pizza."

"Sure, with what money?" Teddy laughed coldly. "You don't have a job, and you've already drained my trust fund. Oh, sorry, was I not supposed to know about that?"

His mother paled, lifting her hand to the rosary around her neck and fiddling with the beads. "I…I was going to put the money back, dear. Once we got caught up."

"Which time? Because I went to the bank and they showed me the statements. Funny how every time you made a withdrawal, it was after you got fired from one of your jobs. And funnier still, each time you sobered up and got back to work, there was never a deposit. Not one."

She was silent, clearly at a loss for words, and Teddy didn't blame her. There was no excuse. Still, his anger wouldn't let him stay silent as well. "You know if you'd have asked, I'd have given it to you. You didn't have to steal it. How could you let me make plans when you knew… When you *knew* that money was gone?"

"Baby…" His mother tried to placate him but he refused to be calmed.

"I'm not a baby. I'm not your honey or your Boo Bear. I'm your son, and you should have asked me first." Teddy's fists curled again. Rather than strike the wall, or worse, his mother, he pushed past her and started up the stairs.

"I'll do better, baby. I'll get clean this time. I really will," she promised, trailing him up to his room.

Teddy flung open his closet and dragged out his suitcase, tugging his clothes and toiletries out of drawers and stuffing them inside. His *Shiloh* file got stuffed down the side, where it hopefully wouldn't get bent.

"Where are you going?" his mother asked, her voice small.

"I'm going to Shiloh's. Then…I'll probably get an apartment, I guess." Teddy stilled, freaking out for a second. He'd never lived away from home. He'd always kinda anticipated his mother helping him through his recovery. The last few years, though, were proof enough that she wasn't capable of it. He returned to packing, pushing the thought from his mind. Maybe Shiloh would help, though he hated to ask.

"Why?" Mother whined, rushing into his room and gripping his arms tightly.

"Ow, Mom!" Teddy yelped and tried to tug free as her nails, sharp and untrimmed, dug into his skin. One had bitten so deep that a small rivulet of blood streaked its way down his arm.

His mother's grip, rather than loosening, tightened, and anger flashed across her face. "You can't leave me. It's not fair. I'm your *mother*."

"Right now, you feel like a parasite." Teddy tore himself free and grabbed his bag.

His mom clawed for his arm again but he avoided it. He wasn't expecting the slap that cracked across his face, snapping his head to the side. His cheek burned where her palm connected. Tears burned in his eyes, his breath choking in his throat. It wasn't the first time he'd been hit—his father had been fond of slapping him around—but it was the first time the hit had come from *her*.

He stumbled back a step, his heart in his throat. He watched the horror spread across her face as she realized what she'd done. She reached out for him, but he stepped back again. He wasn't a little kid anymore, too small to defend himself, and he sure as fuck wasn't going to be like his mom, going back to the same bad situation over and over again. He'd promised himself, when he was old enough to understand that not every dad showed his love in bruises, that when he grew up, he'd live by a 'one-and-done' policy.

One hit and he was done.

He brushed past her and headed for the door. Like a broken record, she trailed behind him, muttering apologies over and over.

He shut the door on the sound.

He was halfway down the sidewalk before he remembered that Shiloh was at a stranger's. He fumbled for his phone and thumbed Shiloh's contact until the number pulled up. He listened to it ring.

"Shiloh's phone, hit me up later."

Teddy cursed and ended the call without leaving a voicemail.

He glanced over his shoulder, back toward his house.

The light was on at the Romeros'.

Mama Romero didn't ask questions. When she saw the bag flung over his shoulder, she held the door wider. "I'll make up the guest room, *dulzura.*"

Chapter Nine

Ian woke to the sound of cheerful whistling coming from the kitchen downstairs, mingling with the rattling of pans. He rolled out of bed and stretched, his spine popping. He'd been working late and honestly could do with another few hours of sleep, but he had an online exam at ten and he'd have to study a bit after breakfast.

Rubbing his eyes, he didn't bother to put on a shirt before he padded across the hall to the bathroom. His brother barely woke up early enough to run down to breakfast, so he didn't pay much attention to the sound of the shower running until he'd already pushed open the door and gotten an eyeful of skin—long, slender limbs and lithe muscles barely hidden by the frosted glass.

He sucked in a breath, arousal stirring even as he quickly backed up, silently shutting the door before Teddy—because it was undeniably Teddy—could notice his intrusion. Heat coursed through his veins and burned his skin. He didn't know why Teddy was there, unless he'd spent the night with Lucas, but it had been nearly a year since they'd had a sleepover. Was it still a sleepover if they were both fully grown?

Ian groaned at the thought of Teddy being over often—Teddy naked in the shower, Teddy sleeping in the room right beside him. It was both a blessing and a curse. He pressed the heel of his hand against his rapidly hardening dick, but the pressure didn't help. He closed his eyes and sucked in a breath, holding it as he counted. *Baseball. Abuela's house at Christmas. Pimples...*

Nothing he was thinking of was making the swelling of his dick any less noticeable. He gave up and returned to his bedroom to pull on a pair of jeans instead, hoping they would hide his erection better than running shorts, then headed downstairs, the sound of water thrumming into the tub a melody with his steps.

Mama was in the kitchen, sliding a stack of silver dollar pancakes out of her cast-iron frying pan and onto an already-heaping serving plate. Beside it, a small mountain of eggs topped with cheese waited to be carried to the table.

"Can I help, Mama?" Ian asked, eyeing the spread.

She waved her spatula at him. "No, *mijo*, it's nearly done."

Propping a hip against the counter, he crossed his arms and watched her dig out a glass bottle of syrup from the fridge. "I didn't know Teddy was staying over."

Mama sighed, dropping her hands to the countertop and bowing slightly. "Poor boy. Showed up last night with a duffel bag and all the fear in the world on his face." *So not a sleepover, then,* Ian realized, a frown growing on his lips. He scratched the steadily growing stubble on his chin. Before he could say anything, his mama continued to speak. "I want him to take the guest room, but he's a stubborn kid. Never has been good at asking for help."

"I know," Ian agreed. "Remember a few years ago? After their power was shut off and we didn't know anything about it for weeks?"

"*Si*. Poor thing had been showering in the hose out back. I still remember the expression on his face." Mama tutted, shaking her head.

"I'll ask him after breakfast." Ian resolved to get Teddy to agree, one way or another, even if it would mean several more uncomfortable erections to hide. Something told him he'd be taking a lot of cold showers.

Mama swatted him with the dish towel. "*Mijo*, are you even listening? I said go get the boys. Breakfast is ready. And tell that brother of yours to get his butt in a seat or I'll hide his phone."

"Got it." Ian started for the stairs. The bathroom door opened just as he passed and Teddy, clearly planning on sprinting across the hall before he got caught, slammed right into Ian's chest. Instinctively, Ian grabbed him, keeping him upright by snapping his arms around the younger man. Only when his hands met hot, naked flesh did he realize that Teddy was wearing only a towel — and a small one at that.

"Well, good morning to you too," Ian teased, grinning down at Teddy, whose face was fire engine red, his eyes wide.

"I...I forgot to bring cl-clothes," Teddy stuttered, skin somehow growing even redder, though Ian hadn't thought it was possible.

Reluctantly, now that Teddy was stable on his feet, Ian let him go. Teddy clutched at the towel wrapped around his midsection. It hung barely to the top of his thighs. "Don't worry. Nobody's complaining." Ian winked but forced himself to turn his back, to give Teddy the privacy he knew the younger man wanted. He started for his brother's room, pausing just to call over his shoulder, "Mama says breakfast is ready."

Teddy cursed himself for his forgetfulness as he gripped the towel tight and darted into the guest room, slamming the door behind him. He was used to his own home, with his own bathroom where he didn't have to worry about embarrassing himself. He hadn't even realized that his sleep-deprived brain hadn't grabbed clothing when he'd stumbled from bed until he'd climbed out of the shower to a bare counter. With growing horror, he'd lingered in the steamy bathroom for several minutes, debating on taking his chances in a sprint across the hallway or waiting it out and hoping someone would walk by and he could admit to the situation.

In the end, he'd chosen to risk the sprint, and now look what had happened. Ian, the *one* man Teddy didn't want to see him like this, in this body that he hated so much, was the one to catch him.

Because...fuck his life.

At least when he'd looked up, he'd not seen the expected disgust in Ian's eyes. Just humor, and beneath it, he didn't think he was imagining the appreciation. Teddy leaned against his door and took a few deep breaths, calming his still-pounding heart. He refused to go down to breakfast like this.

He was grateful that he'd taken a few minutes to calm down, because once he got downstairs, he ended up squished between Lucas and Ian at the breakfast table, close enough that his thigh brushed against Ian's every time he shifted.

Mama Romero bustled in and out of the kitchen, carrying platters of food. Teddy offered to help but she waved him back to his seat. "You're a guest, *mijo*. Sit down. Relax." She'd gone to pat his cheek, but her hand hesitated over the reddened skin. Instead, she'd dropped her hand to his shoulder and squeezed instead.

He felt guilty watching her work, but apparently, this was standard in the Romero house. Ian leaned over when his mother returned to the kitchen after dropping off a heaping bowl of fluffy, cheese-coated scrambled eggs. "Don't worry. She loves serving breakfast."

Lucas snorted on Teddy's other side. "What he really means is that she's bat-shit crazy and needs everything on the table to be put in the right spot."

"Lucas!" Four throats chorused together — one amused, three scandalized. Only Mama Romero seemed to find the comment funny. She'd slipped unnoticed from the kitchen door behind Lucas just in time to hear him. She pinched Lucas' cheek between her fingers and squeezed.

"What would I do without my brat to keep me on my toes?"

"Wither away," Lucas said dryly, rolling his eyes and rubbing his cheek, like he could scrub away the affectionate gesture. Still, his cheeks turned pink in a flush that made Teddy suspect he rather enjoyed the attention.

Ian leaned across Teddy, their sides pressing flush to each other, to squeeze Lucas' other cheek. "Wittle Mama's boy."

Lucas swatted Ian's hand away with a groan. "Shut up."

"Aw. Did I hurt little Lou-Lou's feelings?" Ian teased, tugging on one of Lucas' curls. Noa giggled across the table.

Mama Romero swatted the back of Ian's head. "Don't tease your brother or I'll tell Teddy all about your doll collection."

"Action figures!" Ian immediately corrected, voice lifting a decibel in embarrassment.

Teddy snickered at the red that painted Ian's cheek and couldn't resist teasing him. "Can I play with your dolls, Ian?"

"They were *action figures*. Collectible ones," Ian mumbled.

"Did they wear pretty dresses?" Teddy asked playfully.

"No," Ian said immediately, just as Lucas rebutted with, "Some of them did. Like Princess Leia. You *loooved* dressing her up in Noa's Barbie clothes."

"I know where you sleep." Ian leaned around Teddy again to threaten his brother. Teddy's breath caught in his chest when Ian's arm draped along the back of his chair, his thumb skimming across the back of Teddy's neck.

"I should hope so. It's the room right next to yours. I know you're bad at directions, but I didn't think you'd get lost that easy." Lucas gave a devilish grin and turned back to Teddy. "Did I tell you about that time he was seventeen and —"

Ian cut off whatever story Lucas was going to tell by quickly straightening then reaching around Teddy to drag his brother out of the seat. The pair wrestled on the floor behind them. Ian pinned Lucas almost immediately before giving him a noogie while Teddy stared at the strip of toned skin revealed as Ian's tank top crept up.

"Boys!" Mama Romero scolded the pair, shaking her head. Her lips twitched in a grin. "Teddy is going to think I raised a pair of monkeys. Come on. Breakfast is getting cold."

Ian kept Lucas pinned a moment longer but lifted his head in time to catch Teddy staring. His playful grin turned sinful as his eyes caught Teddy's. Now it was Teddy's turn to blush.

Ian stretched, his shirt creeping up his abdomen to reveal the deep V cut into his hips and the happy trail that teased down into the waistband of his pants. Lucas scrambled free of Ian, but they both ignored him.

"So, Teddy," Ian said as he climbed back into his seat beside him, "what are your plans for the day?"

Teddy wet his lips, clearing his throat before replying. "Umm, probably apartment hunting?" It was a question, though he didn't mean it to be. "Why?"

Ian glanced at his mother before answering. "I'm sure Mama won't mind if you stay in the guest room for a while. We don't use it anyway. Right, Mama?"

"Of course, dear. I'd love for you to stay." Mama Romero answered immediately. Teddy wondered if the pair had already discussed it. He pushed his eggs around his plate for a moment, deep in thought.

Not having to rent somewhere would help him save him money, money he couldn't afford to be wasting.

But he couldn't help but think it was charity. "I...don't want to impose..."

"Oh, nonsense. Stay, dear. I'd hardly call you an imposition." Mama Romero clucked over him for a second. "Besides, you're too skinny. I'd like to fatten you up a bit. Really, you'd be doing me a favor. Set my mind at ease."

Teddy glanced, not at Lucas, who he really should have been worried about, but at Ian. Ian just smiled reassuringly.

"I...I guess, if you're sure I wouldn't be in the way..."

"It's settled then." Mama Romero nodded and turned to Noa, starting a conversation about some talent show the younger girl was involved in, discussion dropped.

"So, now that your afternoon has freed up, you should come hang out with me. There's a street festival on Sixth Street. It could be fun," Ian suggested.

"Could be fun," Teddy echoed, his heart thumping at the thought of spending time with Ian.

Ian smirked. Teddy's skin flushed and he swallowed, wondering how easy it was to read the infatuation on his face. From Lucas' playful gagging beside him, he suspected it was far too obvious.

* * * *

They took Sally, Ian's truck. It was a beat-up red Chevy with a dent on the off-color passenger door. Unlike the piece of crap Teddy's mom drove, each ding and scratch told a story, and Teddy knew Ian kept the engine in tip-top shape. But as much as he'd seen Ian work on her, he'd never ridden in Sally before. The leather seats were worn but clean, the dash layered in scratches but not dust. Teddy tucked his hands under his thighs to avoid running his fingers over the freshly polished chrome gear-shaft, which was clearly not factory installed.

Ian swung into the driver's seat, the muscles of his forearm flexing. While Teddy had changed into a pair of dark-wash jeans and an only slightly tighter-than-normal sweater, Ian now wore a pale button-down with the sleeves rolled to his elbows, leaving plenty of forearm for Teddy to ogle.

And don't get me started on Ian's fingers. Teddy barely held back his moan when he watched Ian spin the key in the ignition then curl them around the leather of the steering wheel. Heat pooled between Teddy's thighs and he struggled not to squirm as they drove, traffic growing heavier the closer they got to the festival. If Ian noticed, he was kind enough not to comment.

Teddy had never been so grateful to find a parking spot. It was too hot in the cab of the truck, the air sparking with electricity. He almost stumbled as he scrambled down onto the asphalt.

Ian jumped down and rounded the front of the truck with a grin. "Excited?"

Teddy was, but not for the reasons Ian thought. He was looking forward to spending the day with him, to seeing what got Ian excited. He supposed the festival would be fun too, though, so he nodded. "Yeah, can we go now?"

Ian, rather than getting upset about his impatience, just laughed. "Sure. From what I've heard, we've got a few options, so pick your poison. There's a bunch of displays from local artists or a few music stages. Or, if you want, we can start with the vendors."

"Do I have to pick?" Teddy asked, wavering. What if he picked the wrong one, and Ian decided not to hang out with him anymore? What if he picked one Ian didn't like?

"Not if you don't want to. We can just wander around and see what strikes us in the moment," Ian held out his hand. Teddy took it immediately, before Ian could change his mind.

They started walking and Teddy was almost immediately overwhelmed. He'd lived in Austin his whole life and had somehow missed this the whole time. He didn't know where to look first. There was a line of white-top tents on either side of the road, brightly colored canvases, glass-beaded jewelry and found-art sculptures spilling out from beneath them, and everywhere, people crowded together so tightly they jostled him, until Ian tugged him closer to his side, protecting him under the shield of his arm.

"See anything you like?" Ian murmured over the ambient laughter that surrounded them after they'd walked past several tents and ooh'd over the contents.

"There's too much to look at," Teddy whined, stopping abruptly to watch a rainbow-colored clown blowing up balloon animals for a small crowd of children at his feet.

"Do you want one?" Ian asked, following his gaze.

Teddy pouted but shook his head. "No. It'll pop." Immediately, he realized that he was giving away too much. His first protest was that it wouldn't last, not that it was for children. He flushed and peeked up at Ian, who looked down on him with a warm smile. He relaxed when he realized Ian wasn't going to mock him, or worse, look at him with disgust. He knew there was nothing wrong with what he liked, nothing shameful, but that didn't stop him from being afraid of being rejected for it.

"How about I try to win you one of those, instead?" Ian pointed over his shoulder and Teddy spun to look, eyes widening when they landed on the booth.

The top of the tent was striped red and white, and from it dangled dozens of stuffed animals, ranging from small ones the size of his finger to ones nearly as tall as him. Immediately, Teddy locked on to the teddy bear. It was pale brown with a blue ribbon, and its fur looked so soft. Teddy's fingers itched to stroke it, so, instead, he chewed on his thumbnail.

Ian tugged Teddy's thumb away from his mouth and said, "Come on. I bet I can win on the first try."

"Everyone knows these games are rigged," Teddy protested as Ian dragged him over to the booth, standing at the chest-high bar. Across from them was a table topped with glass bottles.

The man under the tent was tall, taller still because of the two-foot stilts he stood on. They brought his head nearly to the top of the tent, and his suit was a garish red-and-black striped thing that made Teddy cringe, but his smile was genuine. "Afternoon, folks. Wanna play some ring toss?"

Ian glanced up at the sign advertising three rings for five dollars. He threw a ten down on the bar. "Yep. I wanna win my boy here a teddy bear."

If Teddy's skin got any hotter, he was going to be on fire. He buried his face in Ian's side and groaned. He felt, more than heard, Ian's laugh.

"Six rings, six tries!" Teddy peeked out to see the carnie lay six red rings, about the size of bracelets, across the counter. He peered at the bottle rims, then back at the rings. They *looked* like they would fit.

"How many do I have to get to win the big one?" Ian nodded toward the bear that had caught Teddy's eyes. His heart fluttered when he realized just how close attention Ian was paying for him to notice.

"Six on the blue bottles, four on the green or one on the red," the carnie explained. Now that Teddy looked closer, he realized all the bottles were different sizes. The blue were the biggest, with the smallest mouths, the green were somewhere in the middle, and the red, of which there were fewest, were the smallest, with rims barely smaller than the rings.

Ian examined them critically as well before dislodging his arm from around Teddy's shoulder to pick up the first ring. Ian weighed it in his hand then cocked back his wrist, letting it fly.

It missed.

So did the next three.

Teddy giggled as Ian glared at the last two rings in his hands like they'd betrayed him. "That's okay, I just need two."

Unfortunately, he ringed one around the blue bottle near the edge, but the other circled the red rim for several long seconds before slipping off to the side.

Ian tossed another bill on the counter. "Just needed some practice. That's all," He said, winking at Teddy before picking up his next set of rings.

He ringed three greens and a blue, enough to win him a smaller prize if he wanted, but he shook his head resolutely, even after Teddy protested that the little elephant was more than cute enough. "Nope. I'm winning you the bear — unless you doubt me. Are you doubting me?" Ian glared playfully at him.

Teddy pursed his lips and tapped his chin like he was thinking. "Well…" He drew out the word for a few seconds, then laughed when Ian clutched his chest like his words had physically hurt.

"Just for that, I'm keeping the bear if I win it." Ian stuck out his tongue but threw another bill down.

Twenty dollars later, they walked away from the booth, both laughing, with the giant teddy bear riding on Ian's shoulders.

"I feel like I've got the wrong Teddy Bear on my shoulders," Ian said after they'd walked for a few minutes.

Teddy laughed but scrambled back several steps. "Uh-uh. Nope. I am not riding around on your shoulders."

"Why not? Afraid I'll drop you?" Ian asked, stalking after him, heat in his gaze.

Teddy wasn't afraid Ian would drop him, not at all. He was afraid that having Ian's head between his thighs would stir up thoughts of a different sort. So he lied and nodded, "You've dropped Mr. Blue twice already."

"Mr. Blue?" Ian smirked, closing the distance between them while Teddy was trying to back away without tripping over anyone. "We've named your teddy, I see."

"Duh. Can't keep calling him Teddy. It'll get confusing." Teddy pointed it out like it was the most obvious thing in the world as he struggled to dodge Ian's hand. He failed, and Ian grasped him around the waist, pulling him forward until they stood, chest-to-chest, the stuffed animal—which truly was almost as big as Teddy—tucked, forgotten, in the crook of Ian's arm. The fur brushed against Teddy's skin, soft and warm. He couldn't help rubbing his face across it.

Ian pushed it gently into Teddy's arms. "Happy late birthday."

Chapter Ten

Ian couldn't help watching Teddy. The young man was all smiles as they made their way through the festival, the teddy bear clasped to his chest. Ian had offered to bring it back to the truck but he saw the way Teddy's face fell at the suggestion, even though he'd agreed. Ian had retracted the offer immediately, not wanting to see anything but happiness on the boy's face, and they'd kept walking.

After filling up on kettle corn and ribbon fries, they finally headed home after dark, despite Teddy's protests. Ian had watched him start yawning hours before. He tried to hide them in the cowl of his sweater and the baggy sleeves, but Ian had noticed, the same way he'd seen his smile dimming. Teddy was exhausted, and it was time to get him home.

He wasn't surprised when Teddy fell asleep before they even left the parking lot, curled up in the passenger seat with his knees to his chest, his head pillowed on the bear. Ian couldn't help smiling at the sight.

Teddy didn't even wake up when he pulled the truck into the driveway and turned it off. Ian debated waking him, but Teddy looked so peaceful that he couldn't bring himself to do it. Instead, he climbed out and rounded the truck, carefully opening the passenger door and unbuckling Teddy's seatbelt so he could gather him into his arms, the bear still tucked against his chest, then carry him across the lawn to the front door. It was a bit of a struggle to get the door open, but he managed it.

He passed Mama in the living room. She looked up from her knitting but didn't comment. She just smiled and shook her head before dropping her eyes back to the richly dyed yarn in front of her. Papa was snoring in the armchair.

Ian carried Teddy upstairs to the guest room, depositing him gently in the center of the bed. Teddy woke just enough to help him get his shoes off, though it was clear from the blurriness of his eyes that he was still mostly asleep. Ian urged him under the covers, tucking Mr. Blue in beside him, and smiled at the sleepy yawn.

"Night, Daddy," Teddy mumbled, curling into the bear.

Ian's heart thudded in his chest as he backed out of the room, his eyes wide. Surely, there was no way Teddy had meant that. Teddy must have been dreaming, probably thought Ian was...well, not his father, because Ian knew Teddy's dad had been dead for years, so...

Had Teddy meant it?

Ian had never explored the world of Daddy kink beyond porn. He had to admit that the few videos he'd watched had been hot, but there was something clinical about watching it on his laptop. He wanted…more. He wanted to wrap Teddy in his arms and keep him safe, wanted to help him get dressed in the morning, wanted to make him dinner at night.

Ian hurried into his bedroom for a change of clothes, then into the bathroom. He needed to take a cold shower now, because there was no way he could indulge in the fantasy that Teddy was into the same things he was. Teddy was too young to know what he wanted and Ian knew, if he let him, that he would take absolutely everything the boy had to give. Maybe, eventually, it was something they could explore, but not until he was sure Teddy was ready.

He groaned as the icy water pelted his skin, doing little to curtail the throbbing erection. Finally, it wilted, but the lack of physical evidence of his arousal did little to curb his thoughts. Shivering, he finally climbed out of the shower when it was clear it wasn't helping. The only thing that was going through his mind was Teddy.

Teddy giggling at the street shows at the festival.

Teddy curled up in bed, wrapped around his teddy bear.

Teddy on his knees, his eyes wide as he stared up at him, begging for Daddy's cock.

Ian groaned as his erection started to grow again.

* * * *

Teddy woke up in bed, aching with arousal but burning with embarrassment over his sleep-addled admission, and immediately escaped to the Beckett Estate, Mr. Blue forgotten in his haste.

"So, you really did it? Moved out?" Shiloh sat on the side of the pool, kicking his feet lazily in the cool water.

He leaned back on his hands, his elbows locked and his face tilted up to the brilliant sunlight. A pair of custom Bulgari frames in black cherry with rose lenses perched on his nose, reflecting the light that glinted off the pool.

Teddy shrugged, though Shiloh didn't see it. Out loud, he said, "Yeah. It was time. She's been getting worse. I feel more like her parent, and, dude, I am *so* not ready to be a parent." Teddy tried to make it sound joking but it came out flat. He didn't want to be anybody's Daddy. "She slapped me."

"Bitch," Shiloh cursed, though he didn't sound surprised. To be honest, once the shock had worn off, Teddy hadn't been either. He'd been more surprised it hadn't happened sooner. "What about your surgery? Will the Romeros be there to help?"

"I'm not going to ask them to do that," Teddy immediately rejected the suggestion. That was too much to ask of anyone, especially Ian, especially after he'd accidentally called him 'Daddy'. "I'll figure it out. I'm hoping to have found an apartment by then. I've got a week or two."

"I thought they asked you to stay?"

Teddy shrugged. "They did. But I'm sure they just meant until I got on my feet again."

Shiloh sat silently behind him for several moments, the only sound the splashing of his feet in the pool. Eventually, he rolled onto his side and propped his head on his hand, his elbow on the cement. "I'll come stay with you. I can help you keep your stitches dry and make sure you eat. I won't cook for you, but I can order in." Shiloh shrugged. "I need a break from all this anyway." He waved his hand halfheartedly at the mansion.

"So you want to come play nurse for me?" Teddy pulled his feet out of the water, propping them on the edge so he could rest his arms on his knees. "I've been taking care of myself for years. I'm sure it'll be fine."

"There's a difference between packing your own lunch and recovering from major surgery. They won't release you without home care. You know that." Shiloh frowned. "It was in your hospital packet. I know. I read it."

"They don't have to know." Teddy shrugged. He'd lied to people in suits before, so what was one more time?

"Come on, Teddy. It's not a big deal. It's not like you don't take care of me when I'm hungover. You've cleaned up my puke. I can take care of you for a few weeks."

"This is all dependent on whether I find an apartment in time anyway, you know," Teddy pointed out.

"You'll find one. It might not be a great one, but I'm sure you'll find something."

* * * *

A week before his surgery was scheduled, Teddy signed the lease on a dingy apartment a few streets over. It was, to put it nicely, a dump.

The air conditioner was stuck permanently on, the water heater banged ominously at random times and he was positive he had a handful of skittering roommates. Ian had asked to come with him to check the place out but Teddy cringed at the thought of admitting how shitty the place was, especially to him.

He told Ian that he was subletting from a lovely couple going on an extended honeymoon, because there was no way in hell he was letting Ian within a hundred feet of it. He liked Ian, even if he shouldn't, and he definitely didn't need the older man judging him. Not that he thought Ian would be mean about it, but no way did he want to see pity.

Not from Ian, anyway. He was dealing with it already from Shiloh, who'd come with him while he signed the paperwork. Shiloh hadn't said anything, but he didn't have to. He just stood uncomfortably in the space between the kitchenette and living area, like he was afraid of catching a disease if he touched anything.

The ad had said it was fully furnished, which meant there was a refrigerator from the last decade and a microwave. No stove, but honestly, Teddy couldn't see a space for one anyway. He figured the only thing he'd need to get right away would be a mattress. Everything else could come later, if he bothered. He didn't plan on being there long anyway.

The landlord, a balding man with thick glasses, passed him a pair of keys. "If you need something, call the super. His name's Vik. He can get here right quick if there's an emergency."

Under his breath, Shiloh muttered, "The emergency is the health code. I swear I saw a rat."

Teddy elbowed his friend, but thankfully, the landlord didn't seem to hear. He just waddled out into the hallway, leaving Teddy and Shiloh alone in his new apartment. He'd paid first and last month's rent, so it was his for at least two months.

"I need a bed," Teddy decided, looking around the barren room.

"Yeah, you do." Shiloh leered. The look slid into laughter, though, when Teddy just dug his elbow into Shiloh's side again. "Okay, okay. No more comments."

* * * *

Ian helped Teddy carry the last of his boxes out of his mom's house to the small moving van idling by the curb. Teddy seemed skittish, looking toward the door the whole time, like he expected his mother to come home from wherever the hell she was and stop them.

Outside, Teddy's friend Shiloh was already waiting, a pair of dark sunglasses swallowing half his face, a beanie pulled down over his ears. With one leg propped casually against the side of the van, he looked like he belonged in some magazine.

"Ready?" Shiloh asked, straightening as Ian tucked the last box away.

Ian wanted to yell that no, he wasn't ready. He didn't want Teddy to move out, especially not to some small apartment where he was going to be alone and vulnerable. He didn't care that the older couple he was leasing it from had left all the furniture or that it was within walking distance of a bus stop that would drop him off near the University of Texas at Austin School for Architecture, where Teddy had been accepted on scholarship for the fall. He wanted Teddy to stay with him.

Teddy had called him 'Daddy', and everything in him screamed for Ian to ask if he'd meant it.

But he bit his lip on the words, smiled and nodded when Teddy waved goodbye then silently cursed himself for a fool when Teddy climbed into the moving van and it started trundling away. He understood that

Teddy wanted to stand on his own two feet. He even understood that he didn't want to feel like a burden. He just wished Teddy understood that to Ian, he would *never* be a burden.

Mama clapped him on the shoulder when he eventually wandered back inside and said, "Oh, *mijo*, don't worry. That boy looks at you with stars in his eyes. He'll be back. You'll see."

Chapter Eleven

Two months later

Mama had never listened when he told her he was too old for birthday parties. She'd promised that year not to throw one. But when his boss met him outside the club he worked at, Ian knew what he'd find when he got home. The man stuttered his way through an excuse about a *scheduling error*, so his surprise party wasn't much of a surprise in the end.

It seemed like the entire neighborhood had been crammed into their house, overflowing into the backyard and into their neighbors' yards as well. He swore he only recognized one in three people. He was pretty sure the dark-haired teenager by the picnic table, picking her way through the fruit salad, was one of his cousin Valerie's children, although she could have belonged to Cousin Theresa as well.

A small body rocketed over to him, ricocheting off his knees and onto his diapered rump. Ian scooped the child up with a rowdy laugh. "Alejo, my little firecracker. I nearly squashed you into butter!"

"Not a squash, not a squash!" Alejandro squealed, giggling. He latched his tiny fists onto Ian's ears like handles. "I'm a big boy! Watch, I *zoom*!" He wiggled to get down until Ian lowered him onto his feet.

The child held his hands out from his sides and plunged into the yard, zigging around legs without care. Mama separated from the women to greet Ian with a kiss, her face twisted with concern. "*Mijo*, I know you said no party. I hope you're not angry. I just couldn't bear to think of my boy sitting alone on his birthday."

"I'm not angry, Mama." Ian promised. "I just don't want you to go to so much work."

"It's never work, *mijo*." Mama gripped his arm like she thought he was going to escape and urged him into the yard. "Greet your guests. Aunt Jada and I will finish dinner."

Ian's stomach rumbled at the thought of food. He had planned on eating before his shift.

Mama laughed and patted his stomach. "My growing boy. I've left snacks out, so don't even think about sneaking into the kitchen."

"I haven't tried to steal my birthday cake since I was ten, Mama," Ian protested.

"Only because I threatened you with a *chancletazo*. And don't think you're too old for one now." Mama straightened her spine. It brought her only to his shoulders, but that didn't stop the residual tingle of fear left over from his childhood.

"I'll stay out of the kitchen, Mama," He promised.

"Good. Go find your brother. I worry."

"Yes, Mama."

She left him, heading back to the kitchen, and Ian smiled fondly after her before turning to look for his brother. It seemed the younger man was finally starting to show maturity. He'd been home more over the past month, ever since Teddy had moved out. He didn't seem to be getting in as much trouble, and more often than not, he was turning down offers to hang with his friends.

Of course, Ian wished he would hang out with *one* friend, in particular, if it meant getting to see Teddy more. Teddy had spent over a month in recovery after his surgery, refusing to let Ian see him until he was healed. Afterward, he had picked up a second job washing dishes at a restaurant over on Loop Blvd that specialized in Mexican cuisine. It meant more money for Teddy but less time.

A handful of children rocketed around the lawn, clutching leftover sparklers from the *Dia de la Patria* celebration earlier in the week, and Ian nearly collided into Cousin Monique trying to dodge them. She wished him a happy birthday with a kiss on the cheek, then ushered him along.

Several minutes of mingling later, he finally spotted Lucas in the back of the yard, sitting on the grass by the fire pit. *Tio* Carlos was crouched across from him, arranging logs to start a bonfire. Ian's gaze softened when it landed on Teddy, who was sitting stiffly on a folding chair by his brother.

Teddy looked fully recovered, but, more than that, he looked happier. He practically glowed.

Ian grinned, grateful that Mama's order to find his brother gave him an excuse to approach. He would have anyway, but it was nice not to have to make up a reason. A small part of him worried that Teddy didn't want to see him, but the larger part knew he was being stupid. It was his birthday party. If Teddy didn't want to see him, he wouldn't have shown up.

Teddy met Ian's eyes and a wide smile crossed his face. It wasn't fair how sinfully perfect he looked in those too-tight jeans.

"Hey, brat," Ian said, stepping over his brother's legs to stand closer to Teddy, close enough to see that Teddy's hair was no longer buzzed tight to his scalp, but growing out in gentle curls. It wouldn't take much to thread his fingers through them and urge the younger man forward, to press his face against the crotch of his jeans. He wouldn't do it—not in public, certainly not at his family birthday party—but he could. And the way Teddy looked at him, the soft parting of his lips, the small breath he released before he wet his lips with his tongue, made him think that Teddy wouldn't mind if he did.

"Are you talking to me or Teddy?" his brother said dryly from where he sat, leaning back on his hands. There was a teasing grin on his face that had been missing for a while.

"I don't know. Teddy, are you a brat?" Ian turned back to the boy, his lips twitching.

"I could be...for the right person." Teddy leaned forward, bringing himself closer with a glint in his eyes.

"Oh, gross. Wait until I'm gone before you flirt with my brother, at least." Lucas faked a gag then pushed himself up.

"You better run away fast, then. It's about to get hot over here." Teddy smirked and leaned back, lifting his finger to Ian's chest, tugging the already-low collar of his shirt farther down.

Lucas rolled his eyes and walked off toward the snacks. A moment later, *Tio* Carlos chuckled and followed.

"It's already hot," Ian rumbled now that they were alone — or as alone as they could be, in a crowded back yard — and he leaned down, planting his hands on the arm of the folding chair. He scanned the lithe stretch of body presented to him like an offering. It was firm and slender, compact but strong. Ian knew the younger man would fit perfectly tucked beneath his chin, or under his arm...or under his body, stretched out on a bed. He caught the glimpse of a compression binder beneath the low collar of Teddy's shirt, a reminder that his fantasies would have to remain so for a few more weeks at least.

"Do I get a kiss?" Ian asked.

"Only if you say the magic word," Teddy teased. He bent his head backward, revealing the long, pale line of his neck. Ian wanted to bury his face there, to lick and nibble and leave his mark all over it.

"You want me to beg?" Ian's voice deepened, practically a growl. "I don't beg, *pollito*."

Teddy flushed, but then his eyebrows pulled low over his eyes in confusion. "Did you just call me *little chicken*?"

"Perhaps." Ian grinned. "It's an endearment, love."

"Little chicken?" Teddy seemed put out, eyes flashing. Then he was closing the distance between them, Teddy's mouth slamming into his with more than a little fire. The little moans Teddy was making, combined with the feeling of his slim fingers clenching the fabric of Ian's shirt, held him in place.

For a few moments, anyway. Then Ian shifted, resting a knee on the edge of the lawn chair to give him a better angle. He lifted his hands to the sides of Teddy's face, tilting his head back, opening his mouth for the taking. Ian didn't kiss him, he *possessed* him. He wanted the younger man to think of him whenever he pressed his lips to another.

A thought that immediately had his hands tightening, tugging the man up so their chests were nearly flush, though he was mindful of Teddy's recovering lacerations. He didn't want to think of Teddy with another. Already, he felt like Teddy was *his*.

"How was that for a *little chicken*?" Teddy's voice was breathy as he broke away.

"Beautiful, *cielito*," Ian murmured. "Beautiful."

Teddy felt like all the air had been pulled from his body and replaced with helium, because surely he was floating. Ian's hands cradling his face were large but gentle.

A throat cleared beside them and Ian leaned back, freeing Teddy to draw in a breath. "Yes, Mama?" Ian asked. Mama Romero had a straight face, but there was a glint in her eye. Teddy didn't know whether or not to feel embarrassed.

"Nadine would like to know if Teddy is feeling okay. She said you were performing mouth-to-mouth on your friend." Mama Romero's lips twitched, and Teddy flushed. Nadine was one of Ian's many cousins. She was seven or thereabouts—Teddy couldn't remember.

"I think I fixed him," Ian smirked, looking back at Teddy. "What do you think? Is your heart beating fine or do we need to try again?"

Mama Romero huffed and swatted her son's arm. "Go mingle with your guests, *mijo*. Take your pretty friend with you, if you want." Mama Romero winked at Teddy.

"Yes, Mama." Ian agreed as his mother walked away.

Teddy couldn't help his chuckle. Ian lifted an eyebrow. "You laugh, but you've never had her chase you with a *chancla*. She's a brute of a woman."

"Your mother is an angel," Teddy corrected. He stood up and dusted off the seat of his jeans. "Come on. Let's go mingle. I'd hate to make your mother mad."

They made it only a handful of feet from the shadowed seats near the back fence before getting swarmed. A half dozen children of varying ages were soon hanging off Ian's arms and back, while a young boy giggled and sat on his left shoe, arms wrapped around Ian's calf. A girl in a lacy pink dress tugged on Teddy's pant leg, talking rapidly in Spanish. Teddy could get by with it, if pressed, but it required a good deal of patience, as well as quite a bit of repetition, from the speaker. The little girl, while adorable, had neither.

"*Mas lento, por favor... No entiendo*," Teddy said, crouching down in front of her to try and catch the movements of her lips.

The little girl huffed. "*Estabas besando a mi prima. Vas a casarte con el ahora?*"

"Um... *Si?*" He didn't quite understand what she was asking. He knew *besando* was kissing, and...*prima* was cousin. He wasn't sure about the rest, and he felt stupid asking her to say it again.

In front of him, Ian laughed, looking back at him. His eyes were bright with amusement. "Good to know, sweetheart."

"Wait! What did I just agree to? Ian!" Teddy protested when Ian mimed locking his lips and throwing away a key. "Come on, no fair!"

"All's fair in love and war," Ian called over his shoulder. He set the children down that he held in each arm and they scampered off to play. Then he crouched down in front of the giggling girl by Teddy. "Mayumi, *cuando nos casemos, vas a llevar las flores para mi?*"

"*Si!*" Mayumi squealed and ran off to a woman in a brightly colored dress near the fire. "Mama, Mama! *El Tio Ian prometio que puedo llevar las flores para su boda!*"

The woman smiled and ruffled the little girl's hair. "English, baby. You need to practice."

Mayumi huffed, sucking in a breath and rapidly switching over. "Uncle Ian promised that I can carry the flowers for his wedding! Can they be dandelions? I like dandelions. They turn my fingers yellow and yellow is my favorite color!"

Teddy choked on nothing and spun toward Ian. "You told her we were getting married?"

"No, sweetheart, *you* told her we were getting married. I just agreed. I would never dream of arguing with my *pollito.*"

Teddy snagged a thin slice of watermelon off the party platter on the picnic table beside him and chucked it, without thinking, at Ian's shirt. It splattered in a spray of red, dripping down the cotton fabric. Ian sucked his lower lip into his mouth for a moment, like he wasn't sure whether to laugh or screech, then released with a pop.

"Oh, it's *on*. You better run now, boy." Ian grabbed a handful of ice cubes from the bowl near the punch and approached with a threatening grin.

Teddy shivered, not at the sight of the ice but at the purposeful way Ian called him *boy*, then backed away with raised hands, shaking his head. "No, wait…you *wouldn't*."

"Oh, you don't know me very well at *all* then." Ian's smile grew wide and devilish. Teddy turned and sprinted away, a scream escaping his throat as he tried to escape.

Ian caught him easily, dropping the large handful of freezing cold cubes down the back of his shirt. They slid down his spine in a frigid deluge. Teddy yelped, hopping from foot to foot as he tried to get free. Laughter echoed around them.

"Dance, baby, dance," Ian crowed.

"You, Ian Romero, are an evil, evil man."

"An evil, evil man you already agreed to marry," Ian corrected. "So I'm not worried."

"I'm not good at Spanish!" Teddy cried, spinning around to face him, burning with embarrassment. He hoped Ian didn't think he was serious, not that he would mind marrying Ian, someday—the key word being *someday*. He didn't want Ian to think he was clingy. He needed to prove that, even though he was only eighteen, he was mature enough for a relationship.

Ian grinned and shoved his fingers in his ears. "La la la, not listening."

Teddy rolled his eyes and held up his middle finger instead. Ian tugged his fingers free. "Is that an invitation?"

Teddy shrugged. "Kiss me again and find out."

Ian feigned a gasp, "In front of the children? How risqué." Despite his pretend outrage, he stalked forward, a lion to his prey, and captured Teddy's mouth in a bruising kiss. It was short but not sweet at all. It made Teddy want to drag him upstairs to his room — or the bathroom, or the pantry — and *do* things.

Ian must have seen his desire on his face, because his eyes darkened, his hands twitching like he was going to go caveman and throw Teddy over his shoulder. Instead, he stepped back, though Teddy could read the regret on his face, and put some distance between them. Teddy wasn't sure whether or not to be grateful for the breathing room.

"Come on. Let me introduce you around. I'm sure you haven't met everyone yet." Ian held out his hand.

A small smile curled up the corners of Teddy's mouth as he grasped it tightly. "Well, *everyone* is a lot of people. Might take a while." Teddy was used to his own small, nuclear family, just him and his mom — no cousins, or aunts and uncles. Ian's was like a village.

"Good thing we have all night, right?" Ian said.

Teddy liked the sound of that.

* * * *

Mama Romero and her sisters — all six of them — carried out the main course well after dark. It was closer to eleven than ten, the yard lit by dozens of strands of colored lights strung through the trees and, of course, the warm glow of the large bonfire. The youngest children had been packed away to bed hours before, while the rest ran barefoot through the grass, uncaring of the small sparks spat out of the fire and the misplaced pebbles from the garden. Most of the adults sat in groups around the fire or gathered by the food. Spirits were high and the air was filled with laughing and dozens of conversations in Spanish, spoken too rapidly for Teddy to follow.

Ian eventually settled on the ground by the patio, tucked between the wooden stairs and the small hydrangea bush near the corner. He had tugged Teddy down into the space between his thighs, encouraging him to lean back against his chest. The ground was hard and rocky, and the light from the fire made Teddy feel sleepy, but he wouldn't change a thing. In Ian's arms, he felt safe, far removed from his distant worries and fears

Ian leaned down and nuzzled into his hair. A second later, he brushed his lips against the back of Teddy's neck, below his ear. Teddy's whole body quivered at the intense feeling, like there was a straight shot from his neck to his dick, and he moaned.

Ian shifted behind him and he felt the hardness press against his back. He fought the urge to lean back into it, to roll his hips and tease. Then, he remembered the ice cubes sliding against his skin. He rocked his hips backward, rubbing the growing erection behind him until Ian gave a strangled groan as well.

"Shh..." Teddy whispered, grinning evilly. "Think of the children."

"You're trying to kill me," Ian murmured behind Teddy's ear before nipping the lobe. Teddy sucked in a gasp, tilting his head and exposing his neck farther. Ian slid his tongue over the pulse point, just for a second, then it was gone. Teddy whimpered at the loss.

"I'm trying to kill *you*?" Teddy protested. He arched his back, knowing it thrust his ass directly into the crotch of Ian's jeans. "At least I'm not *torturing* you."

Ian chuckled, the sound strained. He gripped Teddy's hips and tugged Teddy back, planting him firmly against him. Ian rutted against him once, then twice. He closed his lips around Teddy's ear and sucked until Teddy shuddered again.

Teddy didn't care that they were visible to anyone who walked directly in front of them. He dropped his hand to the front of his jeans, pressing the heel down gently on his throbbing dick. His doctor had cleared him for this, even if Teddy hadn't thought it would happen. The pain of his nearly healed incisions was worth the burst of satisfaction.

At least it *was*, until Ian tugged his hands out of his lap and spoke into his ear. "Uh-uh. Be a good boy, now, and keep your hands to yourself."

Teddy didn't need hands. As soon as the words 'good boy' slipped out of Ian's mouth, he was gone, his body racked with the effects of his climax. They hardly seemed like strong enough words but it felt like an explosion, like the burst of fireworks that had lit up the sky last month.

Ian clamped down tight, stilling his hips behind him. "Did you just…?"

Teddy flushed hot and red, covering his face immediately. He'd just come in his pants like a teenager. Well, he *was* a teenager, but if he had been hoping not to remind Ian of that, he'd just failed epically.

"Oh, baby." Ian gripped his wrists and tugged his hands away from his face. "I don't mind, I'm just surprised. I didn't realize how responsive you'd be." He pressed his lips gently to Teddy's shoulder. "It's not a bad thing, not a bad thing at all."

Teddy couldn't protest. Before he could even think up an excuse, he heard Mrs. Romero calling from the other side of the yard, "Someone find the birthday boy. It's almost time for cake."

"That's our cue," Ian murmured, carefully hoisting Teddy to his feet before following him. Teddy patted down his hair and brushed off his jeans, trying to look as if he'd been doing anything but what he'd actually been doing. But no amount of rearranging his clothing could dull the likely fire-engine-red blush he still felt on his cheeks. He was grateful it was dark. Ian, at least, looked as composed as ever...if a bit more well-endowed than usual.

Teddy trailed behind Ian over to the large cake placed at the center of the folding table in the back yard. Twenty-one candles encircled the top. Mama Romero bustled around like a drill sergeant, prodding people into place and dictating the lighting of the candles, all while keeping a careful eye on the shiny silver watch on her wrist.

"It's almost midnight. Everybody in place!" Mama Romero didn't quite clap, but Teddy expected her to. Ian smirked at Teddy but stepped up to the table.

"Who's going to sing? Daniela, you have a pretty voice. You should show it off more often. Why don't you start us off? No, don't be scared. Here, scootch forward. There you go." Mama Romero urged the young teenager forward, ignoring her reluctance. "On the count of three, okay? One, two..."

Daniela's voice was shaky, but under the nerves, it was pretty. "*Cumpleanos Feliz, Te Deseamos a ti...*" The rest of the guests joined in. Teddy hummed along. When the song ended, Ian closed his eyes and thought for a moment, then leaned forward and blew hard.

Smoke trailed upward in the night from the extinguished candles. The last flickered, then guttered in the face of Ian's determination. The guests clapped, the children whooping, and Mama Romero hurried off for a knife.

"I'd ask what you wished for," Teddy murmured to Ian beneath the excited chatter, "but then it wouldn't come true."

"I already got what I wished for," Ian murmured back, curling his fingers around Teddy's. His eyes were soft as they met Teddy's gaze. Teddy's cheeks warmed again. He wondered if the affection he saw was real.

Chapter Twelve

"Teddy, man, wait up," Lucas called after him a few weeks later. Teddy slowed at the crosswalk, checking his watch. He was running late and really didn't have time to chat. "You gotta sec?"

"A quick one," Teddy said, shifting his weight. "I'm on my way to work."

"Oh. Um, I'll walk with you?" Lucas shoved his hands into his pockets then out, before fiddling with the hem of his baggy shirt.

"Okay. It's not far." Teddy glanced both ways before crossing the street at a jog.

"Julian wants to see you," Lucas said once they were back on the sidewalk again.

"Why? It's only been three months…" Teddy had saved up some of his first payment, but he was still a few hundred short. Hopefully, his payments would be smaller when he was paying monthly.

"I don't know. He didn't say but he was pretty set on it. Said to tell you to meet him at the warehouse tonight at eight." Lucas scratched his nose. "He didn't seem very happy."

"I work until eight." Teddy frowned.

"Can you get off early? Come on, man. Julian…" Lucas gnawed on his lip. "I don't know… He's changed lately. I don't want to see him mad."

"I'll see what I can do, but I mean, it's not like there's someone to cover for me. If I don't get the work done, it doesn't get done…" Teddy hesitated, rubbing his palm over the no-longer-prickly fuzz on his scalp. "I'll get done as quick as I can, I guess."

"I'll meet you at the bus stop," Lucas promised. "Just…be there, okay?"

Teddy agreed, waving Lucas off before jogging the last few feet to the entrance to Blood, Sweat and Shears. He was a few minutes late but the salon wasn't open on Wednesdays, so he didn't need to defend his tardiness. Not that his boss Joel would mind—the part-time fitness instructor-full-time hair stylist was pretty laid back. But Teddy felt guilty anyway, since he hadn't been working there long.

Teddy spent most of his shift scrubbing down the upstairs fitness studio with his stomach twisted up in nerves. He hadn't even had the opportunity to make a late payment, so he knew he had no reason for them, except for Lucas' sketchy behavior. But the nerves made Teddy rush, and he managed to get out a few minutes early.

When he met Lucas at the bus stop, his friend was even more agitated than before. Teddy wondered if he was tripping.

"Shit, something's wrong, man," Lucas muttered as he paced. He jerked around when a dumpster lid dropped down an alley. "Fuck. I ain't never seen Julian like this."

Teddy stopped and grabbed Lucas' arm. "Dude, calm down. What's wrong?"

"Jules. He's off his rocker, raging about some *gringo* on fifth who poached his corner and ragged on some of his *gwallas*. He lost a lot of money and he ain't happy. I don't know, man. I don't get involved in that shit. You know that." Lucas flinched as a car drove slowly past. "We gotta go, man. They're waiting."

"You didn't say they were involved in anything illegal," Teddy protested, his grip tightening on Lucas' arm. He ignored Lucas' wince. "What did you get me into?"

"Nothing, or… It shouldn't have been anything. I didn't know, I swear. I found out about the *basuco* last month, and I haven't touched it." Lucas rocked back on his heels.

"*Bas*… Cocaine? They deal *cocaine*?" Teddy asked, letting go of Lucas' arms but only so he could swipe his fingers over his scalp. He tilted his head back and glared at the sky, trying to calm himself. "Fuck!" He cursed and started pacing.

"I'm sorry. I know I fucked up, but we gotta go, man. We're going to be late." Lucas grabbed Teddy's arm, dragging him in the direction of the warehouse.

Teddy yanked away. "Maybe we should go talk to someone? Ian, or…or the police?"

"No! They'll kill me. I shouldn't even have told you. They warned me to keep my mouth shut. Shit, I'm so fucked. So fucked, man." Lucas grabbed his arm again. "Just…just come with me and talk to him. It'll be fine. He probably just wants to know how you're doing on getting the money around. It'll be fine." He said the last quieter, like he was trying to reassure himself.

"It's not going to be fine if we walk in there and you look like you're tripping acid," Teddy hissed, shaking his arm free a second time. "So calm the fuck down, okay? We'll go talk to him."

Lucas dragged in a breath. "Yeah, yeah. Calm down. Got it."

When Lucas looked less like a skittish rabbit about to bolt, they started walking again. He saw the warehouse looming in the distance and a kernel of fear sprouted in his stomach, like Lucas' panic had stretched out trembling fingers and infected him. The warehouse looked worse than it had a few months ago. Across the grungy siding, someone had tagged a large, obscene graphic of a middle finger stuck up to the sky, blood dripping from the knuckles. Two of the bay doors were closed, obscenities in Spanish a neon splash against the white.

The third bay stood open. Teddy found himself walking slower the closer they got. A handful of men loitered around the entrance, their red bandanas easy to spot, even from a distance. Cigarettes dangled from fingers and out of mouths. A heavyset man leaned against the siding, sipping from the neck of a naked vodka bottle, not even clothed in a brown paper bag.

They weren't all men, Teddy realized, when he got close enough to hear the electric guitar spilling from inside, grating out the chords of some *brujeria* song from cheap speakers. At least two were women, baggy cargo pants drooping around their hips.

Teddy squeezed through the narrow gap between the men bracketing the edge of the bay door, angling his shoulder to avoid touching either. They snickered as he passed, wolf whistles following him into the warehouse. A shiver crawled down his spine. He wondered if he'd done the right thing by not calling anyone. But adding Ian to the picture didn't make him feel better. Safer, yes… But knowing Ian was involved? Well, he didn't think he'd like that.

Lucas followed him inside so closely that his breath dampened the back of Teddy's neck. The interior of the warehouse was laid out much the same as he remembered it. To the right was a series of scratched and stained sofas. On one, a man in a tank top and heavy gold chains sprawled, his jeans unbuttoned. A skeletal woman with a white dress hitched up over her hips rode him there, in plain sight of everyone, grunts and moans spilling from her lipstick-smeared lips. On another, a burly man sat with his legs spread, a man — a boy, really, because if he was more than eighteen Teddy would be shocked — on his knees between them. Teddy tore his eyes away from the sight, heat flooding his face.

His gaze landed on the other side of the room. Eight men sat around two folding tables, one on each side, playing cards.

Teddy stiffened his spine and headed that way, spotting Julian at one. A small pile of coins sat in the center of the table. Julian laid down his hand of playing cards just as they approached. "Three of a kind," Julian said, glaring at the other three men, who all folded immediately.

Teddy noticed that at least one had a better hand.

Julian scooped the coins over in front of him before looking up. Like the warehouse, he looked different from the last time Teddy had seen him — grittier. The nice jeans and polo had been replaced with black cargo pants and a white tank that bared his muscles and exposed several dark, blurry tattoos. He was no longer clean-shaven, and the scruff made him look older.

"Ah, pretty boy." Julian leered at him. He waved a hand at the man to his right, gesturing for him to vacate his seat. The man stood, flicking his cigarette butt onto the cement before wandering off. "Sit down. Sit down."

Teddy carefully lowered himself onto the folding chair, perching at the edge like he was preparing to run. "I was surprised to hear from you. I thought I had another three months…"

"Pleasantly surprised, though, right?" Julian leaned back in the chair, his knees spread.

"Yeah," Teddy lied, forcing a grin.

Julian let his chair rock back forward, the legs slamming back into the ground with a clang. "See? Here's the thing, *amigo*. I lost some money recently. This economy…am I right?" Julian laughed but it was cold, chilling Teddy to the bone. "So I need to call in your first payment early. Five thousand dollars by the end of the week."

Teddy paled as Julian quoted the number. It was high…much higher than he expected. "That's…that's not what we agreed on."

The smile slid like water off Julian's face, leaving it hard. "Well then, I guess we're making a new agreement, aren't we?"

"I don't have that," Teddy admitted, clenching his hands on the edge of the chair. If he didn't pay his rent or his electric bill, he might be able to scrounge up three. "I just got back to work."

"*Amigo*," The smile was back. It was as bright as a fluorescent lightbulb and twice as fake. "Maybe we can make a deal."

Teddy bit back the comment that they already *had* a deal, one they'd both agreed on. Julian didn't seem like the kind of person who'd laugh it off. Instead, he tried to soften his grip and shrugged. "Maybe."

"See? Here's what I think." Julian leaned forward, arm planting on the table. "I think you're a pretty boy." He turned to the older man beside him. The red-headed man looked Teddy over and grunted an agreement. "See? Mikey likes you, and Mikey don't like no one."

Teddy heard Lucas whimper behind him before his friend spoke up, his voice shaky, "Julian, I don't think…"

"Shut up," Julian barked over Teddy's shoulder, his eyes flashing. "I don't pay you to think. I pay you to keep your mouth shut." Julian turned back to Teddy. "Where was I? Oh, yeah. Pretty boy. Maybe you come work for me. Maybe you work your debt off on your back, yeah? Maybe you enjoy it, and maybe I make some money. Maybe everyone's happy, yeah?"

"Umm-m. Well, lovely as that sounds, I think I'll have to pass on that…" Teddy was so going to end up murdered. He could see it already. He should keep his mouth shut. Instead, panic spilled down his skin like gasoline. It pricked his fingers like thorns until he slapped them against his thighs, then pried his mouth open instead, loosing the words he meant to contain. "Great offer, though. Real strong first bid. How about I pay you what I have now, instead?"

Jesus Christ, who did he think he was talking to, a teller at his friendly neighborhood credit union? Julian's hands twitched on the table, drawing Teddy's eyes to the black revolver he'd been trying to avoid noticing. It sat heavy by a glass ashtray, inches from Julian's wrist. Teddy shuddered, but met Julian's eyes with as much steel as he could. The cold contemplation sent icicles into his vertebrae but he refused to bend.

He wasn't going to let anyone pimp him out. God had given him teeth and he wasn't afraid to use them.

The entire warehouse was quiet—or maybe Teddy's fear was just too loud. When Julian laughed, the sound broke the silence like a clarinet reed, tension draining out of the room. "You got big *cajones*. I'll give you that, *amigo*. I like you."

Teddy, feigning a confidence he didn't feel, propped his right ankle on his left knee and struggled to relax— to pretend he hadn't pissed himself just a little. "*Gracias*," he said, the word mangled by the tightness of his throat.

Julian's smile stayed in place. "White boys, all the same. You butcher my language. Stick to English, my friend. Get me my money by the end of the month and our relationship will stay…friendly. *Comprende*?"

"Understood."

* * * *

Teddy had the door to his ratty apartment closed and locked behind him before he allowed himself to slump against the warped wood He didn't have that kind of money just…lying around. He should have known better than to get involved with Lucas' friends. He'd known they were sketchy. But there was a difference between defacing-abandoned-buildings sketchy and selling cocaine out of trunks.

He would have to work double the hours he was working now to come up with that much, and if anything, his hours were going to get cut at one of his jobs soon. He'd heard the maintenance man at the college talking about it a few days earlier. Money was tight everywhere. He would never be able to convince them to keep him on longer.

His gaze shifted around the apartment. Three months, and he had barely started to furnish it. The one-bedroom apartment was only not a studio because of the rickety wall hastily put up across one half of what was now the living room to make the small bedroom in the back. Teddy hadn't risked hanging so much as a picture frame on it, just in case it fell over. He had a couch that smelled strongly of ammonia and a coffee table with uneven legs, stabilized partly by a thin stack of magazines slid under one of them. The fridge and microwave had come with the apartment and both were older than he was.

There was nothing he could sell for a few extra bucks. He was going to have to pick up a third job and push college back a semester. If only he had taken out loans, rather than relying on scholarships. The scholarships would vanish when he couldn't attend. The loans might have at least bought him some time. The thought caused a dull ache in his chest. He rubbed it briefly before straightening his spine. He'd start sending out applications in the morning.

Chapter Thirteen

Ian crouched in the shadow of the stairway. He'd pulled the living room blinds — and the curtains for good measure — and turned off all the lights nearly an hour before. This had seemed like a good idea then, before the leg cramp started pulling at his calf muscle, yelling at him to break position to massage it back to normal. It would be just his luck to hatch this plan the one night his brother actually stayed in for a change.

He didn't know how else to get his brother's attention. He'd tried talking to him like a normal person half a dozen times over the past month, but his brother was being shifty. It wasn't just the sneaking out at all hours of the night. It was the jumping at every little sound, the bruises forming below his eyes and the fact that his normally overweight brother had dropped enough pounds that he was damn near skinny.

Ian couldn't do anything about the fact that Teddy had been ignoring his calls or making excuses that he was just *super* busy. Ian was afraid he'd pushed the younger man too far, too fast at his birthday party.

Beyond a few short conversations on the phone—which had left Ian concerned about Teddy's health because, frankly, he'd sounded *exhausted*—they hadn't been able to hang out again.

So while he couldn't fix the distance growing between Teddy and him, he *could* fix his brother.

Maybe.

If he could just get him to stand still and talk for two minutes.

Hence his painful crouching like a crazy person beside the stairs, listening to the sounds of distant traffic and—a floorboard creaked above him. Ian's heart thumped faster as adrenaline started coursing through his bloodstream. This was it. He was going to figure out what his brother was up to, one way or another.

He just hoped it wasn't drugs.

Footsteps started down the stairs, slow and timid. Ian tensed, waiting for them to reach the bottom step before he leaped up and reached out to grab—his mother, who clutched her chest and let out a deafening, ear-piercing scream.

"*Dios mio*, are you trying to kill me?" She slapped him over the head as soon as he released her.

"Sorry, Mama. I thought you were Lucas," Ian apologized, ducking out of the way of her palms as she slapped at him again.

"He snuck out hours ago. Stupid boy thinks his mother don't know when he leaves. I hear him, you know, prying up his window with that rusty old screwdriver. It whines like a dog." Mama rolled her eyes and reached out to flick on the light. "But I did not think you would take to lurking in shadows like an *asesino*, trying to give your poor mother a heart attack.

Shame on you," She swatted at him again but couldn't seem to stop the smirk on her lips.

"Sorry, Mama," Ian apologized again.

"Next time you should lurk under his window in the bushes. Maybe then you scare him enough to crawl back into bed, yeah?" Mama wandered toward the kitchen, digging around in the cupboard before pulling down a small tin of sugar. With hands used to the practice, she threw it into the blender with milk, fruit and ice. She split the *licuado* between two glasses and pushed one across the counter to him.

"So you are worried about your brother too, I see," Mama said after taking a sip. She frowned, staring at the rim of her glass, looking deep in thought.

Ian spun his glass on the counter without drinking, more to give his hands something to do than anything. "He's been acting funny for a while. I was hoping I could convince him to talk to me."

"Lucas has too much of your father in him — stubborn like a bull and as angry as one, too. He won't talk until he's ready." Mama sighed and poured the rest of her drink down the sink. "Is this really about your brother, *mijo*? Or is this about your young man? You should tell him to come to dinner."

Ian's frown deepened at the mention of Teddy. "They've both been acting weird. Lucas is as skittish as a colt, and Teddy…? Well, I know he started college last week, but I didn't realize it would keep him this busy. He sounds exhausted. I just…"

"You worry. It's in your nature. You've always been my little protector, always trying to fix people." Mama reached up and patted his shoulder. "But I do not think this is something you need to fix. Sometimes you need to let people come to you on their own. Go to sleep, *mijo*. You can pick up your troubles in the morning."

Ian kissed his mother on the cheek, cleaned up his glass and went back to his room, but, despite his mother's urging, he couldn't seem to leave his troubles behind. He couldn't wash them away in the shower or dry them off after, couldn't surrender them when he closed his eyes in bed. They clung to him like a leech, whispering that something was wrong.

He sighed and rolled over, punching his pillow until it caved to the form of his skull. Maybe his mother was right and he was worrying over nothing. Maybe Lucas had taken up jogging, and that was the cause of his weight loss and quick escapes out of the door whenever Ian tried to talk to him. Maybe Teddy was just overwhelmed with the newness of college, the stresses of academia at a university more than he expected.

The stone in his chest didn't think so.

* * * *

Ian finally ran into his brother two days later. Literally, unfortunately. He was heading downstairs after having stripped apart his bedroom to find his black boots with the *cascabeles*. Too small for him, they would be just about right for Noa. She wanted someone to practice her dance with, and Ian had allowed himself to be roped in, riding the high of finally hearing from Teddy.

He was so distracted thinking about his date with the younger man later that evening that he didn't even notice his brother descending the stairs in front of him. And his brother was too distracted with whatever *he* was thinking of to notice Ian, even with the bells jangling off his boots.

"Jesus fuck, man!" Lucas screeched, spinning with his fists ready to swing.

"Next time, open your ears, *manito*." Ian reached out and messed up his brother's curls.

"*Jodete!*" Lucas knocked his hand away.

Unfortunately for Lucas, Mama rounded the corner from the living room just as the curse slid from his lips. "Lucas Oliveira Sousa Romero! Apologize to your brother!"

Lucas' shoulders pulled up, tension radiating off him like heat on blacktop. "I'm an adult, Mama. I can curse if I want to!"

"*Mientras tu vivas en esta casa—*" Mama started to threaten, but Lucas' hand sliced through the air, palm flat as the blade of a dagger, cutting off her words.

"Then I'll move out!" Lucas set his jaw, tendons in his neck popping out from the tension. "It's not like you want me here anyway. I'm just…just a *tarado*. A fucking *pendejo*. I fuck up everyone's life." Rather than anger, it was sadness that crossed Lucas' face. Ian swore he saw the shine of tears in his brother's eyes before he turned away from them to stomp back up the stairs.

"Oh, Lucas," Mama sighed, reaching for him, but Lucas twisted out of reach.

"Leave me alone!" Lucas said bitterly. His voice was like gravel in the blades of a lawn mower—ready to damage either itself or the person standing closest. A part of Ian told him to follow his brother to his room, to dig into the root of his unreasonable anger, but a larger part of him told him to duck for cover. It was probably best to let the kid calm down. Besides, Lucas had been avoiding him for weeks. It would serve him right to wait on Ian now.

"I'll talk to him tomorrow," Ian murmured to Mama, plastering on a smile he hoped was reassuring.

Mama frowned, eyes skimming over Ian. "Going somewhere?"

Ian was in his best jeans, artistically distressed across the thighs. He'd paired it with his nicest shirt, a coral button-down that looked great against his skin. "I'm helping Noa with her dance," Ian said. His gaze drifted from Mama's. He was not quite willing to lie, even by omission, while staring her in the eyes. Mama didn't need to know he was going to take Teddy to a matinee. He didn't know why he wanted it to be a secret, except that he felt like speaking it out loud would jinx it.

"Mm-hmm."

up her lips Mama's pursed lips and dry hum made it clear that she suspected that Ian was not being wholly truthful anyway. "Well, *mijo*, after you are finished helping your sister, don't forget to tell Teddy to stop in for dinner soon, hmm?"

"I didn't say—" Ian protested, his face heating.

"You didn't have to." Mama curved. "I see things, you know? You think I don't see the way you look at that boy and how he looks at you? You think I don't see you skulking around the hydrangea bushes instead of mingling? Maybe I should plan weddings instead of birthday parties."

"Mama!" Ian's skin was going to melt if he got any hotter.

"What? You think I don't know what it's like to be young? Your father and I first made love in the back seat of a—"

"Mama!" Ian clapped his hands over his ears.

"What? Did you think you were adopted?" Mama's smirk developed into a full-fledged to a grin. "You were conceived in a Winnebago ten miles south of the American border, and your brother on a loveseat in the backroom of a—"

"You've never had a Winnebago, Mama." Ian cringed.

"I didn't say it was ours. You remember Papa's friend, the one who sponsored him for his visa?" Mama chuckled when Ian started humming to block out the words. Of course he remembered Papa's friend Jack, the American who'd sponsored the pair for their green cards. He was hard to forget, an older man with Irish roots, hair dark and kinky and— Oh God, he couldn't think that word now, not after hearing of his mother's exploits in the back of old Jack's rusty house on wheels. Last he knew, the man was trundling through the so-called wilds of South Dakota now that he'd retired.

He didn't think there were many wilds near Aberdeen.

"I gotta go, Mama. Noa is waiting..." Ian said, not sure he'd survive this conversation.

"Give Teddy my love," Mama called after him.

"Yes, Mama," Ian said between groans and shut the door behind him.

* * * *

Helping Noa with her dance took his mind off his brother's attitude, and by the time he drove her back home from the dance studio and dropped her off, he was more than ready for his date.

Teddy stood nervously on the sidewalk outside his apartment complex. Ian frowned as he pulled up to the curb, eyes moving past the young man to the rather rundown building behind him. The paint was peeling, the grass withered. It didn't look like a place that a *'lovely, young married couple'* would be subletting out. Maybe that was why Teddy always made excuses if he spoke of coming over.

He was stopped from continuing that thought when Teddy tugged open the passenger door and slid inside the car, fastening his seatbelt before fixing him with a bright grin. "Ready to go?" Teddy asked, nearly bouncing in the seat.

"I don't know. I wasn't sure you really wanted to go. I thought maybe we could just—"

Teddy interrupted Ian's teasing with an Oscar-winning pout. "No, I want to go. We have to. It's the *last* movie!"

"What if it's boring and I need a distraction?" Ian asked with a grin as he pulled away from the curb.

"I'm sure we'll think of something." The look Teddy gave him was hot, his eyes heavy-lidded. Ian groaned when Teddy slid his tongue over his lower lip, leaving it glistening, taunting.

"Will you hold my hand if I get scared?" Ian asked, smirking.

"I'll hold *something*," Teddy promised.

Instantly, the car was filled with a scorching heat, and Ian wondered if Teddy could scent his arousal the way Ian swore he could Teddy's. He bit back a groan. "I'm holding you to that."

The small theater was tucked at the end of a dying strip mall. They walked past the skeleton stores, barely noticing the boarded-up windows or tumbleweed newspapers in the walkways. Ian listened to Teddy chatter excitedly about the movie. It was the eighth and final installment, a bittersweet culmination to a nearly decade-long franchise. It had been playing for two weeks already, so the line to get into the theater was short.

Ian passed over his card to the teller, then handed the bucket of over-buttered popcorn to Teddy to hold. "Save some for the movie," Ian teased, watching as Teddy immediately snagged a handful and crammed it into his mouth, his cheeks bulging like a chipmunk until he swallowed. Ian preferred his popcorn plain, but he'd caved to the pleading eyes.

"Free refills," Teddy rebutted, his smile flashing.

"You're going to get a stomachache." Ian rolled his eyes and accepted his card back, returning it to his wallet, which he slid back into his pocket. Maybe if he kept his hands busy for a second, he'd resist the urge to smack Teddy's ass for not listening. They were only on their first date, and he wasn't sure how Teddy would feel about him 'daddying' him already.

Teddy's lips twitched. "No, I won't."

"Yes, you will." Ian held his hand out for the bucket.

Teddy shook his head. "Nope."

"Yep." Ian abandoned his effort and slid his finger into the belt loop of Teddy's jeans instead, guiding him into the theater. They headed down the center aisle. "Where do you want to sit?"

"Center, obviously." Teddy turned about halfway down and flopped into one of the seats, lifting his feet immediately to the back of the chair in front of him.

"Obviously," Ian grinned and sat down beside him.

Teddy snagged another handful of popcorn. He waited, as if making sure that Ian was watching, before sliding out his tongue and using it to capture a kernel, drawing it back into his lips. Then, Teddy did it again, but kept the fluffy, golden treat between his lips. He leaned closer, as if offering it to Ian.

Ian groaned. He held out for a moment before bending forward and snagging it, pulling it into his mouth. He didn't pull back, leaving his mouth gently pressed against Teddy's, stroking the plush, pink lips with his tongue, enjoying the salty remnants left behind. He wondered what Teddy would taste like with a different type of salt on his skin.

Teddy moaned, pressing closer to him, then Teddy's hands were slipping up over Ian's chest, skimming along his neck, clasping his fingers together to hold Ian in place — as if Ian were going anywhere.

A throat cleared behind them and they broke apart. An usher stood in the aisle, weight shifting, face uncomfortably red. Ian smirked but pulled away, settling back into his seat. Teddy's eyes, heated, darted longingly toward Ian, but he settled back as well.

"Sorry, folks. Feet off the seats," the blushing teen stammered.

Teddy huffed but dropped his feet to the ground, waiting until the usher left to mutter, "The floor's sticky."

Ian laughed, but the lights dimmed before he could comment, the first preview rolling across the screen.

The dimness of the theater only made the spark between them burn brighter. Every nerve ending on Ian's body made him crave the man beside him. He longed to skim his fingers over the soft skin, to steal Teddy's breath into his mouth, to stroke the soft strands of hair slowly growing on the young man's scalp where before only stubble had grown. It took all his will to keep himself confined to his own seat. He wanted to pull Teddy into his lap, to settle him astride and consume him. He just...*wanted*.

Partway through the movie, though, his phone thrummed in his pocket. He lifted his hip to slip it free. His younger brother's photo flashed across the screen. Ian, still annoyed with his brother's earlier attitude, shoved the phone back in. He would call him back later.

It rang again a few minutes later and Ian ignored it. Instead, he curled his fingers through Teddy's and settled back to watch the movie.

* * * *

The sunlight was bright when he stepped out of the theater with Teddy. "I can't believe it's over," Teddy said, his expression melancholy. Ian understood the feeling. It felt like a portion of his life had just ended.

In his pocket, his phone vibrated for what seemed like the hundredth time. He stopped on the sidewalk and dug it out, frowning at the screen. "One sec, it's Mama."

Teddy stopped beside him, pulling out a cigarette and lighting it up as he waited.

Ian, only half listening to the ringing in his ear, reached out and tugged the slender white death stick out of Teddy's fingers, dropping it to the ground and scuffing it out.

"Those things will kill y—" he started to say, but Mama's voice cut him off, broken though it was by sobbing. Ian froze, all of his attention on the call.

"Ian, your brother, he… Oh God, they're taking him to the hospital, but they don't…" She hiccupped, her words choking off.

"Slow down, Mama. What happened? Is Lucas okay?" Ian tried to soothe her, concern surging inside.

"He shot himself! My baby, he... I heard the doorbell, and I thought... I thought... Where did he get a gun, Ian? Where did my baby get a gun?"

Chapter Fourteen

Teddy stood silently in the hospital waiting room. He had to clench his hands into fists to keep himself from sliding one of them into Ian's and squeezing. Ian seemed barely aware of his presence at his side. Teddy felt out of place, like at any moment one of the Romeros was going to turn to him and ask him what he was doing there. Or worse, tell him to get the hell out, that he wasn't family.

Mama Romero cried quietly, slumped in a chair near the door. She looked too small, like at any moment the chair was going to swallow her. Papa Romero sat stoically at her side. The only sign of emotion he allowed himself to show was the way his large hands clenched the chair's arms. Noa was curled up beside him, her knees pulled to her chest. Mascara tracked its way down her cheeks.

Ian hadn't sat down in the three hours they'd waited. He'd paced for a while, until even that seemed to take too much energy. Now, he just stood, his arms crossed, eyes skipping from the empty door to the clock ticking slowly on the wall then back again.

Teddy, for the first time since his surgery, wished he were wearing his sweater. Too-large, frayed at the edges and faded from years of acting as his security blanket, it could hide his shaking hands in the pockets and his face in the cowl-neck collar. He'd gotten rid of it weeks ago, but now all he wanted was the reassurance it offered.

He didn't believe Lucas had shot himself.

He'd overheard the police officer talking quietly to Lucas' parents shortly after they'd arrived. Lucas had been found alone, in a one-bedroom apartment supposedly leased in his name, down on Twelfth. There'd been no sign of forced entry, no evidence anyone had put the gun in his hand and forced it to his head.

Teddy knew better. Lucas might have changed lately, getting more skittish in the few weeks since he and Teddy had been dragged down to see Julian, but he wasn't suicidal. Teddy picked at a small hole at the bottom of his front right pocket. He'd just talked to Lucas a few days before and his friend, nervous and looking over his shoulder, had muttered something about going to the police.

Maybe Julian had found out Lucas' plans. Maybe that was what happened when someone tried to flip on dangerous men. Teddy had almost spoken up and told the officer everything, but something had weighed down his tongue, keeping it silent in his mouth. He didn't want to burden the Romeros with the knowledge of what Lucas had gotten up to lately, not if he wasn't sure he was right.

He would go to the precinct in the morning, he decided. He looked up when he saw someone enter, but it wasn't the doctor. It was just an orderly, coming in to change out the coffee before leaving.

Mama Romero kept crying.

Noa tucked her knees in tighter.

Ian started pacing again.

* * * *

Two hours and eighteen minutes later, a solemn-looking doctor came into the waiting room. Teddy knew that it wouldn't be good news.

He was right.

"I'm very sorry. We did everything we could," the doctor said to Mama and Papa Romero. "We were able to keep his heart beating, but he is on a ventilator. There appears to be no brain activity. I would advise you to say your goodbyes."

Mama Romero let out a keening cry, and Papa Romero sagged in his chair, face shattering for a second before he put it back together again into a steely mask. Ian bent at the waist, his hands propped on his knees for support. Teddy heard the half-smothered cry of pain. Unable to stop himself, he rested a hand on Ian's shoulder in comfort, but Ian jerked beneath it like he'd been stung. Teddy tore his hand free, wrapping it around his waist instead. Ian didn't seem to notice.

Teddy watched the family trickle out. He hesitated, wanting to go with them and say his own goodbyes but doubting he'd be welcome. He closed his eyes and smothered his own sob as it welled in his throat.

Then a small, delicate hand curled into his and squeezed. He opened his eyes to meet Noa's. They were the same height, though Noa was five years younger. "He would want you to be there," Noa whispered, her eyes glistening with tears. "You were…his *best* friend."

"I'm not family…" was all Teddy could muster to say.

"You might as well be," Noa squeezed his hand again. "Come on."

Teddy trailed along, his hand clasped in hers, down the hallway and into the intensive care room. Lucas looked small in the bed, attached to wires and tubes and beeping machines, his head swaddled in thick white bandages. Plastic tubing attached to a mouth guard blocked much of the remainder of Lucas' face. The sound of it gasping in and out made the hair on Teddy's arms raise.

Teddy stayed back out of the way as the family said their goodbyes. Inside, he felt like screaming or breaking down into shoulder-shaking sobs. It wasn't fair, and all he wanted was to see his friend open his eyes, sit up and say, "Surprise! I really fooled you, didn't I?"

But Lucas wasn't into practical jokes, and his eyes never opened. Teddy would have the sound of the heartbeat monitor stuttering, screaming loud in a reminder that the heart it attached to was no longer beating, in his nightmares for years. The siren wasn't loud enough to drown out his guilt, nor was the sound of nurses hurrying in, wheeling Lucas' body out of the room, preparing to harvest the bits and pieces that could save someone else. But Teddy didn't want to think of Lucas' heart beating somewhere else, without him. Of someone else getting Lucas' liver, or lungs or eyes. He didn't want to think that somewhere out there, someone would benefit from Lucas not existing anymore.

"Fuck!" Ian cursed, turning and slamming his fist into the wall by the door. Teddy flinched at the sound. Ian stormed out of the room without looking back.

Teddy hesitated a moment, torn between letting the man grieve and following. His feet moved without his input. He followed Ian into a small, two-stall bathroom down the hall. Ian was standing at the sink, his hands on the counter like it was the only thing keeping him from collapsing. His shoulders shook and tears tracked their way silently down his cheeks.

Teddy approached slowly, stopping at his side, but he didn't speak.

Ian stayed silent as well, until suddenly he turned, pulling Teddy into his arms and holding him almost too tight, but Teddy didn't say anything. He just clasped Ian closer and held on while he cried.

Eventually, Ian spoke, his voice broken, "Tell me why, baby. Why would he do that?"

Teddy felt ice crystallize in his throat, freezing his voice until he cleared it. "I...I don't think he did," Teddy whispered. "I think... I think...*someone* set it up."

Ian sucked in a breath and jerked back slightly to look at Teddy. "Why do you think that? Do you know something?"

Teddy's skin grew chilly. "I... He was involved with some...not-so-nice people. I... They... He was talking about going to the police. I don't know if...if they'd have let him."

"What do you mean? *Not-so-nice* people? Was he being bullied again?" Ian tightened his grip on Teddy's arms but didn't seem to realize it. "Do you think they did this?"

"No, I mean… I think it's a gang. Or a cartel. They… Ian, they scare me, and…I think he was in trouble." The words tumbled over each other in his rush to get them out.

"How long was he involved?" Ian's voice was chilly and it was clear by his eyes that his mind was already working, circling through the bits of information Teddy had given him and formulating a theory.

"A year, at least? I only met them twice, but…I don't think they're good people," Teddy admitted.

"You knew he was involved and you didn't say anything?" Ian frowned, his mouth flattening into a thin, white line.

Teddy hunched inward. "He asked me not to."

Ian's look was thunderous as he let Teddy go. Teddy felt the blood rush back to his skin but the relief was drowned out by the wish that Ian would have kept holding him, even if it was painful. "You need to talk to the police. Tell them what you know so they'll look into it."

"I…I was going to go tomorrow," Teddy said. "I didn't think they'd—"

"You didn't think at all," Ian interrupted, his voice raising until he cut it off at the end, turning his face away, his jaw clenched. "I think you should go home. I'll pick you up in the morning. We can go to the precinct together."

"I…I can go myself."

"Teddy," Ian snapped, "I'm not asking again."

Teddy jerked his head in acceptance. Ian pushed past him, shoulder not-so-gently brushing him aside, leaving Teddy alone in the chilly bathroom.

* * * *

Teddy let himself into his dark apartment and closed the door behind him. His body felt heavy, like he was carrying an invisible weight on his shoulders. The weight got no lighter when he heard a chair scrape in the corner of his apartment that he'd dubbed his kitchen.

He froze for a second before spinning around, his heart hammering in his chest. Two men were in his place. The nearest was a hulk of a man who looked like he belonged in a boxing ring, cauliflower ears and a broken nose adding credence to the image. He was white, though he clearly spent a lot of time outside, and the color of his hair was a mystery, since it had been shaved to the skin for long enough that the scalp was the same color as the rest of him.

Julian sat in one of the two kitchen chairs beside the behemoth. His foot was propped casually on his other knee, like it was perfectly normal for him and his goon to have broken into Teddy's apartment.

"Sit down, *amigo*." Julian gestured to the remaining chair.

Teddy sat, already noting the holster at the larger man's side. His eyes lingered on the black matte grip, his mouth growing dry.

"You don't look happy to see me, *amigo*. Surely we are still friends, yes?" Julian's voice was friendly…too friendly. It left Teddy cold. He gave a small, barely-there nod of acknowledgement, but his lack of enthusiasm didn't deter Julian. Like a snake, Julian's grin widened.

"Good, because you see, I thought Lucas and I were friends, then I heard about his little plan to rat me out to the cops. You wouldn't be thinking of ratting on me, would you?" Julian's smile vanished, like it had never been there in the first place.

"No. Of course not," Teddy lied. Sweat beaded on his forehead.

"Good, good, but see, I'm not sure I believe you, *amigo*. I think I need a little reassurance... Or maybe just some insurance, yeah?" Julian sat back in his chair, one hand resting on the table. He held the other one out to the large man, who dropped a small, clear baggie into his palm. Teddy saw three brightly colored pills inside. "Have you met Hugo yet?"

Teddy shook his head silently.

"Well, that's about to change." Julian smirked and dumped the three pills onto the table, halfway between Teddy and himself. "Do you know what these are?"

Teddy shook his head again. "I don't do pills."

Julian shrugged. "And I don't like rats. Maybe you take the pills, and you play with my friend Hugo here—or you end up like your little friend."

Teddy shuddered at the casual admission, even if Julian didn't actually say the words. His eyes dropped to the pills, one blue, one green, one pink. "What...what are they?"

"Just a little bit of molly. It won't kill you. It's just to make you have a real nice time." Julian toyed with the pills, his eyes sharp. "I'm sure you don't want a video of you tweaking on his dick getting out. Your friend told me you want to be an architect. I don't know many companies who'd look kindly on that..." Julian pulled the gun and set it on the table, hand curled loosely around the grip.

Ice crept down Teddy's spine as he reached out and picked up one of the pills. His heart thudded wildly in his chest, his breath racing. It seemed to take forever to bring the pink pill to his mouth and swallow it. He felt every second of it sliding down his throat.

"All of them," Julian ordered.

A small sob slipped from his lips as he obeyed. Another slid free when Julian grinned and pulled out a camera with his free hand. "Don't worry, pretty boy. This little video will stay between us, as long as you keep your mouth shut."

Hugo chuckled and the sound was loud like thunder. "He's got a pretty mouth. Maybe I want it open."

Julian laughed. The world seemed to rock beneath Teddy and he whimpered, gripping the edge of the chair. The world spun around him and suddenly, he felt like laughing as well. The two men no longer seemed quite so threatening. In fact, he was overcome with the sudden urge to dance.

And it was never fun to dance alone.

* * * *

Ian drummed his fingers on his steering wheel, staring through the windshield at the ratty complex that housed Teddy's apartment. It was nearly noon. He should have been here earlier—hours earlier. But every time he'd picked up his phone to message Teddy, guilt had swelled in his chest.

If he hadn't been so worried about his date with Teddy...

If he hadn't ignored Lucas' phone calls...

The *what if*s kept circling in his mind, over and over. He didn't want to take his guilt out on Teddy. He already felt bad for yelling at him yesterday at the hospital. No matter how angry he was that Teddy had known that his brother was involved in shady things and kept quiet, it wasn't fair to hold it against him. Teddy probably thought he was doing what was best by not betraying a friend. It wasn't like Ian had known either, and Lucas was his *brother*.

Ian clenched his fists on the leather, and he resolved to do his best to be understanding. He climbed out of the car and locked the door. It was a shitty neighborhood. If he didn't, he might not have a car to come back to.

He pulled out his phone and scrolled through his messages. It had been a few weeks since Teddy had reluctantly sent him his apartment number—and only after eliciting a promise that Ian wouldn't drop in unexpectedly.

Teddy's apartment was on the third floor, in the corner. A half-dead fern separated it from the apartment beside it. Ian glared at the warped wood. A well-placed kick would split the door in two. Some security that was.

Ian knocked soundly on the door and waited.

And waited some more. There was no movement on the other side of the door, so Ian knocked again, louder.

He frowned when he had to knock a third time. He pulled up the apartment number again, checking that he had the right one. He'd told Teddy he was coming. He reached down and tested the knob. It twisted open in his hand, the door swinging open. Ian frowned, peering into the apartment, his concern growing.

It wasn't like Teddy to leave the door unlocked. Or at least, it didn't *seem* like something the responsible Teddy he knew would do, but he supposed it was possible. "Hello? Teddy?" Ian stepped into the apartment and looked around.

The place was a dump. No wonder Teddy didn't want him visiting. It was obvious that Teddy at least tried to take care of it. The floors were worn but clean. The wallpaper peeled in places, but Teddy had hung a few picture frames. A few knickknacks, clearly several owners away from new, sat on a practically empty bookshelf.

Ian resolved to talk to Teddy later, after they went to the police, about moving back into Mama's. They had a guest room and Mama loved Teddy. He hated to think of the young man wasting money on a crap hole like this when he could be saving.

"Teddy?" He called again.

A groan sounded from one of only two doors. Ian hesitated before following the sound into what turned out to be a bedroom.

At first, Ian refused to believe what he was seeing. The mattress on the floor was bare—just like the pair of bodies tangled on it. One was large, covered in low-quality tattoos—the other small and slender, and all too familiar.

The larger man was on his stomach, one arm tucked under the pillow, the other thrown loosely over Teddy's waist.

And Teddy... Teddy blinked his eyes open and struggled to sit up, not seeming to care that he was nude or that he had clearly been busy the night before while Ian was at home grieving. Ian could see the dried cum on his thighs that Teddy made little move to hide.

"Ian!" Teddy's words slurred together, and Ian had worked in a bar long enough to spot the blown pupils, a clear sign of drug use. He watched Teddy shiver in the cold air. Disgust warred with disbelief. Teddy's mother was an addict and all he'd heard was how much that frustrated Teddy. He found it hard to believe that Teddy would toy with drugs, but he couldn't deny the evidence before his eyes.

Teddy pushed up onto his knees and reached for Ian. There was so much need in his eyes. Half of Ian wanted to snag him from the bed and toss him into a shower, then spend the next week claiming him, over and over, until Teddy knew without a doubt who he belonged to. A larger part forced him back a step, clenching his jaw.

The stranger on the mattress woke, rolling over. He leered at Teddy, his eyes lingering on his ass, before he turned a cold gaze onto Ian. "Who the fuck are you?"

"I'd ask you the same thing," Ian replied, turning to Teddy for an answer.

But Teddy, it seemed, was still at least partially caught in the haze of whatever drug he'd turned to the night before. The young man blinked, rubbing his eyes, then peered at him again. "Ian?" Teddy turned to the man in his bed, his skin paling.

Ian took another step back, "Oh, don't get worried now on my account. It looks like you had a fun night." His voice sounded icy, even to him. Later, he might regret the words, but all he felt now was anger.

Teddy flinched, stumbling over his words. "It's...it's not what it looks like."

"Oh, it's not what it looks like? Because it certainly looks like you went straight from the hospital, where we watched them unhook my brother — your friend — from life support, to popping molly and riding a stranger's dick. So tell me, if it's not what it looks like, then what is it?"

The stranger cleared his throat and Teddy's gaze snapped between them. His expression was torn, and Ian, despite his anger, couldn't help noticing how frail the young man looked, cowering on the mattress. He steeled himself against the thought.

Teddy's voice was small. "Ian…"

Ian waited a second for an explanation that never came. He straightened his shoulders. "Are you coming down to the precinct?"

The stranger curled his arm around Teddy's shoulder and tugged him against his side. Ian's jaw clenched at the sight. "Come on, baby. I got another round in me still."

Teddy seemed to flinch away from the man's touch but stayed silent, dropping his gaze down and away from Ian's, his shame evident. And Ian got his answer. Teddy wasn't going with him, and without Teddy, he would have no way of convincing the police to open an investigation. They would only see his brother as a troublemaker with a slew of misdemeanors under his belt.

"Fine," Ian snapped and spun on his heel. He paused in the doorway, his fists clenched at his side. "The funeral is on Saturday. Lucas would want you there, but after that, maybe it'd be best if you don't come around for a while."

Chapter Fifteen

The wall Ian was leaning against swayed behind him, unsteady as the deck of a ship in a storm. He snagged another shot off a tray one of his cousins was carrying around — either Niki or Noel, their face too blurred to make out. It didn't matter, so long as they kept bringing him liquor. He tossed the shot back, throat too numb to feel the burn any longer. His gaze followed the tray of shots as it got farther away.

The living room furniture had been pushed against the walls and all the seats were taken. Papa looked small in his armchair. A pair of cousins spoke quietly on the couch, their words drowned by the pounding in Ian's ears. The room smelled strongly of bitter cigars.

Ian's attention drifted to the dining room chair wedged into the corner. A half-smoked cigarette was gripped in white-knuckled fingers, dangling between a pair of jean-clad knees. Shoulders slumped, head bowed, Teddy looked like a broken doll. Ian had been ignoring him for the past several hours, but now, he couldn't remember why.

What right did Teddy have to look like that, to tug on Ian's frayed heartstrings? He wanted to be angry. He didn't want to feel like this, like he needed to scoop the young man in his arms and offer comfort.

He didn't mean to act on the stray thought, but he found himself ignoring the way the room spun. He found himself kneeling awkwardly in front of the young man. The moment he touched Teddy, something inside him cracked. He felt it like the snap of a guitar string on his fingers, like a razor blade slipping on his jaw, like the gravel-bitten bruises after he'd crashed his motorcycle in senior year. He sought comfort in the folds of Teddy's sweater, in the warmth of his chest. He curled his fingers into the soft fabric of Teddy's jeans.

Someone was crying.

He didn't realize it was him until he felt slender fingers gently caressing his scalp, soothing him like a skittish animal. There were muttered voices echoing over his head, then he was being lifted. A small body propped up his left side and a larger one carried his weight on the right.

He was vaguely aware of the flight of stairs they stumbled up before he collapsed on his mattress. He blinked up. The larger body — cousin Israel — said something in a soft voice, then left.

Teddy stayed, standing by the edge of the mattress. His shoulders were slumped, weighed down by the somber mood of the *velorio*. His face was blank, like summoning an emotion would be too much effort. The younger man looked lost.

"Stay?" Ian asked, voice slurred.

Teddy didn't answer for a long moment. Then, he nodded silently and lay down beside Ian, facing away. Ian knew that come tomorrow, he would be sober but aching, and somehow he would need to make it through the funeral rites. The long service at Saint Mary's Cathedral and the burial would be bad enough — but watching the women pull out his brother's clothing to wash in the sink, the forced gaiety in the back yard while they dried, then worse, watching clothing that had touched his brother burn… He didn't know how to get through it sober.

But he didn't want to think about it. Instead, he curled his arms around Teddy's slender chest and buried his face in the younger man's short hair, smothering his sobs in the scent of lavender and honeysuckle.

* * * *

Teddy woke the morning after the wake to the sound of rustling. He pried sticky eyes open to see Ian standing at the foot of the bed, shoving clothing into a duffel bag, his jaw clenched.

Teddy sat up, tugging at the hem of his newly purchased Goodwill sweatshirt. "You're leaving?"

Ian roughly tugged the zipper closed and swung the bag over his shoulder, but he didn't answer.

"Are you coming back?" Teddy asked, his voice hoarse.

The muscle in Ian's jaw jumped before he sighed, glancing at Teddy. In his eyes, Teddy still saw anger, but beneath it was an ocean of pain. "I can't stay here. Maybe I'll come back, someday. I don't know." Ian ran a hand over his close-cropped hair. "Not for a while, anyway."

Ian left, leaving Teddy alone on his bed. Teddy's cheeks were damp, his eyes stinging. This was his fault.

Maybe if he hadn't gone with Lucas to meet Julian—or if he'd talked to Ian about the gang earlier… If he'd gone to the precinct as soon as he heard Lucas had died, rather than waiting…

But no matter how guilty he felt, a small part of him knew it wasn't his fault. Lucas had joined the gang on his own, and Teddy wasn't his keeper.

And there was no way for Teddy to have known that Julian was going to show up at his apartment to blackmail him. He couldn't change the past.

It didn't, however, stop him from hurting as he heard the loud rumble of Ian's truck roar then fade into the distance, out of his life.

Chapter Sixteen

Four years later

Ian smoothed out the last strip of packing tape, closed the final box then carted it out to the moving truck. The driver held out a clipboard. "Just need your autograph," the man grunted.

Ian scrawled his name across the bottom line then watched the truck trundle away. He shot his apartment a final glare before he climbed into Sally, his rusty red truck, and left it behind. It had never felt like home anyway.

A pang in his chest reminded him why that had never bothered him. Home would always be Austin, with its hot winters and hotter summers and the smell of Mama's cooking on the air. Where he knew every corner of every street, knew where to find every mural painted on the brick siding—where everywhere he looked, the memories mocked him. He'd left the city four years before and not once had he convinced himself to go back. He'd talked to Mama on the phone and video chatted with Noa. Papa called every month or two. But every time he'd thought to visit, he'd canceled his plans at the last minute.

Work, he'd always said. He was too busy at the office. One of the other accountants was on maternity leave. He had to housesit. He had an excuse for everything — anything but the truth.

The ghost of Lucas haunted the Austin streets. He saw him there, even in memories, taunting him. Begging him. Crying for him to save him, but Ian couldn't. Even when time numbed the sting of his brother's death, Ian had stayed away.

His brother was a ghost but Teddy wasn't. And the pain of Teddy's betrayal still stabbed at his chest like a bullet wound. Worse, actually, because Ian's one and only bullet wound had healed to an only slightly puckered pink scar.

Ian's phone rang on the passenger seat and he answered it without bothering to look. "Romero."

"Ah good, I caught you. Wasn't sure if you'd left yet," Tennyson said. His partner's voice was always slightly mocking, though Ian was starting to think it was just the way the man spoke, nothing personal. "Just wanted to go over a few last-minute details."

"Go ahead," Ian said, half listening. He flicked on his turn signal, cutting off a silver SUV going well above the speed limit to merge onto the expressway. *Fucking Chicago traffic.* It wasn't New York, but it sucked just the same.

"You have a place to stay when you get here? The department just finalized the sale this morning, so construction on the club isn't slotted to start for another week."

"Yeah, booked a hotel. Won't be the first time. I thought the department wanted us to hit the ground running on this thing?" Ian felt a weight land on his shoulders as he left Chicago behind him.

"Forgot they gave me a probie," Tennyson laughed into his ear. "Six weeks is still pretty damn fast for an op like this."

"Two years," Ian reminded him. "I've been on the job for over two years."

"Make it to five and I'll let you graduate to rookie. The first six-to-eight weeks you'll spend getting settled. It'll be awfully suspicious if you move back home and the next day start asking questions. Go visit your mom, go furniture shopping. If you absolutely have to, start looking into financials, background checks — paper shit that won't get nobody's nose in your business. Leave the legwork to me. That's why they sent me out here last month, yeah?"

"I hate paperwork," Ian grumbled.

"So do I. That's why I give it to the probies."

"Anything else we need to talk about or can I get back to driving?" Ian asked.

When Tennyson answered, his voice was more serious. "For real, though. Visit your mom. I know it's hard, but better to rip the Band-Aid off than draw it out."

"I'll think about it," Ian said before hanging up. It wasn't that he didn't want to see her. He just knew that when he did, she'd start crying, then he would start crying. Then she would tell him to visit his brother, like the stone they'd placed at the cemetery would somehow know. His brother's body wasn't even there. They'd scattered his ashes, letting the breeze in the back yard at home carry his brother away on the wind.

Home.

For the first time in four years, he was going home.

He wished the thought didn't cause stones to grow in his stomach.

* * * *

Teddy was about to settle into bed on his first free evening of the month—not counting the date he was planning to bail on later tonight—when someone knocked on his door. Teddy sighed and swung off the mattress, padding on bare feet into what he called his living room. He took one look at Shiloh through the peephole before yanking the door open. Shiloh's tousled pink hair fell into his face but did little to hide the blood trickling from a split near the corner of his lower lip.

"I'll get the peroxide." Teddy knew better than to ask what had happened. He was used to this. Sometimes it happened every day, sometimes they could go a month or two, but it always happened. Shiloh showed up, bruised and vacant-eyed. The only thing asking questions did was make Shiloh stammer a lie and disappear again.

He hurried into the bathroom and grabbed his first-aid box. At least this time, it didn't look like Shiloh would need stitches. Teddy hesitated in the bathroom doorway, staring out at his friend. Shiloh was huddled on the corner of the couch, his heels digging into the edge. He looked blankly toward the window. Teddy pulled his phone out to discreetly snap a picture before returning to the living room.

He dropped onto the couch beside Shiloh. "Let me see?"

Shiloh swiped his hair back from his face, his eyes averted. "The floor in the pool house was wet. I slipped."

"Okay," Teddy acknowledged the lie. "Close your eyes."

Shiloh obeyed, flinching when Teddy carefully lifted a cotton round soaked in peroxide to a shallow cut on his forehead, centered in a dark bruise. "Sorry," Teddy murmured.

Teddy cleaned up the bloody cuts as quickly as he could, not wanting to prolong Shiloh's discomfort, then returned the first-aid kit to the bathroom cabinet. He detoured into his bedroom on the way back to grab his faded, worn comforter from the mattress on the floor. He carried it back out and draped it around Shiloh's shoulders.

"Hungry?" Teddy asked, infusing his voice with as much fake cheer as he could.

Shiloh shrugged, picking at the threads of the blanket. Shiloh bit his lip, which was for once naked of gloss, then said in a small voice, "Will you sit with me?"

Teddy abandoned his plan to feed him and hurried back to the couch. He sat near the armrest and, a second later, Shiloh folded into him, collapsing against his chest like a marionette with cut strings. He was shaking.

They sat in silence. Teddy didn't know what to say. After years, he still hadn't found the right words to make Shiloh trust him enough.

This time, though, Shiloh spoke on his own. "Don't worry. I've got a plan."

Teddy tightened his grip around Shiloh's shoulders. Shiloh could say 'don't worry' all he wanted, but of course Teddy worried. "A plan?"

"Mm-hmm." Shiloh gave a small nod.

Teddy thought of the other plans he knew of — like the plan Shiloh had made to move in with Teddy right after they'd graduated high school. Shiloh had crashed on Teddy's couch for almost two weeks, until his father and a lawyer had showed up, threatening to cut Shiloh off from his trust fund if he didn't move back home. Then after that was Shiloh's plan to transfer to the California Institute of the Arts. Teddy wasn't sure what had gone wrong with that one. He just knew that Shiloh was only in Los Angeles for three weeks before his father had dragged him back.

Teddy wished there was something he could do. Instead, he stayed on the couch, Shiloh in his lap, and sighed. "I'll tell Victor you're off for a few days."

Shiloh nodded, but a few seconds later he jerked up, glaring at Teddy like he was offended. "Didn't you have a date tonight?"

Teddy shrugged. "Wasn't going anyway." It was a blind date, set up through AJ, one of the dancers at Nik's, the club Teddy bartended at during the evenings. Teddy didn't have high expectations. He'd been accepted mostly because Johnny — the bar manager and Teddy's asshole ex — had been standing there smirking.

Shiloh stood. "Come on. Get up."

"I'm not going." Teddy rolled his eyes and collapsed back against the armrest. "I was going to text AJ and ask him to cancel."

"Nope. You haven't had a good dicking since Johnny. That was, what…six months ago?" Shiloh was clearly trying to pretend everything was back to normal. Teddy wondered if it was healthy to let him but decided against arguing.

"Ten," Teddy admitted. And honestly, he wasn't sure he could count Johnny as a 'good dicking'.

Shiloh shuddered visibly, like the thought of going so long was torture. "It's with AJ's cousin? The lawyer?"

Teddy frowned. "I think he's a paralegal."

Shiloh waved it off. "Same difference. He'll have his own place to go back to then."

"I'm not going back to his house. It's a first date. We haven't even met yet," Teddy protested, his cheeks heating.

"That's the best kind of sex." Shiloh shoved at Teddy's shoulder. "Come on. Do you honestly want to date a paralegal?"

"He could be nice..." Teddy said, trying to sound hopeful.

"He could be *boring*." Shiloh rolled his eyes. "Better to find out on the first date, right? Now get up. I'll do your makeup."

"I'd rather stay here. We can watch a movie."

"We've seen *Glitter Nation* three times already. Go on your date, get laid and give me all the details in the morning." Shiloh pursed his lips then grinned. "Or afternoon, if you decide you want some hot, sweaty morning sex for breakfast."

* * * *

Teddy did *not* decide to have hot, sweaty morning sex for breakfast, nor did he decide to get laid. He barely made it to the end of dinner without bashing his head in with a wine bottle.

The expensive red wine was about the only part of dinner he didn't hate. It had been obvious from the second Teddy walked in that AJ had not told his cousin several key details about him—the first being that Teddy was equally as likely to wear heels as he was combat boots… The second, that Teddy didn't give a fuck what anyone said about it.

Jeremiah didn't comment, but he didn't need to. The disapproval was clear in his eyes, in the tenseness of his jaw and the way he flushed with embarrassment when the waitress complimented Teddy's pumps.

Jeremiah was exactly what Teddy had expected from a paralegal. He wore a nice suit, not quite off the rack but not bespoke either, which highlighted a slender frame gained through calorie counting, not crunches. His blond hair was perfectly coiffed, and a pair of thin-frame glasses perched on a straight nose— a straight nose that seemed stuck far too high in the air.

Teddy kept his mouth shut, except to reply politely to Jeremiah's awkward attempt at dinner conversation—mostly about the case he was working on, which was supposedly going to be his big break in the legal field—until dessert arrived. Teddy ordered something he rarely got to eat, an ice-cream-topped slice of devil's food cake.

Jeremiah's spoon hesitated over his own bowl of plain vanilla ice cream. "You're going to eat all that?"

Teddy's spoon was halfway to his lips. He lifted an eyebrow, glancing between the heaping mouthful of cake and Jeremiah. "You got a problem with that?"

Jeremiah flushed. "No, just…calories."

Teddy laughed and shoved the mouthful into his mouth, savoring the rich chocolate flavor dancing on his tongue. He swallowed before saying, "Not worried." He'd always had a good metabolism.

Besides, he ate so little throughout the week that one indulgence wasn't going to tip the scale.

Jeremiah grimaced then tried to hide it in his wine glass. He placed it back on the table with a clink, an uncomfortable smile on his face. Teddy glanced down at his nearly gone dessert and held back a sigh. He wanted their time together to be over, but he also wanted more dessert. Something told him it would be rude to order one to go. He scraped the last drizzling of chocolate sauce out of the bowl, then licked the spoon clean while Jeremiah flagged down a waiter and took care of the check.

"Ready to get out of here?" Jeremiah asked, dropping his napkin in a crumpled heap on the table after dabbing his mouth.

"Sure." Teddy was ready. *So beyond ready.* He now knew way more than he ever wanted to about legal briefings and proceedings. He stood and followed his date out of the restaurant. The night was hot, but it was a mild heat, the kind that warmed his skin without overwhelming him in humidity.

He stood awkwardly beside the fancy black Lexus Jeremiah had picked him up in. "Thank you for dinner."

Jeremiah smiled politely. "I had a pleasant time." *Liar*, but it wasn't like Teddy could blame him since he was going to lie too.

"Me too. Maybe we can do it again...sometime..." *Please don't take me up on it. Please don't take me up on it...*

"Maybe," Jeremiah replied noncommittally. "So" — his date shifted his weight, hand on the driver's door, clearly uncomfortable — "do you need a ride home?"

Well, it wasn't exactly like he lived within walking distance, since Jeremiah had dragged him halfway across town to eat at a pretentious restaurant with portion sizes fit for a toddler, but Jeremiah's tone of voice made it obvious that he was hoping Teddy would say no.

"Nah, I think I'm going to hit Nik's, say hi to AJ."

Jeremiah looked relieved. "Good, that's good. Cool. Tell him I said hey."

"Sure."

"Well, have a good night..." Jeremiah climbed into the car and drove off before Teddy could answer, leaving him stranded on the sidewalk in a pair of shoes not fit to walk home in.

"Asshole," Teddy mumbled and pulled out his phone.

Shiloh answered on the second read. "Teddy, dude, there's like...a giant cauliflower man in your living room."

"A giant...cauliflower man?" Teddy was confused for a second until he realized what day it was, then felt himself go pale. "Shit." It was the second week of August, which meant he was a week behind on his payment. *Again.* He cringed at the memory of the last time. He still had a scar on his wrist from where they'd forced it over the stove in threat.

Shiloh's voice got quiet and slightly tinny, like he was speaking away from the phone. "Well, I'm so sorry if I hurt your feelings, Mr. Cauliflower, but if you don't like what you hear, then maybe don't eavesdrop on private conversations, hmm-m?"

Teddy grimaced and hurried across the street, angling toward the bus stop. The last thing he needed was for Shiloh to irritate Hugo. He didn't think the man took well to insults...and he wasn't willing to find out for sure. "Tell him I'll be there as soon as I can. I'm getting on the bus right now. And, Shiloh...please, *please*, don't irritate him."

"Me...irritate him? I'm fabulous, darling."

Teddy slid onto the bus just before the doors squeaked closed and dropped a few bills into the slot. He slumped onto the cracked leather seat. "Please, Shiloh. Just...get him a glass of water or something and go into my bedroom. Tell him I'll be there as soon as I can."

Shiloh was silent for a second. It sounded like he was walking, and his voice was lower, more serious, when he finally came back on the line, "Teddy, who is he? Are you in some sort of trouble?"

Teddy could lie, but even the thought made him feel like shit. He absently swiped a hand through his hair. "Don't worry about it. I'm getting it figured out."

"Teddy..." Shiloh sounded concerned. Teddy knew that Shiloh had enough to worry about without him burdening him with his problems as well.

"I'm almost home," Teddy promised. "Please, *please* be nice."

"Bitch, I'm always nice." Teddy didn't need to see him to know that Shiloh was pouting. There was a brief moment of dead air, then Shiloh hummed in his ear. "If you ignore the ears, he's not so bad looking..."

"Do *not* flirt with him," Teddy snapped harshly. "Just...please go into the bedroom. He shouldn't bother you if you don't mess with him. Please, Shiloh." His mind conjured up one worst-case scenario after another, from Shiloh flirting with Hugo and ending up on the wrong end of his fist, to him ending up under the large, violent man in Teddy's bed.

"You'd tell me if you needed help, right?" Shiloh asked seriously.

"Of course." Teddy winced at the lie. The only way Shiloh could help him was by paying off Teddy's debt, and Teddy refused to take a cent. It had been his mistake, and he was going to pay for it.

He was grateful to find the living room barren of anyone but Hugo when he finally got home. He heard the shower running in the bathroom and assumed Shiloh had retreated there, following the lure of moderately warm water that only occasionally spat cold.

Hugo dwarfed the cushions of his ratty couch, where he sat with one leg propped on the other, tapping on the keyboard of his phone. He glared at Teddy when he burst through the door.

"You think I ain't got other places to be, boy?" Hugo growled, shoving his phone into the pocket of his jeans before standing. Teddy cowered on instinct, not liking the way the word *boy* sounded on Hugo's lips. It was a word he longed to hear as an endearment, not a curse.

"Sorry. I didn't... I..." Teddy sucked in a breath and forced his spine straight, feigning courage he didn't feel. "You didn't tell me you were coming or I'd have been here."

"Who's the other one?" Hugo didn't bother pointing out that he wasn't obligated to tell Teddy anything — that Teddy should have expected his visit, since he hadn't made his regular drop time.

"Not your business," Teddy replied sharply, ignoring the kernel of fear that grew vines in his stomach. "Leave him out of it."

The look Hugo shot him was searching, eyebrows tugged low to shadow his dark eyes. "Watch your tone, kid. You're late."

Teddy ran his finger in circles over his jeans — the nicest pair he owned, a black pair that clung to his curves just right and only had one hole, near the pocket. He could make the payment, but only if he didn't pay his rent. If it came down to an eviction or a lesson learned at the end of Hugo's fist, though... Teddy sank his teeth into his lip and dropped to his knees in front of the couch, tugging a small wad of bills from a tear in the underside of the left cushion.

Hugo took the stack and thumbed through it. "You're short, kid." He sounded almost sad, which didn't make sense to Teddy. Hugo had never seemed to care much for Teddy, so why he cared if he was short was a mystery.

"No, it's there, I promise. A thousand dollars." Teddy stumbled over his words, tongue tripping.

"Boss added a late fee. Ten percent," Hugo said, and damn it if his voice didn't sound gentle enough at the explanation to make Teddy tear up.

"I... That's a hundred dollars. I don't have that. That's all I have," He nodded to the bills already clasped in Hugo's hand. "I don't get paid again until Friday."

Hugo shifted his weight, and it reminded Teddy of a boulder rocking precariously at the edge of a cliff, threatening to fall, to crush anyone standing beneath him — like Teddy. "Friday, you say?"

Teddy nodded quickly, hope flaring. "Friday, I promise. I can have it on Friday."

Hugo stepped closer, his shadow falling over Teddy and leaving him chilled. His large hand gripped Teddy's hair, tugging nearly to the point of pain but not past. "I'll be back on Friday for the money. Make sure you have it."

Chapter Seventeen

Friday night, after dropping off the extra hundred dollars to Hugo at the gym that fronted for the cartel — money he'd earmarked for bills — Teddy headed to his third job of the day. Nik's was a cross between a grunge bar and a nightclub, somehow managing to stay open despite not being successful as either.

There, Teddy tugged at the hem of the too-small, shiny-blue shorts, trying to adjust his packer without making it obvious. He didn't like wearing it. He was happy with his small but functional dick, but the packer got him better tips and fewer looks. Well, more looks but fewer *looks*. He was four years post-op and finally felt comfortable in his skin, most of the time. Wearing the packer felt like going backward.

Shiloh bounded off his platform, dancing over to the bar where Teddy was mixing drinks. He leaned against the faded wood. "Teddy Bear, I need something to wet my mouth."

A sleazy man — okay, Teddy admitted, he probably wasn't sleazy, but in Teddy's mind all the men who drank at Nik's were sleazy by default—looked Shiloh over with heated eyes. "I've got something you can wet your mouth with."

Shiloh pursed his glossy lips as he looked the man over, "Sorry, babe. I'm working."

"All night?"

Shiloh shrugged. "Maybe."

The man turned to Teddy and slid a twenty across the table. "Whatever he wants. Keep the change."

Teddy rolled his eyes as Shiloh gave the man a once-over again. "The odds of me getting out early just shifted in your favor. Meet me by the door at one, baby. I'll give you the ride of your life." Shiloh winked at Teddy when the man groaned and shifted on his stool.

Teddy flipped his friend off, covering it up by sliding him over a Coke. Shiloh couldn't drink on the clock, even if he was just dancing. Shiloh, however, pursed his lips and leaned over the bar, snagging a bottle of rum. Several men behind Shiloh stopped moving past to watch, dropping their gazes to the thinly concealed globes under Shiloh's lace panties, clearly on display. Shiloh added a shot or rum into his glass then waved his fingers at someone behind Teddy.

Teddy glanced over his shoulder to see Victor, the owner—or the owner for a few more days, at least, until the business changed hands—watching Shiloh with a leer. Victor was nearly twice their age—and half again their size—and had an unhealthy obsession with the dancers, which Shiloh took advantage of often.

"Dick," Teddy said under his breath, just loud enough for Shiloh to hear.

Shiloh chuckled evilly and grabbed at his crotch, stretching the lace over the dick in question. "*This* dick?"

Teddy rolled his eyes and went to answer, but Victor spoke before he could. "Joey called in, so you're on the platforms in ten."

Teddy scrunched his eyes closed and hoped that Victor was talking to someone else. He hated the platforms. But Victor's voice grew sharp when he didn't answer. "Teddy, are you listening?"

"Yes, sir," Teddy spat the words out and pulled the rag out of his apron strings, tossing it onto the bar for the other bartender to deal with, then stripped off the apron. Victor had strict rules about his dancers...mainly that they wore makeup and skimpy underwear, and nothing else.

Except Shiloh, who also wore enough glitter to keep a craft store in business.

"The new owner will be stopping in to inspect the property, so don't embarrass me," Victor said before Teddy could slip into the dressing room. "No half-assing it tonight."

"Yeah, yeah." Teddy muttered.

"Wear the jock," Victor yelled after him.

Teddy threw a hand up in acknowledgement before closing the door firmly behind him. It didn't take long to strip out of the neoprene shorts and into a blue satin jock. He hated it — and not just because it cost twice as much as one he could buy in the store, since it had to accommodate his packer. At least the panties gave him an illusion of coverage. The jock left him feeling exposed.

Thankfully, he was a subpar dancer. Unlike Shiloh, who lived and breathed ballet, Teddy's skills started — and ended — on a pole. It meant Teddy only ever got the platform nearest the bathrooms or the one near the darkened alcoves on the opposite side. Shiloh accumulated the majority of the gawkers near the center.

Teddy used the pole more for decoration than utility. He had a few tricks he used near the end, things he'd learned from Shiloh. Other than that, he ignored the pole and hoped it didn't trip him.

He was near the end of his second set, hanging upside down and gripping the pole with his thighs, hoping not to fall and crack open his skull, when a voice from his past startled him into letting go.

He fell, every muscle clenching in preparation for a hard landing. Instead, he heard a curse before a pair of arms grappled at him and he struck a hard chest, the breath knocked out of him.

He'd swear it was Ian's voice that had startled him from his routine, but that wasn't possible. The last he'd heard from Mama Romero, Ian was an accountant at some firm in Chicago. Of course, it had been over six months since he'd spoken to her, and that was just because he'd bumped into her in the grocery store. He'd done his best to respect Ian's wishes and stay away.

The arms around him tightened. Then he was shifted around so he could slide down the toned body until his bare feet landed on the sticky dance floor. He opened his eyes.

Ian looked exactly as he did in Teddy's memories, but for a small, white scar that bisected his eyebrow, and an intensity in his gaze that had been missing before. His jaw was clenched, and as soon as Teddy's feet were under him, Ian released him, like the thought of touching him a moment longer disgusted him.

"Teddy," Ian murmured, confusion softening the hard lines of his face for a moment. Then they snapped back into place. "Following in your mother's footsteps?"

"Mom never stripped," Teddy cut back, flinching like he'd been struck. "And you left. You have no right to judge me or my life." He brushed past Ian, not caring that he still had ten minutes left of his set and several more left of his shift. It wasn't like working in a club was his first choice, or second. But it was the only job he could find that didn't need more than a high school diploma and was willing to work around his other two jobs. He couldn't afford to be picky.

Ian gripped his arm and tugged, forcing him to stop and face him. "You're right. Just…what happened to college? I thought you were going into architecture."

"Life happened," Teddy muttered, pulling his arm free before crossing them, more on display than ever. "What about you? I thought you were living in Chicago."

Ian's face darkened. "It was time to come home."

"Well, good for you." The music changed from the seductive sounds of the dancers' track to a more upbeat one, the lights over the platforms flicking off. "I gotta get back to work. I heard the new owner's a bigger asshole than the old one."

A choking sound echoed behind him and Victor cursed, "You little *prick*!"

Teddy's face scrunched as he realized Victor had heard every word. At least it was the last day he'd be working for the sleazy bastard.

Victor hurried to make up for Teddy's remark. "I'm so sorry, Mr. Romero. I promise the rest of the employees will show more respect to their new boss."

It took a second for the words to click in his head. He narrowed his eyes at Ian. "New boss? *You* bought Nik's?"

Ian's lips quirked up, but there was no humor in the smile. "Surprise."

Teddy hated surprises.

* * * *

Teddy paced his empty apartment, torn between anger, uncertainty…and a small dash of elation. Ian was back, and Teddy didn't know what that meant for him. The rational part of him said that it meant nothing. Ian had left him. It had been four years since they'd spoken. Ian had changed his number and left without a forwarding address. Teddy had the same battered flip phone he'd had then, and the same dump of an apartment. If Ian had wanted to contact him, he knew how to get ahold of him. He hadn't. So clearly, the fact that he was here—that he was Teddy's new boss— meant nothing.

The smaller, more anxious part of him feared that Ian was here to punish him for not stepping forward all those years ago and speaking to the police. It wasn't like Teddy could even hold it against him, since he felt the need to punish himself daily for the same damn thing.

And the stupid part of Teddy, the one that was ruled by the tiny corner of his heart that remained unbroken, hoped that Ian was back for him.

The rational part of him overruled that voice as well.

Teddy didn't feel like being rational.

He pulled out his phone, hovering his thumb over Shiloh's name in his contacts. He wanted to speak to someone and Shiloh was the only person he had left in his life. He hadn't spoken to his mother since his twentieth birthday, when she'd shown up at his apartment, drunk off her ass, and left with the hundred dollars he'd had hidden in his cookie jar. That was back before he'd sold the cookie jar for an extra five bucks.

He broke down and pressed the button. He listened to the phone ring, and ring, and ring, before Shiloh's cheery voice came over the voicemail. He hung up without speaking and collapsed back on the couch instead. A spring dug into his spine until he shifted.

What he needed was to think this through. Could he keep working at Nik's if it meant he'd be working under Ian? *And not*, he thought, *under him in the way I want to be?*

Could he afford not to?

His debt to the cartel was larger now than it had been when he'd started. He could barely make the interest payments each month. It was all he could do to keep them off his back — and keep off his back for them.

The money he made in tips alone at Nik's was more than he made at either of his other jobs. There weren't many other bars in the city that would give him as many hours and, for as seedy as Nik's seemed, at least he was never expected to 'thank' high-tippers in the men's room, like he'd heard happened at some of the others.

Leaving Nik's wasn't an option, not without consequences too high to accept. He was just going to have to bury the attraction that had rekindled with a single glance and try to keep it professional.

"Well, shit," he cursed.

He wasn't very good at professional.

Chapter Eighteen

Ian watched the workers lay the final strips of paint along the base of the front door. He'd left the murals from the original building — a tattoo parlor, before it had become a small, seedy club — except to have them touched up in places that had faded or chipped. The walls that separated the old club from the abandoned storefront next door had been removed, and the stained, pockmarked linoleum had been stripped, replaced by gleaming hardwood.

The old bar, squat and short, had been replaced with a mahogany one that curved elegantly along the side of the club, giving the illusion of depth. Instead of three platforms for dancers, there were now six. They were narrower but taller, putting the dancers even more on display.

The grand re-opening was only three days away. Waiting felt like torture, but he'd waited four years. He wasn't going to fuck everything up by getting impatient now.

If getting justice for his brother meant playing the part of shady business owner, he'd do it in a heartbeat. He'd done his research. The best way to launder money was through businesses, so he'd make his business irresistible. And when the cartel came crawling, he'd be sure to answer. He might not be allowed to go completely undercover in his hometown—not when getting discovered could put his family in danger—but he was going to prove he could still be valuable. While Tennyson worked his way up the ranks, Ian would follow the money.

He left the foreman to his work, reassured that everything was still progressing on schedule, and unlocked the door that lead to the upstairs.

When he'd told Mama he was coming back to Austin to stay 'indefinitely', she'd pressed for him to move back in. He knew she didn't like having an empty nest. With him gone and Noa off at college, she was feeling lonely. But he couldn't. There were too many memories, and he couldn't afford the distraction—not to mention that the last thing he wanted was for danger to follow him back to his family. It wasn't like he could change his name here and hope nobody recognized him. He had community ties—not many, but enough. It was what made him the perfect mole. He didn't need to invent a cover story. He had one that didn't need to be faked.

Instead, he'd spent two weeks in a hotel while they'd renovated the floor above the club into a usable apartment. It had two bedrooms, a large living space and a small but modern kitchen. It was far fancier than he needed, to fit his new image—that of a rich club owner with too much money. It wouldn't be a stretch, by any means, for anyone who'd known him *before*.

Before his brother had died and his life had taken a hard one-eighty.

Ian bypassed the kitchen and headed into the spare room. It was the first room he'd furnished. A weight bench sat against one wall, a treadmill on the other, and he'd screwed a pull-up bar in the doorway. A punching bag sat in the center. After taping his wrists, he let loose on the blue canvas, the strikes hard enough that he felt them in his bones.

Six weeks, and he still couldn't get the frustration of seeing Teddy on a podium, practically nude, out of his head. Not just because Teddy looked sexier than ever — though he did, with the sapphire blue jock outlining the perfect globes of his ass, the muscles of his abdomen chiseled like a Roman sculpture, hair longer than Ian ever remembered seeing it. The honey-gold hair had fallen in waves over Teddy's shoulders, soft and teasing, daring Ian to run his fingers through it.

It was only one of several reminders that the Teddy on the podium was not the same Teddy he'd left behind. This Teddy, in the moments before Ian had broken the spell and said something, had looked more comfortable in his body, even beneath the very obvious discomfort at being on display. The Teddy he'd left behind would never have worn makeup or had hair longer than stubble. The Teddy he'd left behind wouldn't have worn gloss that drew Ian's eyes to his pouty lips or nail polish that made his slender fingers look even longer.

And the Teddy he'd left behind wouldn't have been caught dead in a bar.

He wondered what else had changed.

* * * *

Ian checked the liquor shelves for the third time. It had been four years since he'd tended bar, and he kept feeling like he was forgetting something. He needed this opening to go well. Ian shifted a bottle of top-shelf whiskey a few inches to the left.

"Mm-m, right there, Daddy," a sultry voice purred behind him. Ian knew without looking that it belonged to Teddy's mouthy friend Shiloh. Ian found himself wishing that the brat had been one of the ones to take his offer of severance pay. Instead, the spoiled boy had accepted the several smaller payouts spread over six weeks as an incentive to return once construction was finished.

Ian nudged another bottle into place before turning around. Shiloh straddled a barstool, scantily clad in a pair of pink suspenders attached to metallic silver booty shorts. Sometime in the years Ian had been gone, Shiloh had died his normally blond hair hot pink.

"Place looks nice," Shiloh acknowledged, gesturing to the much cleaner, larger club.

"Hopefully the patrons agree," Ian said, turning to watch the pair of bartenders carefully prepare their stations. Besides Shiloh, the other five dancers were still back in the dressing room, getting ready.

"You kept your best dancer. I wouldn't worry." Shiloh shrugged and slid forward, propping his elbows on the bar. "What do I have to do to talk you into a drink?"

Ian poured him a Coke and slid it over.

Shiloh bat his eyebrows but his eyes were more cunning than flirty. "Rum?"

"Not on the clock." Ian went back to work, resorting to straightening the napkin dispensers. His eyes caught and held on Teddy as he left the dressing room.

Like the club, the employee uniforms had gotten an upgrade. Lycra shorts had been replaced by spandex — different colors of the rainbow for each day of the week. The look was just as skimpy, just as sexy, but hopefully more comfortable. Looking at Teddy in the tight purple fabric, he wished that he had picked uniforms that covered a bit more skin.

Teddy flushed as his eyes met Ian's but didn't stop his approach. He slid onto the stool beside Shiloh. Teddy snagged the glass from Shiloh and sniffed it. "No alcohol?" he verified.

Shiloh's pout deepened. "Nope." Teddy downed a swallow before sliding it back. "So, boss," Shiloh turned back to Ian, "when do we get our assignments?"

"Hmm-m?" Ian had been too busy watching Teddy's tongue clean drops of Coke from his glossy lips.

"Our assignments. For the platform?" Shiloh asked.

"Oh. Talk to Johnny. He knows your strengths." Johnny had managed the bar for the past two years, according to Victor. Ian hoped he was as good as the previous owner claimed, otherwise Ian would be spending more time in the bar than he'd intended.

Shiloh nudged Teddy's shoulder. "You'll be on a platform then."

"Fucker," Teddy huffed and slid off the stool, heading toward the other side of the bar, where Johnny was quietly speaking with one of the bartenders.

Shiloh just chuckled, clearly not offended.

"They not get along?" Ian asked, watching Teddy walk away. He tried to tell himself that he was just curious, but he couldn't help that his eyes drifted lower, down Teddy's back to the firm ass highlighted by the spandex.

"They dated for a bit." Shiloh shrugged and downed the last of his drink. "Johnny knows Teddy prefers the bar, so he puts him on the platforms whenever he gets the chance. Not that Teddy's a bad dancer," Shiloh hurried to clarify.

Ian frowned as he watched the pair at the other end argue. Teddy was clearly unhappy, and Johnny looked far too smug about it.

"I'll have a talk with him."

"Teddy?" Shiloh asked.

"Johnny. If Teddy doesn't want to be on the platforms, then he can work the bar," Ian corrected absently.

Shiloh laughed, the sound pulling Ian's attention from the other end of the bar. He frowned. "Something funny?"

"Everyone's going to know you're boning if you do."

"We're not boning," Ian immediately replied. The last thing he needed was that rumor spreading about.

"Then everyone will think you are. I mean, I guess if that's what you want." Shiloh shrugged but then his eyes narrowed critically, assessing Ian with a seriousness that Ian hadn't realized he possessed. "You trying to win the pool?"

"What pool?" Ian had no idea what Shiloh was talking about or why who he was sleeping with was anyone's business.

"There's a bet going on between Victor and a few of the regulars. Who can bang the most dancers. Teddy's the only hold-out." Shiloh's eyes grew distant for a second as he thought. "Actually, I think Johnny's the only one who got that notch, and that was because he wasn't part of the pool at the time." Shiloh's gaze darkened. "Though he certainly bragged about it enough after. Which was a pity, because now I have to hold out on him just out of spite." Shiloh sighed, staring at Johnny with regret. "Have you seen his arms?"

Ian felt a growl in his throat at the thought of someone trying to sleep with Teddy for a *bet*. It made him want to introduce the manager of his club to the end of his fist. He reigned the thought in quickly.

Shiloh bounced off the stool, hips swaying as he joined Teddy and Johnny in their maybe-an-argument. Ian watched the trio until it was time to unlock the doors and he had to concentrate on the club. Teddy wasn't his boyfriend, he reminded himself as the first patrons entered. It wasn't his responsibility to keep an eye on the younger man or worry about his relationship with an ex. He had a job to do.

* * * *

"Come on, Teddy. It's not your first time on the platforms. I don't know why you're making a big deal out of it. Just do two sets, then you can hop back behind the bar." Johnny smirked, the expression greasy. "You want the tips, right?"

"I'm not a dancer," Teddy said for what felt like the thousandth time. He knew this was Johnny's way of getting back at him for ending things—not because Johnny actually wanted to be with him, but because Johnny didn't like being cut loose first. Though seriously, how on earth did Johnny not realize that telling Teddy on their third date that—how had he phrased it? *'If you want to be a man, then maybe you should stop dressing like a bitch'* — was not the best way to stay in his pants.

Two years ago, it might have been enough to make him reconsider what he kept in his closet. Now, his closet was extremely happy with the number of stilettos it held.

"But you got a great ass." Johnny leered down at him. "So go shake it for an hour and then you can come hole up behind the bar again."

Teddy sighed. "Last time, though, right?" If he saw that rat bastard Joey again, he'd be having words with him. The only reason Johnny got away with putting him on the platform so often was because the other dancer kept calling off.

Johnny shrugged. "Sure, babe. Last time." It was as believable as his claim that he had a ten-inch dick.

The warning notes sounded over the sound system that the doors were opening soon, so he sighed and headed to his platform. At least Johnny wasn't completely stupid. It was the one closest to the restrooms. Getting him on the platform was one thing—putting him center stage was something even Johnny wasn't stupid enough to try. Even if Teddy managed not to vomit on the crowd, his moves—or relative lack thereof—would be more of a turn-off than a turn-on.

The new platforms were higher than the old ones. It took all his thigh strength to clamber up. When he straightened, he wobbled slightly. The platforms were only three feet off the ground, but that was still a whole foot more than he was used to—and the old platforms had been more than high enough for him.

At least Ian was somewhere behind the bar, not watching him flounder like a dead fish on the podium. And he only suffered through two sets before jumping—okay, awkwardly crawling while trying to ignore the hands that groped at him as he slid, feet first, on his belly — off the platform.

His hope that Ian hadn't seen him was dashed when he rounded the bar. Ian was unsuccessfully trying to bury his chuckling.

"I see you," Teddy said pointedly.

Ian dropped his hand, his mouth still spread in a wide grin. "I see why you don't like the podiums."

"It's not my fault I'm short." Teddy tugged the service towel out of Ian's hand and started wiping down the bar, mostly to avoid looking at the familiar smile. It made him want to go hide in the stock room for a few minutes...hours...days...preferably with the larger man pressed against him in the cramped shelving.

An arm landed on his head as Ian used it for an armrest. Teddy huffed when he realized Ian didn't even have to go up on tiptoes to manage it. He shook his head, dislodging the elbow, and glared. He lifted the towel in his hand threateningly. "I still remember how to use one of these, you know..."

Ian chuckled, probably remembering the same thing Teddy was — Teddy and Lucas, barely fourteen, chasing Ian around the community pool with soaking-wet towels, in retaliation for Ian dunking them.

Ian's smile dimmed slightly. Teddy flushed, guilt welling as he wondered if he should say something. He visited Lucas' headstone every couple of months. He was careful about when he went, so he wouldn't run into Mama Romero or Noa. He'd sit against the headstone while it drizzled, talking things out, like maybe, somewhere, Lucas was listening. He tried to pretend he wasn't just talking to stone. He wondered if Ian ever visited, but as far as he knew, since Ian had skipped out of the funeral four years ago, he hadn't come back.

Teddy cleared his throat and scrubbed at an invisible spill on the counter, averting his eyes from Ian's to avoid seeing the sadness that had dimmed them.

Ian cleared his throat as well. "So, how have things been? Mama said you've been busy…"

Teddy wondered if Ian was genuinely curious, or just trying to change the subject. He shrugged. "Yeah, I've got a couple of jobs. Just trying to pay the bills, you know how it is." Or maybe he didn't. He clearly had enough capital to come in and buy a club, then completely renovate it.

"Yeah." Ian trailed off, an awkward silence spreading between them. Teddy was grateful when a slew of men spilled off the dance floor and approached the bar, giving Teddy something to do besides dwell on Ian's presence at his side. He wondered if Ian was going to hover around him every shift, because the years had apparently not dampened the spark that flared to life inside him with Ian's presence. It had only been one day and Teddy already felt weak-kneed and out of sorts.

He glanced at the clock under the bar. *An hour and a half down…only five more to go.*

* * * *

Teddy glared at the bright red letters stamped across the front of the envelope on his coffee table. *Final Notice*, his ass. It was at least the third 'final notice' he'd gotten. Unfortunately, there was little to nothing he could do about it. Six weeks of not working at Nik's—or Envy, as it had been renamed—had fucked up his budget. Hopefully, not irreparably. The severance checks he'd gotten every other week during the six-week construction had helped, but they'd barely covered half his pay, not even factoring in tips. They weren't enough to pay both his rent and Julian, and he'd had to choose.

Between the two, his landlord was less scary. Even giving nearly every cent of the checks to Hugo, he was still behind.

Unfortunately, he didn't think his landlord would accept that as an excuse. He snorted at the thought of trying to explain that to him. "Yeah, sorry, sir. Can't pay you the rent this month because a big guy with a bat will break my kneecaps. But yes, your letters are very intimidating." *Yeah.* Likely, wouldn't go over well.

Teddy pinched the bridge of his nose. He already worked three jobs. He wasn't sure where he could squeeze in a fourth. Between washing dishes at Antonio's in the morning, cleaning the kickboxing studio in the afternoon and working at Envy at night, he already struggled to find time to sleep.

Sleeping is overrated, he thought.

But damn, he missed sleeping. He imagined he could orgasm just thinking about getting a single good night's sleep. He was more likely to win the lottery, at this point.

Which would really be something, since he couldn't afford to play the lottery.

Teddy brushed his hair out of his face and got back to work organizing the envelopes on his table. Bills in one stack, spam in the trash, correspondence in another stack. The majority of the envelopes were bills. He threw a half-dozen away, then stared at the final ones remaining.

His mom's name was written neatly across the top left in a familiar hand. He clutched it by the edges. She wrote to him occasionally. Sometimes, it was drunken ramblings, mostly apologies intermingled with pleas for him to come home. Sometimes, it was a drunken plea for money and empty promises. He dropped the letter into the trash. He wasn't curious enough about which way it swayed to open it.

He abandoned the bills. He stood and crossed the room to stare out of the window, not paying much attention to the view outside. Mrs. Tanlin was walking her dog again, a Doberman with a weak bladder. Mr. Waverly was leaning into the window of a rusty Chevrolet, probably buying weed. Nothing new, nothing to draw his attention.

Instead, he stared blankly in the direction where he knew his mom's house lay. He missed her. Not the drunk, childish woman she was now. He missed the mother who'd told him bedtime stories and always tucked him in, even if it was the third time in the same night, the woman who'd taken him out for ice cream after one of his father's fits or gone with him to each and every one of his therapy appointments, at least until the drinking had started.

Teddy rested his fist against the windowpane but not hard enough to risk cracking it. The drinking had started before his father had passed away after a particularly violent fit of his father's had sent her tumbling down a flight of stairs. It wasn't the first time it had happened—but she'd been a few months pregnant. He could still remember the blank stare she'd walked around with for weeks.

It was the reason Teddy hated the smell of chrysanthemums. His father had felt more guilty than usual and filled the house with them, until the smell had clogged Teddy's nose, filling the house with the cloying scent. She'd started drinking when the flowers had died.

Teddy stared out of the window, lost in thought, until his phone jarred him from his memories, ringing behind him. He scooped it off the table and flicked it open, lifting it to his ear. "Hello?"

"Hey, Teddy. I was hoping I'd reach you before you left." Santiago, his boss at Antonio's, sounded apologetic, and Teddy already knew he wasn't going to like what was coming. "It's been a slow night. I'm afraid we won't need you to come in."

Teddy closed his eyes and took in a deep breath to keep from cursing. "Okay, thanks for letting me know."

Santiago wished him a good night before he got off the phone. Teddy clenched his cell in his hand, fighting the urge to chuck it at the wall. It seemed like every time he turned around lately, his hours were being cut somewhere. If he believed in God, he'd think it was a punishment.

Fortunately, the only thing he believed in was karma, and this must be karma coming back around to bite him in the ass.

He decided to head to his room to take a nap, but before he did, he dug his mother's letter out of the trash, placing it back on the table to deal with later.

Chapter Nineteen

I'm not here for Teddy.
I'm not here for Teddy.

But damn, no matter how many times he tried to remind himself why he *was* there, his eyes kept skipping back behind the bar. It was Friday, so Teddy was in blue, but that only highlighted the blue shadows below his eyes. Ian dropped his gaze lower with a frown. Teddy had always been slender, but now, he seemed closer to skeletal. Even through the thin, glittery top, Ian could count his ribs...or nearly.

"Boss?"

Ian blinked, reluctantly turning his attention to Johnny. His manager was looking curiously between Ian and Teddy.

"Do you need something?" Ian asked, voice coming out harsher than he'd meant. He winced and softened it. "Sorry. I spaced out."

Johnny smirked, glancing toward Teddy again. "Can't blame you. I just wanted to let you know that the office phone was ringing. Someone named Sam is asking for you."

His spine straightened at the mention of his boss' name. "I'll be right there, thank you." He circled behind the bar, bypassing Teddy to enter his office nook. He'd had it built there intentionally. It was close enough to the bar for him to keep an eye on everything, but thanks to the clever use of lights and shadows, he couldn't be seen from the club floor.

He sat behind his desk and picked up the phone. "Ian Romero speaking."

"Mr. Romero. The delivery is on track, as scheduled." Sam's voice was stern, even through the receiver. Ian could practically see the strict line of his mouth, the closely cropped salt-and-pepper hair.

"I'm glad to hear it," Ian acknowledged his agent's coded phrase implying that all was going as planned. "Will you be reaching out to new suppliers this week?"

"I'll keep you posted. Our investors are hoping to see a quick return on their investment."

There was a click, then the line was filled with the sound of a dial tone. Ian replaced the receiver but didn't leave the office. Instead, he opened his laptop and entered his password to log in. He pulled up the inventory program. He navigated through a series of hyperlinks hidden in a random pattern of items — the third number in the UPC for Redd's Red Apple Ale, then the 'B' in Bacardi Rum, and so on — until he navigated to the sleeper program embedded inside.

A secondary login box popped up on the screen. He carefully typed in his username and password. It was a one-and-done. No option to re-enter if he tapped the wrong key — the program would just self-destruct until a security team had time to set up a cover and re-install it, costing time and money he couldn't afford to waste.

It took a few seconds for the program to boot, then the computer connected him directly to headquarters' servers. He pulled up the file Tennyson was assembling. It was thinner than Ian would have liked, but he knew he was impatient. Either he was getting better at recognizing the patterns or the *La Familia* cartel was just sloppy.

He was hoping for the second, if only to get this done and over with so he could move on with his life.

The files on known members were easy to access, if only because there weren't many of them. There were ten confirmed members — four already in police custody and six suspected. They were all low level, or at least seemed to be. Ian had marked two for Tennyson to follow up on. One, Joey Alvarez, was suspected of transporting cocaine during his business trips into Mexico. Rather than arresting him, though, he'd been placed on a watchlist.

The other, Hugo Ward, was a known enforcer. He'd been arrested for everything from petty theft to assault, but none of the charges had ever stuck.

He frowned at the attached photograph. He'd flagged this one because there was something uncomfortably familiar about the man. Six-foot-five inches, with corded neck muscles and fists the size of mallets, he wasn't someone Ian would have spent time with, so the familiarity nagged at him. Had he seen him with his brother, during one of the rare instances he'd spotted Lucas stirring shit up in the neighborhood? Lucas had never introduced him to his so-called friends. Looking back, that probably had been because he knew Ian would never have let him keep hanging around them. If this Hugo had been one of the bastards his brother had been running with, then maybe he knew something about Lucas' death.

He hurriedly closed out of the program when someone hesitated in the entrance to his office. Johnny awkwardly cleared his throat. "Hey, boss? Can we get a hand at the bar?"

"Of course." Ian closed the laptop and stood. He wished he could lock the laptop up, but since only employees could get behind the bar, and they were all on camera anyway, he knew it would look suspicious. The last thing he wanted was to tip someone in the cartel off that he wasn't who he said he was.

He followed Johnny to the unattended bar and started quickly serving drinks, frowning at the number of waiting customers. When the line had dwindled to normal, he pulled Johnny aside and asked, "Where's Teddy? Why were you the only one behind the bar?"

Johnny shrugged, his expression betraying his annoyance. "I don't know. He went on break about thirty minutes ago and never came back."

Ian's frown deepened. That didn't seem like Teddy. The bartenders were given fifteen-minute break every two hours. He was only fifteen minutes late...but the Teddy he remembered would have hated that.

"Is that normal for him? He didn't look like he was feeling well. Have you checked the restroom?" Ian asked, already glancing that way.

"Nah, we've been slammed." Johnny leaned over the bar and flagged down one of the bouncers. "Dude, can you go check the toilets? We're missing a bartender."

The bouncer—a glance at his name tag named him Deacon—nodded and wandered away. Ian wanted to snap at him to hurry, but he bit it back. He wasn't there for Teddy. He needed to remember that. Besides, the last thing he needed was for someone to think Teddy was something special to him and use it against him. He'd seen it happen before, back in Chicago, and it wasn't pretty.

The bouncer wandered back. "Just a pair of blokes having a good time."

Johnny glanced at Ian and shrugged. "Maybe he went home early?"

"Maybe," Ian acknowledged, though he still thought Teddy would have said something first. But he didn't really know Teddy, not anymore. Four years was a long time. He couldn't expect him to be the same person he'd left behind.

Still, he couldn't help scanning the dance floor, hoping to catch a glimpse of familiar blond head that never came.

Chapter Twenty

It was funny—not in the *ha-ha* way—how a night could start out so good and end up going completely to shit. Granted, he considered the night good simply because he wasn't on the platforms. He was still shit out of luck when it came to picking up another source of income—or paying his rent, or making his next payment. But he'd walked into Envy with a determination to look at the positives. So...if not dancing was the only thing he had going for him, he was damn well going to take it.

Unfortunately, his good mood only lasted two hours.

"Alley. Five minutes." One of the bouncers, Deacon, muttered as he passed the bar, giving Teddy a pointed look. Low man on the totem pole or not, Deak was still a full-fledged member of the *La Familia* cartel, which put him above Teddy in any way that mattered.

"My shift's not over until two," Teddy protested quietly, scrubbing at a non-existent spill, his heart pounding. Whatever he was needed for in the alley was bound to not be good.

"And your debt to the cartel isn't over until you cough up your payments." Deak tapped his fingers on the bar. "Alley. Three minutes."

Teddy gave a sharp, staccato nod and dropped the cleaning rag into the soiled bucket behind the bar. He rounded it to go to the changing room but Deak gripped his arm tightly to stop him. "No need to change."

Teddy cringed, wiping his hands on the booty shorts. "I don't have shoes."

"You won't need them. Go."

Teddy's nod was small. He picked his way through grinding bodies, ignoring the drunk hands that reached out to prod his skin and grope his ass.

"Dance with me," a slurred voice screamed into his ear, large hands wrapping around his hips, nearly pulling him off balance.

Teddy glared and tugged free. "Hands off!"

The man was large and reeked of alcohol but wasn't drunk enough to ignore the house rules. Mainly…don't touch. The bouncers let it go, if it was clear the dancers didn't care, but if Teddy made a fuss, the man would be kicked out on his ear immediately. "Bitch," the man cursed but turned away, setting his eyes on a different twink.

Teddy skirted the edge of the dance floor and stepped into the narrow hallway to the side. He made his way down the dimly lit passage, bypassing the bathrooms to reach the black door. It was lit only by the neon green of the exit sign. He shoved the push bar and the door opened with the squealing of hinges, spilling him out into the back alley.

Ian had added a single streetlight to the small parking lot during renovations, which gave the alley an illusion of safety. The parking lot was small, big enough for six cars — or the four cars and one blue SUV it held now. The paint was faded, the asphalt riddled with potholes.

The entrance to the alley was narrow, wide enough for a single car to pick its way down, and was narrowed farther by the pair of large green dumpsters across from the back door. They were surprisingly neat.

Three men were spread around them. He recognized Mike from his ginger hair, though he'd only had to deal with him a handful of times over the past few years, but it was impossible not to recognize Hugo. His shoulders were set, his muscles corded in tension, and there was a grimness to his expression that made Teddy hesitate to approach. He let the door fall closed behind him, cutting off the pulsing dance music like a power switch. The alley seemed to hold its breath at the sudden silence.

The third man was a stranger.

With his long, dark hair tied back in a ponytail and shredded blue jeans, Teddy could have passed him on the street without a second look. He was as tall as the pair beside him but lacked their breadth, slender in hip and shoulder, which should have made him less threatening. It didn't.

Teddy shivered at the calculating expression on the stranger's face as his eyes scanned Teddy, then seemed to dismiss him as a threat.

"This is Teddy De Luca?" the slender man asked, voice strangely blank. Bored, like he haunted alleys for fun every night.

If he worked for the cartel, maybe he did.

"Yes, sir," Mike answered. His voice was crisp and professional. Teddy almost expected him to snap a salute at the end.

The slender man pulled out his phone, glancing on the screen before he tucked it away. "Get him in the van."

Teddy instinctively looked to the alley's mouth then back to the doorway, tracing his escape route. Barefoot, he would be slower, and God only knew how much broken glass littered the pavement, but if he headed inside, he could make it. His muscles stiffened, pulling taut, but he restrained himself, except to clench his hands into fists.

They knew where he lived, so his escape would only be temporary. Likely, the punishment for running would be worse than meeting with Julian anyway.

Mike and Hugo approached from the sides. Their hands, heavy as hammers and just as capable of breaking bones, gripped him by the biceps, tightening almost unbearably. A whimper escaped his tightly pressed lips as their fingers dug into his flesh.

"I...I can walk..." Teddy said, but they ignored him, frog-marching him to the back of the SUV. It had to be stolen. His eyes caught on the sticker on the rear-view window, a stick figure family complete with dog.

Hugo's grip tightened as Mike's released, keeping him in place as Mike popped the hatch. It opened and Teddy's breath choked in his throat.

A bundle of rough-hewn rope.

A roll of duct tape.

A spade.

Teddy wasted a moment wondering if being a month behind was bad enough for the cartel to make an example of him, then shoved the thought away. He yanked at his arm, struggling to free himself without success. Hugo just grabbed for his other arm and lifted him clear off his feet.

Teddy kicked out, his bare heel colliding with Hugo's hip. The man grunted as it landed, but Teddy didn't have the leverage or training to do enough damage. "Get the rope," Hugo snapped, shaking Teddy like a doll. A second later, he spun Teddy around and forced his wrists together. Mike twined the rope around them tightly, knotting it off, then worked the rest around Teddy's chest and hips. The knots dug into his skin, constricting his breathing, and Teddy panicked, kicking out again.

Mike, unlike Hugo, cursed, though the kick didn't even land, then slapped Teddy hard across the face. His head snapped to the side, his vision blurring with tears. "Knock it the fuck off," Mike cursed, grabbing the last length of cord. He snagged one of Teddy's ankles and yanked it forward, binding his legs together. He didn't seem to care that the ropes were too tight.

"Please, don't do this. I'll ride in the back seat, and I'll be quiet, you don't have to do this. I'll be good," Teddy rambled, pleading. However, the only thing his words did was remind them he could speak.

Hugo tossed him roughly onto the coarse carpet behind the back seat and grabbed a rag, shoving it into Teddy's mouth before Teddy could clamp it closed. It reeked of gasoline and Teddy gagged at the chemical taste where it burned his tongue. Before he could spit it out, Hugo tore off a strip of duct tape and plastered it over his lips.

Teddy's cries were too muffled. He tried to enunciate his pleas, but all that came out was a garbled moan. Hugo backed away then slammed the hatch closed. Teddy flinched back, the metal missing his face by inches, rustling his hair in the breeze.

The SUV rumbled to a start, jolting back and forth as it turned around in the cramped lot. Teddy rolled, his shoulder blades digging into the sharp edge of the shovel, then rolled the other way when the SUV sped up, smacking his face into the back.

Tears slid down his cheeks, dampening the edges of the duct tape, and he struggled to breath through the snot caking his nostrils when the panic set in. He pulled at the ropes, but the knots only tightened, digging into his joints. He would have welts later — if he lived long enough to care.

Maybe his tears would loosen the duct tape enough to free his mouth, but he knew it was unlikely. Even if it did, he doubted he was flexible enough to reach the knots with his teeth anyway.

When he got out of there, he was starting yoga.

It was hard to tell how long they drove for. The sounds of Austin traffic dwindled, the stop-and-go of traffic lights and stop signs smoothing out into the steady rush of the expressway before slowing. The road grew rougher. He felt it in the bouncing of the struts beneath him that sent him rocking back and forth painfully, heard it in the pinging of gravel against the SUV's peeling paint.

Eventually, the van lurched to the side, pulling off the road into...somewhere. All he could see through the dark windows was what looked like tree branches. They were in the woods, somewhere outside the city.

Teddy's panic, briefly abated by the length of the drive, flared back to full force. He cried out as the brakes screamed and the van abruptly stopped. He couldn't keep himself from colliding with the back hatch again, his cheek smacking into the metal. He grunted at the pain.

He heard the doors open then slam shut. There was nothing but silence for several long seconds — silence and the ragged sound of his breathing. Then the hatch opened.

Mike and Hugo were two dark, looming silhouettes against the night sky. Teddy felt like a mouse trapped in a cat's house...or an ant, about to be ground beneath their heels. Then the larger shadow bent over him. He cowered back but couldn't escape the hands that gripped him like vises.

He huffed out a whimpered breath as Hugo — it had to be Hugo from the glint of reflection of the crescent moon off his scalp — threw him over his shoulder, crushing his ribs with the impact, knocking the breath free from his lungs. Tears resumed their wayward course down his cheeks.

He couldn't see much from his vantage point. Just the blades of grass that looked black in the darkness, and the occasional scattering of stones. If they were on a path, it was one rarely used.

They were carrying him into the wild.

Teddy fell without warning. One moment, his body swayed precariously, jostled with each step Hugo took farther into the desert, then he was falling. He landed with a pained cry, stones biting into his flesh. He supposed he should be grateful that it was the only injury he suffered, but all he felt was pain and terror. He looked up with wide eyes, his vision hazy around the edges. For a second, the looming silhouette stretched and twisted, morphing to a monster with dagger claws, but then it crouched. Moonlight glinted on the sharp knife held in Hugo's hand.

Hugo sliced at the ropes. They parted with only a moment's protest, falling to the ground. Teddy pulled his arms inward and tucked his knees to his chest, furtively rubbing at the raw, tender flesh of his wrists but unwilling to take his eyes off the man in front of him.

He lifted his hands to pull the duct tape free, but Hugo swatted them, shooting him a stern look. "Leave it." Teddy tried to plead with his eyes, but the man was unmoved. After a second, though, his eyes softened. "I'm real sorry, kid, but you brought this on yourself. You should have made your payments. I warned you. Didn't I warn you?"

Teddy nodded hurriedly, afraid of making him angry. He flinched as heavy footsteps approached. Mike stood over them. "You just going to sit there, or can we get this show on the road? I got shit to do."

Anger passed over Hugo's face, but it vanished, fleeting as a shadow on the moon. He stood and dusted his jeans off. Mike threw the shovel down between them. It clattered to the ground by Teddy's knees and he flinched.

Teddy's eyes darted between the men and the shovel, heart a thundercloud in his chest. He tried to plead through the gag but it came out a pathetic whimper. For a moment, nobody moved.

Then, Mike grumbled and leaned down, twisting his fingers roughly into Teddy's hair and yanking, dragging him to his feet. Teddy cried out as stones dug into his bare feet and several strands of hair separated from his scalp.

Mike let him go with a glare. "Grab the shovel."

Tears slid down Teddy's cheeks but he shook his head. He didn't want to touch it. He didn't know what they wanted him to do with it, but he suspected, and he wasn't ready to die.

Mike's palm cracked across Teddy's cheek, hard enough that it tore off the duct tape. Teddy cried out, feeling the layer of skin separate. Before they could cover his mouth again, Teddy spat the rag on the ground, his cries no longer muffled.

"Please, I'll pay the money. I'll get it. Please don't do this. *Please* don't do this," Teddy rambled, stumbling toward Hugo with a whimper. Of the pair, Hugo was the one he'd spent the most time with and the one who seemed the most sympathetic. He'd barely touched Hugo's shirt before Mike grabbed him by the hair again and pulled him back.

"Shut the fuck up," Mike barked, spit flying from his pudgy lips, joining the mess on Teddy's face. "Grab the fucking shovel or I will. And I'll shove it so far up your tight little ass that you'll choke on it."

Teddy—crying, aching and petrified—stumbled back. He scrambled for the handle of the spade, yanking it toward him and holding it to his chest, like it could shield him from their anger. "Please..." He tried one last time.

Hugo sighed, "Sorry, kid, but we got our orders."

"Oh for fuck's sake," Mike snapped, stepping forward menacingly. Teddy cringed, but the man just glared. "This ain't a date. You don't got to warm him up first. Either fuck him, or let's get on with it."

Hugo glared at the shorter man, his fists clenching, but nodded. Teddy's last thread of hope that they would change their minds withered and died. Mike gave a feral grin and turned back to Teddy.

"Dig."

He did.

Teddy's shoulders burned as he heaved a small shovelful of dirt over the tall side of the hole. Deeper than his elbows and wider than his waist, it was the biggest hole he'd ever dug.

Grave.

His mind rotated the word around it, rolling it around on the tips of his tongue and the back of his throat, no amount of burying it keeping it down. He was digging a grave.

He shuddered at the thought, nausea burning at the base of his ribs. He didn't realize he'd stopped, leaning on the shovel to keep himself upright, until Mike cursed from his position on the edge.

"The fuck you stopping for, boy?"

Teddy cringed and glanced up at the same time as he stabbed the point of the shovel into the dry, cracked dirt. Mike was alone. He'd snapped at Hugo some time back to '*Go get the box,*' and since then, he'd been a statue looking down on him. The furtive glances Teddy shot him showed him staring at the illuminated screen of his phone with a frown, his pistol held loosely in his other hand.

Now, Mike looked eerie in the pre-dawn light — shadowed, except for the hazy reddish light that outlined him like fire. Teddy gripped the shovel and flung the dirt onto the growing pile. Mike watched then glared at his phone again.

Teddy tightened his hand on the blood-and-sweat-stained shovel. He wondered if he could get enough leverage to make it a weapon... He couldn't reach Mike's head, but maybe he could strike the knees, take his feet out from under him and run.

As if sensing the thought, Mike looked up at him again, his eyes narrowed. Mike lifted the pistol, aiming it at Teddy's head. Teddy went still, fear freezing his muscles into unmoving ice.

"*Bang*," Mike crowed, his hand flexing around the grip, and Teddy flinched. No bullet tore into his flesh, but still, it left him a quivering mess. "Get back to work."

Teddy quickly stabbed the ground again, frantically hurling clumps of dirt over the side, thoughts of escape dwindling. He'd end up with a bullet in his spine before he could even make it out of the hole.

He flinched when something *thumped* above him. He glanced up instinctively, but it was just Hugo. Teddy dropped his gaze again. Mike dragged him out of the hole and tossed him onto the scratchy grass.

Teddy yelped when a scorpion scuttled by his nose and disappeared into the craggy bush nearby. Mike laughed.

"You think it's deep enough?" Hugo said quietly, speaking over Teddy's head.

"Ain't like they going to be bringing out dogs or nothing, right? You think someone's going to miss the fucker?"

Hugo didn't answer.

The pair turned to Teddy. He cowered away, scuttling on blistered palms and heels to no avail. Mike just grabbed his arms and yanked him back.

Mike forced him to look at the pine box. It was maybe three foot by four, and half as deep, closer to the size of a suitcase than a coffin, and for a second, Teddy's hopes soared. Maybe they weren't burying *him*, but just contraband — something illegal, something they didn't want their sweat on.

His hope died when Hugo let him go to pry off the lid. It was empty. Mike shoved him forward until his knees struck the box. "Please, please, please…"

Teddy's emotions were running too high for him to formulate any other words but a plea. He'd heard stories of people being buried alive. He scratched at the skin he could reach, arching his back as he struggled to get away, to run. He kicked at empty air.

A bullet in the spine would be better than this.

Mike shoved him forward, sending him sprawling into the box. He jolted like he'd been electrocuted, arms and legs flailing in his attempt to get out, to make it impossible for them to shut the lid. He banged his wrist into the rough edge, gaining him splinters embedded in his skin and a few precious inches closer to freedom.

He didn't care that he probably looked like a fish flopping on the deck of a ship. He was long past worrying about his pride. It could go fuck itself with a broom, and while it died, he would live on, free and clear.

He didn't see the fist coming until it slammed into his temple. Mike, a wild savagery in his hazel eyes, the bowstring-like cords of his neck pulled tight, leaned over him.

Dazed, Teddy watched as Mike gripped his ankles, folding his legs to his chest, arranging him like a rag doll into the pine box.

"Get the lid," Mike ordered. His voice sounded like it was coming from a tunnel, distant and meaningless. Then, the early dawn light vanished, and the only sound Teddy heard was the pounding of a hammer, nailing him in.

Dirt struck the top of the box. It sounded like rain on an umbrella...but only if the umbrella was sealed over his face and each drop threatened to fill it until he drowned.

Teddy had been buried alive.

Chapter Twenty-One

Late the next morning, Ian sat in his unmarked black sedan outside Shorty's Gym. Ian knew he shouldn't be there. He should leave it to Tennyson. But he itched to do something, anything, to bring the cartel down. He was used to working in the field, not at a desk. He might only be quasi-benched, but it was enough to make him long to be in the thick of things. This was his compromise with himself.

He'd planned on observing the first mark, Hugo Ward, but the man had shown up several hours after his shift had supposedly started, dark jeans stained with what looked like mud.

Not that his mark had gone into the gym he allegedly worked at. Allegedly, because not only was he certain that the gym was a front—the only customers had been a series of men in suits, none carrying gym bags—but Ward hadn't stepped a foot inside. He'd leaned against the brick wall, a cigarette—unlit—dangling from his lips. He looked even larger in person.

Definitely, he spent a lot of time at a gym—just not here, at this gym. Not on the machines, at any rate.

When Ian had sat through his first stakeout nearly three years earlier, his heart had pounded in anticipation, as though at any moment a window would shatter and he'd have to give chase or duck for cover. It was what the TV shows had prepared him for. Five minutes of waiting, followed by a miraculous break in the case.

It hadn't prepared him for the five hours of sitting on his ass developing hemorrhoids, a camera poised at the ready to take photos of nothing or the fact that he couldn't step out for a piss break without risking missing the only important thing he'd see that day, which today, was just pictures of a series of boring men in suits filtering in and out.

At least he no longer had to spend hours later analyzing the photographs and uploading them to the department servers. The latest update had synced all their phones automatically. Any photograph he took automatically uploaded, then deleted itself at midnight. Since he only used this phone for work anyway, he didn't have anything to worry about.

Though he had laughed at the last meeting before he went undercover when his boss had scolded a pair of rookies who'd apparently forgotten about the upgrade and had used their work phones at a strip joint.

It was a few hours after noon before Hugo finally left the gym. Ian followed him through a drive-thru, where Hugo got a pair of burgers and Ian ended up with a salad. Then he trailed the large man to an apartment complex that was far too nice for a man on a minimum wage salary. The address matched the one he had on file. Ian snapped a few photographs of the man heading inside then pulled back out onto the street.

According to the dossier Ian had on Joey Alvarez, the man was a late riser. He spent his evenings prowling nightclubs for hookups, then slept well into the afternoon. Hopefully, Ian would catch him at home.

Ian had done his research well enough to know that there was a nice running path through the park behind Alvarez's condo. Ian switched his heavy, steel-toed boots for running shoes, double-checked that his holster was secure on his ankle and took off at a jog. If he had to stop and tie his shoes just off the path directly behind Alvarez's house, well, what were the odds?

Ian crouched, keeping an eye out for other runners, and peered through the large bay window into the living area. With the sun behind him and the lights on in the house, it was easy to see through the glass. Fortunately, Alvarez was home. Unfortunately, Ian was staring at nothing immediately important to the case.

Alvarez was in his early thirties. He was a pilot for a small airline, which was what allowed him to transport drugs so easily. It was also, apparently, how he picked up women. Alvarez was butt-ass naked on the couch, his pilot's cap cockeyed on his head, while a busty brunette bounced on his dick. Ian felt a bit like a pervert snapping the pictures…but they needed to know all the cartel members' associates, clothed or not.

Ian didn't spare the couple another glance after he tucked away his phone. He stepped back onto the path and started running. He had several hours until the club opened and he needed to return to his cover job, but there was somewhere he knew he needed to go first.

* * * *

The grass was too green.

Ian stared at the perfectly manicured lawn and fought the urge to tear clumps of the perfectly straight blades free, scatter dirt over the perfectly tended headstones and scream into the perfectly calm silence of the cemetery. Everything was too perfect.

Lucas would have hated it.

Ian lowered himself to his knees, his gaze drifting over the dead and dying flower arrangements carefully arranged at the headstone's base. He hadn't brought any. Lucas hadn't liked flowers.

He'd liked Slipknot and Korn. He'd liked dark-wash jeans and well-worn combat boots. He'd liked movies with Brendan Fraser, chasing squirrels into storm drains and painting shitty graffiti on semi-abandoned buildings — but he not flowers.

Shame welled in Ian's chest. It grew into a knot in his throat then burst, sending saltwater tears leaking out of his eyes. He wiped them away with a heavy swipe of his hand. Ian hadn't gone to the funeral — he hadn't even come back to visit, not once. Something had always stopped him, nailing his feet to the ground when he thought of buying a plane ticket. This wasn't the kind of visiting he wanted to do with his brother.

Lucas should be off at college somewhere, terrorizing his teachers and getting shitty grades and…and defacing public monuments with gaudy graffiti.

"You shouldn't be here. You should be alive," Ian said to the headstone. He reached out to smooth away a streak of dirt. "It's been a while. Funny how four years can feel like a decade. I've been busy."

Ian looked around, but the cemetery was empty, as dead as the bodies interred there. "I joined the FBI…for you." He added, though it had to be obvious. "I work on a task force that targets gangs. I took one down in Chicago last year. You should have seen the shit they were into."

Ian sighed as his words stirred up uncomfortable memories. While the *La Familia* cartel he was investigating now was horrible, at least they seemed preoccupied with their drug operation. There were some violent offshoots, sure, and they were still deadly, but so far, he'd seen nothing as bad as the trafficking ring he'd helped shut down. He could still see the faces, scared and dirty, some far too tiny, crammed into the train car when they'd finally tracked it down. It had made him both love and hate his job.

"They finally let me come back to work the case I really wanted. I think they knew I was considering retirement. This shit is… God, Lucas, I never thought people could be so evil." Ian closed his eyes, drawing up his memories of Lucas. He could practically see his little brother rolling his eyes.

"Did you know what they were into when you joined?" It was the question he wished he could ask his brother, the question that rolled itself over in his head at night. Had his brother just gotten in over his head, or had he known the entire time and just…thought the risk was worth it? He felt sometimes like he hardly knew Lucas, because the Lucas he remembered played Pokémon and Mario Kart with the neighbor boy, not with gangs.

Ian sighed. "I just… I can't believe you had a secret this big and never told me. I thought you told me everything. You told me when you got your first chest hair, and…and when you accidentally jizzed the bed before you knew what that meant. But you couldn't trust me to talk about this?"

Ian clenched his hands into fists at his sides, a cold, pained laugh-that-wasn't-a-laugh slipping free. "You could sure talk to Teddy about it, though, couldn't you? I shouldn't be angry. It's been four years, but…it still hurts. He knew, and he didn't say anything. He should have put a knife in my back. It would have hurt less. Am I wrong to still hold a grudge?"

Ian listened to the silence. A crow cawed in the distance, but his question sat unanswered. He sighed. "You should see him, Luc." The nickname rolled off his tongue unintentionally and it speared his chest like a dagger. He rubbed the ache below his diaphragm. "He's really grown into himself. He's still too skinny, of course. He must not visit Mama much. But…he looks happier now. Sometimes." There were still moments when Teddy looked distant, lost in thought, but Ian had yet to see a sweater make its appearance.

"Would you believe he's a bartender? You'd laugh if you saw it. He works for me." Ian laughed, the sound coming easier now. Lucas would have found great irony in that. He'd always said Ian had too big a stick up his ass about following the rules. "He should be completely out of my reach. I'm his boss, and…and my job is dangerous. Really dangerous. I shouldn't drag him into it, but…every time I see him, Luc. Every time, I just want to drag him upstairs and show him that he's mine. But I know I can't do that, not until I forgive him."

Ian leaned back on his hands, tipping his face up to the sunlight. "I really want to forgive him, Luc."

A car door slammed shut and Ian sighed, pushing himself to his feet. He swiped the dirt clear from his jeans. He stood in silence until he heard the approaching footsteps of an elderly woman holding the hand of a child. He watched them head a few rows over.

Ian kissed the tips of his fingers, then brushed them against the stone. "*Te amo*, Lou-Lou." Not for the first time, he wished he lived somewhere else, somewhere it rained, so the weather could match his mood.

* * * *

Ian drove aimlessly around the city until the needle on his fuel gauge hovered on empty. It was after three. He had a few hours yet before he needed to open the club, but he was too restless to sleep. He left his car in the lot and headed for the back entrance, deciding to head upstairs and wear himself out on the treadmill. The energy that coursed through him was not the useful sort. It was frenetic, the kind that urged him to do something dangerous.

He pulled out his keys to unlock the door but frowned when the knob twisted on its own. Had he forgotten to lock it? He was positive he'd checked it. A glance at the alarm had him pulling his service weapon from its holster. It was disarmed and he knew for certain that he'd armed it before he left. Someone had been inside.

Ian nudged open the door. He darted a glance around it. The hallway was dark with shadows that clung to the walls and crawled across the floor, but there was no movement. Ian crept his way inside, his eyes peeled. The thrill of adrenaline — of danger —

swelled in him, urging him onward, whispering for him to take risks, to keep the adrenaline flowing. With the ease of practice, he buried it, keeping his hands steady.

Faintly, he heard the sound of water running. He followed it to the employee dressing room. Pressing his ear against the wood, he listened. It sounded like the showers. He twisted the knob slowly, inching the door open. The room was dark, so he risked opening it farther.

He peered inside. The sound grew louder, the only light spilling out from the shower room to the side. Keeping his service weapon at the ready, he stepped inside, moving quickly. He pressed himself against the wall beside the archway. Drawing in a steadying breath, he peered into the room, preparing to duck if he was met with a spray of bullets.

Chapter Twenty-Two

How long until the air is gone?

Panic made the box seem smaller, and no amount of pushing with his knees and elbows had budged the lid. He had neither the strength nor the leverage to break free, and when the sound of dirt smothering him had died, the panic had only grown.

It had really happened.

He had been buried alive.

How long until the air is gone?

He couldn't breathe.

The air was hot, sticky from re-breath. It stuck in his mouth like cotton. The walls pressed against him, binding his chest, reminding him of days when he'd been weighted down by breasts, no amount of suffocating them able to smother his curves. But now, the binding was suffocating him. Like the teeth of a bra, it dug into his spine, cutting into fragile flesh like an underwire.

How long until the air is gone?

His chest heaved faster, but the more he gasped for breath, the less air he drew in. It was completely black, but spots still speckled across his vision.

It had to have been hours… His fingers were numb and he couldn't feel anything below his knees. It was hot. Not hot, like he'd sat too long in the sun and really wanted a glass of lemonade hot—hot like he'd been crammed into an oven that was about to melt his face off.

Even his sweat was sweating, the bitter scent strong enough that he could taste it. He gagged, too sudden to swallow it down. Pain flared down his spine at the jerking movement, and he hurled. Vomit, rancid and odorous, splashed over his arms and chest, then streaked down his chin, and the stench made him heave again.

Unfortunately, the act of heaving was enough to trigger other muscles to spasm as well, and he cried out as his body clenched and shuddered. Wetness trickled between his thighs as his bladder, which had been protesting for hours, finally gave out.

Urine dampened his thighs, the dampness triggering memories of his puberty, and he hated it. He hated it, but he couldn't escape, too weak and dizzy to do more than futilely shove at the wood. His head felt disconnected, floaty, like it was a balloon about to drift away, and even though he wasn't moving, he felt like he was spinning. Buzzing filled his ears, quiet, then louder.

A shudder wracked his whole body at the thought of the box filling with bugs, creeping, crawling creatures with too many legs scuttling across his skin.

Maybe he passed out. He wasn't sure what was real and what was memory—fading in and out like a flashback film across his eyelids.

He was in his living room, cowering between the legs of an armchair while his father screamed, "No daughter of mine... No daughter of mine..." Teddy's hands clamped to his ears to block out the chanting he'd heard too many times.

He regretted not standing up to the asshole before he'd died. That was real, a knowledge that grew stronger, mingling with the acidic stench of vomit.

He was standing in his apartment, a plain white envelope swimming in front of his vision, his name in his mother's hand scrawled across the front, until he threw it in the trash.

He should have opened it. He should never have let her weakness become his. He missed her.

He missed her hands, the callous on her ring finger born from scrawling vitals on doctor's charts, and teaching a young boy to write. He missed her scent—vanilla and chamomile. He just...missed her. He regretted not opening the letter when he'd gotten it. Any of the letters. He regretted not answering the dozens of missed calls.

The words he wished he'd spoken were needles in his mouth. They stabbed his tongue, slid down his throat like a prick. He wanted to spit them out.

How long?

The urine itched where it clung to his thighs but he couldn't even shift to alleviate it. His muscles ignored his attempts to move, except to spasm painfully.

There were so many things he regretted, though ironically, the one thing he didn't regret was the decision that got him into this mess in the first place. He couldn't regret getting his surgery, not even if it had brought him to this.

Thump.

He wished they would have shot him first. He found himself insanely grateful that they'd crammed him into such a small box—the oxygen had to run out soon, surely.

Thump.

Thump.

The box shook, jarring Teddy from his half-dazed stupor. His heart thudded in time to the strikes. It sounded like...

A shovel.

Hope soared in Teddy's chest. He was being rescued. Maybe someone from the club had seen him get grabbed. Maybe the police had somehow tracked him.

"Help!" His voice was coarse, rough from crying and frantic breathing. He struggled to produce enough spit to coat his throat, then tried again. "Help, please! I'm in here. Please let me out!"

The box shifted around him, tipping and swaying. He was grateful for the narrow space. Despite the rough rocking of the box, he didn't move, didn't collide painfully with the sides like he'd done in the van.

The box landed with a heavy *thud*. Then there was silence.

Teddy held his breath. The prongs of a crowbar slid into sight near his eyes. A thin slit of brilliant light appeared where the lid met the sides, growing wider.

The nails strained audibly, then broke free with a series of pops.

Light burned Teddy's night-blind eyes and he cringed, his hands reflexively covering them. He was dragged roughly from the box and he cried out as his muscles, unprepared, stretched. They cramped immediately, spasming in pain, and his stomach followed. He twisted, heaving the meager contents onto the dirt. The thin, watery bile burned, bitter on his tongue.

Before he could force his eyes open, he was tugged roughly upward. He blinked, his vision watery but clear enough to reveal, not a savior, not a police officer, but the burly silhouettes of Mike and Hugo.

"Best hope you learned your lesson, boy, or next time, I won't waste my time digging your ass back up." Mike snarled, shaking his loose-limbed frame. Teddy couldn't summon the energy to do anything but dangle, limp. Mike's nose screwed up as it caught the disgusting scent that Teddy reeked of. He dropped Teddy like he'd been burned. "Get him in the van. I'll clean this shit up."

Mike dropped him. Hugo didn't bother waiting for Teddy to figure out how to get his muscles working. He just scooped him up and threw him over his shoulder. Teddy heaved again, a thin trickle of vomit spilling from his mouth and over the sleeve of Hugo's shirt.

For a terrifying moment, Teddy thought Hugo was going to kill him. The man froze, his shoulders quivering with anger, and Teddy cringed, unable to hold back a fearful sob. But Hugo just started walking again.

This time when they reached the SUV, Hugo didn't throw him in the trunk. He opened the back door and dropped Teddy onto the bench seat instead. Either he knew Teddy lacked the energy to run or he wanted to see the results of his handiwork.

Hugo shut the door and immediately, Teddy wheezed. The metal seemed to lean in, closing in on him like a junkyard trash compactor. There was no air.

No air.

But then, suddenly, the driver's door opened and the walls snapped back into place like they'd never moved. Teddy's breath sucked in on a gasp. This time, when Hugo shut the door and started the engine, the walls stayed in place. Teddy scrunched his eyes closed against the illusion, burying his face into the cracked leather seat.

His muscles twitched uncontrollably, clenching tight enough to draw pained whimpers from his lips, then released without warning. There was no rhythm to the process, no pattern, just a seemingly endless cycle of pain and relief that distracted him from the driving. He didn't look around, not even when the sounds of Austin traffic permeated the air, until the van squealed to a stop.

He heard the door slide open on its rusty tracks, then felt himself get lifted. He clenched at arms that held him, terrified that they were just going to drop him again, but instead, he was surprised to be set gently down against cold metal, pavement grating against his bare skin.

"Thank you, thank you," Teddy mumbled, over and over. He blinked his eyes open to find himself leaning against a green dumpster, back in the alley behind Envy, Hugo crouched in front of him. His lips were pressed tight together, brows lowered with concern.

His large hands fidgeted where they rested between his knees.

The man's voice was achingly gentle when he murmured, "Teddy, you need to be careful. I can't help you. I can't, but I don't want to watch you get hurt again, okay?"

Teddy's nod was little more than a tip of his head. He didn't know how to be more careful. He didn't know how to make more money or how to spend less. He was poorly balanced on a tightrope and any second, he was going to trip.

This might have only been a warning, but it felt like a death sentence.

Hugo was silent. When he finally spoke, his whispered words were as loud as a shovel in the desert. "Go to the police. Tell them what you know. They can help you."

"I...I c-can't," Teddy whispered. "The video."

"They won't care. No one will care once they know the whole story. Just tell them the truth." Hugo glanced around nervously, like he was afraid someone would hear him.

"The ecstasy..." Teddy reminded the larger man, as if he would forget. He'd been there, the other half of the porn show.

"They won't arrest you for it, not once you explain. I know it's embarrassing, and...shit, nobody would want a video like that floating around." Hugo's jaw clenched and he looked away, his shame easy to read. Teddy didn't remember everything they'd done, but he remembered enough—remembered the high, the words that he couldn't seem to control. "But it's better than dying. You should go before Julian can stop you permanently."

"He'll kill me like he killed Lucas." Teddy didn't know for sure that was what had happened, but he suspected. It was confirmed when Hugo answered.

"Lucas was careless. He spoke to the wrong person about it first. Julian has no reason to think you'd narc, not after this long—and not if you do it quietly."

"Why are you telling me this?" Teddy cried, his body racked with shivers he couldn't control. Hugo was the enemy. Teddy wanted to hate him, but he couldn't, not when Hugo always seemed so concerned, so empathetic, not even when Hugo was watching him get buried alive, if this was how he was going to act after.

Hugo stayed silent, his eyes haunted, for a long stretch of pounding heartbeats. Finally, he lifted a thick finger and trailed it gently along Teddy's swollen cheek. "I like you, Teddy. More than I should. More than I ever meant to." Teddy opened his mouth, his heart tumbling, to explain why that would never happen, but Hugo shook his head. "I know. I know you don't feel that way. *Won't* feel that way. Don't worry. I can't disobey Julian. I would, but... What he's got on me is worse than a video. So please, get out before I have to do something that will break both of us."

Teddy didn't answer...couldn't answer. His mind was too fuzzy to make that decision, and Hugo seemed to realize it. His face fell. "Can you pick a lock?" Teddy gave a small nod. "Do you know the alarm code?" Teddy hesitated, then gave a smaller nod. "I'm going to leave. When I'm gone, go inside. Take a shower, get your things. Consider going to the police."

Hugo stood, dropping a fancy-looking hairpin into Teddy's lap before crossing the alley. He looked back at Teddy. "Take care of yourself, okay?"

Teddy obediently waited until Hugo left before dragging his abused body onto his feet and picking his way, barefoot still, across the dirty alley. He fumbled with the lock pick, his hands shaking almost too badly to move the right tumblers. He was grateful for Shiloh's adamant insistence that every gay boy needed to know how to pick a lock so that they never ended up locked in the closet again. He'd humored him and now, well…it looked like he was going to owe Shiloh a chocolate cake or something.

The alarm beeped in warning beside the door and he dropped the hairpin in his haste to get the code thumbed in correctly on the first try. His fingers shook as they pressed the keys, but finally, the beeping cut off. He sighed in relief and entered the dark club.

It was kind of creepy being in it alone. It looked larger when it was empty of bodies, and the slap of his bare feet on the flooring seemed to echo. He found himself holding his breath as he tiptoed to the dressing room and kicked himself for being a coward. There was no one here. The place didn't open for hours yet. He had no reason to worry. Even if he got caught, he found it hard to believe that Ian, of all people, would call the police. It wasn't like he was stealing anything.

Still, he didn't breathe easily until he closed the dressing room door behind him and slipped across the darkened room to the showers. He flipped on the light.

The bathroom used to be smaller, just a single, large cubicle, like what he'd had in gym class. Three nozzles forcing the dancers to huddle uncomfortably close together. Ever since the remodel, though, the fights over hot water had dwindled. There were still fights, since some of the dancers were drama queens, but not over hot water. The room was double the size, with six shower heads spread equidistant from each other. Half-walls separated one from the next.

He didn't bother drawing the curtains. The rare times he showered here, he always did, but he didn't have the energy.

He spun the nozzle on all the way to hot and stepped under the powerful stream. The water burned as it beat away the dirt, the vomit and the piss. It was scalding, leaving his skin scarlet, but he didn't spin the water down.

He sagged under the spray. He leaned against the wall for support, his hands bracketing the faucet, his hair spilling over his face, shielding it from the rivulets of water that tracked their way down his skin. He closed his eyes, letting the last tears he held in his body slide down the drain with the water.

His shoulders shook from the strain of holding back his sobs until he let them go. He folded his elbows until his forehead rested against the tiles, bowed under the burden of his thoughts. He just wanted to let them go — to think about nothing just for a bit, to forget the fear and the pain and the stress.

To just, for a while, not have to make a decision.

Chapter Twenty-Three

Ian slid the gun back into his holster but stayed otherwise frozen, his eyes locked on the bowed back. He would recognize Teddy anywhere, and for a moment, Ian's eyes saw only the smooth expanse of golden skin, the arched spine...the firm, round globes of a perfect ass.

For a moment, Teddy was a Monet in a roomful of forgeries.

For a moment...until Ian's eyes caught the ugly, raised welts that reddened Teddy's skin, coiling like snakes around his ribs, down his thighs, up his arms — then fury roared to life in Ian's chest.

It was hot, a California wildfire burning its way through Ian's self-control. He didn't realize a growl had spilled from his lips until Teddy spun around, his eyes wide with fear. Before Ian could silence the noise, Teddy slipped, skidding through a puddle of water. His slender arms cast outward for something to grab onto but met only empty air, and fear turned to panic.

Ian jerked forward, grasping Teddy by the hips and pulling him into his body, not caring that the shower pelted him, sticking his shirt to his skin and plastering his jeans to his thighs in an uncomfortable tightness that only worsened at the feel of Teddy pressed to him. Teddy fit into the curve of his body like he was made for him…like a puzzle that had always been missing a piece had finally been completed.

"Ian?" Teddy gasped, curling his small hands tightly into the damp fabric of Ian's shirt, like he was afraid that if he didn't, Ian would shove him away…not knowing that all Ian wanted was to hold him ever closer.

"Teddy Bear," Ian murmured, brushing the wet strands of Teddy's hair off his face. His hair still smelled strongly of *Teddy*, the honeysuckle and spice that was always so distinctly *him* that Ian had learned to hate it in Chicago, whenever it tickled his nose and Ian couldn't find the one person he wanted the most.

"I'm sorry," Teddy stuttered when Ian dipped into memories for too long. Teddy's face dropped, hiding in the shield of Ian's chest.

"No," Ian murmured, holding the smaller man close. "Don't be sorry. Never be sorry for coming to me. I'll always be here when you need me." He made the promise, knowing full well it was hypocritical, knowing that Teddy had needed him before and he'd left—packed his bags and driven until he ran out of gas.

He wasn't driving away this time.

Teddy shivered. Ian reached out and spun off the water, then forced himself to step back from Teddy long enough to grab a towel off the shelf. He wrapped it around him, draping it around the slender shoulders. It fell past his hips, but not far enough to stop Ian's gaze from lingering. He frowned at the bruising that stood out so obviously in contrast to his pale skin.

"Come upstairs," Ian said, then winced when he heard the way he'd said it. He had no right to order Teddy around — but Teddy just nodded.

Ian found himself filled with an unfamiliar hesitance, an indecision he wasn't used to. He was so confident, normally, always did what he thought best without worrying about consequences that may or may not come. But he was afraid to touch Teddy again. He had reacted without thought earlier, fear of Teddy falling, of getting injured further, overriding his rationality.

But now, he feared that if he stretched out his hand... If he took Teddy's in his to lead him to his apartment, Teddy might flinch and recoil from his touch. Ian wasn't sure he could handle Teddy pulling away, not when all he wanted to do was hold him close, protect him from whatever horrible things he'd been through.

Teddy chose for him. The younger man's spine seemed to straighten, drawing on the core of steel Ian had always been so proud of, and Teddy stepped forward, plastering himself to Ian's side. Teddy's hand slid into his and gripped it tightly.

"Upstairs," Teddy agreed, eyes darting up to meet his, uncertainty clear in their blue depths.

Ian hurried Teddy out of the chilly dressing room and across the hall to the door that led to the upstairs apartment. He unlocked it quickly. He reluctantly locked it behind them, his hurry to get Teddy upstairs and into something warm outweighed by the knowledge that he needed to take basic security measures, now more than ever. The delay cost him precious seconds, then he was hustling Teddy up the stairs and into the living room.

Inwardly, he grimaced. It was cold, not in temperature but in style, nothing like the cozy apartment he wished he could be bringing Teddy back to. Still, it wasn't like he had time to go shopping for new furniture, so he deposited Teddy on the leather couch. "I'll be right back. Stay here?" Ian said, half a question and half an order. Teddy nodded, so Ian hurried into his bedroom.

He locked up his weapon, then grabbed a pair of sweatpants with a drawstring and a black shirt that he knew Teddy would drown in. After a second's hesitation, he grabbed a sweatshirt as well, just in case. He carried the clothing back out and set them on the oak-and-glass coffee table.

Teddy was still on the couch, but he was examining the apartment—or what he could see of it. Curiosity danced in his blue-sea eyes, and Ian found his shoulders relaxing slightly. The fear, if not completely gone, seemed to have diminished. Teddy sat up straighter when he noticed Ian coming back in.

Teddy stood, letting the towel sag free of his body. He peered at Ian through his lashes. "Help me dry off?" he asked.

Ian swallowed, taking the offered towel and running it along Teddy's body, confusion just strong enough to outweigh the desire that touching Teddy, even through a thin cloth, stirred.

"Will you tell me about these?" Ian asked as he carefully dried around the welts. He was grateful that none seemed to have broken through the skin. They looked like rope burns.

"I don't want to," Teddy answered immediately, flinching back for a second before regaining control of himself. Ian didn't miss the fear that returned. "Not now, anyway. I just..." Teddy clenched his eyes shut for a few seconds and the only sound was their breaths mingling. "I just want to forget, for a little while. Make me forget?"

Fire flooded Teddy's face. He knew what he looked like — barely attractive on a good day, let alone covered in bruises and rope burns. The silence that followed his plea dragged on, each silent second causing his embarrassment to grow.

"Never mind," he said suddenly, lurching for the sweater Ian had left on the coffee table. He fumbled the fabric. *I'm such an idiot.* "I shouldn't have —"

"Teddy," Ian groaned, the towel fluttering to the floor between them. Teddy froze, his gaze darting up to Ian's and sticking. The look on Ian's face wasn't anger or disgust or discomfort. It was... It was desire, hot and naked, tinged at the edges with reluctance. A reluctance, Teddy suspected, to hurt him.

Teddy slowly straightened, gathering the shredded remnants of his courage, and lifted his trembling fingers to Ian's face. He skimmed his fingertips over the five o'clock shadow, enjoying the way it scratched his skin, then lifted himself onto tiptoes. He rubbed the unmarked side of his face along the stubble, letting it scratch him like sandpaper. He wondered how it would feel on his neck or his thighs, if it could smooth out his rough edges to something softer.

"Ian," he whispered, half-plea, half-promise. "Please..."

Ian groaned, but then his mouth was on Teddy's. Teddy allowed Ian to take control, to slide his tongue along the seam of his lips until they parted on a gasp, to capture Teddy's breath in his mouth and drink it in, drowning in it like a parched man in the desert finally finding an oasis.

Teddy melted beneath the heat of Ian's kiss, if it could even be called that. It was like no kiss he'd ever had—no schoolyard dare or heavy-handed make-out session. Ian lifted his hands to Teddy's waist, and beneath them, Teddy's skin burned. The only thing that could soothe the ache was Ian. He needed more.

He arched into the touch. His chest, always so small, so delicate—not ripped like Ian's, no matter how many crunches he forced himself to sit through—bumped into Ian's in a wordless, demanding plea. He tangled his fingers together behind Ian's neck, trying to pull him closer. Ian broke away with a groan, and Teddy growled at the distance that grew between them.

"Are you sure?" Ian said, and it was obvious that—while he wouldn't like it, while it might leave him hard and uncomfortable if Teddy changed his mind—Ian would back away in an instant. It just made Teddy want him more. He needed this, to forget about the terror and panic, to forget about the decision he knew he needed to make. He wanted to drown in Ian, to never come up for air.

With a strength he didn't know he had, he grabbed a fistful of Ian's shirt and used it to shove the larger man onto the couch then planted himself astride his lap. The feel of the jeans between his thighs brought out a moan and he couldn't help from rocking his hips.

"Never been more sure...of anything in my life," Teddy promised, then released his stranglehold on Ian's shirt. Instead, he gripped the hem and tugged. Ian lifted his arms, allowing Teddy to pull it off his body.

Ian was a god.

His muscles were perfect, like they'd been sculpted out of stone. A bead of sweat trailed from the hollow of

Ian's throat, down between his pecs. Teddy leaned forward, catching it on the tip of his tongue and following it back up. He lived for the gasped breath that he drew from Ian's mouth, the small, nearly inaudible moan that Ian couldn't choke back.

Teddy sucked gently on the skin below Ian's ear, not hard enough to leave a mark, though he imagined it — imagined Ian covered in his marks, imagined tracing every line and hollow of Ian's body with his lips.

"Please," Teddy murmured, trailing kisses down Ian's jaw to his lips. He sucked on the lower one, teasing it with his tongue.

Finally, Ian broke. He dropped his hands to Teddy's hips, dragging him closer, forcing Teddy to rut against his erection. Teddy couldn't hold back the gasp as electricity shot from his core to the very tips of his toes.

"Again," Teddy demanded, flailing his hands until they landed on Ian's strong shoulders. He gripped them, savoring the carefully controlled strength.

Ian dragged him forward against the hardness barely contained by his jeans, thrusting up to meet him. They were uncoordinated at first, until they developed a rhythm. Teddy ground his hips down with a moan, but it wasn't enough. He dropped his hands to the damp jeans, tugging at the button until it popped open.

"Off," he demanded.

"Bossy boy," Ian said. At the words, Teddy moaned, a full-body shudder quaking his body. Ian used the moment to shift Teddy up so he could push his jeans down past his hips and over his thighs. They were thick with corded muscles. Teddy pushed himself off Ian's lap so he could drop to his knees between them. He dotted kisses along each golden swath of skin revealed, until the jeans landed in a puddle at Ian's ankles.

Teddy glanced up, and Ian nodded. Teddy tugged off the running shoes and peeled away the black socks, revealing the sexiest pair of feet Teddy had ever laid eyes on. He wasn't normally someone who noticed feet, except if they were smelly or particularly strange, but on Ian, he noticed everything, from the graceful arch to the long toes. He wanted…

Teddy wanted to worship him, to cover his skin in kisses. Teddy slid his fingers over the sole of his foot and imagined his touch was reaching deeper, into Ian's soul instead. He massaged it, first the right, then the left, stroking along the tendons. The pain of his blistered palms wrote a new story in his head, erasing the feel of splintered wood with smooth skin.

He curled his hands upward. Was it weird to find ankles attractive? Did he care?

He dropped kisses on Ian's calf, on the curve of his knee, trailed fingers over the sculpted thighs. He pressed his nose into the crease of Ian's groin, breathing in the scent that was uniquely Ian. He felt the flex of tendons against his skin as Ian tensed.

Teddy looked up through his lashes, a sultry smile dancing on his lips. He slowly crept his hands over Ian's hips, toward the straining erection inches from his face. He wasn't surprised that Ian was big.

"May I?" Teddy teased, breath ghosting along the throbbing shaft. A smile crossed his lips when it twitched in front of him.

"If I say no, will you—?" Ian's words cut off in a groan when Teddy shifted forward, swallowing him down to the base.

Ian lifted his hands to Teddy's head. Maybe to pull him off, at first, but instead they lingered, cradling his face. Not holding him down, just a caress, a silent plea for more. Teddy obeyed.

Ian was thick and heavy in his mouth, a comforting weight on his tongue. Teddy didn't consider himself a slut, though he wouldn't shame anyone who was, but he'd sucked enough cocks to know his way around one.

Each time Ian rewarded him with a moan or a gasped breath, Teddy doubled down, letting him slide into his throat, swallowing around the sensitive head until Ian couldn't help but thrust upward. He flicked his tongue over the weeping slit, savored the taste, then took him back into his mouth again.

Teddy pressed his thighs together, struggling to relieve the ache in his own dick. He could come just from the feel of Ian sliding into his throat.

But then Ian's hands tightened carefully on Teddy's head and pried him off. He whimpered at the loss, trying to return to the throbbing cock dancing inches from his mouth.

"My turn," Ian murmured. He lifted Teddy, flexing his biceps with the show of strength, onto the couch beside him, then Ian was kneeling.

Teddy ground the heel of his palm into his dick, the biting pain bringing him back from the edge he wavered on at the sight. Then, Ian knocked his hand away and his mouth descended.

"Fuck," Teddy cried, hips surging upward. Ian was going to kill him.

Ian closed his mouth over Teddy's swollen cock. It filled his mouth comfortably, the perfect size to suck on, just long enough to tickle the roof of his mouth if he engulfed it to the base, which he did. Teddy's hips surged upward, until Ian curled his fingers around them and gently pressed him back down. He pulled back, his cock slipping free with a gentle pop.

"Don't worry, Teddy Bear, I got you," he promised, glancing up at Teddy to make sure they were still on the same page, still both wrapped in the heat of desire. Teddy's eyes were hooded, his mouth parted on a gasp. His tongue, pink and talented, slid free to wet his lower lip, a teasing swipe that made Ian want to capture it with his mouth.

Instead, confident that Teddy was still present, still *wanting*, Ian engulfed Teddy to the root again.

It didn't take long for Teddy to cry out, his hips jerking against Ian's hands, his body twitching. It drew into a beautiful symphony of soft cries and fingers flexing against Ian's hair.

Ian dropped his hand to his own throbbing dick. It took barely two strokes and he was spilling onto the rug with a long groan.

His head dropped to the cradle of Teddy's hips as he gathered his breath. Fingers loosened in his hair after a moment, petting over the strands until Ian recovered.

Then he turned his head and pressed a kiss to Teddy's inner thigh, the skin pale and smooth as silk. He dropped a second to Teddy's sharp hipbone, a third to the dip of his navel. He trailed his lips up to the hollow of Teddy's throat before he hovered over his lover's lips.

He hesitated, suddenly concerned that Teddy wasn't ready to taste himself in Ian's mouth, but Teddy didn't wait. He lunged upward, sealing their mouths together in a demanding display of ownership, chasing his climax from Ian's tongue before breaking free with a gasp.

When they separated, heat still flared in Teddy's eyes. Ian wanted to carry him into his bedroom and ravish him, but he knew that now wasn't the time.

Teddy quivered beneath him, and a yawn split his mouth after a second.

"I want you to stay," Ian murmured.

Teddy scanned his face, as though he was trying to read Ian's intentions, before he nodded. "I want to stay."

Chapter Twenty-Four

Ian's bed was the size of a small country. Teddy snuggled into the blankets, stretching his legs toward the foot, his toes pointed. Even with his arms outspread as far as he could reach, he couldn't touch either side.

He was never getting out of this bed.

Ian hovered near the edge. Teddy rolled onto his side, anxiety blossoming in his stomach. Maybe Ian was disappointed. Teddy knew he wasn't large, and even without the remnants of his bindings on his skin, he had scars. Any confidence he had in his appearance had dwindled during his time in the box.

He shoved the thought down. He would take it out later and turn it over, analyze it...piece it together into something he could handle. For now, he needed to ignore it. It was too fresh, an oozing, weeping wound in his psyche.

He smothered it beneath his insecurity, and his insecurity beneath anger, his anger beneath discomfort. He rolled them into a ball and shoved it into a corner, then tugged on a smile.

He lifted the blanket. "Are you getting in?"

"Only if you want me to," Ian answered, the lips that had brought Teddy so much pleasure curving down.

Teddy's smile faltered. "I... Don't you want to?"

Ian's frown softened, his eyes turning liquid. He kneeled on the mattress and crawled his way under the comforter and over to Teddy, folding himself around him like a security blanket. "Of course I want to."

Teddy shifted around until his back pressed against Ian's chest. He grabbed Ian's arm and tugged it over him until he was held completely. Instead of feeling trapped, he felt safe.

Secure.

Protected.

He fell asleep to Ian's fingers tracing patterns on his skin.

Ian sat, propped up on his elbow, and watched Teddy sleep. Whatever ordeal the younger man had been through had clearly left him exhausted. He'd passed out almost immediately.

Ian's eyes followed the path of one reddened welt up Teddy's wrist, nearly to the elbow. He had enough experience to recognize rope burn when he saw it. This wasn't the prickly, reddened mark of *shibari* that left delicate patterns on pale skin but faded quickly. It was the angry blisters of serious bondage. Gently, careful not to wake him from much-needed rest, Ian lifted Teddy's hands, first the right, then the left, lingering over the fingertips.

Loss of circulation over a prolonged period could leave permanent damage, but thankfully, he noticed none of the symptoms that spoke of trauma too severe. The fingertips looked healthy, a pale pink. He flipped the hands over, palms up, and winced at the ragged blisters following the fleshy base of Teddy's fingers and the arch of his thumb.

Ian grabbed one of the half-dozen pillows that decorated his bed — for show more than anything — and slid off the mattress, leaving the pillow in his place. It took him minutes to get the first-aid kit out of the en-suite bathroom and open it, taking the supplies he needed back into the bedroom. Ian laid them on the mattress and sat.

He lifted Teddy's hands again, cradling them in his lap. The kit was FBI-grade, practically a hospital in miniature. He picked up the aerosol analgesic and sprayed the worst of the wounds. Cleaning them out was going to hurt, and he didn't want to wake Teddy while he did it. It wasn't like the spray was hard to come by. It would be easy enough to requisition more later, if he needed it.

While he waited for the spray to work, he combed through the damp strands of hair that fell over Teddy's face. Teddy looked peaceful in sleep, even younger than his twenty-two years. Ian couldn't stop himself from leaning down and brushing a whisper of a kiss across his forehead.

Teddy shifted and Ian pulled back, afraid he'd woken him, but Teddy just breathed a sweet sigh and nuzzled farther into his pillow. Ian let out the breath he'd instinctively held. He forced himself to get back on task, to not get distracted staring at the fey boy in his bed.

He grabbed the antiseptic and carefully started cleaning out the blisters, smoothing on a bandage when he was finished. In the end, he only needed five — one for each palm, where the blisters had broken and wept a clear fluid, one for a sore on his lower ribcage and one for the sole of each foot. No wonder Teddy hadn't limped much, since both feet were shredded equally. He felt uncomfortable as he inspected Teddy carefully from scalp to toes, struggling to remain professional, while at the same time feeling like he was adding to the violation. The prickly sensation in the pit of his stomach worsened when he gently pried apart Teddy's buttocks, looking for evidence of assault. If there were bleeding or tears, they couldn't afford to overlook them. It would mean a hospital trip, followed by a trip to the police station.

Ian nearly sagged in relief at the unmarked flesh and quickly removed his hands. He didn't think Teddy's assault had gone that far, though in his mind, it had gone more than far enough.

He contained his anger in a tightly wound ball in his chest until he'd finished his ministrations and returned the first-aid kit to the bathroom. Then, after checking to make sure that Teddy was still sleeping soundly, he slipped out of the room.

He headed to his study, where his laptop sat innocently on the desk, unaware of the dilemma it stirred in him.

He wasn't allowed to use department resources for personal gain.

But the answer to who'd damaged Teddy could literally be at his fingertips.

If he were caught, it could mean a citation.

But his file was squeaky clean, not a single mark against him.

Obviously, while his mind ran the pros and cons for him, his body decided to act on its own, because he was sitting and logging in to the server before he realized he'd come to a decision. He hesitated briefly before typing Teddy's name into the database.

Part of him was certain that nothing would show up because Teddy wasn't the kind of person to end up on an FBI watchlist. He was surprised, then, when on the screen, a small brown folder popped up, next to the words 'Person of Interest'.

His cursor hovered over the file as he second guessed. This was a violation of Teddy's privacy. If Teddy wanted him to know, he'd have told him, and unless Teddy was directly involved in a case he was working on, Ian had no right to run a background check, let alone scour the FBI database for his activities.

What could Teddy be involved in to land himself on the FBI's radar? Ian's mind flicked back to before he'd run away from Austin. *Drugs, maybe?* Though in the months Ian had been back, he'd never seen a sign that Teddy was using again.

It could be as simple as having witnessed a crime in progress. 'Person of Interest' didn't necessarily mean suspect and didn't necessarily mean Teddy was involved in anything illegal.

Ian closed the browser before he could talk himself fully into opening the folder. When Teddy woke up, Ian would take him back to his apartment for a few days' worth of clothes. If Teddy didn't open up to him himself over the next few days — or if something else happened — Ian would read the file. Until then, the only way he could earn Teddy's trust was to be worthy of it.

He shut his laptop.

Rather than act on the impulse to watch Teddy sleep, he detoured into his gym and jumped on the treadmill, determined to burn the anger away through exercise.

Not that any amount of running was enough to quench the fury.

* * * *

Teddy woke alone.

The room was dark, curtains drawn over the windows and not so much as a nightlight in sight. Teddy sat up, for a moment uncertain where he was. He shivered and gripped the expensive cotton sheets, pulling them up over his nude body. It wasn't until he unclenched his hands from their painful grip that he noticed the white bandages on either palm. He frowned and shoved the blankets back down, examining his body.

A larger bandage followed the curve of his rib on his left flank, and he felt the itch of gauze swaddling the arches of his feet. Someone had taken time to care for his injuries, and immediately, the memories of the night — *day? What time is it?* — before came flooding back. He was at Ian's apartment, after getting caught breaking into Ian's club to use Ian's shower.

He flushed at the other memories — the taste of Ian's salty pre-cum on his tongue, before Ian had deprived him of it to give Teddy the best blow job of his life. The feeling of Ian's fingers owning every inch of his skin.

Teddy frowned, scanning the twisted mess of covers around him, but none of them hid Ian. At some point while he had slept, Ian had slipped out of the room. Teddy squinted at the glowing red numbers on the alarm clock. It was nearly eleven. He'd slept for over six hours, longer than he was used to getting in a night. No wonder his limbs felt like jelly.

Teddy shoved the covers off completely and swung his legs over the edge of the high bed. His feet barely skimmed the floor. He winced when standing put pressure on his tender soles. Ian was probably downstairs, either behind the bar slinging drinks, since Teddy had clearly slept through the first half of his shift, or in his office downstairs, finishing up the never-ending paperwork he always complained about.

Teddy padded out into the living room to find the clothing Ian had set out for him earlier still where they'd been left, in a neat pile on the coffee table. His muscles ached, fire tearing through his shoulders as he pulled on the baggy black shirt stamped with Envy's logo. His thighs screamed as he struggled to step into the legs of the sweatpants. They sagged low on his hips, even after he tightened the drawstring as far as it would go and knotted it off.

A bit of searching led him to a pristine bathroom, where he straightened out his hair as best he could. He struggled not to look at the red-and-purple bruise that spread from his jaw to his cheekbone. It was so obviously a handprint. A second, smaller but blacker bruise covered his temple, disappearing into his hairline. Teddy lifted his fingers to prod at it, poking the tender flesh before pulling his finger away with a hiss.

Of course it hurts, dumbass.

If he kept his head down, maybe he could slip unnoticed into the dressing room downstairs before finding Ian. He kept a small makeup kit in his locker for the days he ended up running too late to go home before his shift.

He made it into the dressing room undetected — but then came face-to-face with seven half-dressed dancers.

The laughter and rough-housing trickled away as one after another, they glanced over and caught sight of him. It wasn't like the bruise was hard to see, and unlike some of the guys who lived by the motto 'work hard, play harder', he wasn't one to engage in kinky sexcapades — or at least, not ones that ended up leaving marks.

Shiloh dropped the heels he was carrying with a curse and hurried over. "Shit, Teddy, what happened?" Shiloh grabbed Teddy's wrist in a none-too-gentle grip and dragged him over to the bench at the far end. "Talk."

Teddy flushed, catching the way the dancers glanced at him from the corner of their eyes. This wasn't the best place to have a private conversation, and he still hadn't decided if he wanted to tell Shiloh in the first place.

Shiloh fidgeted, his hands fluttering like he was going to touch Teddy, then dropping to scratch at a scab on his thigh, then lifting again.

"Just… Stop, Shiloh." Teddy knocked Shiloh's hand away from the now-bleeding sore. "Just help me cover it up and I'll talk to you later, okay?"

"Promise?" Shiloh asked, hands finally stilling.

"Yeah."

Shiloh hesitated, his eyes scanning Teddy's face like he thought he was lying before he stood and grabbed his makeup kit. It was larger than Teddy's and several hundred dollars more expensive, and it didn't take Shiloh long to have it spread out across the bench on either side of them, taking up enough space for three people. Teddy winced as Shiloh spread primer over the bruise. No matter how gentle Shiloh tried to be, it stung like a motherfucker.

"Sorry," Shiloh mumbled, his lip caught between his teeth as he started dabbing concealer over the marks. At least by the time he got to foundation, Teddy's skin was so on fire that it hardly made a difference. "Are we just hiding them or do you want a full face?"

Teddy thought of Ian waiting somewhere behind the bar and hesitated. He wanted to look pretty for Ian, but he didn't want his love of makeup to run off someone who had already become one of the most important people in his life. He straightened his spine, tensing his jaw. Ian had never complained about his makeup or the way he dressed, and if he tried to start now, then he didn't deserve Teddy anyway.

"Full face," Teddy answered with confidence.

Shiloh grinned and Teddy closed his eyes, letting him paint his face. They sat in comfortable silence, settling into the routine. He couldn't see, but several times Teddy heard the door open and shut as dancers came and left, as the time for their sets came up. He felt muscles he didn't know were tense relax at the feel of the makeup brush's bristles dancing their way across his eyelids or along his cheekbones, even tracing the shadows of his neck. He trusted Shiloh to use his discretion with the makeup, knowing his friend would only ever make him look his best.

The door opened again, but the voice that spoke wasn't a dancer, it was Johnny. "Jesus Christ, Teddy, you were scheduled to start hours ago, and Shiloh, your set is five minutes overdue." He sounded exasperated but Teddy didn't bother turning to look. Ian knew where he was. He could have woken him if he was worried about it, and everyone knew that Shiloh worked here for shits and giggles.

Shiloh, to his credit, was much politer in his reply to Johnny then Teddy expected. He just said, "Fuck off, duckweed," and went back to applying a sheen of lip gloss to Teddy's lips.

"Watch your mouth or I'll dock you," Johnny snapped.

Shiloh probably rolled his eyes, but then there was the distinct sound of a door shutting as Johnny left.

"Okay, all done," Shiloh said, and Teddy heard the cap twist back onto the lip gloss. "Now, tell me you're not wearing that."

Teddy opened his eyes and glanced down at the baggy sweatpants and T-shirt combo. "I was going for shabby-chic."

"You tripped into full-on guttersnipe, babe." Shiloh said, voice caught between apology and playful teasing. "Here... I have an extra pair of shorts you can borrow." Shiloh hopped up and bounded over to his locker, tugging out a pair of neon-pink silk panties that were *so* not regulation.

"Ian gave you permission for those?" Teddy asked, doubting it very much.

"I asked Johnny. He didn't answer, but that might have been because he was too busy drooling. Here... Try them on." Shiloh tossed them into Teddy's lap.

Teddy barely stopped himself in time from biting his lip and screwing up the gloss. "How much concealer you got?"

Shiloh frowned, planting his hands on his hips, fingers bracketing the piercings over his hipbones. "There more bruises you need me to work my magic on?"

Teddy shrugged, his gaze drifting downward. He tugged off the shirt, then hesitated before dropping trou. He wasn't embarrassed to be nude in front of Shiloh. They'd both seen each other naked too many times to count, and both of them had agreed years ago that they weren't each other's type.

"Damn, Teddy," Shiloh breathed, stepping closer. "Whose ass do I need to kick?"

Teddy would have laughed at the thought of Shiloh kicking anyone's ass if he didn't sound so serious. And when Teddy looked at him, a frisson of fear jolted down his spine. Shiloh was short and slender, but with the pissed look on his face and his clenched fists, Teddy actually believed Shiloh could do some damage if he wanted to.

"No one's." Teddy mumbled. "I got myself into a bit of a pickle with some people I owe money to." He grabbed the pink panties and tugged them on to give him something to do besides see the judgement that surely was on Shiloh's face.

"People you... Damn it, Teddy, what did you do?"

Teddy glanced up and glared at Shiloh. "I'm not going to tell you if you start acting like a bitch about it."

Shiloh glared back, crossing his arms. "A bank would repossess your car, or...house or whatever, and since I know you don't have either, you clearly didn't take a loan out from the bank. Who the hell do you owe money to?"

When Teddy opened his mouth, he planned on lying, spinning a tale about losing money at the horse races or some shit. Instead, maybe because he was tired of keeping the secret, maybe because he wanted someone to tell him what to do...maybe just because it was Shiloh, the truth spilled out in all its ugliness. When he finished, Shiloh looked stunned—and not in the good way, the 'oh-my-God, what a nice surprise' way.

In the 'I don't know whether to yell at you for being so stupid or wrap you up in bubble-wrap because you're clearly incapable of making good decisions' way.

"Oh, Teddy." Shiloh stepped forward. Teddy flinched, certain Shiloh was about to cuff him over the head like an errant child, but instead, Shiloh tugged him into a tight embrace. Teddy returned it, letting his head drop onto Shiloh's shoulder for a second, like it could fix everything. "I'll get you the money you need. It'll take me a few days, but I can make it work, and—" Shiloh rambled.

Teddy shook his head and pulled back. "It's my debt, and I'll pay it. I'm not taking your money."

"Don't be an idiot. Of course you are. I'm not going to just sit here on my pert little ass while you get yours beat over something as stupid as money." Shiloh's face darkened for a second. "It's not like I'll need it much longer."

"What the hell do you mean, you won't need it much longer?" Teddy reached out and grabbed Shiloh's arm in a tight grip, fear stirring in his chest. He knew Shiloh took risks—did reckless things like go home with strangers and self-medicate, but that sounded too final.

"Relax. I don't mean it like *that*. Just that I'm halfway through my plan to finally get out from under Dad's thumb." Shiloh shrugged free from his grip. "I'd rather put some of my trust fund to use before I lose it. I'll tell Dad I crashed my car and need a new one or some shit."

"Then donate it to the Drop-In Center, or...or the Red Cross or something. I'm not taking your money." Teddy shook his head. His debt was over two hundred thousand dollars and counting. Not exactly pocket change.

"Teddy," Shiloh started, his eyes sharpening.

"Don't 'Daddy' me, you're not good at it," Teddy said, hoping that joking would make Shiloh drop it.

Shiloh rolled his eyes. "Better at it than you, brat. Take the money."

"Suck a dick," Teddy shoved at Shiloh's shoulder and rolled his eyes. "Not taking your money."

Shiloh's lips pursed in his signature pout. "You're my best friend. Let me help you."

Teddy narrowed his eyes and considered for a second. "I'll let you help me when you let me help you."

"I don't need help," Shiloh immediately replied, arms crossing defensively.

"You show up with worse bruises than mine on a regular basis." Teddy stepped toward Shiloh, but his friend jerked back, out of reach. "Is it your dad? I'll go with you to the police station. You don't have to do it al—"

"You don't know what you're talking about. My dad would never hurt me. Fuck," Shiloh cursed, turning around and lacing his fingers on his head, drawing a breath in so ragged that Teddy could hear it. He spun around a second later, his expression angry, "Money's about the only useful thing I have going for me. Why won't you let me help you?"

"Because I'm not going to be just another asshole who uses you. I'm not going to let you throw money at me and end up hating me like everyone else." Teddy narrowed his eyes and changed the subject back to the one he thought was the most important. "If it's not your dad, then who is it? Do you have a boyfriend I don't know about, or…or is it one of your professors?" He struggled to think of who would have had access to Shiloh over the years. It had to be someone close since Shiloh seemed adamant to protect them.

"Just drop it, okay? You can't help me. No one can help me, okay?" Shiloh's voice was devoid of hope, so filled with resignation that Teddy's heart cracked. "I just… Let me fix this one thing, okay?"

"I can't," Teddy whispered. "I'm not taking advantage of you."

"Damn it, Teddy!" Shiloh cursed, brushing his hands through his hair until it was a wild pink halo around his face.

The door opened before they could speak again. "Guys, you—" Johnny started to scold them.

"Shut up!" Teddy and Shiloh both snapped together, shooting twin daggers.

Johnny glanced between them then slowly backed out of the room and shut the door. Teddy watched, astonished. "Really? That's all it took?"

Shiloh held on to his glare for several more seconds before he snickered, subject dropped and tension dying.

Chapter Twenty-Five

Ian's eyes drifted to the ceiling for what had to be the sixth time since his shift had started. Well, Teddy's shift, that Ian was covering. He could have explained that to Johnny, but a small, jealous part of him enjoyed watching the man storm around behind the bar in what could only be described as a tantrum.

Ian's phone buzzed in his pocket. He finished pouring the last few drinks before he pulled it out and glanced at the screen.

It was a text message from a blocked number. He thumbed it open.

Storm on the radar.

Four words.

Ian frowned, tightening his hand on the cellphone. It was a code he and Tennyson had agreed on before he'd flown back to Austin, one of several. It meant that trouble was brewing in the ranks of the cartel and a warning to be on guard.

Ian slid the phone back into his pocket and wiped at the bar. Tennyson had a few leads to follow up on, and Ian had made several not-so-subtle comments over the past few weeks, dropping money into less-than-clean hands. This was always the hard part—the waiting, the days and weeks before he made first contact. He had learned patience over the years, but had never learned to like it.

If things went to shit before he even managed to get an in with the cartel, that would be months of research down the drain. Hundreds of thousands of dollars wasted…and that wasn't even taking into account the personal reasons he couldn't afford to fail.

He would have to work harder.

"About damn time you got here," Johnny snarled.

Ian looked up to see Teddy, still barefoot, bandages peeking out from his soles, circling the bar. He wore the baggy shirt Ian had left out for him. The collar gaped, sliding off his shoulder, and the hem was long enough that Ian caught only peeks of pink panties beneath it. There was something alluring about the faux innocence, something that made Ian want to slide his hands beneath the shirt and trace over the panty lines. The bruises on Teddy's face were gone, hidden by makeup like they'd never existed, and a hesitant smile wavered on Teddy's lips when his eyes caught Ian's, like he wasn't sure he was supposed to be here.

"I had to look pretty," Teddy said, curving his lips up in a smile that was all for Ian, if the direction of his eyes was any indication.

"I'm sure the boss would rather you show up and do your job," Johnny rebutted. "And where the fuck are your shoes?"

Teddy just rolled his eyes and pushed past him, walking right up to Ian. His chin was lowered, but he looked up through the fan of his eyelashes at Ian. "Sorry, boss."

Ian chuckled and pulled off the plain black apron he always wore when he managed the bar, tossing it to Johnny. "You're in charge." Then, he lifted an eyebrow to Teddy and lowered his voice. "You can finish your shift here, if you'd like, or we can go back to your apartment and pick up whatever you need for a few days." He hesitated. "If you still want to stay."

"I want to stay," Teddy replied, cheeks pinking. He cleared his throat, "I mean, I want to go get my stuff so I can stay. Not I want to stay and finish my shift because I don't want to stay."

"I know what you mean," Ian said, his grin widening.

"Oh good, because now I'm not even sure what I mean."

Ian brushed his fingers over Teddy's as he passed. "Coming?"

Teddy groaned. "I will be."

Ian laughed. "Come on, brat."

Teddy huffed, "You're the second person to call me that today." He jutted out his bottom lip in a pout and his eyes skirted to the dance floor. Ian followed his gaze to the podium that Shiloh was dancing on.

If what he was doing could be considered dancing... Sometimes, the pink-haired man moved with a grace too perfect to be real, his body sinuous and untouchable. At others, like tonight, he was a pistol. There was nothing graceful about the way he rutted against the floor, his ass round and on display. He was a flame, and the crowd were moths. Ian supposed he could see the draw. Maybe, if Ian had never met Teddy, he'd have bought the illusion. But, while Shiloh was a flame, Teddy was the sun.

"Are you sure he was talking to you and not the mirror?" Ian teased after a second, lifting an eyebrow and glancing back at Teddy.

Teddy laughed and lifted a shoulder. "With Shiloh, you can never tell."

Ian started walking, the logo on the arm of his shirt meaning most eyes, when they landed on him, almost glazed over and ignored him. They might scan his body in appreciation, but it hadn't taken long for the customers to learn that the employees were off limits.

The eyes lingered longer on Teddy, though he wore the same logo, but Ian could hardly blame them. Teddy walked in front of him and Ian couldn't help but groan at the peek of pale skin flirting in and out of sight. The shirt fluttered with each step, revealing the pert, cheeky globes of his ass straining against the pink satin.

They made it nearly to the back entrance before he noticed Teddy stiffen, his hands clenching into fists at his sides.

"Something wrong?" Ian asked, immediately on alert. He scanned the empty hallway for signs of a threat but came up empty.

"Just...Um, can you go first?" Teddy's voice was small, tinged with embarrassment.

"Yeah. Of course." Ian slipped around him and pushed open the door, scanning the alley and lot. It was empty.

He held the door open for Teddy, then led him over to his truck.

"I can't believe you kept her," Teddy murmured, running his hand over the faded maroon paint of the passenger door, a slightly darker color than the rest of the vehicle.

"You thought I'd trade in Sally?" Ian asked, peering over the hood with an arched eyebrow. "This old girl's been with me since Papa dinged the bumper and Mama banned him from driving."

Teddy shrugged. "I don't know. I guess I thought when you left that you cut ties with everything." He traced a ding along the passenger door, vaguely remembering a conversation he'd had with Lucas. His friend had been terrified Ian would notice. Lucas had ridden his bike too close on the driveway, after Ian warned him a half-dozen times to be careful. "I'm just glad you didn't leave everything behind."

"Not everything," Ian agreed, and there was something in his voice, some double meaning that Teddy couldn't quite grasp. He glanced up, and the longing he saw on Ian's face sent a shiver down his spine. "I never quite managed to leave you in Austin. I ran for months, and every time I stopped, the memories caught right back up." One side of Ian's lips quirked up. "I have to say, though, that the memories don't do you justice."

Teddy flushed and climbed into the passenger seat rather than answer. He wasn't sure what to say. Should he be happy that Ian had thought about him? Angry that Ian had left? Something in between?

Ian climbed in as well and started the car. He didn't back out of the lot, though. Instead, he rested an arm on the back of the seat and twisted, staring at Teddy intently. "How come you never went to college, Teddy? I thought you wanted to be an architect?"

Ian had asked before and Teddy hadn't answered. Teddy bit his lip and averted his eyes, staring out of the passenger window with seeing, without speaking, until finally, he sighed. "I could never make tuition. I keep telling myself I'll start next semester. But then something comes up, and...it just hasn't happened yet." Teddy shrugged like it didn't matter, even though each time he pushed his dream back, it died a little.

He was a twenty-two-year-old bartender, and sometimes dishwasher, and part-time cleaner. He didn't know how to fit full-time student into his job description.

"It will. It has to. You're so smart, Teddy. It'll happen," Ian said, but Teddy couldn't help but feel like he was being placated—like Ian thought there was something wrong with Teddy's decision but didn't want to say it.

"I'm not ashamed of my choices," Teddy said abruptly, glancing at Ian out of the corner of his eye.

Ian blinked. "Of course not. There's nothing to be ashamed of. You're a hard worker."

"I'm doing the best I can," Teddy added, determined that Ian understood that.

"I know." Ian finally turned away, putting the car in gear and starting the crawl down the alley and out onto the street. "I'm sorry. I wasn't trying to come across like I was judging you or anything. I just know how much being an architect meant to you. I thought maybe something had changed."

"No," Teddy answered. "Nothing's changed."

The drive to the apartment was quiet but not uncomfortable. Teddy swung his feet in time to the music and Ian tapped his thumb on the steering wheel. It didn't take long to make the trip across town.

Teddy didn't have a designated parking space at his apartment complex. There was a small lot across the street, but it was first come, first served. Normally, that wasn't a big deal, since Teddy didn't drive and Shiloh parked his car wherever he felt like, legal or not. Tonight, it was a monster of a deal, since it was late enough that anyone coming or going had pretty much already done so, and Ian had to circle the lot twice before he found a spot barely big enough to wedge the truck in, between a SUV and a coup that straddled the line. Teddy barely resisted the urge to open his door harder than necessary and hit the double parker in the paint job.

He didn't do it, but only because Ian was watching, waiting for him to inch the door open and slide through the narrow gap down onto the pavement. Teddy's shirt caught the seat and rode up, and he didn't miss the flash of heat that crossed Ian's face.

"My apartment's a piece of shit, but I have a nice mattress. If you want to test it out..." Teddy said, making sure to sway his hips flirtatiously as he moved up to Ian's side.

"Maybe I will. I've been thinking of going mattress hunting," Ian answered, sounding almost serious.

"Noooo," Teddy whined and grabbed Ian's hand, playfully tugging it, "I love your mattress. It's the size of Taiwan!"

"I think the people of Taiwan would beg to differ," Ian replied dryly but didn't pull his hand away.

Teddy bumped Ian's arm with his shoulder. "I think they would also be sad if you hunted your mattress."

"Dork." Ian rolled his eyes, then reached across to ruffle Teddy's hair. They bantered back and forth as they entered the complex. Ian started for the elevator but Teddy stopped walking abruptly.

The elevator, he knew, was narrow, hardly large enough for him and his shopping if there was another resident already waiting. With Ian's broad shoulders, it would be a tight squeeze. Teddy might enjoy being pressed tight to Ian's body, but he feared it would feel too much like the box.

"Can we take the stairs?" Teddy asked in a rush, embarrassed, like the simple request was going to make Ian think less of him.

Ian tightened his grip on Teddy's hand instead. "Oh, great, I hate elevators. Rickety little things just as likely to get stuck as make it anywhere." Teddy's shoulders sagged in relief, and they turned to the stairs instead.

The stairway was wide and cold with cement steps and a metal railing that Teddy knew better than to trust with his weight, even if he'd only previously taken the stairs when the elevator was under maintenance or he was running too late to wait for it. They walked up side by side.

Each contact sent a tingle along Teddy's skin, and more than once he lifted his eyes to see a matching fire in Ian's. He had the sudden urge to draw Ian into the shadowy nook behind the door of the second landing or kneel on the steps between it and the third. Unfortunately, Teddy wasn't looking to spend a night in the county jail if he was caught, so he just sighed and sent a rueful look at the shadowed landing instead.

Ian groaned, and Teddy looked up to find him watching him, eyes dark. Teddy smirked and tugged open the door that led out to the third floor. Ian trailed along behind him. Out of habit, Teddy ran his fingers over the lush green leaves of the potted fern beside his apartment. It had been withered and dying when he'd moved in, but he'd taken it under his wing and nurtured it back to life.

The plant distracted him from the bright orange paper adhered to his front door.

Evicted.

Well, shit.

Chapter Twenty-Six

Ian read the notice over Teddy's shoulder. *Evicted, due to non-payment*. Teddy could see the super on Monday if he wanted to retrieve his things. What did they expect Teddy to do until then? Ian was grateful that he'd brought Teddy himself. He knew Teddy well enough to know that if he wasn't there, the boy would have buried his head and slept in a cardboard box somewhere before admitting he was in trouble. His suspicion was confirmed when Teddy spun around and nudged Ian farther down the hall, like he thought there was a possibility Ian had somehow missed it.

"Um, I'll just…go in and…You don't have to stay," Teddy stumbled for an excuse. Ian crossed his arms, not afraid to use his intimidation skills for good for once. Teddy wilted under the expression. "Okay, so…I guess you read the notice."

"You're staying with me." He could have made it a suggestion or a question, but he was well past that now. He wasn't going to let Teddy check into some pay-by-the-hour motel and waste his money rooming with scorpions, bedbugs and any manner of disgusting diseases.

Teddy was quiet for a second. Ian wondered what was going through his mind. He knew there was a difference between staying with someone by choice — knowing there was a place to go if things ended poorly — and being homeless, subsisting on charity. Not that Ian saw it as charity, but Teddy would.

Ian backed Teddy against the door, bracketing him with his arms. "I want you to stay with me. I'll sleep on the couch, if you feel more comfortable with that, but I want you in my bed. I want to dress you up for work, and cook you dinner." He didn't say the rest, that if Teddy was staying with him, Ian could keep him safe from whoever had marked him up, because he didn't want to lie. Maybe Teddy would be safer from one problem, but Ian couldn't squash the reminder that he would be putting him at risk from another.

Teddy shifted onto tiptoes and brushed his lips over Ian's, then whispered, "Careful, or I might think you like me."

"Whatever gave you that idea?" Ian nipped Teddy's plump lower lip.

"Well, I hate to disappoint you, but you can't dress me up until Monday. I don't have any clothes."

"You'll have to run around naked then," Ian teased. His hands dropped off the wall, sliding down Teddy's spine to cup his ass. He tugged Teddy closer, their bodies joined from shoulder to hip.

"I'll get cold. You'll have to warm me up." Teddy's voice was breathy.

A door opened down the hallway and Ian reluctantly pulled away. "Come on. There's no point standing here…getting *cold*." He smirked and held out his hand. Teddy took it, and together they walked back downstairs and across the street to the lot. Ian opened the passenger door for Teddy, but when Teddy went to climb up, Ian lifted him sideways onto the seat, his feet dangling.

A small squeak slid from Teddy's lips at the show of strength. That, or at the sight of Ian's muscles bulging. Ian slid into the space between Teddy's thighs, until his knees hit the leather. He would never make Teddy wander around his apartment naked, not even if the thought of it made Ian ache. But he could still tease him about it.

"Do you want to be my good little houseboy?" Ian asked, testing the water. His eyes locked on Teddy's for his reaction. Negative, and he would step back, laugh it off. Instead, he saw the way Teddy's pupils blew wider, heard the slight indrawn breath. Teddy flicked his tongue over his lip, so Ian pressed on. "Stay with me, be ready whenever I want to play with you?"

"Please, Ian…" Teddy shifted on the seat. Ian's gaze drifted down, his lips curving wickedly at the small tent forming beneath the baggy shirt.

"What do you want, Teddy? Do you want me to take you home and lay you out on my bed? Let me lavish you in praise?" Ian dropped his hands to Teddy's thighs, holding them open around him. "Be my good boy?"

Teddy moaned, his muscles jumping under Ian's palms as his hips flexed. The reaction was strong enough to confirm a suspicion Ian had been harboring for a while, a suspicion that Teddy wanted someone to take control for a bit.

Then Teddy confirmed it out loud. "Yes, that. I want that."

"Or" — Ian slid his hands farther, circling his thumbs over the pale, sensitive flesh of Teddy's inner thighs — "do you want me to take these pretty panties off you right here and be bad for a while?"

"Shit, Ian," Teddy cursed, his back bowing with a shudder. "You've got a dirty mouth."

"I can make it dirtier," Ian teased, pushing his hands over Teddy's hips. Teddy whimpered when Ian bypassed his erection to grip the hem of the shirt and shove it upward. "Lieback."

Teddy collapsed immediately, sprawling on the leather seats. Ian suddenly wished he'd splurged on a personal phone, rather than assuming he wouldn't need it. He wanted to snap a picture — capture the elegant line of Teddy's arm where it stretched above him, gripping the edge of the seat, the taut flex of his small waist. Instead, he let the shirt drop high on Teddy's chest and trailed his fingers downward.

Teddy either was naturally hairless or kept up on his waxing because the skin was smooth under his fingers, a contrast to his own. Ian flicked one rosy nipple, watching as it hardened into a tight bud, then the other. He lovingly ran his fingers over the barely noticeable scars, leaning down to drop a kiss along the silver line, then let his hands trail down Teddy's body. He wanted to learn Teddy's body, spend hours playing him like a finely tuned instrument, but there wasn't time, not out in the open.

It was late and the dark lot was devoid of lights, but that didn't lessen the thrill. This wasn't like Ian. He'd had hookups over the past few years, he wasn't a saint, but they'd been quick and simple — a few minutes spent in a club bathroom, the occasional lift back to their place. It was rare that he played with the same man more than once, and only with a strict understanding that it wasn't going to go anywhere. He'd always planned on moving back to Texas, and he knew none of the glittering, exuberant men he was attracted to would ever consider following him.

Texas had a reputation for being a hotspot for conservative homophobia that it more than lived up to, even if Austin was surprisingly liberal.

Besides, the risk to his job was never worth the short-lived satisfaction of caving to his exhibitionist tendencies. He thought he'd left them behind, consigned them to the follies of his youth, but now, with Teddy, he couldn't stop. He didn't care if anyone saw them. He wanted to show Teddy off, to show the world that he belonged to him.

Ian toyed with the band of the pink panties and looked up to meet Teddy's eyes. "Do you want to be naughty with me?"

"Yes," Teddy's answer wavered between a sigh and a moan.

"Yes what?" Ian asked. Maybe he was punishing himself, curious to see what Teddy would call him. There was no way Teddy would call him what he wanted... What he needed, if he were honest with himself.

Teddy froze, meeting his eyes. He seemed to hold his breath, his cheeks pinking. "Yes...*Daddy*?"

All the blood left Teddy's head to flood down into his throbbing, pulsing dick. He was harder than he'd ever been in his life, and saying the words — the words he'd only ever thought of saying for real in his deepest, most secret fantasies — felt unreal, like he was going to wake up any second in his shitty apartment and realize that the last twelve hours had been a dream to make up for the nightmare before it.

But then Ian was tugging his panties over his hips, leaving them stretched, straining, across the top of his thighs in a way that felt even dirtier than being stripped of them entirely. And a second later, a hot, wet heat swallowed him down. He cried out, thrusting his hips upward to meet Ian's mouth.

Ian chuckled around him, the sound a throaty vibration that made Teddy shove his knuckles into his mouth to smother his scream of pleasure.

Ian let him slide from his mouth but didn't leave him completely wanting, wrapping his large hand around Teddy's tiny shaft, squeezing just enough to keep Teddy from softening or spilling over the edge. "Stay still, boy, or I'll have to correct you."

Teddy's hips jerked at the dirty words and Ian gave a wicked chuckle. He sealed over his mouth over Teddy's tip just as he laid a stinging *smack* on the exposed curve of his ass, where it hung over the seat. Teddy cried out, his hips jerking again, and he was rewarded with a second spanking.

Ian released him, then he laid a teasing stripe with his tongue up the underside of his shaft. "Careful, boy, or I'll think you like that. Do you want a spanking?"

It was too much—the playful words, the spanking, the threat of getting caught...Teddy exploded, untouched, without warning. His cry was loud, until Ian stood to smother it with his mouth. He barely felt Ian's hands shifting his panties back into place and rearranging him on the bench until he was seated. Ian pulled away to click Teddy's seatbelt on.

"Good boy. You looked so pretty when you came," Ian murmured and Teddy believed him. He could see the straining hardness beneath Ian's jeans.

"I'd look prettier in your cum," Teddy said without thinking, but his embarrassment died before it could flourish. He was too wrapped in the warm cocoon of Ian's praise.

Ian slid his thumb through the dampness on Teddy's abs then he lifted it to Teddy's mouth. Teddy parted his lips and allowed him entry, sucking on the thumb until it was clean and Ian pulled it free.

"Did you mean it?" Teddy asked before Ian could step back and break the moment.

"That you looked pretty?" Ian asked, eyes still dark with lust.

"When you called me 'boy'. Did you mean it?" It was Teddy's most secret wish, that he could be that for someone. He'd always been the grown-up, the adult, the responsible one — the one who cleaned up after his mother, who worked three jobs, who talked his friends out of reckless ideas.

Was he asking too much to want to give that control to someone else for a while? Would it be too much for Ian?

With a kiss to Teddy's forehead, Ian laid his worries to rest.

"I meant it. I would very much love to be your daddy."

Ian drove toward the local superstore, his heart lighter than it'd been in years. He relished the gentle acceptance that had crossed Teddy's face at his promise. He knew some people found it weird, the thought of being called 'Daddy', but he didn't. Maybe because he called his father 'Papa', so 'Daddy' didn't have the same meaning.

He'd never trusted someone enough to admit that his toppy tendencies stretched further than the bedroom.

He'd known since high school that he was attracted to men who were smaller than him. He been afraid at first that it was some twisted way of compensating for his sexuality—that he was gay, but he wasn't one of *those* gays. He'd hated himself for a while, until he'd realized that he wasn't compensating at all.

He needed to be bigger than his lovers because it made him feel strong, like he could protect them. It had taken him falling down the porn rabbit hole to realize how far that need actually went. He was a Daddy, and he wanted a boy to take care of.

Not *a* boy. He wanted Teddy. In one way or another, it had always been Teddy.

Of course, he wasn't a full-time Daddy, not exactly. He wasn't looking for a domestic discipline relationship. He didn't necessarily want to set up a list of chores or plan Teddy's schedule for the week. He wanted to take care of him, to make him breakfast in the morning, to buy him pretty clothes, to run him a bath when he was stressed or tired.

"Where are we going?" Teddy said a few minutes later as they passed the turn-off that led back to Envy.

"To get you some clothes." Ian glanced over at Teddy for a second, just long enough to find Teddy's hand and reach for it, then turned his eyes back to the road. "And whatever else you need to get you through the weekend."

Teddy's hand twitched in his. Ian couldn't tell in the darkness of the truck cab, but when he glanced over, it almost looked like Teddy was blushing. "I don't have any money. I can just borrow your sweatpants—"

"I want to do this for you. Are you going to be a good boy and let me?" Ian asked, testing the waters. Was he moving too fast? Pressing too hard?

"I..." Teddy's hand tightened on his, "Okay. But I'll pay you back."

Ian pulled the car into the parking lot and turned off the ignition before shifting in his seat to face Teddy. "I don't want you to pay me back, boy. Let me do this for you."

Teddy's cheeks darkened further and he dropped his eyes, but unless Ian was misreading him, he didn't look upset. He looked... Ian's gaze skimmed down to the obvious bulge between Teddy's thighs and he smirked.

"Okay," Teddy whispered.

"Okay, what?" Ian asked, confident now that Teddy wasn't opposed to him taking charge.

"Okay, Ian?" Teddy's voice lifted high on the end but his lips quirked up.

Ian playfully swatted the boy's thigh. "Is that what you want to call me?"

"I don't know. Do you want me to call you something else?"

"Well, a boy who's good for his daddy gets rewarded," Ian suggested.

"I can be a good boy, Daddy," Teddy promised, his eyes hooded with lust.

Chapter Twenty-Seven

It was after midnight when Ian finally agreed that they had more than enough stuff to get Teddy through until he could get into his apartment. Teddy's argument that they'd already picked up more than he'd owned in the first place had fallen on deaf ears. Teddy's arms were laden down by bags, not even counting what Ian was carrying himself, and Ian was still mumbling that he hadn't found everything he was looking for. Teddy was torn between rolling his eyes and blushing at the sweetness.

Ian put the bags he was carrying into the truck then waited while Teddy added his. "We'll go to Knickers for Nick soon," Ian said, once the back bench was full.

Teddy sucked in a breath, his voice coming out in an embarrassing squeak. "What? Really? Are you serious?" He'd heard of the new boutique, of course, but had never had the courage — or the money — to go inside. The few times he'd had to buy new panties, either for himself or for the club, he'd ordered them online. It wasn't horrible, and most of the time he got what he wanted, but the sizing could be tricky — even more so when he wore his packer.

Ian frowned, clearly confused. "Why wouldn't I be? I'm sure as hell not going to make you wear anything from in there." He jabbed his thumb back toward the store.

Teddy flushed. He'd assumed they'd avoided the lingerie section because Ian was embarrassed to be seen there with him. It was one thing to put up with him wearing panties or even to enjoy it in private, and a whole different matter to purchase it in public. Shame bit at his chest. He should have known Ian wasn't like that.

"I mean, their stuff isn't horrible," Teddy mumbled, dropping his gaze to his feet, now clad in a pair of pink Converse rather than the too-large sandals he'd borrowed from Ian earlier.

"No, but it's made for women. You deserve to have something made for *you*." Ian reached up and tucked a strand of Teddy's hair behind his ear, lingering on his skin for longer than necessary. "Ready to go home?"

Teddy nodded. He was ready. Beyond ready. "Let's go home."

The drive back to Envy seemed endless, but finally, Ian pulled Sally into the parking lot and shut off the ignition. Teddy couldn't help nervously glancing around the lot before climbing out, but all the cars were ones he recognized. It was nearly closing, so only the staff's vehicles remained. Customers had to park across the street.

Between him and Ian, they grabbed the bags and carted them through the service door and up the stairs to Ian's apartment, after only a brief pause to unlock the door then re-lock it behind them. Teddy expected Ian to drop the bags on the couch, but instead, he carted them directly into his bedroom.

"Hang on a second and I'll clear you out a few drawers." Ian immediately started emptying the top two drawers of his dresser without waiting for a response, which was a good thing, because Teddy stood there for several seconds in stunned silence.

He'd never had anyone willing to clean out a drawer for him. Even in the few relationships he'd considered his 'best' — the ones that had lasted longer than a few weeks — none of his things had ended up anywhere but the floor. Watching Ian carefully fold and tuck away his clothing, not seeming to care whether it was the masc gray button-down or the femme blue blouse, sent his heart fluttering around his chest like a hummingbird.

He didn't deserve this man.

Ian pushed the last drawer shut then folded up the reusable bags, tucking them into the bottom of his closet before brushing his hands over his pants, almost like he was cleaning them of dust. "There, all done." Ian glanced toward Teddy, a soft smile on his face that faded after a second to concern. "What's wrong?"

"Nothing. Absolutely nothing," Teddy replied, then walked over to stand in front of Ian, close enough that he could see the scattering of freckles, barely visible on Ian's terra cotta skin and feel Ian's breath on his lips.

"You're staring at me," Ian murmured.

"Do you want me to stop?"

"Never," Ian groaned and bent down, sealing his mouth over Teddy's. Electricity danced between them, sparking against his tongue, a live wire coiling around their bodies. If it fused them together, Teddy wouldn't mind.

But unfortunately, Ian broke away with a groan when his phone buzzed. Teddy felt it against his hip. Ian slipped his hand between them to pry it free of his pocket. He glanced at the screen, his mouth tightening in a frown. "I'm sorry. I have to take this."

Teddy nodded, stepping back to catch his breath. Ian dropped a peck onto his lips then lifted the phone to his ear. "This is Ian."

Ian slipped out of the bedroom, heading deeper into the apartment. His voice grew quieter until Teddy couldn't hear it. Teddy released a stuttering breath and flopped backward onto the bed. He ground the heels of his hands into his eyes. *Am I really doing this?*

Fucking was one thing. He was good at it. He had lots of practice. He frowned and corrected himself. It wasn't that he'd had a lot of sex, just…the sex he'd had was always meaningless in the end. He was beginning to believe that was all he was good for. In the end, he was always too much.

In the four years since his surgery, he'd had a handful of relationships. There had been Nathan, who'd said he was 'too queer', Victor, who'd said he was 'too boring' because he worked too much to be any fun and, of course, there had been Johnny, who'd said he was 'too femme'.

He was always too something-or-other.

Ian, though… Ian looked at him like he meant something, and there was very little about Teddy that Ian didn't already know. Only one thing, in fact, that Teddy could think of.

It was, unfortunately, the one thing he didn't think Ian would be able to look past.

Teddy shivered and curled up in the center of the bed, dragging the blankets up and around himself to chase away the chill. He was going to have to tell Ian everything. He wanted to wait, to figure it out on his own, but Ian deserved honesty. Even if it meant that Ian was going to kick him out after. Even if it cost him his job at Envy.

He didn't know how Ian would react to the news that Teddy was growing steadily more in debt to the same cartel that was responsible for his brother's death. His breath caught in his throat. He'd never thought of it that way, but...was he *funding* the cartel? He'd always thought of it in terms of paying off a debt. A bad debt, a shitty loan, but...if he was funding them, did that make him responsible for the shit they got into?

Teddy tugged the blanket over his head, tears burning his eyes. How many other people had lost their brothers or best friends because of the cartel? He was so worried about what Ian would think of him, but now, he wasn't sure he could even look himself in the mirror.

He was a horrible person and he deserved to die alone.

He reached his hand out from under the blanket, fumbling around on the nightstand for his phone. He dragged it under the covers and hit speed dial.

"Shiloh?"

* * * *

Teddy hadn't visited Shiloh at the estate in over a year, but it still looked the same—the same wrought-iron fence, the same carefully trimmed grass, the same gilded door. And a good thing for Teddy, the same easy-to-climb trellis next to Shiloh's bedroom window.

He slipped inside easily, unnoticed by anyone but Shiloh.

Shiloh was waiting for him on his bed, lying sideways with his feet kicked up on the wall. He tipped his head back to stare at Teddy upside down. The column of his throat was long and slender but blighted by the darkness of bruises shaped like fingerprints.

"What happened?" Teddy instantly asked, rushing over, though he knew better than to touch. He didn't need to, since Shiloh clearly knew what he was asking about. He immediately tugged up the collar of his shirt with a frown.

"Trick got carried away. That's all," Shiloh shrugged like it didn't matter. Teddy still couldn't make the dual images of Shiloh fit together. The spoiled rich kid with a fancy car and expensive clothes just didn't meld with the one Teddy saw too often—the bitter, oft-bruised young man who sold his ass and throat for cash. But whenever Teddy asked why, Shiloh just shrugged the question off and answered, "Why not?"

There had to be more to the story. Teddy knew that Shiloh liked sex, but he couldn't believe that his friend would turn to prostitution for the thrill. But it couldn't be for money, either, since the jeans Shiloh wore cost more than a month's rent. It was like putting together a puzzle upside down but missing half the pieces.

"Stop worrying," Shiloh snapped. "I can see you thinking, you know, and you're not here to talk about me, so spill."

Teddy slumped down on the mattress and sighed. "I slept with Ian." It wasn't what he'd meant to say, but apparently his mouth bypassed his brain.

Shiloh's brows lifted and he rolled onto his stomach. "All the details. Spill. Now. How was it? Are you going to do it again?"

"That's not…" Teddy flushed. "It was good — better than good. Amazing, but…that's not the issue. I want to do it again. I just… There's something I haven't told him and when I do, he's going to hate me."

"Nobody could hate you." Shiloh rolled his eyes. "You're a teddy bear." Shiloh snickered, "Literally. Everyone just wants to grab you and squeeze you and pinch your cheeks. You're such a boy that it's not even funny."

"Of course I'm a boy. I paid a lot of money to be a boy." Teddy scowled. Being squeezable was not exactly a masculine trait, not in his mind.

"Not a boy, a *Boy*. You know…" Shiloh wagged his brows. "Like…be a *good boy* for Daddy? Come on, Teddy, I put it together ages ago."

Teddy's cheeks went hot and he groaned, burying his head into the covers. "You don't have to make it sound so…so *dirty*."

"It is *dirty*, but that doesn't mean it's bad. Honestly, I'm proud of you for being brave enough to go after what you want. You could have buried your head in the sand and kept having boring vanilla sex forever. There's nothing wrong with wanting someone to take care of you." Shiloh's voice sounded so wistful that Teddy couldn't help but lift his head to peek at him. There was a yearning so obvious in every line and plane of Shiloh's face that Teddy wondered how he'd missed it for years. He'd always seen Shiloh as carefree and energetic, too buoyed by an inner fire to ever be tied down by anything. The look on his face, though, made Teddy reevaluate his friend's desire.

"Do you... Is that something you want? Someday?" Teddy asked hesitantly.

Shiloh's face closed down. "No. Of course not." Teddy flinched at the harshness of his friend's voice and Shiloh immediately softened it, reaching out to squeeze Teddy's shoulder, "Not because it's wrong, or...or because you have something to be ashamed of, just... Who would want a boy like me anyway? I'm a brat who fucks anything that moves. Not exactly *good boy* material." Shiloh must have seen Teddy open his mouth to argue because he rushed onward, dropping his gaze from Teddy's. "But you are. Ian would be lucky to claim you. I'm sure whatever you have to tell him, he'll get past it. What did you do that's so bad, anyway?"

Teddy's palms grew clammy and his skin chilled. "I... You remember Ian's brother, Lucas?"

"The one who killed himself?" Shiloh said after a few moments' thought.

"He didn't kill himself," Teddy admitted, clenching the Egyptian cotton sheets. "He got involved with a cartel and they shot him."

"Oh, shit," Shiloh breathed.

"And...and I've been giving the cartel over ten thousand dollars a year for the past four years..." Teddy said the last on a whisper.

* * * *

It was nearing dawn when Teddy finally crept down the trellis and back out onto the streets. The walk to the bus stop passed in a blur. After he'd explained everything to Shiloh, his face had crumpled and they'd curled around each other, both pretending they weren't crying, for nearly an hour. Teddy was crying because he was ashamed — ashamed that he'd been stupid enough to take the loan in the first place, that he'd never gone to the police after Lucas' death, that he'd kept the secret from his best friend for so long.

Then he was crying because Shiloh had finally confessed his own secret. Teddy had always assumed that Shiloh had money. He drove a new Bugatti, wore designer clothing, bought makeup and lingerie on a whim. But apparently, the expensive car was in his father's name, the designer clothing bought by his father's secretary, the makeup and lingerie swiped on a card carefully monitored by his father's accountant.

Shiloh had no money of his own because his father insisted he didn't need it. After all, he didn't pay rent on an apartment because his father said he was too immature to be trusted not to use it for parties or drugs. He didn't have to pay for his tuition because his father would pay for college, as long as he went for business management. He had an allowance, but it was tied to a debit card that wouldn't allow cash withdrawals, so every purchase he made, whether for shoes or condoms or a gas station cappuccino, was critiqued and criticized during his monthly sit-down with his father and the accountant. And Shiloh's trust fund was untouchable until he was thirty.

Shiloh had finally, after they'd sat in silence for several long minutes, whispered the secret that broke Teddy's heart. He sold his body because it was the only job he could get that his father wouldn't find out about. Apparently, he'd tried teaching a dance class and his father had sent one of his goons — aka bodyguards — to drag him out in front of everyone. He didn't even get paid for dancing at Envy, since he couldn't put his social security number on the application without his dad finding out, so the only money he pocketed was from tips.

Teddy didn't know how to help his friend — and that killed him.

"A fine pair we both make, huh," Teddy had finally said before he left. Shiloh's eyes were red and puffy, like Teddy's probably were as well, but he'd laughed.

The bus dropped Teddy off a few blocks from Envy, though he barely remembered getting on, and too soon, Teddy was standing outside the locked stairway door. He still hadn't come up with the words he needed. He fiddled with his phone, tapping out a message and hovering over the send button several times before deleting it. Finally, he sucked up the threads of his courage and sent it before he could stop himself.

Downstairs, let me in? We need to talk.

Be there ASAP.

There was a brief pause, then his phone buzzed again.

Don't leave.

It was only a few moments longer when he heard the lock tumble and the door was pulled open, revealing a very concerned-looking Ian, who tugged him into the stairwell and re-locked the door. Then Ian was pressing forward, crowding Teddy against the wall while his hands skimmed over his skin like he was searching for injuries.

"Are you okay? Where did you go, baby?" Ian asked, his voice gentle when he should have been angry, should have been yelling at Teddy for leaving without telling him.

"I…" Teddy closed his eyes, breath catching until he cleared his throat. "There's something I have to talk to you about and you're not going to like it. I…I got scared. I went to see Shiloh. I'm sorry. I should have told you I was leaving."

"Yes, you should have," Ian answered, his voice dark, but not, Teddy realized, with anger. He stroked his thumb over Teddy's cheek. "Just because you covered them with makeup doesn't make me forget about these bruises. Someone hurt you, baby, and until I know who, I don't like the thought of you wandering around the city at night, unprotected."

Teddy hunched, dropping his chin nearly to his chest. His hair fell between them like a curtain. "You…you won't care so much when you hear what I have to tell you. I…I deserved them."

Ian gripped his shoulders tightly, though not painfully. "No, you didn't. I don't care what you think you deserve, you don't, baby. And nothing you tell me is going to make me think that, okay? Come upstairs."

A tear slid down Teddy's cheek. Ian said that now, but Teddy could still see Ian's face in his memories — the way it had twisted in disgust that morning he'd seen the person Teddy really was, the selfish, weak man who'd rather let a man fuck him than take a beating. He should have said no, then maybe everything would be different. Maybe Ian wouldn't have left, or…or maybe Teddy would have gone to the police station, battered but with his spine straight, not bowed like a coward beneath a thrusting body that

Teddy barely remembered, blurred by the effects of the drug he'd allowed himself to be given.

Or, the small, rational voice in his head that sounded too much like Ian whispered, *you'd have ended up like Lucas, swallowing a bullet.*

Teddy allowed Ian to lead him upstairs and settle him onto the couch. He protested when Ian left him, until he said he was just getting Teddy something to drink. Guilt swelled further in his chest. He didn't deserve Ian. Ian was going to hate him when he admitted what he'd been up to, and letting him take care of him now would surely only make it worse. He couldn't force himself to stop him, though.

Ian returned a few minutes later and placed a large, steaming mug in Teddy's shaking hands. The hot chocolate was dark and expensive, but small, rainbow marshmallows floated on top...Teddy's favorite. Warmth that had nothing to do with the drink curled in his chest. Ian hated them, always had, so there was no reason to have them. Teddy imagined that Ian had stocked them just in case and smiled.

"There...that's better," Ian murmured. Rather than sit on the couch beside him, like he expected, or standing over him, looming like Teddy feared, Ian sat on the sturdy coffee table in front of him. It was close enough to the couch that Ian's knees bracketed Teddy's thighs, closing him in, surrounding him. Maybe it should have made him feel trapped but it didn't.

It made him feel safe, and the thought was just enough to have him tightening his grip on the mug before setting it safely on the coffee table, just in case. Ian wouldn't hit him, no matter how mad he was. Not on purpose, anyway. But Teddy also knew that if Ian got mad, he was large enough to hurt Teddy by accident.

"The reason I got these bruises is…is because I owe the cartel a lot of money and got behind on my payments." Teddy said it before he could talk himself out of it or try and sugarcoat it.

Ian's brown eyes blazed with lightning and he went still. Even his breath seeming to freeze in his lungs. Then he leaned forward, hands bracketing Teddy's hips and digging into the couch. "I think you'd better start at the beginning."

Chapter Twenty-Eight

Ian hadn't felt this angry in years. It seemed that every time he found something good, his happiness was shattered because of that goddamn cartel. He wanted to dismantle it, tear it apart with his very hands. They'd taken his brother from him. He refused to let them lay another finger on Teddy.

"I think you'd better start at the beginning." Ian scowled, wondering how they'd managed to get their hooks on the boy in front of him. Because unlike his brother, who had always flirted too heavily with the wrong side of the law, Teddy was a good boy. Ian doubted he even jaywalked.

But Teddy flinched back from him, his pale skin growing even whiter, and Ian cursed himself for allowing his anger to color his voice. He gentled it and lifted one of his hands from where it was fisted against the leather to gently brush through Teddy's hair. "Baby, I'm not mad at you, I promise. Just tell me what happened, okay?"

Teddy sucked in a breath, as though gasping in the oxygen would give him courage, and he nervously wet his lips. "You...you remember when I came to stay with you guys for a bit? Just, um...after high school?"

"How could I forget? I had to stare at your cute little ass traipsing down the hallway to the bathroom every morning." Ian smiled, hoping it looked more honest then it felt. That had been a long few days, trying not to get caught staring at the younger man, and Ian had gotten far too acquainted with his hand in the shower.

Teddy's skin pinked, a color that looked much better on him than the ghastly whiteness of his nerves. "Did Mama R—I mean, did your mother ever tell you why?"

"You can call her Mama. She misses you." Ian knew he wasn't lying, since his mother still spoke of Teddy often. Maybe it was time for him to finally visit. Since moving back, he hadn't managed it yet, partly because he was busy with getting the club off the ground and laying the groundwork for his cover, but partly because he was afraid seeing her would bring up memories he didn't want to have. "But no, she never told me. Just said you were having some problems at home."

"Oh. Well, my mother was — *is* an alcoholic. She has been since I was a kid, and... Well, once my dad died, she lost her grip on it. She'd go through phases. Sometimes she was okay, but then she'd get worse and end up losing her job. I didn't know it, but every time she got fired, she'd dip into the money that had been set aside for me from my father's life insurance policy. It...it was the money we'd both planned on me using for my surgery."

Teddy looked down, fiddling with the hem of his shirt, and Ian's heart broke a little. He remembered watching Teddy, both before and after his physical transition, and the thought that Teddy's mother had knowingly almost prevented it from happening made him glad the woman had moved to a trailer park somewhere on the other side of the city a few years before. Otherwise, he didn't think he could stop himself from storming over and banging on her door the next time he went to visit Mama. "That must have been horrible for you."

"Yeah. I think what made it so hard was not knowing about it. I found out about it so close to my surgery date that there wasn't much I could do, you know? And I knew that backing out of the surgery until I could come up with the money again would make it look like I was having second thoughts, and...I was afraid the surgeon wouldn't do it if I waited. I was in a really bad place, and Lucas saw me crying. He...he told me about this friend of his."

Teddy trailed off, darting his gaze up to look at Ian, like he was afraid Ian would be angry that he'd brought up Lucas. And Ian was, but not in the way Teddy thought. He was angry at his brother for dragging Teddy into something that clearly neither of them had been prepared for. So Ian just schooled his face and nodded. "Go on."

"This friend, his name was Julian. He said that he'd give me the money for the surgery, and that I wouldn't have to pay it off for a while, and...it seemed like such a good deal, you know? I was never going to convince a bank to give me a loan, and it wasn't like I could come up with the money that quick, not even if I picked up another job. So I took the deal, but...then things got strange. Julian raised the payments, and Lucas kept saying that he was acting weird. Like...on edge, and that he was involved with cocaine, and...I thought I'd finally convinced Lucas to go to the cops, but the next thing I knew…"

Teddy choked on a sob and bent forward, collapsing like a rag doll against Ian's chest. "I didn't know that they would do that. I didn't mean to get him in trouble. I shouldn't have said anything—"

"No, baby, no. It wasn't your fault." Ian stroked through Teddy's hair, petting it while Teddy cried. "Lucas was in over his head. I've looked into it, you know…what happened. He was doing some really shady things and probably was already drowning before he even brought you to see Julian. It's not your fault."

That was one of the hardest things he'd had to come to terms with since investigating the cartel. In his head, his brother was a kid who didn't know better, a causality of something he didn't understand. Finding out his brother had been one of the cartel mules, helping sell drugs to the local schools, robbing convenience stores…whatever it took to keep his so-called 'friends', he'd had to come to terms with the fact that his brother wasn't a victim. Eventually, if the cartel hadn't gotten to him, the police probably would have.

Ian let Teddy cry against him until the sobs quieted, then shifted back slightly to wipe at the tears that smeared the boy's makeup. "So you owe the cartel money? For your surgery?" Teddy nodded, digging into his lip with his teeth until Ian plucked it free. "If you paid them off, would they leave you alone?"

Teddy shrugged. "I…I don't know. I owe them more money now than when I started. I think…" Teddy dropped his gaze to his wringing hands. "Julian said at the beginning that…that I could pay him off in…in a different way, and I said no, but…I keep wondering if that's why he keeps upping my payments?"

Ice formed in Ian's stomach and he barely recognized the growl that came out of his mouth as his. "No. Not happening. I promise, baby, that we'll get this figured out without resorting to that." Ian hesitated, not wanting to make Teddy angry by asking the question that circled through his mind, but knowing, both as a boyfriend and as a federal agent, that he had to. "Why didn't you go to the police, baby?"

Teddy cringed, looking away in what appeared to be shame. "After…after Lucas died, I think Julian knew I wanted to. He showed up at my apartment with one of his men, Hugo. And…and he had a gun. I thought… I thought he was going to shoot me too. But he just gave me some molly and told me to…to make a little video with his friend. For *insurance*." Teddy spat out the last word in disgust. "I didn't…I didn't want anyone seeing that. Seeing *me* like that, and…and I didn't want to get arrested for using drugs."

Ian sat back slightly, thinking for a few moments before asking, "Are you still worried about it?"

Teddy shrugged. "I…I don't know. Hugo said that I should go to the police — that what they had over me was nothing, not in the grand scheme of things, and that they probably won't arrest me for using a little molly under duress. But it seems so dangerous, and — "

"Hugo… Hugo Ward?" Ian frowned, wondering why one of the cartel enforcers would be telling Teddy to narc.

Teddy stilled, his eyes darting up to Ian's. "How do you know that?"

Ian was torn, balanced on a cliff. He could shrug, lie…or he could trust Teddy and throw himself over the edge. "I'm going to tell you something. You can't tell anyone, not even Shiloh. It's very important, okay?"

Teddy gave a small nod.

"When I left, I didn't go to Chicago to be an accountant," Ian admitted. "I was pissed that the people who killed my brother were going to get away with it, so I finished my degree online and joined the organized crime division of the FBI. I've been working undercover for the past three years to put away gangs and cartels."

Teddy flinched back, though Ian suspected it was from surprise. "You... So, you're back in Austin to..."

"To investigate the *La Familia* cartel. Yes."

"Which is —"

"The cartel that killed Lucas. I thought I was here to get justice for Lucas, but...maybe I'm really here to save you instead." Ian didn't care if it sounded cheesy. He meant every word. Now that he knew Teddy was involved, he felt his priorities shifting. He wanted to bring the cartel down, but now it seemed even more important. He wasn't going to let the cartel take someone else he loved from him.

Someone else he... He felt his heart jump at the realization that he loved Teddy. That he'd loved Teddy for years, and no amount of running had been enough to bury his feelings completely.

"You...you should hate me," Teddy whispered, his words shaky but filled with enough self-loathing that Ian knew he believed the words wholeheartedly.

Ian lifted his hands to cradle Teddy's head, leaning forward to press a gentle kiss on the quivering lips. "How could I hate you, Teddy? I love you."

Teddy pulled back from Ian's lips with a gasp, his eyes wide in disbelief. "You…you love me?"

Ian's lips were curved like a Cupid's bow and soft as silk. "Of course. You don't have to say it, but you *do* have to believe it."

"I've been in love with you since I was sixteen," Teddy immediately answered, his voice coming out stronger than he realized. He'd dated during Ian's absence, but he'd always known that whoever he ended up with would always come in second to his memories.

Ian laughed. "Don't make it creepy, *papillo*."

Teddy blushed. "What can I say? I was an early bloomer."

Ian smiled, but when he took Teddy's hands in his, his expression grew more serious. "No more secrets between us. This…this thing we have… It won't work without honesty."

"No more secrets," Teddy agreed, squeezing Ian's hands. His own smile slid from his face like water. "I don't know what to do."

"You need to report this—not to the police, though. I think that you were right to be worried. A cartel this size definitely has moles in the police force, and I can't be sure that we've uncovered all of them. They'd know within minutes of you showing up. But I can make the report to my supervisor, and you'd officially be an FBI informant. That would keep you out of trouble for the ecstasy. Hugo was right about that part. There's not much that can be done about the video, though." He frowned, hating the thought of Teddy having to deal with that and not being able to fix it.

"I…I don't care about the video as much anymore. It's not like anyone will care about a bartender's sex tape, right?" Teddy gave a shaky laugh. "It's not like I'm an architect now."

"Baby, if you want to be an architect, we'll make that happen," Ian promised, stroking his thumb over Teddy's palm. "But as for the cartel, I want you to let me get you caught up on your payments. Don't argue. I have the money. I make a good salary and I don't use it for much. I've been too focused on getting back to Austin. I'm not letting anything happen to you when I have the means to prevent it."

"That's... It's a lot of money, Ian." Even just getting caught up would take several thousand dollars.

"When you called me Daddy, did you mean it?" Ian repeated the question Teddy had asked him earlier, looking straight into Teddy's eyes.

Teddy bit his lip but nodded. "Yes..." he finally whispered.

"Then let me do this. I can't bring the cartel down yet, not without more evidence, but I can do this much." Ian waited for Teddy to nod again, then smiled. "Good boy."

He leaned back so he could reach the coffee table drawer, tugging it open and pulling out a yellow legal pad and a pen. "I know this will probably be difficult, but I need you to tell me anything you can about the cartel, starting with Hugo."

Chapter Twenty-Nine

Monday morning rose cloudy and gray, foreshadowing a much-needed rain unlikely to fall. Teddy was glad that despite the bleak weather, the atmosphere between him and Ian was cloud-free. He kept waiting for Ian to treat him differently, to finally be angry over his revelations, but Ian was as thoughtful as ever, going so far as to remind him to have a healthy breakfast before heading downstairs to work on some paperwork for the club. Teddy had offered to help, but Ian had just shaken his head and told him to 'rest.' He could totally rest downstairs at the club, though, right?

Teddy drank half a pot of coffee before he even started digging through his drawers — God, it felt strange to say *his* — to pull out a pair of lavender skinny jeans and a Tiffany-blue blouse that matched his second favorite Chucks.

He wasted just enough time on his makeup to cover the still cringe-inducing bruises on his cheekbone and jaw, but there was nothing he could do about the partially healed split on his lower lip, so he gave up and headed downstairs. The club was quiet without the pulsing of bass — and without the attempts to holler drink orders over the top of it. It was almost too quiet, and Teddy shivered as he slid onto one of the dozen barstools, his back to the empty dance floor. The flesh on the base of his neck itched and he fought the urge to scratch it.

Instead, he twisted around, his gaze probing the darkened shadows beside the DJ booth, then drifted to the Stygian hallway. The ominous red pinpricks of light were likely the exit sign, but he couldn't *not* see a pair of glowing scarlet eyes. He shuddered — then shrieked as something touched him. If it weren't for the hand that gripped his arm, he'd have fallen off the stool.

"Shit, sorry!" Ian cursed, guiding Teddy fully back onto the stool and spinning it to face him. He must have left the office and rounded the bar without Teddy even realizing it. "I thought you heard me.".

"Sorry," Teddy flushed, embarrassed that Ian, of all people, had seen him jump.

"You're supposed to be resting," Ian said, after brushing a strand of hair out of Teddy's eyes.

Teddy tried to look properly innocent as he glanced up through the fan of his lashes. "I am resting. My butt is resting on this stool."

"Cheeky brat," Ian teased. "You're lucky your butt is on the stool or I might decide to *rest* my palm on it instead." Heat surged through Teddy's core and he whimpered before he could stop himself. The smirk that lifted the corner of Ian's mouth didn't help, either. "I think *someone* likes that idea."

Teddy bit his lip to hold back a moan, then winced as his teeth caught the tender flesh.

Ian's fingers gently soothed the soreness away. "The only one allowed to bite that lip is me," Ian murmured, "so let it heal for me like a good boy."

Teddy's lips parted on a gasp and Ian took it as an invitation, slipping a finger between them. Teddy's arousal waxed higher and he sucked on Ian's finger the way he wanted to suck something else.

"Naughty boy," Ian scolded, but his eyes glimmered with amusement. "I didn't tell you to suck. Open those pretty lips for me."

Teddy whimpered but he parted his mouth. Ian rested two fingers on his tongue, stroking over it just firmly enough not to tickle. There was something so perfectly dirty about sitting submissively while Ian used his mouth with his fingers. He shuddered, a keening, pleading cry escaping from his throat as Ian ran his fingertips over his teeth, then petted the inside of his cheeks, as though he were mapping out Teddy's mouth.

"You've got such a hot mouth, baby," Ian groaned, pulling his spit-dampened fingers free. "Can't wait to feel it wrapped around my dick. Is that what you want, baby?"

"Please," Teddy whimpered, unable to stop his hips from thrusting upward, unconsciously humping the air.

"You want it, baby? Or is this what you want?" Ian flicked open the button of Teddy's jeans before shoving his hand into the waistband, curling his wet fingers around Teddy's cock. He moved it slowly, jacking Teddy off with his own spit, and the thought alone was enough to push Teddy right to the edge.

"Yes, that. I want that…this. Please, Daddy, don't stop." Teddy's hips jerked up, until Ian's other hand curled around his left thigh, pinning him.

"Uh-uh. Be a good boy and take what Daddy gives you." Ian worked his hand faster, driving Teddy closer and closer to his climax, until —

He stopped, pulling his hand free just as Teddy was almost there, nipping his orgasm in the bud right before he could spill over. Teddy cried out at the absence, but Ian chuckled. "Naughty boys who don't listen to their Daddy don't get rewarded, do they?"

"I can listen," Teddy promised, struggling to keep his hips from chasing his orgasm on their own. "I can listen so good, Daddy."

"I don't know. What did Daddy ask you to do this morning?" Ian stepped closer, into the cradle of Teddy's thighs, and rested his hands on the bar behind him, effectively closing him in. Rather than feeling claustrophobic, however, Teddy felt safe. Protected.

"To…to rest?" Teddy said, though it came out like a question. It was hard to think with Ian so close, his scent filling Teddy's nose. Teddy's gaze dropped to the straining zipper of Ian's jeans, where the large erection was practically begging to be released.

"And?" Ian prodded when it became clear that Teddy was distracted. Though Teddy hardly thought that was his fault. Ian was large, and his jeans were so tight that Teddy wanted to trace the prominent bulge with his tongue.

"And…" Teddy struggled to think, then his stomach dropped nearly to the floor. "And to eat a good breakfast…"

"And did my boy eat a good, healthy breakfast this morning?" Ian asked, and he sounded so certain that

Teddy wondered if he'd been watching the cameras he'd noticed tucked into the corner of nearly every room upstairs.

Teddy's chin dropped to his chest as he shook his head. He'd been so preoccupied with getting ready to come down and see Ian that he'd forgotten. "No, Daddy." Tears burned his eyes at the realization that he'd disappointed Ian already.

Ian dipped his fingers under his chin and lifted it until Teddy's eyes met his. "Oh, baby, I'm not mad. I just want you to be healthy. Come on. Hop down."

Teddy curled in on himself as he carefully slid off the stool. "Are you going to spank me now?"

Ian smoothed his thumbs over Teddy's cheekbones, wiping away the dampness. "No, we're going to go get breakfast."

* * * *

Teddy crossed his legs under the table in an attempt to hide the obvious erection pressing against the front of his tight lavender jeans as Ian ordered for both of them. "I'll have the Tortilla Espanola, substitute egg whites, with a black coffee." Ian glanced at Teddy over the top of his menu, then passed it to the waiter, a young, bespectacled man with a Clark Kent curl. "For him, we'll have the veggie frittata with a side of sausage and a"—Ian paused, lifting a brow at Teddy in question—"chocolate milk?"

"Coffee," Teddy corrected.

"You already had half a pot," Ian pointed out, proving that he had indeed been watching the security videos. "Juice or milk."

"Chocolate milk is fine," Teddy agreed, feeling his skin pinken at the show of dominance. He'd wondered if Ian daddy-ing him in public would make him uncomfortable, and now he had his answer. The only way it made him uncomfortable was in the tightening of his jeans.

The waiter took the menus and left to get their drinks. Ian waited until they were alone to turn to Teddy. "Should I have asked before ordering for you? I hope I didn't make you uncomfortable."

"You didn't," Teddy looked down, feeling his cheeks warm even further. "I...I liked it."

He heard the relief in Ian's voice when he answered, "Good. But don't ever hesitate to tell me if I go too far, okay?"

Teddy shifted in the booth, less than subtly rearranging himself, then smirked up at him. "I don't think that's possible." Heat darkened Ian's eyes as he seemed to recognize the source of Teddy's discomfort. "Actually, I'm hoping we can go a bit...*farther*...tonight."

"Oh, I'm sure we can come to an agreement." Ian murmured, dropping his hand below the table, and Teddy had a feeling there was some rearranging going on over there, as well.

Before Teddy could make a flirty comment, though, their waiter returned with their drinks. Teddy groaned.

It was going to be the longest meal ever.

Ian loved the flushed, almost desperate look on Teddy's face. It made him want to dirty the boy up, lay him out across the table in front of everyone and feast on him. Thankfully, the larger, more rational, part of him was still thinking with his upstairs brain. So he settled instead with teasing his boy throughout the meal.

He couldn't lie and say that he wasn't doing it for enjoyment, because he certainly loved the way the pale cheeks turned pink and the lust-dazed blue eyes that blinked back at him, but a smaller part of him hoped that keeping Teddy on one edge would keep him off another. He couldn't get rid of the sight of Teddy the night before, shaking and scared as he recounted his experiences with the cartel, starting from the beginning and ending with Teddy nearly in panic mode as he recounted being buried alive. All Ian wanted to do was tuck Teddy away safely into bed before tracking down each and every one of the people involved until he could put them in graves of their own.

Since he couldn't act on that desire without compromising his honor—and his duty as an agent— he settled on keeping his boy distracted instead. He waited for Teddy to clear his plate before he lifted his foot and ran the toe of his black oxfords along the outside of Teddy's calf and up to his thigh, enjoying the visible shudder his boy made. "Ready to go?"

"Ready for something," Teddy mumbled, eyes half closing, throat moving as he swallowed.

Ian left enough money on the table to cover the bill, plus a substantial tip, then stood, holding his hand out to Teddy, who took it without question. Teddy's blissed-out look stayed firmly in place as they climbed into the truck and started driving, only fading when Ian parked in the lot outside Teddy's apartment.

Ian reached over to carefully remove Teddy's delicate lip from his teeth. "Remember what Daddy said about that lip." Teddy whimpered, and he seemed to lose some of his trepidation. Ian ran his finger over the lip one more time before pulling away. "Let Daddy get the door for you."

"Yes, Daddy," Teddy whimpered, and obediently stayed in his seat until Ian rounded the car and opened the door. Ian depressed the button on the seat-belt hooker, curling his fingers around the belt as he guided it back into place, skimming his knuckles along Teddy's chest, so he felt the shiver that spread through his boy's body and heard the indrawn breath.

Ian palmed the rock-hard bulge beneath the soft jeans. "The sooner we get your apartment cleared out, the sooner we can go home."

"What are we waiting for, then?" Teddy's voice was breathy, but a wicked smile lit up his face and he practically leapt out of the seat to run toward the door.

"Look for cars!" Ian called after him, shaking his head as Teddy skidded to a stop, barely on the sidewalk, head bobbing as he looked both ways, before taking off running again. Ian refused to give chase, mostly because he didn't want to look like a creeper. Teddy didn't go far, anyway. He stopped at the door and rocked back on his heels to wait, his hands finding their way into his back pockets.

Ian moved up behind him and slid his hands over Teddy's, not-so-subtly gripping the perfect globes of his ass until Teddy arched back into him. Ian leaned forward to nip at the shell of Teddy's ear before murmuring a secret.

"Boy, you ever run across a street like that without me again and you won't be able to sit on this ass for a week." He gave it a squeeze for emphasis.

Teddy moaned. "Yes, Daddy."

"Go on, then," Ian slid his hands free and stepped back. "Show Daddy up to your apartment so we can get started."

After listening to Teddy's story, he now understood why he refused to use the small, cramped, rickety elevator. The stairs were hardly better, narrow and bleak, but thankfully, they only had to go to the third floor.

The super was already waiting, leaning against the wall across from the door, staring at his phone. He was a large man — not fat, just heavily muscled, bulging arms on display beneath a blue tank top, thighs that threatened to split the seam of his jeans. He was taller even than Ian. An ID card was clipped to the hem of his shirt, the name 'Vik' printed across in large black letters.

Vik tucked his phone away as they approached. He frowned at Ian before his gaze landed on Teddy and softened. "Hey, kid. Sorry to hear about the eviction."

Teddy shrugged. "My fault, anyway."

"Still sucks. I'd have been here to let you in earlier, but I was out of town visiting my sister." Vik said all this while he pulled out a key ring and sorted through them, finally inserting the right one into the lock and twisting it until it clicked.

"She have her baby yet?" Teddy asked as the door was pushed open.

"Nah. She's big as a house now. I told her she better pop my niece out soon or she won't fit through the hospital doors." Vik smirked and stepped out of the way to let Teddy and Ian into the apartment.

"I bet she had something to say about that." Teddy said with a laugh.

"She kicked her shoe at me then made me put it back on her since she can't reach her feet." Vik smirked, then sobered slightly and sighed. "Call when you're ready for me to lock it back up, yeah? I have to go up to 4C to fix a toilet, but I'll be around."

"Thanks, Vik."

Ian closed the door behind the superintendent then lifted an eyebrow at Teddy, trying hard not to be jealous. "You guys seem close. Ex-boyfriend?"

Teddy laughed. "You're funny. I am *so* not his type."

"Oh, really? I find it hard to believe that a sexy little thing like you isn't *anyone's* type."

"Trust me. Vik and I might be great friends, but he and I have way too much in common to be compatible." Teddy's eyes roamed over Ian's body with a hungry look. "Let's just say that we'd both rather be put on our knees than put someone else there."

Ian raised an eyebrow and glanced back at the now-closed door that Vik had left through. "Huh."

"Shows what you get for stereotyping." Teddy sniffed like he was insulted, but broke off into the cutest little giggle.

"Boy, you best start packing or the only thing you'll be leaving here with is a sore bottom," Ian said with a groan, adjusting his painfully tight jeans to accommodate his erection.

"Promises, promises," Teddy shot him a wicked grin before heading to the kitchen to pull out a handful of garbage bags. When he returned, he was sporting a more serious expression, though his eyes still glinted with humor. "There's not much I'm worried about, mostly my clothes, some books. Everything else is replaceable."

"You go get your clothes. I'll pack the books." Ian snagged one of the garbage bags before swatting the tempting ass in front of him as Teddy passed by.

"Careful, or I'll lose more clothes than I pack..." Teddy said over his shoulder.

"Promises, promises..."

Chapter Thirty

Teddy sank onto the bare, dingy mattress that took up most of the space in his — or what was formerly his — bedroom. He'd packed a whole quarter of his closet before he'd stumbled on the mouse-nibbled shoe box that he'd shoved under a particularly ugly pair of green suede ankle boots. Quite literally stumbled, and he had the bruise on his shin to prove it.

Part of him wanted to carry the box to the nearest window and dump it, contents and all, into the alley below. A larger part of him resisted. It was not, however, strong enough to make him open it.

He knew what was inside — stacks of old pictures, some of him and his mother, some of him and his dad, before the bastard had passed away, some of grandparents he barely remembered. And nine letters, all unopened.

Reading them wouldn't change anything, wouldn't *fix* anything, wouldn't bring back his inheritance to pay off his debt or strip him of the memory of his mother's palm cracking across his face. Reading them wouldn't take away the nights she'd been too drunk to make dinner or the school plays she'd missed, or the feeling that he'd never been *quite* good enough.

He tightened his fingers painfully on the edge of the box as anger boiled over. He almost didn't hear the door opening, or the soft footsteps approaching the mattress, until a pair of jean-clad knees entered his field of vision. Ian crouched down in front of him, concern on his face.

"Everything okay?" Ian asked.

Teddy shrugged. "Part of me says these would make really good kindling."

Ian reached for the box but hesitated before touching the lid. "May I?"

"Go for it." Teddy shoved them out, letting Ian remove the lid and peer inside. The letters glared at him from their place atop the pile. Nine white envelopes with his name written in a messy scrawl across the front.

Ian picked one up and stared at the stamp, then flipped it over to see the seal still in place. "From your mother?"

Teddy nodded. "She's sent one every year on my birthday…and Christmas. Except this year I've gotten three already."

"Do you want me to read them for you?" Ian asked.

Teddy almost bit his lip but caught himself, nodding instead. Ian sank onto his butt, crossing his legs. He slid his thumbnail beneath the seal and pulled it open.

"Wait," Teddy interrupted and Ian froze. "Can you… I mean…will you read it out loud?"

"Of course." Ian pulled a folded piece of white copy paper out of the envelope. Teddy couldn't read the words from his place on the bed, but he recognized his mother's messy scrawl, traveling uneven across the page, and knew the water stains were more likely caused by spilled whiskey than tears.

"This one was from…three years ago," Ian explained before clearing his throat.

"Dear Teddy,
I hope you're having a good holiday. The house feels really empty without you. I miss you. I don't remember why you left, but I know it was probably my fault. I've stopped drinking. I would love to hear from you.
Love, your mother."

The next few letters went in a similar vein. Greetings and platitudes, reminiscing about good times Teddy barely remembered. A promise that she'd stopped drinking. The unsteadiness of her handwriting made him doubt it. He shivered, wrapping his arms around himself as he listened to the first six letters.

But Ian hesitated when he got to the next one, the one sent back in February—the first letter she'd sent off schedule. A frown crossed Ian's face. He glanced up at Teddy before patting his lap. "Come sit on my lap, baby."

Teddy didn't hesitate. He slid off the bed and crawled into Ian's lap, grateful that his small stature let him tuck himself securely under Ian's chin. He felt the ghost of a kiss part his hair before Ian cleared his throat. If Teddy wanted, he could look down at the crisp, sterile paper Ian had pulled from the envelope, could read along, but he didn't. He just listened to the rhythmic notes of Ian's voice as he started to read.

"My Dearest Teddy.
I hope this letter finds you happy and healthy. I have had some time to think recently, and I know that I don't deserve

your forgiveness. I've been going to meetings for a while now. I like to think you'd be proud of me. I'm on step nine now. It has been three months since I've touched alcohol. It's not a lot, but it's a start. I'm supposed to make amends now. I don't know how I can fix what I've done, though. I don't remember a lot. And what I do remember makes me want to reach for a bottle to forget again. I remember h – "

Ian's voice broke for a second before he started reading again.

"I remember hitting you. I thought that was something I'd never do. I always promised I'd never be like your dad, but I was, and I'm sorry. I know you must hate me. But that's okay, because I hate myself too. I'm working on it. I just want you to know that I'm sorry, and I love you."

There was no signature at the bottom of the letter, just an XO. Teddy couldn't help the tears that clung to his eyelashes before spilling down his cheeks. It was how she'd always signed his birthday cards, too.

"The next one," Teddy whispered, fingers curling in the cotton of Ian's shirt, clinging to it like a security blanket.

"Are you sure? We can—" Ian started to say, hand hovering over the second envelope.

"I'm sure. The next one. Please."

Ian opened the next envelope. It had been sent in early May. It read much the same as the first— apologies that seemed more sincere than the usual ones, an update on her meetings. His mother mentioned her sponsor, an older man named Finnick, often. She wrote about struggling often with her urges, shame bleeding through the ink of her words, but that, more than any of her earlier promises, made him think that maybe, this time, she was serious. Again, she signed it with hugs and kisses.

The last envelope was the one from the end of August, just over a month ago. Ian pried it open and pulled out the letter.

"Dearest Teddy.

I know you're probably not reading these. I wouldn't read them either. I just wanted you to know I have been sober for eight months now. I find myself reaching less and less for the bottle, and more and more for your baby pictures. I put that picture of you – the one you hate, I know, but it's just too cute – on the mantel. You know, the one of you in your princess costume. I'll never forget the tantrum you threw or how cute you looked pouting. I knew then that you were going to be special. I remember how angry your dad was when you came home in the neighbor boy's Batman costume, and how Mrs. Knowles laughed at little Timmy trying to walk in your slippers. I guess I'm rambling now. I just miss you.

Hugs and Kisses,
Mother."

Teddy tried to subtly wipe away the tears tracking their way down his face. "I miss her too."

"Have you thought of visiting?" Ian asked, and for a moment, Teddy tensed, hearing an undercurrent of judgement that reason told him didn't exist. Mutely, he shook his head. "You could, you know. Sometime." Teddy shrugged. Ian circled Teddy's wrist-bone gently with his thumb. "I'll go with you, if you want. If you change your mind."

Teddy stilled, biting his lip before he remembered Ian's warning, then nodded. Maybe, he could visit his mother if Ian was there beside him. He thought maybe he could do anything if Ian was there beside him.

"I...I gotta finish packing," Teddy mumbled, scrambling from Ian's lap before he agreed to something he wasn't ready for yet. Ian didn't argue. He just returned the letters to the box and carefully put the lid back on, tucking it under his arm as he stood.

Ian dropped a kiss on Teddy's forehead as he passed. "Take your time. I'll be out here when you're ready."

Teddy nodded mutely, no longer paying attention to what he was throwing into the garbage bag at his feet, just wanting to be finished. He tied off the bag, grunting as he hefted it and carried it out into the rest of the apartment, dropping it by the door. Already, there are two smaller, oddly bulging bags waiting, the corners of his books threatening to tear the flimsy plastic. Thankfully, Ian had been smart enough to fill the bags only a third full, so hopefully, they would make it.

He turned and stared at the rest of the apartment with mixed feelings. Mostly, he was happy to finally be leaving it behind. Staying with Ian for the past few days only highlighted how bad his apartment really was. Still, it was — or had been, at least — *his*. He couldn't help the pang of sadness, nor the smaller kernel of fear that thrummed through his chest at the thought of leaving. There would be no more cuddling on the ratty couch with Shiloh, watching movies on his friend's table or impromptu dance lessons to the thumping bass from the downstairs neighbor at three a.m. And if Ian left him again — with his job, Teddy knew he couldn't make any promises — Teddy would be on the streets.

"Ready?" Ian said, pulling Teddy from his thoughts.

Teddy rubbed the heel of his hand over his sternum then nodded. "Ready."

* * * *

Teddy felt better after Ian had helped him cart his belongings upstairs to the apartment. The first thing he did was shuck his jeans, enjoying the feel of air on his skin. Then he started unpacking. His clothes found a home in one half of Ian's closet — or two thirds, if he was being technical. Ian's clothes lined one side of the walk-in, mostly dark jeans and dark suits, and dark button-downs and dark tees. After Teddy hung his final sequined top, he turned, hands on his hips, and looked over Ian's wardrobe with a critical eye.

"Ian!" he yelled out into the bedroom. "Daddy!"

There was a thump, like Ian had dropped something, then heavy footsteps as he hurried to the closet. "What's wrong? Did you hurt yourself?"

Teddy shot him a scathing glare. "Yeah, I pinched myself on the hanger. I need you to kiss my booboos."

Ian, rather than laugh or scold him for his sarcasm, stepped closer instead and grabbed Teddy's hand, looking over his fingers critically, though there was a spark of humor in his dark eyes. He lifted each fingertip to his mouth and brushed his lips gently over them. "Better, baby?"

"Um…" *Shit, am I supposed to be able to speak now?* "No. Not better. Need more kisses." He had called Ian in for a reason. A very important, wardrobe-malfunction-related reason, but now all he wanted was for Ian to —

Ian sucked Teddy's pointer finger into his mouth, sliding his tongue teasingly over the pads of his fingertips and the crease under his first knuckle, the suction a heady push-and-pull that made Teddy's dick throb in his jeans. Ian released it with a *pop*.

"Daddy..." Teddy moaned and slid closer, plastering himself to Ian's chest. His eyes widened when Ian shifted, sliding a large thigh between Teddy's knees, forcing his legs farther apart until Teddy's groin was firmly pressed against Ian's thigh. Teddy couldn't help rocking against it.

Ian dropped his hands to Teddy's waist, encouraging him to move, to thrust his hips back and forth against his leg. A small part of him whispered that he should be embarrassed, humping Ian's thigh like a dog in heat, but a larger part of him shook in pleasure. The embarrassment seemed to feed into it until he could hardly think of anything but the feeling of Ian's thigh between his legs. He curled his fingers tightly into Ian's soft cotton shirt and somebody was moaning desperately. Him, he realized, and the realization made him grind his hips harder.

"That's a good boy. Fuck Daddy's thigh. Daddy wants to make you feel good. Come on, baby." Ian's words had Teddy shaking. And his hands, urging him faster, had Teddy quivering through an orgasm that left him boneless, collapsing against Daddy's chest with a sigh.

Daddy stroked his hands down Teddy's spine, petting him in soothing circles. Teddy knew he should get off him but his muscles refused to move, unless it was to snuggle closer. "Feel better?" Ian asked eventually, after Teddy's shaking had stopped and he'd gone boneless instead.

"Mm-hmm," Teddy agreed.

"Sounds like it's nap time." Ian chuckled.

Teddy huffed, his eyes drooping. "I was going to yell at you for your clothes, though." His voice was whiny, and he shifted his head to glare at the dark side of the closet. He snickered.

"Mm-m. And what's wrong with my clothing?" Ian sounded amused.

"Darth Vader called. He wants his wardrobe back." Teddy cackled. "Look. It's the *dark* side!" He pointed at Ian's side of the closet.

"Brat." Ian smacked Teddy's butt, then practically carried him out of the closet to drop him in the center of the bed. Teddy laughed as the mattress bounced under him. He wasn't laughing when Ian propped a knee up on the foot of the bed then crawled forward until he sat astride Teddy's hips. A devilish smile danced on his lips.

"I thought it was nap time, Daddy," Teddy teased, working his hands under Ian's shirt to play with the soft fur on his chest.

Ian's smirk widened and he shifted up onto his knees. He skimmed his hands down Teddy's sides before taking his waist. Then Ian was flipping him over onto his stomach. Teddy gasped as he spun, a gasp that turned to a moan as Ian snagged the waistband of his briefs, lacy and pink and tight. Teddy lifted his hips so Ian could slide them down, but Ian only pulled them low enough to expose his ass, letting them snap into place around his thighs. Teddy panted fast at the restraint, minimal though it was. He felt Ian shift forward, his jeans scraping against Teddy's bare skin.

"It's nap time for little boys," Ian said, breath ghosting over Teddy's neck. "Daddy wants to play."

Teddy couldn't see him, but he could hear the grating of a zipper being pulled down slowly, then he felt it…a thick, weeping shaft nestling into his crease. He moaned, and a wet tongue slid from the base of his neck to his ear. "You can stop me whenever you want, baby. Just say…anything."

Teddy shivered. Ian wanted him to stay *quiet* through this? He sank his teeth into the pillow to smother a protest.

"Don't worry, baby. Daddy won't fuck you yet. Daddy just wants to play." Teddy felt Ian's hips thrust as he spoke, sliding his dick through Teddy's cleft, and it was like lightning coursing through his entire body.

God, Ian was going to *murder* him.

Ian could watch his dick sliding between the firm cheeks of Teddy's ass all day. Already, it was weeping, leaving clear streaks along the paler flesh he slid between. "Such a pretty ass, baby," Ian murmured, sliding his hands down Teddy's sides and over his hips, until he was kneading the fleshy globes with each thrust.

He could tell Teddy wanted to speak—to urge him to go faster or harder. Teddy was biting the pillow hard enough that Ian was surprised he wasn't inhaling feathers. Ian slowed his thrusts instead, leaning forward until he lay, chest to back, against Teddy. He pressed a kiss to the back of Teddy's neck, savoring the taste of his sweat, the sound of his breath drawing in. "Such a good boy for me."

Teddy's whole body shook at the words, and the telltale signs of his climax—the curling of his fingers in the sheets, the broken breaths, goosebumps along his spine—spurred Ian faster, until he spilled his seed across Teddy's lower back.

Teddy unclenched his jaw from the pillows to say, "Daddy made a mess."

"Then Daddy should clean it up." Ian slid lower, until he could trace the milky white trails painting Teddy's flesh with his tongue. His cum was bitter, but it was worth it to feel the shiver that spread through Teddy's body. "Better?"

Teddy smirked over his shoulder. "I'm still sticky."

Ian landed a playful slap to Teddy's ass, watching it jiggle. Teddy yelped in surprise. "You can take a bath later. It's nap time."

"I'm not tired," Teddy protested. But his eyes, still shadowed in bruises, drooped from fatigue.

"Tell you what, baby. Close your eyes for fifteen minutes, and if you're still not tired, you can get up." Ian slid off Teddy to lie beside him instead, shifting the smaller man around until he fit comfortably under his chin, his head on his chest.

Teddy grumbled under his breath but didn't protest. Instead, he snuggled closer and sighed. Ian wasn't surprised when he fell asleep well before the fifteen minutes were up. Besides the stress of moving, he was still recovering from his ordeal at the hands of the cartel. It only made Ian more resolved to see them brought down.

He tightened his arms around Teddy. He would do whatever it took to keep his boy safe.

Chapter Thirty-One

Teddy woke alone, one arm stretched across the mattress, like he'd been reaching for Ian in his sleep but had come up empty. He yawned and rubbed the sleep from his eyes. "Ian?" he called, levering himself up. He was met with silence.

He swung his legs over the edge of the bed, a second yawn teasing its way free. His jaw clicked as it stretched. "Ian?"

He padded on bare feet out of the bedroom and into the rest of the apartment, peering into each room. Maybe Ian had headphones in or something.

Instead, what he found was a small yellow square stuck to the fridge.

Out for work. Dinner in fridge. Be a good boy and EAT.
XO.

Teddy glared at the sticky note. Apparently, he'd slept longer than he meant to if Ian had left before he woke, but seriously? Ian thought he was going to be able to sit here and eat like nothing was wrong, all the while knowing that Ian had left to go play with gang members? Or…provide backup for the agent playing with gangsters, but whatever…

Fuck that.

He'd go downstairs and see if they needed help at the bar, instead. At least then, his hands would stay busy.

He was halfway dressed when his phone rang on the nightstand. Teddy crawled across the mattress and snagged it, then cursed as he spotted the caller ID. Blood, Sweat and Shears.

He thumbed the green button and yanked the phone off the charger hard enough that it disconnected from the wall in his haste to get it to his ear. "Oh my God, I'm so sorry, Joel. I wasn't paying attention to the day, I totally forgot I had a shift I'll be there as soon as I get dressed, I am *so sorr*—"

Joel interrupted him, "Calm down, Teddy. It's not a big deal. I was just worried when you didn't show up. I thought maybe something happened since you're never late. Show up whenever, okay? I don't have any classes scheduled until tomorrow anyway."

After a few more apologies, Teddy disconnected the call. His stomach dropped when he saw the bright red missed call from Antonio's. Santiago must have called when he was sleeping. He held his breath when he opened the voicemail, preparing for the tirade.

"Hey, Teddy. Sorry to call so close to your shift, but don't bother coming in this morning. Actually, the boss doesn't need you back until Monday, but make sure you report to his office first thing."

Teddy let out a gasp of relief. At least he hadn't missed his shift, even if there was a knot in his stomach at the thought of not working through the weekend then having to see the big boss himself. He had a sinking suspicion that he knew what the man was going to say. He'd lost more shifts than he'd worked lately, ever since the man's nephew had started working and they'd cut his hours.

He stripped off the booty shorts he'd just tugged on and scrambled into the closet for a pair of plain blue jeans instead. He threw on a pair of his new Chucks that Ian had insisted on buying him—not that he was complaining, because he loved them, especially because they were pink—then topped it off with a pretty blue Henley. He spent longer than he'd hoped reapplying his makeup to cover the bruises, then shoved his phone into his pocket.

He left the apartment and took the stairs two at a time. He was in too big a rush to do more than hesitate at the back door, then sprint, his heart pounding, through the alley and out onto the sidewalk. He slowed to avoid running into a businessman thumbing through his phone hurrying in the same direction he was in, but otherwise he moved as quickly as he could.

Joel might not be worried about him being late, but *he* was. He hated being late to anything, but especially to work. Thankfully, *Blood, Sweat and Shears* wasn't too far away from Envy.

Blood, Sweat and Shears looked like a boutique from the outside. Its skeleton was a Queen Anne house in miniature, complete with a slender portico on the verandah, an octagonal tower so small it was *surely* only decorative, and a single gable. What color it had originally been was a mystery. It had been repainted in shades of bubblegum pink and ivory.

Teddy pushed through the glass door that completed the house's transition from home to business. He'd been working here for nine months but still got stuck in the entryway each time, unable to pull his eyes from the interior. He guessed from the slate mantel left in place behind what was now the line of hair stations on the left, the elegant mahogany wall behind the washing stations to the right and the remnants of the gold-embossed wallpaper behind the check-in desk, that the large, open floor salon had once encompassed the entry way, gentlemen's lounge and parlor.

Teddy loved the way the salon somehow managed to transition from Victorian splendor to modern chic in a way that blended so beautifully. If he looked, it was easy to see the history left in the details — the scrollwork carved into the wooden door frames, the marble flooring, the elegant cornices. But the salon had been built seamlessly around those details.

"Excuse me." A petite woman carefully shifted to get around him.

Teddy flushed, stepping out of the doorway. "Sorry." How many people had watched him stop and gawk like a tourist at the Governor's Mansion?

He hurried over to the desk.

Delia looked up with a pleasant smile that widened when she spotted him. "Teddy!"

Teddy's cheeks flushed further at the warm greeting. He liked Delia. She was always friendly, but he suspected she was more Shiloh's friend than his. The two could get lost in conversations about gay romances for hours.

"Hey, Delia. Your hair looks nice." It was pink now, much brighter than the magenta she'd sported when he'd seen her at the beginning of the week. It made her olive skin glow.

"Thanks." She reached up to play with a few of the strands for a second. "Amy's coming home tomorrow." Amy was Delia's girlfriend. She'd been away since the beginning of the year, visiting her mother in Michigan, so he'd never met her.

"I think she'll like it." Teddy hurried to reassure her, sensing a bit of uncertainty in Delia's voice.

"You think?" Delia's smile wavered for a minute before it snapped back in place. "Yeah, I bet she will. Oh, um...here... I'll let you upstairs. You probably want to get to work."

"Thank you." Teddy followed her around the half-circle desk, waiting while she unlocked the door that led to the upstairs. He started up, then paused, turning back around. "But seriously, Delia. Don't worry. Your hair looks great. Amy will love it."

Delia blushed, but this time, she looked like she believed him. "Thanks, Teddy." He started up the stairs, the click of the door shutting behind him echoing like a gunshot. His spine stiffened, a sweat breaking out on his forehead.

He'd never noticed how narrow the stairway was — how dark, with the doors at both the bottom and top shut tight. He swallowed and looked up, and up...the stairs stretching like a mountain above him, walls leaning toward him.

He squeezed his eyes closed. "It's fine," he muttered. "Everything is fine. One step at a time." Eyes clenched shut, he stepped up, then again. His hand stretched in front of him, he didn't open his eyes until his palm struck the wooden door and he fumbled it open.

He drew in a shaky breath as he staggered into the studio on the other side. The tight band around his chest unclenched, his breath releasing. He was fine. Everything was fine. He rubbed his palm over the center of his chest, taking a second to calm down before analyzing the studio like he did every time.

The original carpeting had been torn out, the hardwood floor refinished and polished until it shone. Several exercise mats were stacked, awaiting cleaning, against the row of mirrors built over the windows on the far wall. A pair of ballet barres stretched along the mirrors on the side walls.

The studio wasn't hard to clean, just time-consuming. He had worked out a pretty good system, though. Mirrors first, though the cuts on his feet stung when he stretched on tiptoes to reach the top. Then he wiped down the mats and put them away. A quick sweep later, and the only thing left to do was polish the floor. It was the most difficult part of the job, since it required him to get on his hands and knees and work the entire surface with small circles. And missing a spot could leave it streaky or off color. Today, it was even harder, since the homemade polish — olive oil and vinegar — stung his still-sore hands.

"Looking good," a familiar voice said from the doorway when he was just over halfway finished.

Teddy sank back onto his heels and swiped at the hair that sweat had plastered to his forehead. He turned to smile at his boss over his shoulder, "Thanks, Joel. It should be dry enough to walk on in a few hours, but I would stay off it until then."

Joel was the owner of both the kickboxing studio, where he taught self-defense classes twice a week, and the salon downstairs. Teddy thought he looked more suited to one job than the other, even if he felt guilty for stereotyping. But Joel had muscles on his muscles and wore tight tank tops that showed them off. He looked like he should be on the cover of a bodybuilding magazine, not dying and cutting hair. Despite his appearance, Teddy knew Joel had a whole host of awards for the salon.

Joel's near-permanent smile slid off his face. "Are those bruises?" He stepped closer, not caring that his shoes scuffed the freshly polished floor.

"You're leaving marks," Teddy pointed out, rather than answer.

Joel stopped walking immediately, chagrin crossing his face for a second. "Sorry. I'll fix it later. But seriously, Teddy, what happened?"

Teddy shrugged. "Nothing to worry about."

Joel looked clearly torn between whether to press the issue or not. "I know that I'm your boss, and it's not really my place, so stop me if I make you uncomfortable, but if you're in a bad situation, I can help, okay? There's a place called HOPE. They provide housing, counseling, anything you need, really." Teddy frowned, not sure why Joel thought he'd need help with housing, since it wasn't like he'd advertised that he'd been evicted. Then it cleared up when Joel added, "You don't have to stay with someone who's abusing you."

"Oh. Oh! No, no one's abusing me. Not like that. I…I mean, obviously, you can tell the bruises aren't from like, tripping or something," Teddy felt himself flush, "But it's not like, domestic violence or anything. It's more like a mugging. Not really a mugging, but… Well, I'm perfectly safe in my living arrangement. But thank you for worrying. I appreciate the thought."

Joel eyed him for a minute, clearly trying to figure out if he was lying, then nodded. "Okay. If you say so.

But seriously… If you need anything, just let me know, okay?"

"Promise. But I don't." Teddy smiled brightly back, then waved the rag he was using to polish the floor with. "I'll just finish this up, then I'll get out of your hair."

"Take your time. You're not in my hair at all," Joel lingered awkwardly in the doorway before slipping back downstairs.

* * * *

Ian was still gone when Teddy meandered into the kitchen. He had an hour or so still until his shift at Envy was due to start, so he pulled the plate Ian had made for him out of the fridge, stomach growling at the delicious smell that wafted off it, even cool.

It was some type of fish—not salmon, or cod, but he couldn't tell what it was—grilled and plated with rice and a yellowish bean on the side. It looked like something he'd eat at Mama Romero's, and when he tasted it, he nearly moaned. It was the perfect blend of spices, something he'd never be able to replicate, no matter how hard he tried. Not even with a recipe at his fingertips.

As much as he wanted to savor the dinner, he was hungry enough that he practically inhaled it. The only good thing about eating so fast was that it gave him time to linger in the shower, letting him wash off the stench of vinegar and sweat before it was time to head downstairs. He wished Ian were there. Johnny had picked up quickly that Ian didn't want Teddy on the platforms—mostly because it was obvious how much Teddy didn't *want* to be on the platforms—so it was rare that he was stuck there lately. Unfortunately, with Ian gone for the night, Johnny met him before he'd even rounded the bar.

"I want you on the platforms." Johnny's leer widened at Teddy's grimace.

Teddy knew Johnny wanted him to beg to work the bar. The bastard was a sick fuck who got off on his discomfort. He refused to play that game. He stripped off his apron and tossed it at Johnny rather than hanging it back up, then turned to cross the floor.

He was stopped by Johnny's hand clamping down on his bicep, hard enough to hurt.

"The fuck, man?" Teddy snapped, yanking it free and rubbing the already-red skin.

"Aren't you forgetting something?" Johnny's eyes dipped lower, staring pointedly at the crotch of Teddy's panties.

"Like…?" Teddy trailed off, not sure what the issue was. He always wore the pink Spanx on Mondays.

Johnny leaned over the bar. He cleared his throat uncomfortably, then lowered his voice. "Your, um…your packer?"

Teddy frowned, arms crossing. "What about it?" He hadn't worn it since *that* night, the night he'd thought was going to be the last. He wanted to live true to himself. He would never begrudge someone else their packer. He knew that for some men it was the only way they felt comfortable in their masculinity. It just wasn't for him. He didn't need — or want — one for himself.

"You're not wearing it." Johnny said it like he thought Teddy had just managed to overlook it.

"I know. What about it?" Teddy straightened his spine and glared at the taller man, daring Johnny to comment again.

Johnny, however, was an idiot who didn't know when to let a subject die. "You're not wearing it. You should go and get it. You'll look weird without a...um," Johnny waved awkwardly at Teddy's crotch again.

"Without a dick?" Teddy prompted with exasperation. "I *have* a dick. I don't need a fake one to make it bigger. So, unless you're going to tell me to go find a pillow to shove in my panties to make my ass look bigger too, why don't you just chill the fuck out and let me go embarrass myself, hmm?"

Johnny's face turned a shade of red Teddy'd never seen before, which looked remarkably odd, considering his mouth had pinched tight enough to turn his lips white. Rather than wait for the outburst, Teddy spun on his black satin heels and strutted away from the bar, letting his hips sway as they wished, then ascended as elegantly as he could — which was to say, not at all — onto the platform closest to the bathrooms.

He peered through the dimness of the club at the other platforms, trying to figure out which dancer had called off to land him on one. He frowned and skimmed over them again. *Where is Shiloh?*

AJ caught his eye from the platform that was usually Shiloh's and lifted an eyebrow. Lips moving with exaggeration, he mouthed, "Where's Shy?"

AJ shrugged. Teddy had left his phone in his locker and wouldn't be able to check it until after his first set, at the earliest.

Twenty minutes had never crept by so slowly. The first thing he did when the spotlight above him flickered off and he'd safely clambered back down onto the dance floor was hurry into the dressing room and dig out his phone.

No missed calls, no texts, which was odd because Shiloh almost always let him know when he wasn't coming. Teddy tried to call him twice, but it just rang and rang until he reached Shiloh's voicemail both times.

Teddy flinched and pulled his thumb away from his mouth, not realizing he'd been chewing his nail until it tore painfully. "Ouch." He shook his hand, which always seemed to help, even though it really did nothing.

The dressing room door opened and AJ slipped in, his thumbs hooked in the waistband of his Spanx. "Hear anything from Shiloh?"

Teddy shook his head. "No. Maybe he got held up after class…or something."

"Yeah, maybe." AJ sounded as confident as Teddy, which wasn't very confident at all.

Teddy tried calling Shiloh one last time before he had to return to the floor, but he got nothing but voicemail.

Chapter Thirty-Two

Ian had left the apartment that evening with far more reluctance than he was used to. He'd never intended on working for the FBI, would likely never have applied if not for his brother's death, but it hadn't taken him long after graduation to realize that he loved it. He loved the smell of gunpowder on the range, and he loved the thrill of chasing down a suspect. Most of all, he loved knowing that his actions were putting bad men where they belonged, keeping other people's little brothers safe. He'd never expected that there would come a day when he'd dread it. But everything in him protested the thought of leaving Teddy behind, sleeping curled up in the center of his bed.

It was a distraction he didn't need and couldn't afford. He sat outside the bar where he was meeting Tennyson for a few minutes to get his mind back on the job. It wasn't just the case at risk if he didn't have his head in the game. It was people's lives. Tennyson's, his...anyone put at risk by the cartel's operations.

When his head was as clear as it was going to get, he climbed out of the truck and headed into the bar. Tennyson was already waiting, a tumbler of whiskey sitting untouched in front of him.

Ian almost didn't recognize him. Gone were the bespoke suit and Bemer shoes he wore around the office, replaced by a leather jacket and dusty black motorcycle boots. Typically clean-shaven, his jaw was covered with a layer of scruff and steel-streaked bangs hung over his forehead, shadowing his eyes. A silver ring glinted on his lip.

Ian slid into the stool beside him. Tennyson lifted a hand to the bartender and a few seconds later, a second whiskey was slid in front of him. Tennyson pushed it over to Ian. "Nice work on the De Luca boy," Tennyson grunted. "Don't know how you convinced the kid to flip, but with his info, it looks like we might finally have some leverage."

Ian, halfway through lifting the tumbler to his mouth, slammed it back down on the bar. "He ain't a kid."

Tennyson lifted a brow, lips twitching on a grin. "Sorry, Romeo. I forgot you're barely legal yourself."

"Shut your mouth, asshole," Ian growled, but his own lips twitched as well. "You ready for tonight?"

Tennyson had slowly worked his way up from providing part-time security for lower level runners to driving for one of the enforcers. If all went well tonight, he'd be joining DeAza's personal security team. They'd arrested one of the crew a few weeks prior for possession, rather than wait for a position to open naturally.

Normally, things like this didn't bother him, but Ian's gut kept insisting that something was wrong.

He'd taken every precaution he could think of. Tennyson was bugged, a small listening device hidden in a pen in his pocket. If they scanned him for it, all he'd have to do was click it and it automatically deactivated for sixty seconds. Ian would be in the van outside, and he'd — or rather, his boss had, since his name wasn't officially connected to the FBI while undercover — convinced the local police to keep a SWAT team on standby, just in case. They would be only three minutes out.

Three minutes, though, could be the difference between success and failure, life and death.

Tennyson clapped him on the shoulder, dislodging him from the morbid thoughts of everything that could go wrong. "Stop stressing. This isn't my first rodeo."

Ian drew in a calming breath that didn't end up being so calming, but it at least kept him quiet long enough to pretend. He swirled his whiskey around, ice clinking on glass. "Sorry. You got everything you need?"

Tennyson patted the pocket of his jacket. "All ready to go."

It didn't take long to outfit the surveillance van and double-check the supplies. Soon enough, the plain black van was parked in the shadowed alley across from the paint-tagged warehouse that DeAza's crew occupied. Ian made the final few tweaks on the surveillance equipment.

Tennyson's voice came loud and clear through the bug, his voice tight with what Ian thought were nerves, just as a sleek, black Ducati Diavel peeled too quickly around the corner, neatly cutting off a black sedan from the other direction. "Ten on site."

Ian glared at the Ducati through the screen. "I should write you a ticket for that stunt."

Tennyson just subtly lifted a finger in the direction of the nearest hidden camera, then pulled off his helmet and locked it into one of the panniers. The warehouse had four closed bays and a single small door that was propped open by a brick. Tennyson headed for it. He was met before he reached it by a pair of men Ian recognized from the files. DeAza's guards — or two of them at least. The thinner was a man named Nicolas Garcia-Reyes, who had a series of misdemeanors for drug possession and assault, while the taller was Diego Ayala. Unlike his partner, Diego's record was clean.

If things went well, it wouldn't be clean much longer.

As Ian expected, they patted Tennyson down, and there was a tense sixty seconds of silence while he waited for them to scan for bugs. When the sound clicked back on, partway through DeAza laughing about something, Ian relaxed. So far, everything was going to plan.

DeAza seemed in good spirits, joking around with Tennyson and his other men, and Ian found himself tuning out the back-and-forth banter, wondering how Teddy was doing back at Envy. He tuned back in, however, when the sound on the bug went silent. Ian flicked the speaker and was just about to start fiddling with the settings when he realized the silence was real, not a malfunction.

"I'm sorry... You want me to *what*?" Tennyson asked, his voice low. Ian heard the underlying anger buried beneath faux confusion. Whatever they'd asked, Tennyson had clearly heard them perfectly. Either he was repeating it for Ian, somehow knowing Ian had tuned out, or for emphasis on the recordings. Either way, it couldn't be good.

"I said if you want me to do something for you, you gotta do something for me. You expect me to pay you, to trust you with my business, then you need to earn that trust." Julian's voice was slick. Somehow, he sounded reasonable.

"Sure, what do you need me to do?" Tennyson's voice was back to a smooth drawl. They'd known there was the possibility that he would have to do something incriminating to get into the cartel's good books. It had already been cleared through the higher ups that he had *some* leeway.

"Some people owe me money and it's time I taught them a lesson," DeAza said. There was the sound of shuffling as something was passed from one hand to another. "There's a few fuckers who owe me big. We're going to make an example out of them and show people what happens when you fuck with *La Familia*."

Ice slid down Ian's spine and wrapped around his chest until he couldn't breathe. Teddy could be one of them. Ignoring protocol, Ian yanked his cell phone out of his pocket and dialed Teddy's number.

It rang, and rang, until it hit voicemail. He hung up rather than leave a message, then he dialed again, and again, until he ended the call again with a curse. "Fuck, Teddy." He started dialing again, this time the number to the bar. It rang for a long dozen seconds until it was finally picked up.

Johnny sounded out of breath. "Envy, can I help you?"

"Johnny, it's Ian. I need you to put Teddy on—" Ian started.

"Teddy," Johnny hollered away from the phone. There was a moment of mumbling, then Teddy came on the phone, confused.

"Hello?"

Ian breathed a sigh of relief. "God, I thought something had happened when you didn't answer your phone."

"Sorry, I left it in my locker. What's wrong? Why would something have happened?" Teddy's voice rose at the end, fear leeching into the words.

Ian hurried to soothe him. "Nothing's wrong, baby. I want you to go upstairs and lock the door for me. Don't let anyone in but me."

"My shift—" Teddy started.

Ian interrupted, "I'll talk to Johnny, but I need you to listen to me, okay?"

"Okay…" Teddy's voice wavered. Clearly, he didn't like the idea, but Ian would rather lose money at the bar than put Teddy in danger. His superiors had authorized him paying off Teddy's debt—not that it had mattered, since he would have done it regardless—but they had stipulations. The money was going to come from the bureau, so they could tag it. They wanted to trace it, see where it ended up. It was unlikely it would end up with any of the cartel leaders without being laundered first, but there was always a chance. This branch didn't seem quite as well-organized as some of the others they'd investigated.

"Love you, baby," Ian said, just in case he didn't get a chance to say it later.

"Love you too, Daddy," Teddy whispered, and Ian could see his boy's blush in his mind, just from the way he said it.

"Give the phone to Johnny now," Ian ordered. He explained that Teddy needed to leave then hung up, letting himself focus on Tennyson's op again.

Chapter Thirty-Three

Teddy hurried upstairs, following Ian's orders to the letter. He twisted the last deadbolt but still didn't feel better. He might be safer up here, but Ian wasn't. Ian was out there, on assignment, and Teddy had no idea what he'd seen or heard that had made him so worried. Thoughts on Ian, Teddy wandered into the kitchen. He opened the fridge and stared blankly at the contents. Should he make something for Ian to eat? Would he be hungry when he got home?

But he didn't know when Ian was supposed to be back, and he'd feel worse giving Ian cold or over-cooked food than he would to give him nothing. He closed the fridge, eyeing the small pile of dishes from his dinner in the sink. He washed them and tucked them into the draining board, then fidgeted with the knobs on the cabinets. Sighing, he grabbed a towel and started drying each dish by hand.

Eventually, he ran out of things to do in the kitchen, so he dusted the shelves in the living room, cleaned the exercise equipment in the spare bedroom and mopped the bathroom. By the time he heard the muted music in the club below switch off, signaling that it was closing time, Teddy was on his knees in Ian's closet, organizing it. Unlike some people who had a junk drawer, Ian apparently had a junk closet. Teddy hadn't paid it much mind when he'd been hanging up his things, except to notice the deplorable lack of color in Ian's wardrobe.

So far he'd found a half-dozen records, even though Ian had no record player, a pair of shoes with holes right through the toes, one half of a pair of boots, and an empty photo album next to a shoebox stuffed with pictures. Teddy had pried off the lid before immediately closing it when he came face-to-photo with a picture of Lucas. Maybe soon he would be ready to face the past, but not now — not alone in Ian's closet.

Teddy shifted a stack of textbooks that Ian had, for some reason, decided to hold on to, so he could reach the far back of the closet. It was shadowed and hard to see, and for a moment, Teddy almost ignored the plain black suitcase standing up in the corner, thinking it was empty.

He nearly missed the tufts of blond fur stuck in the teeth of the zipper. It was only when he bumped it, reaching for a plastic bag stuffed with papers beside it, that he noticed. His fingers itched with curiosity. Part of him said he should leave it be, that if Daddy wanted him to see it, he'd have shown it to him, but Ian had already told him a dozen times to make himself at home — that they had no secrets from each other anymore.

His fingers twitched closer, until he was gripping the zipper in his hand and slowly pulling it down. Slowly, the suitcase opened, until a large blond bear tumbled out, a pretty blue ribbon still tied neatly around his neck.

"Mr. Blue," Teddy murmured as he caught it. Unfolded, it was nearly as large as him, bigger than he remembered. "I can't believe I forgot about you." A second later, he corrected, "I can't believe Ian kept you." The fur was soft under his fingers, nowhere near as matted as he'd expect from a four-year-old stuffed animal kept locked away in a closet. Did that mean Ian took it out occasionally, maybe while thinking of him? Or was that wishful thinking?

Ignoring the rather large mess he'd made in the closet, he dragged the bear out into the bedroom and onto the center of the bed. He crawled atop the comforter and curled around the stuffed animal, a yawn unexpectedly sliding free. He'd just close his eyes for a second.

* * * *

Teddy woke with a start, his heart pounding in his chest. He'd fallen asleep, and anything could have happened. Had Ian tried to call? Had he remembered to take his phone off silent before leaving the club? Had he even remembered to bring it into the bedroom?

"What's the matter, Teddy Bear?" a sleepy voice said from the bed beside him, and for a split second, Teddy's still-sleepy mind questioned when Mr. Blue had learned to speak.

"Ian?" he said when his brain clicked on. He twisted and threw himself into Ian's arms. "I didn't mean to fall asleep. I was trying to stay awake for you." God, he was *so* not going to cry over this. But despite telling himself that, his bottom lip wobbled, a lump growing in his throat.

"Baby, I'm not mad. I never expected you to stay awake the whole time." Ian rubbed his back, but that only made the tears well faster.

"I was so worried," Teddy admitted into Ian's chest.

"I didn't mean to worry you, Teddy Bear. I promise I wouldn't let anything happen to you."

Teddy straightened, swatting Ian's shoulder. "Not about me... I was worried about *you*! Just...anything could have happened and I wouldn't even know about it." Teddy's anger fled as quickly as it had come, his lip quivering again.

Ian's face softened, "I wasn't in danger either, baby, promise. I just sit in the van and listen to boring conversations. The only thing I'm in danger of is falling asleep."

Teddy slumped back down against Ian's chest, his cheek against his daddy's bare skin. After a few seconds, he reached out and dragged Mr. Blue across the mattress to their side. "I found Mr. Blue. I figured you got rid of him. Or Mama R. had him in storage somewhere."

"Of course I kept him. I always planned on giving him back to you, but..." Teddy felt Ian's shoulder shift in a shrug.

"Yeah," Teddy acknowledged the unspoken words. But life had happened and everything had gone to shit.

Ian went back to rubbing his back, but soon enough the feeling grew less soothing. Ian's fingers stroked down his spine, then up his sides, dancing over his ribs and back down, and Teddy shivered, goosebumps swelling. They weren't the only thing swelling, either.

Blood rushed to his cock and it hardened painfully against Ian's hip.

Ian's fingers stilled. His voice was husky when he spoke, "Does someone want to play?"

Rather than answer, Teddy ground his dick against Ian's skin, his panties already wet with arousal.

Ian moved, gripping Teddy's hips tightly. Teddy whimpered at the loss of friction. "Daddy..." Teddy whined, his cheeks flushing. He still hardly believed that he was allowed this, that Ian wanted him the same way he wanted Ian.

"Is that how good boys ask to play?" Ian said gruffly, his own dick pressing hard into Teddy's abdomen where it peeked out of his briefs.

Teddy whimpered, trying to move but held in place by strong hands. "Daddy, please can I play with you?"

"You're such a good boy. How could I say no to you?" Ian loosened his hold, then cupped his ass, urging him into motion, guiding him until they were rutting against each other, his small dick sliding against Daddy's larger one, separated only by the fabric of their underthings. The lace scratched against his skin, which only made his arousal draw higher.

"Daddy, please..." Teddy begged, scrabbling at Ian's shoulders for purchase. It felt too good, but at the same time, it wasn't enough. "I need...I..."

"Mm-m, you need something, baby? Do you want more? What do you want?" Ian thrust against him, his dick brushing a line across Teddy's stomach and Teddy whimpering, feeling the wetness from Daddy's pre-cum. "Do you want Daddy's hand?" Immediately, Ian slid between them, dipping below the band of his panties to stroke him.

Without warning, Ian bucked, rolling Teddy onto his back, and Daddy was nestled between his spread legs. Teddy gasped, his breath catching in his throat. His hips met air as he thrust.

"Or does my Teddy Bear want Daddy's mouth?" Ian trailed kisses down Teddy's chest, pausing only to suck each of his nipples into his mouth. Even though the left had never regained as much sensation as it'd had before his surgery, the feel of Ian's tongue against his skin still made him shudder, and heat flooded Teddy's body, little moans and whimpers leaking from his mouth. Slowly, Ian inched Teddy's panties lower, down over his thighs, past his knees, until they slid free of his ankles, landing somewhere on the floor behind them.

"Daddy," Teddy gasped, arching his hips upward as Ian moved lower. Ian's mouth was close, only inches away, only centimeters, only…Daddy's mouth was on him, sucking him in, and Teddy wanted it, so much…but he wanted something more.

"Daddy, please…I want your cock," he pleaded, any embarrassment he might have felt showing in the face of his want. He wanted Ian, and he wanted him now, more than he'd ever wanted anyone in his life.

Ian chuckled, the sound a tickle against his skin. "Patience is a virtue, baby." Teddy's fingers scrabbled at the bed linens. He was not a patient person, especially not now, not like this.

"Fuck patience," Teddy whined. Ian's eyes met his at the same time as the palm of his hand cracked against the side of his hip, the feeling just shy of painful. Teddy gasped, his breath catching in his throat. "Daddy…"

"Language, baby," Daddy teased, his eyes sparking, before he swirled his tongue around Teddy's dick again. He sucked for a moment, almost in punishment, before he let Teddy slip from his mouth with a pop. "Show me where you want me, baby."

Teddy flushed, heat burning through his cheeks. He didn't know why he felt so shy now, after all they'd done together, but embarrassment coursed through him. Slowly, he slid his fingers over his too-thin stomach and across the sharp edges of his hips, before dipping lower.

He circled his fingertip around his puckered rim. "Here, Daddy."

Ian's smile grew devilish as he stretched over him, reaching across the bed to the nightstand. Ian tugged open the drawer and pulled out a small, unopened bottle of lube and a foil packet. Ian threw them on the mattress. They landed by Teddy's hip.

"Spread your legs for me, Teddy Bear. Let Daddy see you."

Teddy moaned at the words, parting farther. He felt exposed, on display—but not in a way that made him feel dirty, not like on the podiums downstairs. He felt like Ian could see every part of him—not just his body, but his thoughts, his fears.

Ian flipped open the lube and spilled it over his fingers. Then those fingers, always gentle, always caring, dipped into his crease. "Hold yourself open for me, baby."

Teddy jerked, a whimper leaking from his mouth as he reached down, digging his fingers into skin as he obeyed.

"Such a pretty boy," Ian praised. At the same time, he swirled his fingertip over Teddy's rim until it softened and he could slip inside. Immediately, Teddy tightened around the intrusion. Ian stilled, letting him adjust, not moving again until Teddy whimpered, bucking his hips in a demand for movement, for more. For *something*.

Ian slowly fucked him with the digit until Teddy was a mewling mess, only then inserting another. Teddy savored the burn, not quite pleasure but not quite pain. "Please, Daddy. Ian, another. *Please*," he finally begged.

Ian dropped a kiss on the tender skin of his inner thigh as he slipped in a third finger. "Such a good boy, taking my fingers so well. Feel how tight you are, baby." Ian guided Teddy's hand down, encouraging him to slip his own finger in with Ian's, and that alone was enough to have Teddy barely holding back his orgasm. The feeling of his channel tight around Daddy's fingers and his own... It was so dirty, but so hot.

"No more, Daddy. I want you now. Please, Ian." Teddy couldn't wait longer. His climax was held back by a tenuous thread, and the threat of it snapping had him nearly sobbing.

Daddy pulled his fingers free and Teddy moaned at the loss, the emptiness, but only for a second. Just long enough for Ian to tear the condom wrapper open with his teeth and sheathe himself, then Daddy was there, pressing his cock against Teddy's waiting ring. Even with the prep, it was tight. Ian inched in slowly, until his balls rested, hot and heavy, against Teddy's skin.

Teddy cried out at the feeling of Ian inside him to the hilt. He'd never felt like this, like every thrust was reshaping him, consuming him from the inside out until he was something else, something *more*. Then Ian's lips were on his, stealing the air from his lungs in time with his daddy's thrusts. At the same time, Ian dropped his hand down to Teddy's cock, pulling pleasure from his body like water from a well—but it did nothing to quench the fire that burned in Teddy's body. It stoked it higher. Teddy was gasoline and Ian a match.

"It's like your body was made for me," Ian panted, brushing his lips along the crest of Teddy's ear before dropping to his neck, nuzzling the spot that never failed to send shivers down his spine. He clenched down on Ian, grinding his cock against the palm of Ian's hand and unable to speak except to whimper.

"Such a good boy," Ian continued to praise him, each word winding Teddy higher. He was on a tightrope poised to fall, only his will keeping him aloft.

"Come on, baby," Ian's breath came harshly, as did his thrusts, which grew less rhythmic. They were a staccato pulsing, each one pushing Teddy closer. "Come for Daddy, Teddy Bear. I want to see you, wanna feel your tight ass milk me. Come, Teddy."

The tightrope snapped and Teddy fell, pleasure coursing through his veins as he spiraled, his channel clamping down and body shaking. For a second, he thought he passed out, his vision sparking to black, but then Ian shuddered above him, spilling into the condom inside him.

Teddy waited for him to pull out, to roll over and go to sleep now that he was finished with Teddy's body, but instead, Ian dropped down atop him. Teddy should have felt smothered, but instead, all he felt was cherished. Ian was still moving, stroking through Teddy's hair, trailing small kisses over Teddy's cheek and chin until Teddy relaxed.

Eventually, Ian softened inside him.

Teddy winced when he slipped free. "I wish you could stay inside me forever."

Ian licked the seam of Teddy's lips until they parted, then he slid his tongue into Teddy's mouth in a hot kiss. "We can go to the clinic in the morning and get tested. Then I could fill you up, plug you. Keep you full of my cum all day."

Teddy whimpered at the thought of carrying some of Daddy around with him.

Ian laughed. "Little minx. You like that?"

"Please can we? Do you mean it?"

"Always, baby." Ian promised, levering himself off Teddy to climb off the mattress. "Stay here and let Daddy clean you up."

Ian returned with a washcloth. He was in no hurry, swiping it gently around Teddy's ass and dick, even over his inner thighs, removing all trace of lube, as well as the remnants of Teddy's orgasm. After dropping the washrag in the hamper, Ian slid back into bed beside him, folding Teddy back into his arms like he'd never left.

"Sleep time, baby."

Teddy would have protested, but a yawn interrupted his words. Maybe Daddy was right, and sleep would be for the best.

Chapter Thirty-Four

The clinic was clean and quick. It wasn't the one Teddy used—he used the free one over by the university, which was, admittedly, still clean, but nowhere near as fast. They'd barely checked in with the nurse before they were called back to a room. There was only one bed, which Teddy hopped up on with Ian's urging. Ian leaned against the counter, his hands planted on the countertop.

Teddy briefly flirted with the thought of seducing Ian. He didn't have a doctor kink—or didn't think he did—but they were alone, and being alone with Ian was enough to spark his lust.

Unfortunately, before Teddy could let his imaginings of fucking Ian on the hospital bed devolve too far, the door opened and a young man in scrubs entered, holding a pair of charts. He was about the same age as Teddy, and like Teddy, he wore eyeliner. He had a bright smile on his face.

"What are we here for today, guys?"

Teddy felt his skin pinken at the matter-of-fact way Ian answered, and thankfully, the nurse didn't bat an eye. Teddy walked out of the clinic minus a gallon of blood — not really, but it felt like it — less than a half hour after they'd walked in.

Teddy rubbed the crease of his arm, where the weird pink bandage was working hard to strip the area of every stray strand of hair, until Ian swatted his fingers away. "Don't pick at it, baby. You'll make it bleed."

"It's already bleeding. See?" Teddy shoved his arm upward toward Ian's face, until the red-tinted cotton that peeked out from under the bandage tickled Ian's nose.

Ian's mouth twisted, nose crinkling as he tipped his head back and away, "Gross."

"Oh come on. Look at it!" Teddy grinned, leaning up on tiptoes to get closer. "How are you supposed to kiss all my booboos if you can't even look at them?" He feigned a pout.

Ian rolled his eyes but dutifully kissed the bandage that was wrapped around the crook of Teddy's arm. "There… Happy?"

Teddy tugged his arm down and made a face. "Ew, gross. Do you know how many germs are in the human mouth? I mean, *I* don't, but I'm sure it's bunches."

"Do you know how many spankings bratty boys get? I mean, *I* don't, but I'm sure that's bunches too," Ian teased, reaching around Teddy to swat his butt.

"Nope," Teddy disagreed, popping his lips at the end of the word. "Naughty boys get corner time. Spankings are for fun time." He might sound like he was teasing, but in reality, he was serious as a stroke — not just because he enjoyed the feeling of a bare palm on his ass too much for it to be a punishment, but because he'd always vowed not to let anyone hit him in anger, not even for play.

Ian sobered slightly. "Understood. No spankings except for fun."

Teddy nodded. "Maybe if I'm a good boy today, we can practice?" A shiver of excitement trickled down his spine as Ian's eyes darkened with hunger. Ian lunged forward, pressing Teddy fiercely back into the side of the truck—hard enough to steal the breath from his lungs but not so hard as to be painful. It was just the right amount of force, combined with just the perfect amount of care, to have Teddy squirming beneath Ian's palms.

Then Ian's knee was between his, prying his legs apart until he was riding Ian's thigh, unable to stop his hips from rocking. He gasped at the coarseness of his jeans against his cock.

Maybe it was a bad day to go commando.

"Daddy," Teddy gasped and shuddered as Ian clamped his hands around his hips, urging him faster. A tightness spread from his core, from that spot inside him that made everything feel so much bigger, like he couldn't breathe, though his lungs were heaving.

"Uh-uh, Teddy Bear," Ian teased, leaning down to clamp his teeth around Teddy's lower lip and tugging, sucking on the fleshy pout until he cried out. "Good boys don't come until Daddy says they can."

"Please, please, Daddy. I'll be good." Teddy would be good. He would be *so* good. He'd be the absolute best. He just needed Daddy to let him finish.

"I don't know. Only a naughty boy would come out in the open like this, don't you think? Wouldn't a good boy wait until they got home?" Daddy's voice was rumbling thunder that drove the lightning shooting through Teddy's veins higher.

Teddy was vibrating. It started in his hip and spread lower, an intermittent buzzing against his skin, until—

"Your phone is ringing, Teddy Bear. Better get that." Then Ian stepped back, leaving Teddy a quivering mess against the passenger door of the truck, only supported by his own wobbling legs, while Ian looked calm and cool, like he hadn't just had Teddy on the brink of climax.

Teddy fumbled for his phone, his fingers stiff and unwieldy as they dug around the small pockets of his skinny jeans. "Not fair," he muttered before thumbing the answer button without looking.

"Teddy?" Shiloh's voice was muffled as it came through the speaker. "Is everything okay?"

Teddy straightened immediately at the rough sound of his best friend's voice. "You're asking *me* if everything is okay? I called you like nineteen times last night!"

"I know. That's why I'm checking in," Shiloh replied, so much sarcasm riding his voice that Teddy could almost see him rolling his eyes. "I thought maybe you got mugged or something."

"And I thought you got kidnapped!" Teddy half-screeched into the phone, ignoring the way Shiloh whimpered at the loudness. "You didn't show up to Envy. You didn't answer my calls or my texts. I even shot you a fucking e-mail! An *e-mail*, Shiloh. Do you know how long it's been since I used *that*? High school. It's been since high school. If it wasn't for the fact that you ghost me at least twice a year, I'd have been over there banging on the door at two in the morning. And you know I would have done it."

Teddy only stopped ranting because he ran out of air halfway through his tirade and had to suck in a breath.

Shiloh used the opportunity to interrupt, which was probably for the best, because Teddy was nowhere near done. "I know I'm a shitty person. I should have messaged last night. I…I stayed the night with a trick and didn't have a phone charger."

"One of these days you're going to stay the night with a serial killer or something," Teddy grumbled, scuffing his shoe across the pavement. He hated it when Shiloh did stupid shit like this. It was so beyond risky that it wasn't even funny.

There was a long stretch of silence before Shiloh finally spoke. "I need the money."

"Badly enough to risk your life?"

"Look… Just because we're friends doesn't mean I need you analyzing my life choices, okay?" Shiloh snapped, and Teddy's shoulders sagged at the anger in his friend's voice. They didn't fight often, but when they did, he always hated it. "I gotta go. I just wanted to make sure you didn't die or nothing."

The line abruptly clicked off, leaving only silence in his ear. Teddy sighed and shoved his phone back into his pocket.

"Everything all right?" Ian asked.

Teddy shrugged and pulled open the passenger door. "I guess. Just Shiloh being Shiloh."

"Hmm-m." Ian hummed an acknowledgment before helping boost Teddy into the tall cab of the truck, even reaching across him to buckle him in. "Sometimes we have to let people make their own choices."

"Even when they're bad ones," Teddy finished with a sigh.

"Even when they're bad ones," Ian agreed before closing the passenger door and rounding the truck to the other side. Ian climbed in and started the engine, then dropped his large hand onto Teddy's thigh. It nearly spanned it, his pinkie finger tickling Teddy's inner thigh while his thumb ran circles above his knee. It distracted Teddy for several minutes as he silently urged Ian to slide his palm higher.

It did not, however, distract him enough that he didn't notice when Ian took a wrong turn.

"You missed our turn," Teddy pointed out.

Ian just smirked and kept driving. Teddy peered out of the window, watching the familiar streets pass by, trying to figure out where they were going. Maybe Ian was taking him on a surprise date. It made sense in some ways, since Teddy had to work at the club that night and Ian had said something about 'running an errand', which Teddy knew had something to do with his real job at the bureau. But when Ian pulled the truck into the parking lot of what was clearly a university, Teddy's excitement grew into nerves.

"What are we doing here?" Teddy asked, his voice small. He knew this college. Recognized it, though it had been years since he'd meticulously scoured their website, filling out applications. Despite the time that had passed, it looked nearly identical to his memories of the one and only tour he'd taken before he'd had to drop out before he'd even started.

Ian put the truck into park and turned off the engine before he turned toward Teddy. His own anxiety was clear on his face. "Hear me out. I might have overstepped a bit, but I already talked to the admissions office and the financial aid office, and they still have all your information on file. I know the only thing that was standing in your way of coming here was money, and that's something I can fix."

"Back up a bit, just…I don't understand. Are you saying…? What are you saying?" Teddy didn't know whether to laugh or cry or storm out of the truck. On the one hand, Ian *had* overstepped, and by more than just 'a bit'. But on the other…he'd always wanted to be an architect and Ian was offering that to him, on a silver platter no less.

"I want you to go to college, Teddy. Get your degree. Follow your dreams. You'd make such a good architect," Ian lifted a hand to Teddy's face, stroking along his cheek. "It kills me that you spend every night dancing instead of studying buttresses or whatever it is that architects study." Ian's lips quirked up slightly before he grew serious again. "I want you to be happy."

"I am." Teddy lifted his hand, closing it around Ian's, but he didn't pull him away. He just turned his head to brush his lips across Ian's palm. "You don't need to send me to college to make me happy. You did that all on your own."

"Then do it to make me happy," Ian murmured, caressing Teddy's skin, slipping his thumb over Teddy's lips before dipping between them for the briefest of seconds. "Let me do this."

The stubborn part of Teddy immediately urged him to refuse. He'd been taking care of himself for years, since long before he'd realized it wasn't normal for an eight-year-old to make himself dinner, and that part of himself was scared of what it would mean to stop now. But he'd already given Ian control of his body and heart…maybe it wouldn't hurt to give him control of his mind, too.

"Okay," Teddy whispered his agreement and it was as if that one single word, that verbal submission to Ian's will, relinquished him from the hold of his fear and replaced it with calm.

Chapter Thirty-Five

After what felt like hours of filling out paperwork and enrolling for classes — because the fall semester would be starting before Teddy knew it and already the courses were close to being full — Ian pulled the truck up to the curb in front of Envy and let the engine idle. It was late enough that the lights on the sidewalk had already flickered on, and soon enough, the club would be opening its doors.

"I should be back before midnight, but if I'm not, I want you to go upstairs as soon as your shift is over, okay?" Ian fretted worse than a mother hen and it was hard for Teddy to resist rolling his eyes.

"Well, I was thinking of going out back and standing in the alley with a big sign that said 'Mug me,' but — " Teddy started to joke, but Ian landed a swat on his thigh and cut off his words. "Geez, lighten up, Daddy." Teddy laughed and slid out of the truck before Ian could swat him again.

"I'm not afraid to put you over my knee and redden your ass right here, boy," Ian warned, his eyes glinting.

"You'd have to catch me first," Teddy teased, blowing Ian a kiss before he slammed the door and sprinted for the side entrance. For a moment, he thought Ian was going to follow him — the look in his eyes when Teddy took off running was predatory, and Teddy swore he heard him growl — but no footsteps stalked him down the alley. Instead, he heard the soft rumble of an engine as the truck pulled away.

But not, of course, until Teddy was safely inside.

* * * *

Later that night, Teddy slithered off the platform, a dozen hands caressing his ass under the guise of 'helping.' He had to pick his way through a larger-than-normal crowd of already-buzzed clubbers to make it to the bar.

He'd never seen this many customers on a weeknight and Teddy racked his brain to think of a reason as he hopped over the counter to the other side and snagged his apron off the hook. He tugged the skimpy blue fabric over his head and tied it, pausing only to wash his hands before he waded into the fray.

Impatient frat boys crowded around the bar, orange Longhorn shirts stretched tight across swollen chests.

Teddy, under the guise of grabbing a new bottle of Hennessy from under the counter, lowered his voice and whispered a question at the other bartender, Zach. "What's with all the straights?"

Not that no gay men wore Longhorn shirts — plenty of them did, especially this close to the start of the season. But most of the college guys cringed away from any man who stood too close, chests puffing out and jaws clenched, like taking up more room would keep 'the gays' from approaching. Really, all it did was mean that they all had to stand even closer together. In the brief few minutes Teddy had stood behind the bar, he'd already seen half a dozen of them almost come to blows over an accidental brush of arm against chest.

Zach rolled his eyes and thumbed over his shoulder at Johnny. "Dumbass over there picked the theme."

Teddy craned his neck to see the sign hand-written on a chalkboard near the front but couldn't read it over the dozens of heads blocking his view.

Zach saved him the effort. "Masc Night. Half-off drinks for jocks."

Teddy cringed, eyeing the crowd again. "Ian approved that?"

Zach shook his head, then shrugged. "Doubt it. Ian doesn't seem like he'd put up with that shit."

For a second, there was a vulnerability in Zach's voice. Teddy caught the way the other man's fingers skimmed over his pink lace shorts. Unlike Teddy's boyshorts, Zach wore cheekies, leaving the lower half of his ass exposed. He suspected that Zach liked the uniform more than he'd ever admit. Outside the club, Zach wore gym shorts and tank tops religiously, but more than once Teddy had glimpsed lace beneath when his shorts rode too low.

"Hey, *soy boy*," an asshole leaning on the bar hollered over toward Teddy and Zach. "You two done gossiping, or do I have to come around the bar and grab a beer myself?" Teddy didn't need to know who it was directed at to be offended. Both of them were in pink, with glittery makeup and heels, so it could have been to either…or both.

Zach's face closed down in a mask Teddy recognized well, because he saw it too often in the mirror. The other bartender's shoulders tensed, arms crossing like they could protect him from the insults.

Teddy's first instinct was to cave in, but instead he found himself angry. For once, why couldn't Teddy say what he wanted, act how he wanted...*be* who he wanted, without judgement? Ian wouldn't see him this time, but he imagined Ian would approve. Daddy would want his boy to stand up for himself.

Teddy squared his shoulders and strutted over to the asshole. The man might be taller than him, and his shoulders might be broader, but his eyes were blurry with drink.

Teddy lifted a knee onto the bar until he could climb onto the top, drawing the eyes of everyone nearby, knowing it would also get the attention of the bouncers. He lowered his eyes and sank demurely down, giving a coquettish flutter of his eyelashes. His teeth brushed over the fullness of his lower lip, drawing the man's eyes for a moment. Teddy knew that despite his low dose of T, they were still feminine, especially with the gloss, and confusion warred with arousal on the larger man's face.

Teddy lifted his hand and ran it down the asshole's chest from collarbone to waist, "Trust me, baby. I eat *all* the meat."

He couldn't hold back his laugh as the larger man half fell in his attempt to scramble away from Teddy's flirting fingers.

Would Ian spank him later for flirting? And more important, would Teddy like it? Would he enjoy the feel of his skin heating up, the sting of pain pulling pleasure from his flesh?

The asshole, however, looked horrified, before the terror of being touched by a man twisted to disgust and fury. He lunged forward, his mallet-like fists lifting. Teddy tensed, waiting for the blow he knew was coming.

It never landed. He cracked open eyes that he didn't remember shutting to see the asshole hunched over, his arm twisted painfully behind his back by a familiar man.

Hugo held the asshole's wrist in a vise grip, his other hand clenched around the back of his neck. A moment later, he moved, slamming the man's face into the top of the bar so loud that Teddy thought he heard a crack, and he wondered what had broken—the bar or the man's nose.

Teddy lifted his eyes to Hugo's face and shuddered. The hulk of a man was an ice sculpture in the heart of a Midwest February. With his lips pulled tight, no bared teeth or flashing eyes to show his anger, Teddy had to read it in the curve of his jaw, and in the taut, straining tendons in his neck.

Hugo's large hand pressed the frat boy harder into the bar. "Say you're sorry." Behind him, the crowd shuffled back, giving them room.

"Sorry," the asshole whimpered, the word muffled.

"I didn't hear you."

"Sorry!" The asshole's voice, though louder, was still muffled, but Hugo released him. Just in time, since Teddy saw a pair of bouncers pushing their way across the dance floor, headed their way.

The man fell to the floor and scrambled back, shooting daggers at Teddy until Hugo stepped threateningly toward him, his shadow swallowing the man's face. If Hugo had been smaller—or the gun on his hip just a bit less on display—the man and his friends might have caused problems. Instead, with only minor grumbling, a pair of behemoths picked their friend off the ground and half-dragged him out of the club. The bouncers retreated back to their corners.

Johnny glared from the other end of the bar, only now bothering to realize there was an issue. "There went a shit ton of easy money."

Teddy just lifted his middle finger and aimed it at the fucker. "It's a good thing you like dick, because you're a real pussy."

Zak laughed.

Johnny didn't.

Hugo cleared his throat. "Teddy."

The high that Teddy had been riding crashed instantly, his heart plummeting to his feet as the Obviously Bad Thing hit him in the face.

Hugo didn't visit him casually.

Hugo wasn't his friend.

If Hugo was here, it was because... *Fuck.*

"Now?" Teddy asked, sliding off the bar to land in front of him, wringing his hands. "Can... Do I have time to change?"

Hugo shook his head slowly, his cold mask breaking just long enough for Teddy to read what might be sadness beneath it. "No. We have to go now."

Teddy flexed his fingers, wiping his sweaty palms on his thighs. "Okay." Before he could lose control of the panic fluttering to life in his chest, he grabbed a bottle of liquor — he didn't care what it was or how it tasted, he just needed to feel the burn, to let the fire of the whiskey numb him — and drank straight from the mouth.

"Hey!" Johnny grabbed it from his hand and shot him a dirty glare. "The fuck, Teddy?"

"Let's go," Teddy ignored his ex and started for the back hallway, alcohol humming just loud enough in his veins to mute the fearful whispers in his mind. He walked quickly through the hallway and out into the alley, knowing that to the crowd in the club, he'd look eager. They'd wonder where he was going and why, and if he was blowing Hugo out back. But if he hesitated, the meager courage he'd scrounged up would wither and die.

Hugo ushered him to a black sedan, already running, and urged him into the passenger seat. "Don't make me tie you up."

Maybe it was meant to sound like a threat, but Teddy heard it as the plea that it was.

"Are they going to kill me?" Teddy's voice came out small as he voiced the fear that sat like curdled milk in his throat.

"No," Hugo immediately denied, but his hands turned white on the steering wheel.

Teddy turned to stare blankly out of the window. He didn't understand. Ian had told him the FBI was going to pay off the cartel. Why would they still be after him? Unless they hadn't made the payment yet—but what would have stopped them? Was this about something else? His heart beat faster in his chest. Had they found out he was working with the bureau now?

He silently apologized to Ian. Whatever happened— if he died, if they just beat him up—Ian was going to blame himself. Teddy should have stayed out of the other man's life. Should have just…loved him from afar, like he'd done for years without realizing it.

Because he did realize it now. He'd thought the young, innocent love he'd held for Ian as a teenager had passed, thought he'd moved on. Seeing Ian again—

living with him, growing to trust him — made him realize how wrong he'd been. His love hadn't faded. It had just slept for a while, lain dormant, hibernated through the winter of their separation.

He almost missed the turn onto a familiar street, just two blocks over from the house he'd grown up in. Hugo drove up to a warehouse graffitied with curses and gang signs, then honked at a closed bay. The door opened with a loud, grinding rumble, and Hugo drove through. It shut slowly behind him with an ominous bang as it hit the asphalt.

Hugo idled the car for a long, silent second, then spun the key. The ignition died. "Get out," Hugo ordered, his voice like gravel.

Teddy scrambled to open the door with shaking hands. The interior of the warehouse looked much as he remembered it, though the furniture was nicer. There were still women on their knees, still men roughhousing by the pool tables. Still the same faint odor of nicotine and piss.

Teddy didn't have time to get more than a quick glance as he darted his eyes around. Hugo grabbed Teddy's arm just below the shoulder and half-walked, half-dragged him forward.

It had been two years since Teddy had seen Julian face-to-face. The man looked older, his dark hair cropped close to his scalp, silver glinting where it threaded through an eyebrow. A scar stretched from the corner of the man's mouth to his right ear, giving his face a lopsided grin, though his expression was sober.

Teddy barely met the man's eyes before he was shoved down at Julian's feet, pain blooming beneath his kneecaps when they struck the cement. His eyes watered but it didn't stop him from seeing the others beside him.

There were four other people on their knees at Julian's feet, three men of disparate ages and a woman perhaps a decade older than Teddy. The blonde woman was in an old-style diner dress, name tag reading *Delia*. One of the men was in a polo with the logo of a gym stamped on the arm and another wore a cheap, poorly fitting suit. A car dealership badge naming him Carlos dangled from the lapel.

"Tie him up," Julian ordered.

Teddy liked to think Hugo hesitated. It was only a few seconds, though, before a rope was yanked around his wrists, binding him tightly. Teddy scanned the faces of the men surrounding Julian, hoping for a hint of what was to happen.

It was hard to tell. Some were laughing, some leered at Teddy's exposed skin and Delia's heaving cleavage, and some just looked solemn.

Julian himself looked bored. "You must be wondering why you're here, no?" He paced the line, stopping at each one of them before moving to the next. He stopped again at the other end, in front of the man in the polo shirt. He was in his forties at the most, his steel hair smoothed over to hide a growing bald spot.

A dark stain spread from the crotch of his pants already, probably the source of the piss Teddy had smelled earlier. "You've failed me, Silas. You promised me your gym would be safe from the feds, that my *money* would be safe from the feds. But what do I find tonight?"

"I d-don't know, sir. I didn't tip off no one," The man, Silas, said through chattering teeth, his eyes darting from left to right, like he'd see something that would save him—or someone, because he tried to scuttle forward, despite the bindings on his arms and ankles, nearly toppling at the feet of one of the men. "Tell him, Jose. Tell him I don't know nothing."

The man, Jose, cringed away from him, then kicked out, foot connecting with Silas' side and sending him toppling to the pavement. "Get your dirty fucking hands off me."

Silas shuddered, struggling back up onto his knees as he turned toward Julian instead, like his pitiful appearance would inspire mercy. "Please, DeAza. I didn't do nothing, I didn't. I kept my mouth shut. It wasn't me."

Teddy had been trying to stay silent and unnoticed, but he couldn't stop the small cry that escaped his lips when Julian pulled a gun off his hip and pressed the barrel tight against the kneeling man's forehead. The flesh dimpled around the metal.

"You know, it's a pity, because I actually believe you," Julian said but pressed the gun even harder against the man's skin. "A man like you— Well, you're not even a man. You're a rat. You don't have the *cajones*. But somebody ratted, and now there are feds watching your gym. And you promised me... No feds at your gym. Didn't you promise me that?"

Silas nodded frantically, tears spilling down his cheeks. Teddy didn't want to watch but he couldn't tear his eyes away. Fear held him frozen in its grasp.

But Julian pulled the gun away and straightened, passing the weapon to the man in the leather jacket. Teddy's shoulders sagged in relief, thinking the man was safe, that Julian was just teaching him a lesson through fear and empty threats.

He should have known better.

Julian gestured to one of his men. "Jo, what do we do to rats who can't keep their mouth shut?"

Jo reached into the pocket of his leather jacket and pulled out what looked like a fishhook, complete with black fishing line. "We close it for them."

Teddy retched at the sight of the hook piercing the flesh above the kneeling man's lip. He slammed his eyes closed, but not before he saw the hand clamp down on Silas' jaw, forcing his mouth closed when it opened on a scream. He couldn't block out the sounds, the wet sucking sound of the line being tugged through flesh, the muffled screams, the laughter of the gang members.

Whatever Hugo had promised, Teddy doubted he was walking from the warehouse in one piece.

The sound of cries grew quieter. Teddy forced his eyes open, not knowing what was happening somehow worse than the ghoulish sight that greeted him. The older man was a sickly gray, which made the black thread sewn across his mouth even more ghastly, and crimson streaked across his chin and neck. Tears streaked down his cheeks but the sound was wrong, sobs caught behind a mouth that no longer opened. It was like something out of a horror movie that Teddy never wanted to watch.

Jo let the man fall to a bleeding heap on the cement.

Julian waved a hand, and two of his men started dragging the softy sobbing man away. "I'm impressed. I didn't think you'd go through with it."

Julian moved down the line, to the man in the cheap suit.

Teddy tried not to listen and harder not to watch, but he couldn't help seeing the hammer fall on the third man's hands, over and over. Bile burned his throat at the sound of bones breaking.

It was a sound he'd never be able to get out of his head, a wet pop, a snapping *crack* that didn't seem loud enough but, at the same time, was too loud to unhear. It was somehow worse than the man's choked screams.

Chapter Thirty-Six

Teddy couldn't help it.

He leaned to the side and vomited, acid coating his tongue and spilling out his nose, coating his face and shirt before landing in a puddle on the floor. The smell of sick made Teddy's stomach heave again. It also drew Julian's attention to him.

A boot collided with Teddy's side. "And you," Julian snarled, kicking him again until he toppled into the puddle of sick. It stuck to his skin and Teddy gagged again, the sound hollow, empty.

"I lend you money to pay for your little surgery. I even offer you a way to pay me back." Teddy shuddered when a pair of knees entered into his vision as Julian crouched, then the man tangled his fist in Teddy's hair, dragging him closer across the pavement. "I had high hopes for you. You looked so pretty sucking Hugo's dick that you could have paid your debt off twice over. You're just lucky that little video you made is doing so well or I'd have pulled you in months ago."

Teddy stared up at him in horror — not that he had a choice, since Julian was still tugging him up, forcing him to meet his eyes.

He'd thought the video was safely locked away. How many people had seen it? How many people had *paid* to see it? If he hadn't already thrown up, he would now.

Julian must have seen his horror and he widened his smirk before he tugged a bandana out of his pocket and roughly wiped the vomit off Teddy's face. It somehow left Teddy feeling even dirtier.

"You're the hottest thing in porn right now. You should hear what they're saying." Julian straightened, the hand he had clasped in Teddy's hair forcing him back up onto his knees.

"Mikey," Julian snapped with his other hand at a red-headed man nearby. "Read me what they're saying."

The large redhead laughed. "You got it, boss." He pulled out his phone and a second later, started reading. The words were stilted and lumbering but no less horrific for that. *"Teddy's mouth looks so pretty wrapped around that big dick. How much for him to suck mine?"*

Julian clamped his free hand across Teddy's mouth and squeezed, the pain growing until Teddy was forced to open it, unable to bear the pressure. With his other hand, Julian forced Teddy's face closer, until his mouth was pressed tight to his jeans. They tasted of sweat.

"He does have a pretty mouth, doesn't he, boys?" Julian said as he dragged Teddy's face across his crotch. Teddy cried out as the zipper stabbed into his skin, rubbing it raw. A chorus of rough agreements sounded, but they were drowned out by the sound of Teddy's racing pulse in his ears.

"Read the next one," Julian demanded.

"Look at that tight little-boy pussy. Wanna see it stretched around two dicks — one for each hole."

Julian said something and Teddy knew it was crude, but he didn't hear it. Didn't hear anything but those words echoing in his head, a loop that repeated over and over until it threatened to break him.

He'd grown to love his new body. He loved the flat planes of his chest, even if he wished it didn't bear the scars of its old swells. He loved the curve of his hips, even if they were maybe just a tad too feminine, because they made his ass pop in his favorite pair of skinny jeans. He even loved the small size of his penis, because it was *his*. But he'd never grown to love that last part of his old body, the part they had never quite gotten rid of, and knowing that people had seen it —

Worse, that people wanted to *use* it… It was enough to make him ignore being dropped back to the cement, even enough to block out the weight of a heavy, steel-toed boot pressing into his chest.

"You're a perfect little porn star now, Teddy." Julian dug the treads of his boots deeper into Teddy's flesh. "So I'll do you a favor, give you one last chance to make the right choice. You make me enough movies to pay off your debt, and I'll let you walk, free and clear."

Teddy shuddered, a sob escaping from his lips. He couldn't do it. He couldn't.

"Or…" Julian lifted his foot from Teddy's chest and crouched in front of him again. Before Teddy could process it, Julian had a gun in his hand and the barrel was pressed against Teddy's lips. Julian gripped his jaw, digging his fingers into the flesh of Teddy's cheeks until his mouth opened against his will.

The barrel slid between his teeth like an iron cock, resting against his throat until he gagged. Julian cocked the hammer. Teddy's pulse pounded harsh and heavy in his veins. His lungs heaved but drew in no air.

He was going to die.

Julian leaned closer, his breath ghosting over Teddy's cheekbone. He crooned in Teddy's ear. "What do you say, Teddy? Are you going to learn to take a dick for me? Or are you going to learn what a bullet tastes like?"

He was a devil, offering Teddy a choice between two hells, a choice he couldn't make. To agree would betray Ian, to deny would condemn himself.

So he made the only choice he could make and closed his eyes, saying a prayer to a God he did not believe in, not for himself but for the man who held his heart in gentle hands. *Let Ian forget me.*

The sound of gunfire echoed through the warehouse then pain—blinding, biting pain that started in his jaw and spread through his skull until blackness took him.

Chapter Thirty-Seven

Ian had never been so excited to walk into a club, not even when he'd turned twenty-one and had been permitted in for the first time. It had been a nearly three-hour round-trip to meet with one of his superiors, but he'd left the meeting with a small briefcase stuffed with marked bills that would, hopefully, help bring down the cartel—and more importantly, buy Teddy's freedom.

All he wanted to do now was find his boy and celebrate.

Teddy wasn't behind the bar, though. Ian didn't see him on the podiums, either, and nor was he in the changing room. Ian headed back out and flagged down Zach. The bartender slid a glass to his last customer before heading over. "S'up, boss?"

"Have you seen Teddy?" Ian asked.

"He went out back with some big dude an hour or so ago," Zach answered. Heart beating faster, Ian spun on his heel, ready to rush toward the back door, but Zach hollered after him, "The big dude came back a few minutes ago though. Said Teddy wasn't feeling well and would be upstairs?"

Ian changed course, barely restraining himself from sprinting as he headed for the stairway that led to his apartment. Teddy wouldn't have let some stranger up there unless he didn't have a choice, and the only 'big dude' Ian could think of that Teddy would have left with was Hugo Ward, the cartel's enforcer.

He took the stairs two at a time, anxiety only growing when the door at the top was unlocked.

Teddy knew better.

Ian burst through, not even pausing to draw his service weapon as he charged at the large man pacing the living room. Only the element of surprise let him get the drop on the man, and seconds later, he had Ward on the ground, pinned beneath his knee. Now he drew his gun, pressing the barrel to the man's forehead.

"Where is he?" Ian growled, anger fighting with fear.

The big man went still beneath him. "He's fine. Bit banged up, but he's fine."

"Where. Is. He?" Ian pressed the gun harder.

"The bedroom!"

Ian backed off, keeping the gun pointed at Hugo with one hand while he tugged out a coffee table drawer with the other. He pulled out a pair of handcuffs and chucked them at the man. They landed on his chest and bounced. "Put them on."

Hugo didn't argue. He snapped the cuffs around each wrist.

"Tighter," Ian ordered. Hugo looked like he wanted to argue but didn't, just pressing the cuffs closed farther.

"I know where you live. If you're not here when I get out, I will find you," Ian threatened. He didn't like the idea of leaving Hugo out here alone, but he needed to check on Teddy.

His boy was curled on his side, his back to the door. He looked small on the mattress. Ian's shoulders sagged in relief when he saw Teddy's shoulders shifting with each breath. He rounded the mattress and his relief died.

Teddy was breathing, but he was far from uninjured.

Red-stained cotton balls were stuffed into his boy's mouth, enough that Teddy's left cheek bulged out and dried blood crusted around his lips. Ian dropped his firearm on the nightstand and crawled onto the bed. "Teddy," Ian murmured, hesitating as he reached for him. Was that his only injury, or were more hiding beneath the baggy shirt that covered him from shoulders to knee?

Teddy moaned and twisted his face into the pillow, then whimpered in pain. His eyes cracked open, red-rimmed and swollen. He mumbled something. It was inaudible, the words smothered in cotton.

Teddy made a face then whimpered again, pulling at the cotton shoved in his mouth. A garbled "ow," sounded as he pulled out a thick wad. They were dark brown and crusted together, with streaks of scarlet from where he must have opened a wound.

"It hurts," Teddy mumbled, fingers pressed to his lips.

"Don't try to talk, baby." Ian reached out and brushed a strand of hair out of Teddy's face. The ends were stained red. "I'm so sorry, baby." He'd left Teddy alone, and look what had happened. He'd promised

Teddy nothing would happen to him and God only knew what his baby had endured.

"Not your fault," Teddy whispered, lips barely moving. Whatever had happened, it clearly hurt to speak.

"Let's get you to a doctor," Ian said, gathering Teddy into his arms rather than argue. It was his fault. If he hadn't left, Teddy wouldn't be hurt. If he'd urged his superiors to work faster, they'd have paid off his debt already. He should have made sure Teddy stayed in the apartment.

"Pants," Teddy muttered before Ian could carry him out of the room. "Can walk."

Ian sat Teddy gently back on the bed and grabbed the first pair of pants he could find, a pair of sweatpants that would be far too large on Teddy but much more comfortable than skinny jeans. He pushed a pair of boots onto Teddy's bare feet.

He didn't see any other injuries, but everything in him still protested letting Teddy walk. But it was probably better that way. Safer, since Ian refused to let Hugo leave without answers.

Ian grabbed his gun in one hand and Teddy's hand in the other and returned to the living room.

Hugo was still sitting on the floor where he'd left him, skin pale, his hands shaking in the cuffs. "He's okay, right, man?" Hugo asked.

"If you cared, you wouldn't have brought him to them. Get up." Ian gestured toward the door with the gun. "You're coming with us."

"He saved me." Teddy's voice was garbled and hard to understand.

Ian lowered the gun slightly but didn't holster it completely. "It's okay, Teddy. Don't try to talk until we get to the hospital." Ian glared at Hugo. "*You* can explain everything in the truck."

* * * *

Eight stitches and an antibiotic later and Ian was driving Teddy back to the apartment. He'd left Hugo on the sidewalk outside the hospital. He wasn't sure whether to thank the man or kill him. If he hadn't taken Teddy in the first place, he never would have been in danger. But if he hadn't stepped in and shot Julian, his boy might never have made it home. He'd figure out how to deal with the man later, after he got Teddy settled.

It wasn't hard. Between the stress of the day and the painkillers the doctor had given him, Teddy was half asleep when they made it upstairs. Ian tucked him into bed before double checking that all the doors and windows were locked. He was halfway back to the room before he decided to bring Teddy some water in case he needed some pain pills partway through the night. He left them on the nightstand, then went to climb into bed before he paused, worried he would jostle Teddy.

Maybe I should sleep on the couch?

"Daddy," Teddy mumbled and yanked the blanket on Ian's side back. "Sleep."

"I should go g—"

"No. Sleep." Teddy patted the mattress, lips twisted in a mulish pout. "Now."

Ian couldn't tell his boy no. He slid under the covers, though it would be hours before he'd fall asleep.

Chapter Thirty-Eight

Ian was hovering.

It had been over a week since he'd ended up in the hospital for what had amounted to little more than a scratch inside his cheek. Apparently, Hugo had shot Julian before Julian could shoot Teddy, and the resulting jerk of Julian's hand had caused the sight at the end of the barrel to drag along the inside of Teddy's mouth.

Teddy didn't know what to do with his newly bought freedom. In exchange for not getting charged for shooting Julian, Hugo had agreed to be an informant for the FBI. With Julian gone, the cartel was in turmoil. He didn't know what Hugo had said to convince the cartel not to kill him for treason or whatever it was they called it, but he'd managed it. Before letting Hugo scurry back to the cartel, Ian had given him the briefcase of money to take back as well. So Teddy was free, for the first time in years.

Not that it felt like it, because Ian was hovering.

Teddy stood up, planning to head to the bathroom, and Ian was at his side. "Everything okay, Teddy Bear? Can I get you something?"

Teddy didn't know whether to laugh or groan. "I have to pee. Do you want to help me pee?"

Ian flushed. "Oh."

Teddy smirked and headed to the bathroom. When he came out, Ian was standing by the window, one hand planted on the frame as he looked outside. Teddy came up behind him, wrapping his arm around Ian's waist and leaning his cheek — the not-injured one — against Ian's back.

"We should go do something," Teddy suggested. He knew if he stayed inside much longer, he was never going to get up the courage to leave. Ian had pulled strings with some hacker he knew in the FBI to get Teddy's video pulled down, but that couldn't erase it from the minds of however many thousands of people had seen it. He was going to wonder now, every time someone's eyes lingered on him for too long.

It was why he needed to face it now, before he lost the courage to. He couldn't do it alone, but with Ian... He could do it with Ian.

"We could watch a movie? There's a new one on Netflix that I've—" Ian started.

Teddy rolled his eyes. "Something *outside*, Daddy. I want to see *clouds* again, Ian. *Clouds*."

"It's Texas, Teddy. There are no clouds." Ian twisted in Teddy's arms to look down at him with a curious grin.

Teddy continued on, completely ignoring Ian's comment. "And afterward find somewhere quiet where I can finish my book."

"Are you…misquoting *Lord of the Rings*?" Ian's confused expression made Teddy laugh.

"I knew you were a nerd," Teddy playfully smacked Ian's arm. "Next you'll be dragging me to comic-cons and midnight showings of *Star Wars*. By the way" — Teddy waggled his eyebrows — "the Cinema Six is doing a midnight showing of all the *Star Wars* movies…"

"How about we go out for breakfast?" Ian countered. "If you can make it to midnight without yawning, then we can decide whether to lock ourselves into a movie theater for twelve hours."

"Do I get to take a nap? Because I can make it to midnight if I get to take a nap."

Ian ruffled his hair. "We'll see. Go get dressed. I know exactly where I want to go."

Teddy thought it would be somewhere fun. Like mini golf, or the dentist. When Ian instead pulled the truck up outside a familiar house, he'd left Teddy with no choice.

Teddy crossed his arms tighter over his chest and shook his head again. "Nope. Not getting out, and you can't make me." It was Ian's own fault for getting out and leaving the keys in the truck.

"Unlock the door, Teddy."

"Nuh-uh." Teddy pressed the lock down harder. "I don't want to go in."

"Mama misses you." Ian tugged on the door handle like it would suddenly make it unlock.

"Mama…Mrs. R.," Teddy corrected himself, "doesn't miss me. She'd probably be happy to never see me again." That was how she should feel, anyway. If he'd opened his mouth sooner, if he'd followed his gut and convinced Lucas to go to the police earlier, Lucas wouldn't have died. He didn't think he could bear to look her in the eyes and see the anger, or disappointment.

"That's not true. I already told her we were coming, and she can't wait to see you." Ian leaned his arm against the door, his expression annoyingly gentle. "Unlock the door, Teddy."

"I'm scared," Teddy whispered, thought he didn't mean to say it. The words came out on their own, from a place of truth he'd meant to bury.

Over Ian's shoulder, Teddy saw the front door of the Romeros' house open and Mama R. was in the doorway. She looked older. There were new lines around her eyes, her hair was more gray than black, but she was smiling. He could almost hear the slap of her sandals on the sidewalk, the swish of her skirts around her knees, as she hurried toward the truck.

"Ian, you let that boy out of that truck right this instant. What are you thinking, locking him in like that?" Mama R. slapped Ian across the back of his head, her eyes twinkling. "I'm not too old to put you over my knee, you know."

Teddy scanned her face for signs of anger or disappointment. All he saw was humor and a gentle kindness.

Teddy unlocked the door.

He was free, he was safe and he finally had love. Daddy had changed his whole world.

Want to see more like this?
Here's a taster for you to enjoy!

Knights and Butterscotch
Faith Ashlin

Excerpt

Matti pushed his hair back off his face and blew out a long slow breath. Enough—he'd had enough socialising for now. There was only so much wholesome happiness a man like him could take and he'd had his fill for the time being.

It was pretty damned awesome to see Maxim so happy he glowed as he looked at his bride-to-be. To see her looking back, eyes filled with promise for the future, filled with love and possibility. Matti just hoped—no, prayed—that they could have all they deserved. That events would turn out in the right way for them and that the future…but that was for another time. Now was for the simple love between two people. One that burned bright and would be fulfilled tomorrow at their wedding.

A wedding. It was an interesting thought at a time like this. But right now he'd had enough of small talk and playing nice. After the wedding, and its formal reception, his group would gather to celebrate in their own way. That would be more Matti's thing, one where he could really relax.

Now he needed cool air and a glass of something very cold because it was damned hot in the banqueting suite. He stepped up to the bar and asked the bartender for water and ice, smiling when it was handed over quickly. Air, and the relief from being polite, were next on his agenda. He pushed his way between the groups of chatting people and made for the glass doors out onto the big balcony overlooking the city.

The noise stopped as soon as he closed the heavy door behind him and the respite was palpable. Space and peace, cool air on his face, they all drew him forward. Then there were the shimmering lights below. All those people living, loving, dying. They called out something to him that he couldn't understand and wasn't sure he was ready to hear. Or maybe it was all only in his head.

He was being daft again and there was nothing else for it but to laugh at himself. The world below didn't need him, wasn't asking anything of him. It didn't even know he was there.

He rested both forearms on the ledge of the curved, stone balcony edge and looked down. Max was getting married. That was enough to make anyone smile. The amazing Isobel had finally decided it was time and they were making it formal and permanent. It kind of put everything in perspective.

"Anything interesting going on out there?" a voice asked from the darkness at his side.

"Oh." Matti turned but couldn't see the man's face. "I didn't know there was anyone out here."

"Doesn't matter. I just thought, as you were studying it so intently, there had to be something going on in the big wide world."

"Nothing as far as I know. I only came out for a bit of peace and to look at the pretty lights."

"Then I should let you have your peace." The man took a step forward and Matti saw him properly for the first time. "I'll go."

"No," Matti said, louder and with more feeling than he'd expected, intended. "I don't want you to go." Now that was just a plain stupid thing to say to a complete stranger. "I only... I..." He stopped, knowing how foolish he sounded, feeling his cheeks flare and the skin on his face tighten.

"Are you all right?" the man asked.

Matti took a step away as the stranger came closer, and now they were both in the light.

Tall, was Matti's first thought. Very tall with wide shoulders and thick hair and the most startled look on his face Matti had seen outside a comic book. No, not startled. Shocked and a little dazed. "I think maybe I should be asking you if you're okay," he said. He wasn't quite sure how he managed to get the words out in the right order, his mind was whizzing so fast. Tall and right-looking and something else he had no intention of thinking about.

He might not be thinking about it but his blood was pulsing under his skin — he'd swear he could feel it.

"I..." It was the man's turn to stammer, but he didn't take his eyes from Matti's. "I feel like I've been hit by a truck. A big truck. One that's going very fast and landed right on my head."

"Trucks don't hit you on the head, they smack into you. Falling aeroplanes or meteors hit you on the head."

"And you'd know this because?" The man smiled and Matti wasn't sure if he was going to be sick for all the wrong reasons.

"'Cause a meteor just smacked me on the head?" Matti couldn't look away or breathe properly. Yeah, breathing properly—deep and slow—that was a good idea. It might stop him talking stupid crap to a perfect stranger for a start. "That bitch hurt and now I feel like I have my skin on inside out."

"I…" The man put out a hand, not quite touching Matti but looking like he wanted to. "This is…"

"Yeah, it is," Matti agreed, knowing just what he meant.

"Is this weird?" the man asked, his face scrunching up like something was hurting but in a good way.

"Weirdest thing I've ever known." There really wasn't anywhere else Matti wanted to look, anyone else he wanted to look at. He wasn't even sure he wanted to stop the crazy talk.

The man took a deep breath, holding it as he stared at Matti. Then he gave a curt nod, and held his hand out properly. "Jamie. I'm Jamie or my name's Jamie or something."

"You think your name's Jamie?"

"No, pretty sure it's Jamie. I'm Jamie, who are you?"

"Matti. My name's Matti and…" He grasped Jamie's hand and lost the ability to speak. Jamie's hand sat so perfectly in his, it seemed to mould itself to his palm, skin flushing and fusing and tingling as their hands settled together. And when did he think such crap? He guessed it was better than saying it out loud.

He looked up, his breathing still not working right, and Jamie didn't look much better than he felt. Jamie's pupils had dilated to ridiculous proportions, his face was flushed and there was a sheen of sweat across his forehead. He was trying to say something but he didn't seem to be having any more success at forming a coherent sentence than Matti.

"I… You…" Jamie said, clutching Matti's hand tighter.

"Yeah," Matti agreed again, nodding furiously, although he knew it made no sense.

For the longest moment they stood like that, at the edge of the balcony, palms pressed tight in what looked like a handshake that had become frozen in time, with the rest of the world forgotten. They were so still they could have been a photograph, a moment captured forever.

PUBLISHING

Sign up for our newsletter and find out about all our romance book releases, eBook sales and promotions, sneak peeks and FREE romance books!

About the Author

KD Ellis is a professional cat wrangler by day, and an author by night. She moved from a small town to an even smaller village to live with her husband and wife and their two children. She loves reading—anything with men loving men. She writes queer romance in between working her two jobs and cuddling her pets—all six of them, which confuses the turtle.

KD Ellis loves to hear from readers. You can find her contact information, website details and author profile page at https://www.pride-publishing.com